Helen ... any years. Before she began writing she had a range of jobs, including tour guide, army officer and management consultant. Her Lavender Road novels were inspired by a chance encounter with a neighbour who showed her the sites of the air-raid shelters on Clapham Common. She occasionally teaches creative writing and is a Fellow of the Royal Literary Fund.

Helen now lives with her husband and two dogs in Wales.

Helen Carey

HELEN CAREY

Some Sunny Day

headline

First published in Great Britain by Orion in 1996

First published in this paperback edition in 2016 by
HEADLINE PUBLISHING GROUP

1

Cataloguing in Publication Data is available from the British Library

ISBN 978 1 4722 3146 8

Typeset in Bembo Std by Palimpsest Book Production Limited,
Falkirk, Stirlingshire

Printed and bound in Great Britain by
CPI Group (UK) Ltd, Croydon CR0 4YY

MIX
Paper from
responsible sources
FSC® C104740

Headline's policy is to use papers that are natural, renewable and recyclable
products and made from wood grown in well-managed forests and other
controlled sources. The logging and manufacturing processes are expected to
conform to the environmental regulations of the country of origin.

HEADLINE PUBLISHING GROUP
An Hachette UK Company
Carmelite House
50 Victoria Embankment
London EC4Y 0DZ

www.headline.co.uk
www.hachette.co.uk

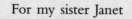

For my sister Janet

Prologue

'AAGH!' Mary Parsons' shriek cut like a knife through the men's patriotic banter and ricocheted round the damp walls of the Flag and Garter cellar. 'What was that?'

Next to her, perched on a canvas camp bed, eighteen-year-old Katy Parsons clenched her fists and tried not to scream as a small furry animal brushed her bare ankle in its flight from her mother's panic.

On the other side of the pile of crates erected to give her and her mother some modicum of privacy, she could hear her father's anxious voice. 'What's the matter, Mary, love? What happened?'

But her mother was trembling too much to speak.

Katy cleared her throat. 'It was a mouse,' she said shakily.

'A mouse?' Malcolm Parsons sounded incredulous. 'Goodness me. Did you hear that fellers? I thought at very least they'd heard a bomb falling.'

As the men laughed, Katy frowned crossly and wrapped her feet in the blanket so she wouldn't feel the mouse if it came past again.

Since the bombing had started in earnest just over a week ago she had begun to hate the Flag and Garter cellar. She hated the eerie swinging shadows, the scuttling rodents, the clammy coldness, the smell of sweat and stale beer. But more than anything she hated the loud, beer swilling men on the other side of the crates,

1

the anti-Hitler jokes, the bravado, the drunken cheers when the guns fired up on the Common at the end of the road.

It was easy for them to be brave from the safety of a reinforced cellar, she thought irritably. But what about their poor wives in the surrounding Clapham streets, huddling with frightened children in those flimsy-looking garden shelters? And what about the rescue workers above ground, the fire fighters, the gunners, the nurses?

A sudden tremor of nervous anticipation coursed through her slender body. Because on Monday she was going for an interview at St Thomas's Hospital.

For a moment she allowed herself the dream of being accepted for nursing training. Imagined herself in the distinctive mauve striped uniform, ministering to the sick and wounded, easing their pain, comforting them, calm, efficient. Best of all she imagined her parents' pride when she qualified as an SRN, gaining her coveted Nightingale badge in record time, despite the rigours of war.

'She has found her true vocation,' people would say in wonder. 'And to think she used to be such a sickly little mouse of a thing as a child.'

Abruptly she shook her head then flinched hard as something exploded in the distance. The hurricane lamp jumped on its hook and shadows swung unnervingly across the cellar walls. Katy tried to relax and failed.

Twisting her tense fingers round the rough blanket, she frowned. If only her dream could be true. More than anything she longed to be the kind of person who could take control, the sort of person people would take orders from and still respect, the sort of person who would do heroic things without worrying about the consequences.

With a sigh she turned her attention to the voices on the other side of the screen. Her father was still chuckling about the mouse. 'Nothing like a mouse to scare the ladies. Not Adolf Hitler. Not the Luftwaffe. Or a Nazi land-mine. Oh no, a little mouse is all it takes.'

The men were still laughing when the crash came. Right above them as though a lorry had driven right through the wall.

And in the sudden shocked silence that followed it, even as her ears sang, even as she waited for the click of a detonator, for the explosion that would blast them all to smithereens, Katy could hear the mouse still scratching at something under her bed.

A moment later the hurricane lamp fell to the floor and plunged the cellar into darkness.

It seemed to Katy as though all the men started shouting at once. She could hear her father's voice telling them to put out their cigarettes, she could hear swearing as they bumped themselves on crates and barrels, she could hear someone panicking about gas and above it all she could hear her mother, only inches away, screaming her name.

'Katy! Are you all right? Katy, where are you?'

Chapter One

Gripping the narrow counter, Joyce Carter winced as the Women's Voluntary Service canteen van was rocked by another explosion. The air inside the van was already thick with smoke and now the sharp smell of burning was creeping through the side serving flap making her wonder if there would be anyone left out there to eat the sandwiches she was laboriously preparing. It was a warm night even for September and with the water boiling in the urn for tea, the atmosphere inside the van was stifling. Already she could feel the sweat pouring off her, the spreading knife was slippery in her hand, and she wished she could stop for a moment to wash her face. But if she did Mrs Trewgarth would be bound to catch her and then she'd feel guilty. Mrs Trewgarth never stopped.

Behind her, brushing bottoms, her daytime employer, Mrs Rutherford, was fighting with the tea urn, grunting as she tried to swing it on to the counter.

'Do you need a hand?' Joyce asked over her shoulder. After a year of charring for her, she'd come to like Mrs Rutherford. She wasn't a bad sort, even if she was a bit la-di-da. It was her who had persuaded Joyce to help on the WVS canteen. Joyce smiled to herself. She still couldn't get used to the idea of a smart, well-dressed woman like Celia Rutherford serving tea and sandwiches, war or no war.

'Bloody thing,' Celia Rutherford muttered now, throwing a quick guilty glance in Mrs Trewgarth's direction up at the front. Luckily the noise outside was such that the other woman hadn't heard her lapse. Celia touched Joyce's arm. 'I wonder if you could just slide the mat underneath, Mrs Carter, if I lever it up slightly?'

The handle-less urn was scalding hot and extremely heavy and their curses became rather less circumspect as they tried to manoeuvre it into position.

A sudden crash, a burst of shouting and a scream made them pause in alarm. And in that second something exploded so close by that the serving flap lifted right up, drawn by the shockwave, allowing them a glimpse of their surroundings, the burning buildings, the jagged scar of a fallen roof, the black figures scurrying about, the distant red sky reflecting in the water gushing down the road.

Over it all they could hear the jarring drone of planes, the wail of sirens, the panicked shouting of the rescue workers. For an instant they could even feel the heat of the flames on their faces. It was like a firework display from hell. And then the flap crashed back, shutting out that terrible pink light, jerking the urn, splashing boiling water on their hands.

For a moment they stared at each other, Joyce, square chinned, red and sweating under her orange turbaned scarf, Celia Rutherford, tall and coolly elegant in her tailored summer jacket and matching skirt. For the first time Joyce felt truly afraid and could see her fear reflected in Mrs Rutherford's eyes. Then as the pain in her fingers began to bite, she quickly turned away and grabbed the butter. 'Here, rub this on,' she offered. 'It takes the heat out.'

A moment later Mrs Trewgarth's stentorian voice came from the front. 'Are we ready, ladies? There's people wanting sustenance out there.'

Celia closed her eyes for a moment. 'Why are we doing this?' she asked helplessly. 'Why aren't we tucked up at home safe and sound in our shelters?'

At once Mrs Trewgarth's face poked round the door. 'Chin up, ladies,' she said bracingly. 'Never forget that the Lord is on our side.'

'Why the hell doesn't he do something to help, then?' Joyce muttered sourly as she turned back to her sandwiches. She wasn't much of a one for the Lord. She knew Mrs Rutherford was a believer, she certainly went to church each Sunday. Those smart, rich sort of women always did, dressed up in their best hats and gloves with their families all in the pew with them. Mr Rutherford was probably on the parish council and all. He was on everything else. And Mrs Trewgarth presumably believed, being as she was the verger's wife and that.

But God wasn't much cop as far as Joyce was concerned. Not just now at least, when he was letting Hitler rain his bombs down on innocent families, and women and children were being machine-gunned in the streets as they fled their blazing homes. Quite a few churches had copped it already, they said, and schools and pubs. Four pubs had been hit in South London over the last two days. Not that you'd expect God to look after pubs necessarily, but you'd think he'd do something about the churches.

Joyce shook her head as Mrs Trewgarth flung up the serving flap, securing it to the clips on the roof, just as a massive sheet of flame lit the sky over the distant docks, momentarily drowning out the criss-crossing searchlights as they circled the sky for prey. She winced. It was bad enough here in Clapham but it looked like a bloody inferno over there in the East End.

She could hear the planes again now and the thump of the guns and she shivered despite the heat in the van, suddenly wishing she was in her Anderson shelter in the back yard. Not that those were bomb proof of course, but they were a damn sight more solid than this WVS tin can that rocked and swayed every time the anti-aircraft guns fired.

And then suddenly they were serving, handing out sweet tea and Marmite sandwiches to the rescue workers, the firemen and the stretcher bearers, and to the victims pulled to safety from burning houses, from crushed shelters, dug out of flooding cellars. Men and women and children all with the same look of shock and despair and a certain raw courage as they cradled their tea in trembling dirty fingers, knowing their homes were gone but somehow determined to survive, if only to spite Adolf Hitler and his vicious Luftwaffe.

As Joyce handed a cup of tea to a man with blood clotted on his forehead and a small child in his arms, she frowned. 'You look like you ought to be in hospital.'

He shook his head, wincing with the pain of it and glanced down at the child clinging to his side like a small charred monkey. When he looked up his eyes were red. 'I had to find our lad first. I knew the missus had copped it, but I couldn't go, not knowing our Charlie was still buried in there somewhere.' He sipped the tea, took a deep breath and smiled up at Joyce bravely, raising his cup in a tragic salute of thanks as he moved away.

Feeling tears in her own eyes, Joyce sniffed and looked away. Suddenly she felt Celia Rutherford's hand on her arm. 'That's why we're here, Mrs Carter,' she said quietly.

Joyce nodded. She was right. It gave you a kick doing good. It was nice to be appreciated. And it didn't happen often at home.

In the darkness of the Flag and Garter cellar, Katy had barely finished convincing her mother that she hadn't miraculously been singled out for destruction, when she smelt the thin odour of paraffin leaking from the fallen lamp.

Nervous someone would drop their cigarette, she clambered to her feet. 'Careful!' she shrieked. 'Keep back! Keep away from here!'

But thankfully all the cigarettes seemed to have been put out already, there were no red tips glowing in the darkness. As she strained her eyes, heart suddenly beating hard, feeling rather self-conscious, she heard someone stumbling towards her. Her father. She recognised the swaying gait caused by his wooden leg. But he was making a most peculiar noise, a kind of awful, breathy grumbling, like something out of a horror movie. It was a moment before she realised that he had his gas mask on and was trying to calm her through the distorting filter.

'It's all right, love. Everything's under control. Now sit down and try not to worry.'

'I'm not worried,' Katy said. 'It's just that the paraffin has spilt and I didn't want a fire.'

'That's right. We've all got to be careful. Now, you put your mask on and sit tight and we'll have you out of here in no time.'

Suddenly irritated by her father's over protective concern, Katy pulled her torch from under her pillow and played it round the room. The cellar was becoming more like the set of a horror film by the moment. If it hadn't been so frightening it would have been laughable. The sight of two dozen gas-masked men nodding and gesticulating to each other in the confined space was completely ridiculous and their wheezing breathy exchanges quite gave her the creeps.

'I don't think there's any gas, Daddy,' she said. After all, she should know. She was the one with faulty lungs, the one who coughed her guts up at the smallest opportunity. Her chest was tight now, all right, but not because of gas. The combination of fear and several hours' worth of concentrated cigarette smoke was quite enough to constrict her fragile airways, without the addition of anything Hitler might send her way.

But her father was already yanking her gas mask out of its cardboard carrying case. 'Come on, Katy, pop it on, there's a good girl. Nothing to worry about, you know. Just to be on the safe side. Look, your mother's already got hers on.'

That wasn't surprising, Katy thought, her mother had been dying to put on her gas mask ever since the bombing started last week. Somehow in her mother's mind the hideous, black rubber mask had become a safety line, a talisman, as though nothing could possibly happen if you had your gas mask on. Even now she was peering anxiously through the visor, flapping her hands frantically at Katy, urging her to hurry.

Wishing her parents would come to terms with the fact that she was eighteen and almost grown up, Katy smiled grimly as she obediently pulled the hated rubber straps over her head, wincing as they tugged painfully at her hair. Little did they realise that the one thing that might finish her off was wearing the gas mask. Because however hard she tried, she couldn't breathe in it. The only way she could get enough air for her thick lungs was by keeping a little gap at the side.

Over the long first year of war, the phoney war they were calling it now, when no bombs had fallen, that little gap hadn't mattered, but now suddenly it was September 1940, the Battle of Britain was raging overhead, and Katy realised that if Hitler did drop his dreaded poison bombs, she was for the high jump. Up shit creek without a paddle, as her friend Jen Carter from across the road would crudely put it.

But this was no gas attack. Katy could feel it in her bones. In any case she could hear someone moving about upstairs in the bar.

So could her father apparently because he grabbed her torch and rushed up the cellar steps, the danger of gas apparently forgotten as he whipped off his mask and shouted through the heavy door.

'Hello there! Is that the ARP? This is the landlord, Malcolm Parsons. There's twenty of us down here, and two women. Nobody hurt. Is it safe to come up?'

The footsteps paused for a moment and then a gruff voice called back, 'No, mate, you better stay where you are.'

'Christ!' someone muttered from behind the stacked crates. 'There must be an unexploded bomb . . .' and at once the atmosphere in the cellar changed. The voices dropped, everyone stood stock still as though one false move would send them all to kingdom come.

Katy could almost smell the fear. Her mother was crying gently, sniffling and gurgling inside her mask like a baby.

Katy slipped off her own mask to whisper words of comfort to her mother. The noises from upstairs were less muffled now, more urgent somehow and she tried to imagine what was going on. She wasn't quite sure what a bomb looked like. Was it big and round and shiny with spikes poking out like in the films or was it long and thin and black and altogether more sinister?

She wondered exactly where it was. Lying on the well-polished counter perhaps, or in the corner of the tap room under the darts board. From the sound of chinking bottles it must be near the bar; they were probably moving the bottles off the dresser in case it exploded, or perhaps they were merely treating themselves to a fortifying tipple before attempting to defuse it.

The same thought had apparently occurred to her father. He approached the door once more. 'Oi,' he hissed, his reluctance to disturb the bomb apparently still uppermost in his mind, outweighing his concern for his precious spirits. 'What's going on up there?'

This time his query was met with no response.

'Oi! You up there!' His voice wasn't quite so conciliatory this time. 'Can you tell us what's happening? Is there a bomb?'

Silence. Even the footsteps had stopped. 'They've gone,' he said blankly. 'They've gone and left us.'

'I reckon as we ought to get out,' someone said moving towards the steps. 'If there's a bomb up there, we're sitting in a bleedin' grave. Excuse my French.'

'We ought to at least have a look,' another voice agreed.

But when they tentatively tried to open the door it seemed to have been jammed shut.

'Something must have fallen against it,' Malcolm Parsons said. 'I hope it's not the grandfather.'

'Good God, have you left him out there?' someone quipped. 'I thought he was well dead and buried.'

Katy giggled. But her father was not amused. 'The clock, you fool,' he growled.

The ornate grandfather clock he'd inherited from his father was his pride and joy. It stood by the cellar door, waxed and oiled and keeping time minute for minute with Big Ben up in Westminster on the other side of the river. Katy knew it was the bane of the regulars' lives. Secretly they called it Bloody Ben. When her father called time of an evening on the dot of ten thirty, it was to the gilded face of the grandfather clock that everyone's eyes went, wishing that for once the damn thing would run a few minutes slow.

Knowing her father would be heartbroken if anything happened to that clock, Katy crossed her fingers, praying silently that Bloody Ben would be spared. She was fond of the clock herself, even though she rarely spent time in the public rooms. Her father didn't like her to consort with the customers and would never hear of her helping behind the bar, let alone doing any of the seemingly endless chores of swabbing and scrubbing, barrel rolling and cashing up. Even washing and polishing the glasses was considered too much for his precious daughter.

Katy knew it was because he cared for her, that he could never really believe that the life-threatening asthma attacks of her youth were a thing of the past. She also knew that he wanted to keep her pure. Pure and unsullied by tap-room talk, in the hope that she might attract a suitably respectable husband. That was why he was so anti the idea of her nursing. He thought it might spoil her chances. The fact that no man had ever given her pale face and drab hazel curls a second glance was beside the point. Her father wanted the best for her, and in his eyes the best thing for any girl was a husband.

Sighing, she looked up at the men on the steps by the cellar door. They were struggling to open it now, all delicacy and care gone in their determination to discover what new terror waited for them on the other side. As someone played a torch over them shouldering the tightly sealed door like a human battering ram, Katy changed her mind suddenly and began hoping that it was the grandfather clock after all impeding their exit, and not some lethal explosive device primed to detonate at the slightest touch.

But if it was, it clearly wasn't that sensitive because the door was moving now, with the weight of three or four men behind it, and suddenly as the crack widened, an ominous ticking noise made itself heard over the general mêlée. At once the men stopped in their efforts and stood back, sweating and white faced, as it dawned on them what that ticking might mean.

In the sudden tense silence someone swore and then apologised as he remembered there were ladies present.

'Is that what I think it is, or is it your friggin' clock?' someone asked suddenly and Malcolm Parsons shook his head nervously.

'It's not the clock. That ticks much faster than this. And not nearly so loud.'

Mary Parsons was crying in earnest now, still in her gas mask. Katy took a deep breath as she turned to hold her hand. Her mother was shaking so badly the vibrations ran right up Katy's arm.

Katy realised she was frightened again, very frightened, and yet at the same time she wished they would get on with it and not just stand about gassing. Suddenly she stood up, peering at the crack they had forced in the door. The atmosphere in the cellar was getting unbearable, the tension mixed with the acrid odour of hot unwashed bodies, old beer, paraffin and the unmistakable smell of urine was getting to her and she wanted to get out, even if it was the end of her.

She was halfway up the steps before anyone noticed her.

'Katy, love, are you all right? What are you doing?' Her father's voice was anxious.

She coughed nervously and her voice came out too fast. 'I'm the smallest person here. If you make the gap a little bigger I could squeeze through and see what's blocking it and maybe get help.'

Malcolm Parsons looked astonished. 'Goodness. Don't be absurd!' His voice was verging on irritable now. He tried to gentle it. 'You go and sit back with your mother, dear. We don't want you getting in the way, or getting hurt, do we? I know you're frightened and you want to get out, but you'll have to be patient like the rest of us. We'll just have to wait for them to come back to us. Help will be on its way, you mark my words.'

For a second Katy toyed with arguing. She longed to say it wasn't her skin she wanted to save, that for once she was trying to help, to show some courage. She wished she had the words to do it tactfully without sounding sulky or peeved, but she knew she hadn't. She also knew that if her father got angry she'd probably spoil it by crying. Reluctantly, smarting, she retreated back to her bunk and the clutching hands of her mother while the men tried to reclose the door.

It was half an hour later before they were finally released. Thirty minutes, with every single slow second of it ticked off steadily from the top of the cellar steps. Bomb or no bomb it was driving them all mad. And by the time the all-clear sounded at five o'clock in the morning and an air-raid warden noticed the broken window on his way home and climbed through to investigate, some of the captives were close to exploding themselves.

'Oi, Mr Parsons,' the ARP warden bellowed through the door. 'Are you down there? Are you all right?'

Malcolm Parsons, close on the other side of the door, nearly jumped out of his skin. 'Yes, we're all right. But keep your voice down. There's a time bomb up there.'

There was a moment's tense pause then the ARP voice came again. 'It's not a bomb you've had, Mr Parsons, it's a bleeding thief. They've cleared the place while you've been hiding down there. They've jammed the door with the clock.'

Katy closed her eyes. Her poor father.

After a moment's tense silence, the ribbing and teasing started as the men let off their tension.

'You'd think he'd know the sound of his own friggin' clock!'

As they filed up the cellar steps a few minutes later, Katy's heart bled for her father.

The tall dresser behind the bar was empty, cleared of bottles, even the measures and optics had gone and the darts trophies. Only her father's precious silver tankards were left where they had fallen, behind the clock.

There was glass everywhere, the blackout curtains torn and flapping in the breeze, clearly the thieves had rammed the back of their truck through the big side window and loaded it up from the inside.

Katy walked over to her dazed father and touched his arm. 'I'll help you clear up,' she said.

Abruptly he straightened his back and brushed off her tentative fingers. 'No, no, I'll deal with it. You go on up to bed while you've got a chance.'

Katy took a step back and bit her lip. Already he was unlocking the door, ushering everyone out so he could get to work with the broom.

'But what about the stock?' Katy asked. 'Can you replace it?' She realised that she had no idea how the pub worked. She knew the building was owned by the brewers, Rutherford & Berry, she knew the beer was delivered once a week on the horse-drawn dray, she knew that her parents held a joint licence, but that was about it. Where the other drinks, the cigarettes and the tobacco came from and how it was accounted for was a mystery.

Her father glanced round, broom in hand, clearly surprised to find her still standing there. For a second she was taken aback by the bleak look in his eyes, but he quickly put on a brave smile. 'Don't worry yourself about it, dear, I expect we'll survive. Now do go on upstairs. I don't need you here and you know how much you need your sleep.'

Katy felt a jolt of disappointment. Was she really so feeble that even in a crisis he couldn't use her help? Not that there was much she could do, admittedly. But it would have been nice to feel needed.

'I won't get much sleep when I'm nursing,' she said suddenly.

But her father merely sighed. 'Katy, we've talked about this before,' he said wearily. 'Your mother's very worried about the whole thing. Why don't you wait another year and see about it then when you're a little bit older and wiser?'

Katy flinched. 'I want to do something now, Daddy. I can't just sit around while people are getting bombed. Four hundred people have died in the bombing already and there'll have been more tonight. I might have been able to help.'

Her father tried to hide his scepticism with a slight smile. 'It's very creditable, love, but I honestly don't think you'd like it, all that blood and what have you. Not for a squeamish little thing like you. And you know you wouldn't like living away from home.'

He saw her stubborn expression and reached over to pat her hand. 'It's for your sake that we're concerned, Katy, love. You're not very strong. It's quite hard work, nursing, and we don't want you to be disappointed if you can't manage it.'

For a moment Katy couldn't trust herself to speak. She felt a self-conscious flush creep up her skin. If she couldn't manage it then at least she would know. Know that she was indeed a feeble, squeamish little thing. But she would never know if she didn't try.

As she turned away, she crossed her fingers silently behind her back and prayed St Thomas's would take her on.

Flushed partly with the heat of the oven and partly with pride, Joyce leaned over to inspect the plum pie she'd carefully set down on the kitchen table. She smiled. Neatly fluted at the edges with a beautiful shiny golden crust held up in the middle by an upturned egg cup and steaming gently, it looked and smelt absolutely delicious.

She'd always been a good cook. Not that there was much call for it in a family of six children, four of them boys. It was quantity they wanted, not quality. And on the money they'd lived on they were lucky even to get that. Years ago before the children were born she had dreamed of opening a little cafe somewhere, but that idea had bitten the dust long ago. Serving on the WVS canteen van was the closest she was likely to get. She sighed slightly as she closed the oven door. You needed cash to set up something like that, and confidence, and after twenty years of marriage to Stanley neither of those was in plentiful supply.

Not that Stanley was around at the moment. Far from it. The stupid bugger was still languishing in Reading jail after falling blind drunk off a getaway truck just over a year ago. He'd be out next month though, the thirteenth of October, they'd said, all being well.

For a second Joyce stopped and stared bleakly out of the small window into the shabby back yard where the boys' spare vests and work shirts were flapping on the line. Behind them, Pete was trying to fix some sacking over the entrance to the Anderson shelter.

Then she shook her head decisively and turned back to her pie. She wasn't worrying about Stanley today. Nor about the war. Today was a celebration. Today her eldest son Bob was being released from Brixton.

Glancing at the clock, quickly she put the cutlery on the table. Then she went to the kitchen door. 'Oi, Mick,' she yelled. 'Come down here a minute.'

At first she thought he hadn't heard her, but then she heard someone thumping down the stairs like a herd of elephants and a moment later Mick's face appeared round the kitchen door. 'Lunch ready?'

'Nearly.' Joyce opened the dresser drawer and took out a tin. 'Here,' she said, taking out half a crown. 'I want you to nip over the pub and get a couple of pints of beer.'

Mick looked amazed. 'Cor,' he said. 'You're pushing the boat out a bit, ain't yer?'

Joyce glared at him. 'It's for Bob,' she said shortly, handing him a metal jug. 'He'll want a drink after all this time. And mind you don't spill it on the way back.'

Of all her sons Mick was the clumsiest. Last week he'd had his wages docked for dropping a crate of bottles off the brewery dray and smashing the whole lot.

'And tell Jen dinner's ready,' she shouted after him. 'She's with those old ladies over the road.'

'I don't reckon she's coming,' Mick shouted back. 'She's practising her singing for tomorrow. She's got one of them auditions. For that Forces Entertainment thing. ENSA.'

Turning back to the stove Joyce stuck a fork in the potatoes. Bloody Jen, she thought, always doing exactly what she wanted. You'd think she was bloody Vera Lynn the way she went on.

And then suddenly Bob was there, standing in the kitchen door, lanky as ever with a kit bag over his shoulder, a short back and sides, and a wide smile on his face.

'Mmmm.' He closed his eyes appreciatively for a moment. 'I haven't smelt home cooking like that in bloody ages.'

'Bob!' Joyce stared at him with pleasure as he dropped the kit bag and stepped into the room.

A wide smile broke on to her mouth as he hugged her. For a moment, as she felt his arms wrapped round her, she felt quite choked. It was a long time since anyone had hugged her. She certainly didn't get any hugs off the boys or Jen. Mick was too sulky to hug anyone. Pete at sixteen was a nice enough lad, a bit on the slow side perhaps, but much too shy to show his feelings. And Jen was far too busy preening herself to become an actress to spare a thought for her poor, careworn mother. Joyce grimaced. As for Stanley, he'd never been one for showing affection, drunk or sober.

No, Bob was the best of the bunch. Bob had always been her favourite. He was twenty now, he'd been eighteen when they'd put him away. She'd seen him in the meantime of course. But not where they could laugh and hug. Not here in her kitchen. Suddenly she wanted the embrace to last for ever.

But Bob was already disengaging and looking around with interest. 'It looks different, smaller than I remembered, and neater.' He frowned. 'You didn't have them net curtains before, did you?'

'No.' Joyce could feel herself colouring self-consciously. 'I only put them up yesterday.' They were made from a spare bit of material Mrs Rutherford had given her. It was nice to have a few pretty things about, she reckoned, even if the thin pink ribbon holding them back did look out of place in a shabby, rundown terraced house with lino floors and walls that were worn to the brick in places they needed re-plastering so badly.

Bob nodded slowly. 'It looks good, nice.' He turned back to her and smiled suddenly in slight surprise. 'Come to think of it so do you, Mum. You look really nice.'

'Do I?' Joyce felt herself flush again. 'I had my hair done last week. That must be it.' For the first time in years. She'd had it set in rollers. It had made a difference. Given her a bit of a lift.

He shook his head. 'It's more than that. You look younger.' He frowned. 'You always used to be in a dirty old apron and looking so tired.'

Joyce grimaced. Yes, she remembered those not so distant days, when she had been permanently on her knees, living off air most of the time, hardly daring to complain that Stanley drank or gambled away his earnings, for fear of a mouthful of abuse or a black eye.

She shook her head and tried to shrug those unpleasant memories off.

It would be better now. What with her cleaning for the Rutherfords four days a week and Mick and Pete both earning, things weren't going to be quite so tight.

She glanced at Bob, perhaps he'd bring in a bit now and all. It was nice that he was back. He was a good lad, Bob, even though he had got into trouble with the law. You could hardly blame him, what with the unemployment and that. She hoped he would mend his ways now, though. It was quite a few months now since the police had come to the door, and she had grown used to living without the fear of search warrants and arguments on the doorstep.

But there were other things to fear now, of course. Particularly for a fit young man. She frowned. 'I suppose you'll be wanting to join up now?'

Bob looked appalled. 'Not if I can bloody help it.' He saw her expression and rolled his eyes. 'Don't worry, Mum. I'll do my duty, but I'm going to have a bit of fun first.'

Fun? Joyce looked at him surprised. What sort of fun did he think he was going to find in a city that was having the guts bombed out of it every night? A city where you couldn't even get a loaf of bread without queuing for it?

But before she could speak she heard Mick's footsteps coming down the passage, heard Pete come in the back door, saw their shy grins as they greeted their long-lost older brother, heard Bob's laugh as he punched them both playfully on the shoulder and suddenly her heart lifted.

Maybe Bob was right. Maybe you could have fun. Even in wartime. Taking off her apron she began to put the food on the table and smiled to herself. Who cared about bloody Adolf Hitler when you were about to eat the best-looking plum pie she'd seen in years?

Katy was shocked when she got off the bus outside St Thomas's hospital on Monday morning. Overnight a bomb had fallen on one of the blocks in the middle of the north side of the enormous hospital. Three floors had collapsed and there was rubble everywhere.

It was the first major bomb site Katy had seen and she was astonished by the amount of damage. It seemed incredible that so much mangled masonry and broken timber could emanate from even such a solidly built building like St Thomas's. Let alone the bricks and pipes and dust. There was dust everywhere, hanging in the thin September sun, dust and the acrid smell of old fires.

'I reckon they was aiming at the Houses of Parliament,' a workman remarked close by, nodding at the wounded hospital. 'On the other side of the river, Big Ben and that, but the hospital copped it instead.'

Two nurses had been killed in the bomb, he said, crushed to death as they slept, and three or four masseuses, no one seemed to know for sure. The X-ray department was out of action and the gas supply was failing.

Bearing in mind the disruption, Katy was sure her interview would be delayed or forgotten. But on the dot of eleven she was shown into Matron's office.

It was a spacious book-lined room with large windows over-looking one of the hospital courtyards. In the middle of the room was a large wooden desk. On one side of it was an upright chair on which Katy was asked to sit. On the other side of it was Matron. 'So you want to become a nurse, Miss Parsons. Can you explain to me why?'

Katy blinked and cleared her throat ready to reply. And then, to her horror, as she glanced nervously across the wide desk at St Thomas's most senior nurse, stern and immaculate in her navy uniform, starched collar and magnificent frilly cap, all her carefully rehearsed reasons for wanting to be a nurse deserted her. Helplessly, after what seemed like half an hour of agonising silence, she watched her interviewer unfold her hands and lean slightly forward, tapping a forefinger on the desk's highly polished surface.

'Miss Parsons.' Matron's voice was brisk, but behind her spectacles her eyes were kindly. 'We won't get very far with this interview if you don't answer my questions.' She glanced down at the fob watch which hung from her ample navy bosom. 'As I am sure you are aware, the hospital was bombed early this morning. I lost two of my best nurses and four masseuses and there are a number of things I have to see to.'

Katy flushed. 'I know, I heard. I . . . I'm really sorry.'

'Yes, well, we're not here to mourn the dead, but to discuss your future,' Matron said crisply. 'Now, Miss Parsons, I need to know your reasons for wanting to undertake nursing training at this hospital.'

Again Katy hesitated and again Matron tapped her finger on the desk, rather more impatiently this time, until Katy finally gave in.

'I don't know what reasons to give,' she said helplessly, twisting her gloves in her hands. 'I . . . I want to do it so much, I don't want to say the wrong thing.'

For a few moments Matron regarded her steadily. 'I see,' she said at last, leaning back in her chair, leaving Katy wondering exactly what she had seen and hoping those piercing eyes hadn't noticed the terrible self-doubt that was filling her mind. How could she, Katy Parsons, daughter of a Clapham publican, ever in a million years hope to convince this powerful, confident woman that she had anything to offer? How could she even presume to believe she might be permitted to wear the prestigious St Thomas's uniform, to take her place on the wards, nursing the sick and injured? It was absurd even thinking about it. She was quite clearly wasting Matron's time.

It seemed Matron's mind was running along the same lines as she glanced through the documents in front of her. 'Your health record is poor. Your academic record is little better than average. And you are at least six months too young.' She looked up. 'On paper you have little to recommend you, Miss Parsons.'

'I know,' Katy said miserably. So that was it. She would be dismissed and that would be the end of her dream. In a moment Matron would get to her feet, walk her to the door, shake her hand with a brisk but regretful smile and then return to her desk to put a firm black cross against her name on the list before calling in the next, rather more promising, candidate.

Suddenly Katy wished she was more like her friend Jen Carter. Jen wouldn't be sitting here in dumb silence waiting to be dismissed. Jen fought for what she wanted and got it. But then Jen was different. Jen was tough. Jen was the sort of person people wanted because she had guts and drive and ambition. Exactly the qualities Matron was presumably looking for, Katy thought sadly. Exactly the qualities she lacked.

She looked up. So why wasn't Matron getting up? Why wasn't she showing her to the door? Why was she still sitting there with a thoughtful expression in her intelligent eyes?

'Why don't you forget about the interview for a moment, Miss Parsons,' she said suddenly, leaning back in her chair, 'and just tell me what's on your mind.'

Chapter Two

Jen Carter sat awkwardly in the Miss Taylors' spick and span little sitting-room with their smelly old dachshund on her lap and a small glass of sherry in her hand. It was meant to be a bit of a celebration. They were celebrating her being offered a solo slot in an ENSA concert party. To start as soon as they got a suitable touring group together.

Jen smiled automatically as Ward Frazer, the Miss Taylors' nephew, topped up her glass. Jen knew she should be delighted. She was delighted. It was a lucky break. And all thanks to a friend of Ward Frazer's. But she deserved it. She had put in a lot of hard work, a lot of heartache, one way and another, to get this opportunity. For years she had dreamed of fame and fortune on the stage and yet now she had her foot on the ladder, she found she was suddenly scared. Not of failing, not of hostile audiences or forgetting her words, but, absurdly, of leaving home.

Not that she could ever admit it to anyone in a million years. If nothing else, they would laugh in her face. Because anyone in their right mind would be delighted to wave the Carter household goodbye. For ever.

Jen had always thought, given the chance, she would be on the first train out. She hated Lavender Road with its shabby Victorian houses. She hated her parents' cold, dingy home with its lino floors and leaking roof. Come to that she hated her stupid, stick-in-the-mud family. And yet now the moment was approaching she found she didn't want to leave. Much as she hated it, she knew it. It was all she knew. It was home. And more than anything she knew she would miss the funny old Miss Taylors who had been so kind to her, taking up her cause with such relish when she'd lost her chorus job for refusing to succumb to the producer's lecherous advances.

She looked at them now, twittering with pride over their handsome Canadian nephew, already tipsy on the sherry he had brought for them. And then there was Mrs Frost, sitting stiff-backed and stern, as usual, there by the piano, who had taught her so much, both professionally and privately with her no-nonsense attitude and perfectionist standards. Mrs Margot Frost whose hawk nose and barking voice concealed a heart of gold.

Jen bit her lip. They were all so proud of her. So fond of her. Their protégée.

And she was fond of them. She had always thought she was so self-contained. That she didn't need or want anyone else. Last year she had even turned down the chance to go and live in Ireland with her then boyfriend. OK, so she had regretted it bitterly since, especially as Sean had lost no time in finding another girl, but at the time she had wanted to prove herself. To show she could make it on her own. And yet now she had the chance, she was dreading it. Dreading having to leave these funny, eccentric, kindly old women. Dreading having to start all over again on her own.

'Where's Katy Parsons?' Thelma Taylor asked suddenly. 'We should have asked her to come and have a glass of sherry with us.'

'We did,' her sister replied. 'She's at her St Thomas's interview, remember? She said she'd come in and let us know how she got on.'

'Is that the girl from the pub?' Ward asked and, jerked out of her reverie, Jen looked up in surprise. Fancy Ward remembering Katy Parsons. To her knowledge he had only clapped eyes on her a couple of times and both of those Katy had been as quiet as a mouse. Mind you, Katy was always pretty quiet. And if a man got within three miles of her, she clammed up even worse. A mute mouse.

Jen smiled at the thought and caught Ward's eyes on her. He had unnerving eyes, grey and very steady as though he was looking right into your brain. She smiled quickly in case he was, and he smiled back. And even immune to men as she was these days, Jen felt a shiver of pleasure. She looked away quickly and then cautiously back again. He was talking to Mrs Frost now, making her smile too.

Jen studied him covertly over the rim of her glass. Tall, well built, with an easy manner, raven-dark hair and those devastating eyes, Ward Frazer was gorgeous, there was no other way to describe him. No wonder Katy disappeared into the background when he was around. Jen sometimes felt pretty tongue tied in his company herself.

'She's going to be a nurse, then?' he asked and she realised he was addressing her again, leaning forward, his elbows on his knees.

Quickly she roused herself.

'She hopes to. Although personally I think she's nuts. As far as I'm concerned nursing doesn't have a single thing to recommend it. It's hard work, dirty, and badly paid.'

Ward smiled mildly. 'Maybe she's hoping to meet a handsome doctor.'

'What, Katy?' Jen giggled. 'I doubt it. Katy would run a mile if a doctor came anywhere near her.' She shook her head. 'No, she'll be far more interested in caring for the sick and wounded, relieving suffering, emptying bed pans, helping with the war effort and all that.'

Ward's eyebrows rose slightly. 'Surely that's rather creditable?'

'Oh yes, of course, terribly,' Jen agreed quickly, flushing. She hadn't meant to sound quite so dismissive. She'd momentarily forgotten Ward Frazer was constantly risking his life for the blasted war effort. 'Terribly creditable.' She grinned. 'But not quite so much fun as chasing doctors.'

She groaned inwardly as his brows rose again and his mouth curved in a faint responsive smile. What was she saying? If she wasn't careful he'd start thinking she fancied him. And the last thing she wanted just now was a flirtation.

And a flirtation was all she was likely to get from Ward Frazer. He had a reputation for it. Loving and leaving. Not that she blamed him. His aunts had told her that he had lost the girl he loved in Germany before the war. Some Jewish girl, they said, killed in that awful Kristallnacht purge on the Jews. Jen felt a sudden stab of pain. She knew what it was like to lose someone you loved. Not that Sean Byrne had died of course. But his defection had been quite enough to put her off wanting to get involved again. In any case Ward Frazer was much too classy, much too educated for the likes of her. He was far more suited to girls like Louise Rutherford who lived in the big house up at the end of the road overlooking the common. Daughter of the brewery owner, pretty and sophisticated, even if she was a spoilt little madam.

Louise Rutherford fancied the pants off Ward Frazer. Or she used to. They'd dated once or twice and then he'd dropped her. Apparently he'd told her she was too young and too innocent and he didn't want her falling in love with him. Jen glanced across at him again now, wondering about him. Wondering what he really wanted. Looking at him leaning back in his chair teasing his aunts about the sherry, you'd never guess his traumatic past, nor that he currently spent half his time on crazy, suicidal missions behind enemy lines. Or would you?

She frowned. Now she thought about it, perhaps there was something behind that languid charm and humorous smile, a toughness, even a hint of ruthlessness. A definite sense of danger. And lurking in those steely grey eyes was a strange bleakness, a certain detachment she hadn't noticed before. She knew the Miss Taylors thought he had a death wish. Suddenly she could believe it.

Jen shivered and caught his eyes on her again.

'Are you OK?' he asked. 'Or is Winston squashing you to death?'

'Oh, I'm fine.' She smiled brightly. 'It takes more than a dachshund to squash me.'

He grinned. 'Is that right?'

Reaching awkwardly over the dog on her lap for her glass, she gulped the last of her sherry. It was time to go, before she dug herself in any deeper. But before she could make her excuses and stand up, someone knocked at the door.

It was Katy Parsons. Jen could hear her in the passage, chattering with uncharacteristic eagerness to Mrs Frost who had let her in. Then the door swung open and Jen saw her friend's mouth shut abruptly as she caught sight of Ward Frazer.

Esme Taylor broke the sudden silence. 'You know Katy, don't you, Ward?'

He was already on his feet. Now he advanced courteously to greet her.

'We've met,' he said, smiling at Katy and extending his hand. 'But we've never been properly introduced.'

On the fifth floor of the Ministry of Information in Whitehall, Pam Nelson was sitting tensely at her desk watching her boss get ready for his regular Monday morning meeting at the War Ministry.

She could hardly wait for him to leave. Why was he taking so long gathering his documents? Why couldn't the blasted man just stuff everything in his case and go?

'I expect they'll be kicking off quite promptly today after all the bombing at the weekend,' she said hopefully, but he refused to be hurried.

'I dare say they will,' he replied distractedly. 'But they're bound to ask questions about this de Gaulle fellow and I must make sure I've got all my bits and pieces. Half the senior bods are always late in any case.' He straightened up. 'Now, do you think I'll need a coat, Mrs Nelson? That's the most important question. What's it like outside?'

Pam glanced out of the window, wincing slightly at the brightness of the light pouring through the small panes. Although bombs had apparently fallen in this part of London over the weekend, there was no sign of it from up here. Everything looked peaceful and green. 'It's lovely,' she said, rubbing her hand over her mouth to hide a yawn. 'There are people in shirtsleeves in St James's Park. You won't need a coat.' Please go, she added silently, please go and please don't come back for a couple of hours.

'I'll probably have lunch with the Private Secretary,' Mr Shaw said, picking up his gas mask box and moving towards the door at last. 'So I won't be back until two-ish.'

Thank God, Pam thought. She smiled as brightly as she could. 'That's fine. I'll be here. I'll field any calls.'

Mr Shaw nodded. 'You're a marvel, Mrs Nelson,' he said warmly. 'I don't know what I'd do without you.'

'And I love you too,' Pam muttered, as he stepped into the corridor. 'But just now I want this office to myself.'

She was already on her feet and halfway round her desk when his head popped back round the door. 'Did you say something?'

Stopping abruptly in the middle of the office, Pam blinked. 'Oh, er, no, I just, um, called good luck, that's all.'

He looked surprised. 'Oh thanks. Well,' he gave a little wave, 'I'll be off then. See you later.'

This time she waited until she could no longer hear his footsteps squeaking up the passage, then she quickly shut and locked the door, took both the telephones off their hooks, grabbed her coat off its peg, rolled it carefully and lay down on the small carpet with it as a pillow.

For a moment she felt guilty and absurdly self-conscious. It would be desperately embarrassing if she was caught, she would almost certainly get sacked. Everyone was tired, they would say, nevertheless work must go on. But she was beyond caring whether anything went on. All she knew was that with the endless night-time racket of sirens and guns and bombs and with her bereaved friend Sheila and her child craving her company all day and occupying her and Alan's air-raid shelter night by night, she hadn't managed to get a wink of sleep all weekend. And she needed her sleep. Because without it she got ratty. Ratty with Alan. And she couldn't bear the pain on his face when that happened.

If only he would persuade Sheila to go back to her own house on the other side of Lavender Road everything would probably be all right. But he was too soft hearted. Too kind.

Pam felt tears of tiredness well in her eyes. Determinedly she closed them. 'Please God let me sleep now,' she murmured, wishing the floor wasn't quite so hard. 'And then I'll be nice to Alan tonight.'

For a terrible second, as she stood there in the Miss Taylors' sitting-room doorway, Katy thought she wasn't going to be able to shake hands. She was horrified to find Ward Frazer there in the first place, and so stunned that he remembered her, that for a second she was entirely unable to move. I'm paralysed, she thought to herself in panic. I'm going to have to spend the rest of my life in a wheelchair.

But then, thankfully, at the last moment, good manners came to the rescue, unlocking her rigid limbs and she touched his hand briefly, mumbling something incoherent and, stepping back, nearly knocking over one of the Miss Taylors' occasional tables in the process.

I'm going to die, Katy said to herself, as Jen giggled and reached out to steady the table. She could feel the colour flooding her face. Any moment now I'm going to lie down on the floor and die. What was he doing here? The Miss Taylors had said he was only staying for the weekend. It had never occurred to her that he would still be here, that she would barge in all flustered and brimming with news to be faced with blasted Ward Frazer.

'Tell us all about it,' Thelma Taylor said, leaning forward eagerly, motioning Katy into a chair.

As she sat down reluctantly, Katy bit her lip. All the way home she had been longing to tell them about it. How embarrassing it had been when the Matron had finally forced her to confess every-thing, all her hopes and fears, how she longed to prove herself, to do something worthwhile, but feared her parents were right when they said she wouldn't be able to cope. How reluctant they were for her to live away from home.

She wanted to tell them how kind Matron had been. Understanding and sympathetic. How she'd said Katy was too young to embark on SRN training in any case. St Thomas's didn't take anyone until they were nineteen at least, and that due to the bombing they were probably going to evacuate the whole hospital into the country anyway. Including the nurses in training. And most of all she wanted to tell them how Matron, sensing her bitter disappointment, had suggested she do a year's probation at a local hospital instead. She recommended the Wilhelmina hospital in Clapham and to Katy's astonishment, she had picked up the telephone there and then and arranged it for her.

But with Ward Frazer sitting there watching her with those unnerving grey eyes she couldn't say any of it. He wouldn't be interested in the Wilhelmina, that it was close enough for her to live at home, that the junior nurses wore a uniform of lilac and white stripes, that she would have to provide her own shoes and stockings and report to a Sister Morris on the Ethel Barnet women's surgical ward at eight o'clock in the morning on the twenty-third of September.

Somehow, by not looking at Ward and prompted by Mrs Frost, she managed to stammer out the gist of it and then coughed in embarrassment as they started to congratulate her.

'Give the poor girl a drink, Ward.' Thelma Taylor nudged him, and at once he got to his feet.

'I'm sorry. I was miles away.' He smiled apologetically at Katy. 'Would you like a glass of sherry?'

'No, no, honestly, I don't really drink,' she stammered. 'I really ought to get home anyway. I only popped in to let you know what happened.'

'Oh go on, Katy, just this once,' Jen urged her. 'We're celebrating after all.'

'Just a small one?' Ward suggested, and Katy was powerless to resist that smile.

'All right, then,' she muttered reluctantly. 'Just a small one.'

For a second he was almost close enough for her to touch him as he reached for the bottle. He had lovely hands, she noticed suddenly, clean strong hands with a scattering of hairs on the back and long competent fingers. As he tipped the bottle, she caught a glimpse of an efficient-looking watch on his wrist and then her eyes were drawn to a nasty little scar on the side of his forefinger and the telltale black circle under the nail.

'How did you hurt your finger?' she asked, pointing. 'It must have been agony.'

The abrupt question clearly took everyone by surprise, including Ward who almost spilled the sherry as he turned his hand as though to see what she was referring to. It was a moment before she realised why. Then she felt a complete idiot.

That bruised nail would be about ten days old. Ward had only come back from his last 'mission' just over a week ago. You didn't have to be a mathematician to work out that he had suffered that small injury abroad somewhere in Nazi-controlled Europe, in which case he was hardly likely to want to discuss the circumstances. Katy cringed, unable to look at him for fear of seeing the embarrassment, the distaste for her tactless prying in his eyes.

But his voice when he spoke sounded relaxed. 'Someone shut a car door on it,' he said putting the bottle down. 'I guess it did hurt at the time, but it's fine now.' He flexed it a couple of times as though to prove his words.

Jen giggled. 'Perhaps you should take a closer look, Nurse Parsons, just to make sure.'

At that moment Katy would willingly have killed Jen. Catching the flicker of amusement on Ward's face out of the corner of her eye, she flushed.

'I don't think that will be necessary,' she said stiffly and Ward grinned.

'Pity,' he said lightly. 'I've got one or two other scars hidden away. I was hoping you might give me your opinion on those too.'

31

Katy flushed again as everyone laughed. He was teasing her, at least she hoped he was just teasing, and not mocking her; it was hard to tell from the faint twist of his lips as he put the bottle back on the dresser. Either way it made her feel most uncomfortable, and she couldn't respond when he turned and smiled straight at her.

Instead she gulped down the drink and stood up abruptly. 'I'm sorry, I really must go. I had no idea it was getting so late. Mummy will be worried.'

Before anyone could object, she had waved a hurried farewell to the Miss Taylors and to Mrs Frost, nodded a see-you-later to Jen and was then stuck on the wrong side of the room not knowing how to say goodbye to Ward.

He didn't seem prepared to help her. 'Shall I see you out?' he said politely as she stood awkwardly at the door.

Katy swallowed. 'No, it's all right,' she said hastily. He obviously couldn't wait to see the back of her. 'I can see myself out.' She frowned as he shrugged indifferently. She had obviously got that wrong too. 'It was nice to meet you,' she said desperately.

For an awful second she thought he wasn't going to answer, then he nodded. 'I think the pleasure was mine,' he said. Then he smiled. 'Goodbye, and good luck with the nursing.'

The extraordinary thing, Katy thought as she let herself out of the front door a moment later, was that nobody else in the room seemed to have noticed anything odd about her hasty departure. But she knew Ward had noticed and she could only pray that he wouldn't guess the reason for it. That she feared if she stayed one more minute in his company she might blurt out something so stupid he would never look at her again. As it was he must already think she was a complete idiot, gauche and naive, stumbling over the furniture and acting so prim and proper. 'I don't think that will be necessary,' she mimicked herself cruelly and groaned.

It was Jen's fault for teasing her like that. Jen was always teasing, but Katy had never dreamt she'd do it in front of Ward Frazer. How could she be so mean? She wished she could take her to task for it but she knew she couldn't. Jen would only smell a rat and Katy couldn't bear for anyone to know the awful devastating effect Ward Frazer had on her. Nobody. Least of all Ward Frazer.

She stopped on the pavement and glanced down the street towards the pub on the corner. As always at lunchtimes there were quite a few bicycles leaning against the wall outside. It would be busy and smoky inside and everyone would be talking about the dreadful bombing at the weekend; the devastating fires which were still burning even now down at the docks; the hundreds of people killed and thousands injured; the vans she had seen this morning outside St Thomas's labelled 'dead only'; the number of planes brought down.

She didn't really want to go home. Her father would be serving at the bar and she didn't want to tell her mother her news without him being present. Her mother would only get flustered and start worrying about what kind of bomb shelters the Wilhelmina had or whether they'd need her ration book for meals or something else equally irrelevant. Katy sighed. She loved her parents, but sometimes they were a bit of a trial. If only they would realise that she had grown up.

Not that she'd shown it just now, of course. When she had walked into the Miss Taylors' sitting-room she had felt about five years old and wished she could have run away and hidden in the cupboard in her bedroom.

Crossly, she looked up the narrow street the other way, towards the smart end by the common where Louise Rutherford lived with her rather frightening parents.

Katy wondered if Louise was still keen on Ward Frazer. She certainly had been last year before her affair with Count Stefan Pininski. Katy could remember the evening just before Christmas when she had gone up to Cedars House to tell Louise that Ward was due to arrive any moment at the Miss Taylors'.

They had run back up the street together and stood hidden by darkness, shivering in excitement, as he got out of his car and knocked at the old ladies' door.

That was the same night the little Whitehead boy had been run over, the first time Katy had ever spoken to Ward Frazer, as they knelt in the gutter together trying to save the child's life.

She had blocked that dreadful scene from her memory, she realised now. The biting cold, the darkness of the winter blackout, the terrible sense of helplessness as she felt the blood from the child's head dripping through her fingers.

Ward had been injured, too, she remembered, saving the other child, the older one, George, grabbing him out of the path of the car, even as the toddler caught the bumper head on. She hadn't known it at the time. It was only afterwards when the ambulance had gone and the crowds dispersed, that she caught, in the sudden unexpected flash of torchlight, the unguarded grimace of pain as he bent to pick something up off the ground.

He had shrugged off her concern then, just as he had tonight and she had never known the nature of his injury. All she had known was the incredible sense of loss she had experienced when he had turned away from her and taken Louise into his arms.

Realising she was standing almost on the exact spot of that tender, emotional embrace, Katy shivered.

Then she frowned.

Damn Louise Rutherford for her pretty face and winning ways.

And damn Ward Frazer too. Perhaps the scars he had mockingly offered to show her today were the very ones he had received that fateful night. Suddenly Katy wished she'd had the guts to agree to his suggestion. She should have whisked him off into another room there and then and told him to strip to the waist. That would have shaken the smirk off his handsome face. And off Jen's too. She chuckled suddenly as she imagined the Miss Taylors' shocked expressions.

And then, just as she was wondering what might have happened next, she heard the sirens start up, in the distance first, and then closer and closer, the ghastly two-tone wail so familiar now after a week of endless raids. At once the street was full of people hurrying back to their own homes, to their own families, to their own shelters. In the early days when Hitler was still bombing the airfields, nobody had bothered much, but since the Luftwaffe had turned its attention to London, people had begun to realise that it was a choice between the shelter or the morgue.

Already over the clamour of the sirens, the shouting and the slamming of doors, Katy could hear the low ominous grumble of aircraft.

For a second she toyed with running up to the shelter on the common. But it was rumoured to be damp and smelly and she knew nobody used it if they could avoid it.

Instead she turned and sprinted for home, longing, even as she ran with her gas mask box bumping awkwardly against her side, for the day, two weeks away, when she would no longer have to spend hours on end cowering underground with a lot of drunken strangers and would instead be whispering reassuring words of comfort to the grateful patients on the Ethel Barnet women's surgical ward.

Chapter Three

Sitting in the reinforced cellar of Cedars House, listening to her parents' low-voiced argument against the repeated thump of the anti-aircraft guns, Louise Rutherford had never been so miserable in all her life. A year ago she had been a happy, pretty, fashionable eighteen-year-old, part of a happy united family, with a wide circle of classy, stylish friends met through her finishing school Lucie Clayton, secretly rather excited that war had been declared, and even more so about the possibility of meeting a handsome young officer to sweep her off her feet.

Now, a year later, everything had gone badly wrong. Her hair had lost its bounce and her skin its colour, she was permanently exhausted and she hadn't had any new clothes for ages.

Most of the handsome boys she had known last year had joined up and disappeared, either to sea with the navy or to RAF training camps in Scotland or, more recently, with the army to North Africa. Two of them were already dead and one was a prisoner-of-war.

Even the girls had deserted her. Some of them like Helen de Burrel had joined the emergency services and were spending their time driving antiquated old ambulances round London collecting up the victims of bombing raids. Others had left London for the relative safety of their country estates; a few of the heartier ones had joined the services proper, and one or two even, incredibly, had joined the new land-army and were spending their days milking cows and digging fields in the government's drive to home production.

Everyone seemed to be doing something. And now even meek, little Katy Parsons was joining the war effort with some nursing job down at the Wilhelmina.

Not that Louise wanted to do any of those things. She felt faint if she set foot in a hospital and as for becoming a land-girl, she couldn't think of anything worse. It was bad enough having to help her mother in the garden with her private Dig for Victory campaign. In any case her father would never dream of letting her to go off and live on some distant farm. He was far too old fashioned. As far as he was concerned women should sit safely at home and knit balaclavas.

That's what he was arguing about now, on the face of it at least. He didn't approve of her mother joining the local Women's Voluntary Service.

'I'm not at all happy about it, Celia,' he was saying. 'I've said before. This WVS business really isn't suitable for a woman of your position. If nothing else, it's extremely dangerous.'

Right from the start he had been anti her mother helping on the WVS canteen van. It hadn't mattered too much over the summer before the bombing had started but now that she was out two or three nights a week he was getting increasingly irritable about it. Though why her mother should want to risk her life in the beastly van with awful old Mrs Carter and that hearty Mrs Trewgarth, Louise could not imagine. She would have thought she saw quite enough of Mrs Carter's sour face with her coming in to Cedars House every day to do the cleaning. It seemed her father agreed.

'I fail to see why it's any less suitable for me than anyone else,' her mother responded stiffly. 'Better that I should take the risk than women with young children.' She looked up from her knitting. 'It would be a different matter if my children were all at home. But with Douglas at school and Bertie away I have plenty of time on my hands.'

Louise blinked and then cringed. Why on earth had she said that? Everyone knew that was the root of the problem. Sure enough her father's mouth tightened ominously.

'Yes, well, the less said about Bertram the better,' he said coldly. But it seemed her mother had raised the subject deliberately.

'He wants to come home,' she said now, glancing up from her knitting, her voice light and artificially casual. 'He telephoned this morning.'

Pressing herself back in her chair, Louise waited nervously for the explosion. She didn't have to wait long.

Her father's fist came down on the arm of his chair so hard it nearly cracked it. 'How many times do I have to tell you that you are not to speak to that boy?'

He stood up, nearly bumping his head on the low ceiling, and took such a violent step towards her mother's chair that, for a dreadful moment, Louise thought he was going to hit her.

'I will not have it,' he shouted. 'Do you hear me? He has disgraced the family and I will not have him thinking we don't mind. Nor under any circumstances will I allow him to set foot in this house.' His voice was controlled again now, but somehow even more frightening in its hushed intensity. 'I hope you are hearing me, Celia, because that's my last word.'

'I can hear you, Greville.' Her mother spoke quietly, but Louise could hear the icy chill in her voice and as her father sat down again the cellar seemed even more claustrophobic than before. Their anger seemed to spread even to the darkest corners.

Louise shivered. She wondered if her brother fully appreciated the trouble he had caused. Having left school in the summer, Bertie had suddenly decided he was going to be a conscientious objector. Her father had hit the roof. He had also hit Bertie. Quite hard, on the side of the head. He had called him a coward. A disgrace. A traitor.

But Bertie refused to change his mind. It looked bad for the family, Louise could see that. The Rutherfords had a certain position in the local society. Her father, as owner of the local brewery, was a highly respected local figure. He held several positions of authority. Louise could see why her father was angry, why he had banished Bertie to Shropshire. But the force of his anger scared her. It seemed to be rocking the very foundation of the family and spreading to other things not remotely connected with Bertie.

Only yesterday he had torn her off a strip for spending time with Aaref Hoch. It was all very well to amuse herself trying to teach the Hoch boys English, he had said, but she must remember that Aaref was not 'one of us'. What he had meant was that Aaref was foreign, penniless and, worse, Jewish.

Louise had nodded dumbly, too startled by his sudden attack to argue. She couldn't even begin to imagine how he would react if he ever found out about Stefan Pininski.

Louise swallowed hard. Stefan Pininski. Even now the pain connected to that name was intense. So intense she could hardly bear to think about that awful day when she had called unexpectedly to see him in his suite at the Savoy and had been greeted by his wife.

His wife. Those two words hurt her even more than the thought of his name.

If she hadn't seen the woman with her own eyes she would never have believed it. Suddenly she had realised why he wanted to keep their relationship secret. At the time she had been put out but now she was glad. If her father had found out what she had been up to, he would have hit the roof so hard he would have shot straight through into the night sky.

The only people who knew about Stefan were Aaref and Katy Parsons. They had both been suitably sympathetic. But then Aaref was half in love with her himself and Katy was sympathetic about everything so it wasn't all that surprising. Neither of them could fill the awful gap left by Stefan's deceit. Nor could they do anything about the nagging worry that had recently started to fill her mind.

As hard as she tried Louise couldn't forget Stefan's love-making. Tender and sincere. His whispered endearments. His passion. His declarations of love. It killed her to think he'd seduced other girls. And boys too, his wife had said. That made her feel sick. But it didn't stop her hurting. Nor did it stop her worrying.

She felt herself blush as she thought of the intimacies he had demanded of her. Glancing quickly at her father, she wondered what he would say if she told him some of the things Stefan had asked her to do. Probably he wouldn't know what she was talking about. Certainly she couldn't in a million years imagine him asking them of her mother.

But it wasn't Stefan's love-making she was worrying about now, worrying so much that she could hardly eat or sleep.

It was the fact that it was six weeks since the last time she had been with him and she still hadn't had a period. Oh, she had tried to convince herself it was the war, the bombing, her heartbreak that had delayed it. But now it was getting seriously late and she hadn't the faintest idea what to do.

She racked her brains. What had Stefan said when she had once asked nervously what would happen if she got pregnant? 'Don't worry about it, my darling. I will take care of it. It's very easy. Very quick. I know a very good man. But I will be careful and make sure you are safe.' He had kissed her then. And like the blind naive idiot she was she hadn't thought another thing about it. She had been so innocent, so trusting. So *stupid*.

And now that she might just be in need of his 'good man', where was Stefan? Halfway across the Atlantic on his way to New York. She had seen the announcement in *The Times*. 'Other recent departures include the Count and Countess Pininski, recently of the Savoy, London, who sailed last week for America.'

Tears blurred her vision. She suddenly felt very alone. She couldn't possibly ask her mother. Anyway she might be wrong. She hoped she was wrong. Prayed she was wrong.

She would have to look at her diary. Try to work it out again.

She glanced at her father again, strict and severe, reading the paper now with a deep frown still on his forehead, and her heart shook.

If he could throw Bertie out without a qualm just for being a conscientious objector, what on earth would he do to her if he discovered she was pregnant? Whatever happened there was one thing she must do for absolute certain. Make sure he never ever found out.

'Alan, please,' Pam Nelson begged her husband. 'You've got to do something.' She saw the dismay in his kindly eyes and steeled herself to be tough. 'We can't go on like this. It's not right. I'm exhausted. Mr Shaw caught me asleep in the office last week. He was nice about it, quite understanding really, but I can't go on like that. I'll lose my job.' She saw his gaze flicker and looked away, trying to keep the bitterness out of her voice. 'I know you wouldn't care about that, but I would.'

Alan Nelson sighed and leaned across the kitchen table to touch her gently on the arm. 'I know you would, Pam. I know how much you enjoy your job. But it's wearing you out. You're so late getting home these days. I know it's because of the raids and that but even so . . .' He tailed off helplessly and Pam bit her lip.

It was true. She was late getting home. Sometimes she couldn't get home at all. When the sirens sounded they closed the floodgates on the Underground lines under the Thames, trapping her north of the river. The buses were no better. They just stopped where they were as everyone ran for nearby shelters.

Sometimes she sat in those dirty noisy shelters for hours. There was one in Vauxhall where she'd been greeted like an old friend when she'd hurried in one afternoon last week as dozens of German planes roared low overhead. Clapham had been bombed to hell that night, even half a mile away in the Vauxhall shelter you could smell the putrid acid smell that hung on the night air. As she'd walked home wearily after the all-clear, the streets had been running with water and sewage from broken mains. On Wandsworth Road, a block of flats had gaped faceless and sagging in the bright moonlight, a stack of open rooms, some even with the furniture still inside, like a dolls' house with its front removed.

Now it was Sunday evening, the sirens were expected to sound shortly, and Pam was facing another sleepless night crammed into the Anderson shelter in the back yard with Sheila and Alan and little George.

Sheila and George were in there already as usual, lying on the wooden bunks Alan had made for them, surrounded by most of their possessions, leaving little room for Alan and Pam.

'It's not fair,' Pam said now. 'It's our shelter. Why can't they go back to their own house? They've got a perfectly good cellar there they can use.'

'She's scared to.' Alan spoke with faint reproach. 'You know that. She's your friend. She's scared of being on her own. She's not as strong as you, Pam. She needs help.'

Pam sighed deeply. Alan was right, she should feel sorry for Sheila. She did feel sorry for her, desperately sorry for her, who wouldn't when the poor girl had lost her husband and her youngest son within months of each other?

But she and Alan had to live too. They had had enough trouble last year with Pam falling for their Irish lodger and Alan taking off for Dunkirk in his little river boat and nearly not coming back.

And now this Sheila problem was causing a new strain between them. Alan with his big heart and endless supply of patience wanted her to stay, and Pam, exhausted and at the end of her tether, wanted her to go. Sheila couldn't stay buried in their air-raid shelter for ever.

The one thing people were learning from this beastly bombing was that whatever happened, life had to go on. People still struggled to work. Even shops that had been bombed opened the next day. On Saturday Pam had bought a pound of apples from the market in Northcote Road and each one had had slivers of glass embedded in the skin. On Tuesday a German bomber had crashed into the tram depot in Clapham, slicing off the top of St Barnabus's spire as it fell, but the trams still went out on time the next day and St Barnabus's was still holding its services as usual.

In his wireless broadcast that night, J. B. Priestley said that Londoners were now the soldiers of the war, fighting the greatest battle. Pam felt she was fighting for her sanity.

'I know she's scared,' she said now, suddenly angry, standing up and going to the sink. 'We are all scared. We're scared of the bombing and we're scared of the thought of Hitler invading. And I know we've all got to do our bit and try to help each other. That's all very well, but nobody is helping me.'

She lifted her hand irritably as Alan went to speak. 'I know it's awful for Sheila on her own without Jo, but why doesn't she go to her relatives in the country? Or get someone in to share her own house over the road? Or if she has to stay here, why doesn't she at least pull her weight here and do a bit of shopping or cooking occasionally? Why doesn't she move her stuff out of the shelter so I might be able to lie down for five minutes after a full day at work?'

She felt tears suddenly in her eyes and brushed them away angrily. 'It's your fault, Alan. You think I'm strong. You think I can cope with everything. Well, I can't.'

Surely now he would understand, she thought as she blinked her tears back and stared at him hopefully.

Expecting some comfort, it took her a moment to realise that far from leaping to his feet full of reassuring husbandly sympathy, Alan was sitting in rigid silence at the kitchen table with his eyes fixed over her shoulder in an expression of absolute horror. Following his gaze, Pam swung round sharply. Her heart sank.

Sheila was standing in the back door with an empty cup in her hand. White faced and trembling, she must have heard every awful word Pam had spoken.

With a stricken glance at Alan, Pam moved forward quickly, but before she could speak, Sheila had yanked an old canvas bag off the peg on the back of the door and turned and run back into the yard.

Catching her up at the entrance to the shelter, Pam took her arm.

'Sheila, I didn't mean . . .'

But Sheila shook off her hold and swung round, eyes blazing. 'Don't worry. You don't have to spell it out. I know when I'm not wanted.' Clattering down the concrete steps, she began pulling her things off her bunk and shoving them into the bag, ignoring her son who sat watching with wide, scared eyes. 'I thought you were my friend. I thought you liked having us here. I thought having George here made up a little bit for not having children of your own.'

'Sheila, I love having you here . . .' Pam started helplessly but it was too late. She could see from the other girl's wild eyes and stubborn chin that her mind was made up. She hadn't been herself since Jo had died and now, watching her scrabbling her things together and shouting at George to get ready, she realised that Sheila was even closer to the edge than she had thought.

'Sheila, please. Let's talk about this.' Alan was there now, his voice calm and practical. 'It's silly to rush off now. They're expecting the sirens to go off any minute.' But it did no good. Jerking George off his bunk, Sheila picked up the bag and pushed past them into the yard.

'But where will you go?' Pam asked helplessly as they followed her back through the house to the front door. George was struggling now, his little arms flailing as he screamed to be left behind.

'Stop it,' Sheila shouted at him. 'It's no good you going on like that. They don't want us. That's all there is to it.' She opened the door and turned back for a second, her eyes cold and hard. 'What do you care where we go?' she hissed at Pam. 'We'll go where we feel safe and where people are prepared to give us a bit of kindness.'

★　　★　　★

The Wilhelmina hospital had been built during the Great War specifically to withstand the Zeppelin bombs. By the time it was finished, the Zeppelin raids were a thing of the past and the Wilhelmina's semi-underground design and reinforced structure had never been put to the test. Now, with the other London hospitals suffering from the nightly Luftwaffe attacks, the sturdy, bomb-proof Wilhelmina was coming into its own.

The Matron of St Thomas's had warned Katy that the Wilhelmina was run along strict, old-fashioned lines but nevertheless Katy's first day wasn't a bit what she had expected. She barely got the opportunity to speak to any of the patients, let alone to whisper words of reassurance and comfort.

Her first shock came when she duly presented herself to the Ethel Barnet ward at eight o'clock on the Monday morning.

As she pushed open the heavy swing doors she realised the Ethel Barnet ward was enormous. At least twenty beds lined one wall and twenty the other. In the middle were two great pillars, a number of metal trolleys covered in terrifying-looking instruments, some kind of enormous copper water boiler and towards the far end a highly polished table at which a tall, stately nurse was standing stiffly with a small book in her hands.

Expecting a room full of bustling activity Katy was surprised by the intense silence that greeted her. Gazing round in astonishment she realised that everyone in bed had their eyes closed and at the very far end of the ward five nurses knelt reverently in a row under the high heavily grilled window.

Before she could absorb the implications of this extraordinary sight, the silence was broken by a stentorian bellow from the nurse with the book.

'What do you think you are doing?'

The words were delivered so loudly that Katy let go of the door and it swung with a terrible crash behind her which nearly made her jump out of her skin. Aware of forty-five pairs of startled eyes swivelling towards her, Katy blushed scarlet.

'I'm Katy Parsons,' she whispered.

'Speak up.' The bellow came again. This must be Sister Morris, Katy realised, and her heart sank.

Repeating her name she added bravely, 'I was told to report here at eight o'clock.'

At this, forty-five pairs of eyes swivelled to the white-faced clock on the far wall. To Katy's dismay although the small hand sat firmly on the eight, the long hand was rapidly approaching ten past. Even as she gaped at it in horror, it moved another incriminating minute.

Dumbfounded, Katy was just about to check her own watch when Sister Morris roared again brandishing her prayer book like a sword. 'Well, don't just stand there, girl. Kneel. Can't you see we are in the presence of Our Lord?'

Stifling a terrible urge to giggle, Katy dropped hastily to her knees, wincing as they made painful contact with the well-polished floorboards. Terrified of laddering her newly purchased thick black stockings, she tried surreptitiously to wriggle a layer of her tweedy coat and sensible grey skirt between her knees and the floor, grimacing as the toes of her regulation Oxford shoes squeaked alarmingly.

It was clear that Sister had been close to rounding off the prayers when she had been interrupted. As soon as the final Amens had been said, Katy got to her feet and began to hurry forward to apologise.

But she was stopped in her tracks by another terrible roar. 'Get out! Get out!' Sister was sweeping down the ward like a tidal wave of rustling starch. 'What are you thinking of? I will not have mufti on my ward. Go at once to get yourself registered and then to the laundry stores and don't come back until you are properly dressed.'

Half an hour later, after signing her enrolment forms in the registry and a hasty visit to the laundry, Katy found herself dressed in a lilac striped dress two sizes too big for her, a crisp white apron with strings so long they almost trailed along the floor and a small folded linen cap that despite the laundry lady's efforts had a tendency to droop at one side. Once again she heaved open the huge wooden doors.

'Not that way!' Sister was advancing furiously. 'Those doors are reserved for doctors and visitors.' She glared at Katy and pointed at the far end of the ward where a small, rather insignificant door led off to one side. 'Nurses come and go that way.'

Not knowing whether to laugh or cry, Katy stumbled away but by the time she'd scurried up and down numerous identical unmarked passages and staircases and finally managed with the aid of a kindly hospital porter to reappear at the right entrance, Sister Morris was nowhere to be seen.

As she hovered nervously at the edge of the ward one of the other nurses glanced at her. 'Sister is in her office,' she said crisply, nodding to a side room. 'Waiting for you.'

'Where on earth have you been?' Sister Morris shouted as Katy knocked and pushed the door open nervously. 'It's gone nine o'clock.' Her eyes widened as she took in Katy's appearance. 'And what do you think you look like?' She frowned. 'I'm not impressed, Miss Parsons. Not impressed at all. You present yourself ten minutes late, improperly dressed, and now an hour later you stroll in again, looking like something the cat brought in. What have you to say?'

Katy blinked. There was a lot she would have liked to say but under the dreadful stare of Sister's ice-blue eyes she couldn't persuade her dry lips to utter a single word. All desire to giggle had suddenly left her. She felt instead as if she was about to burst into tears. She had longed for this day for so long and she couldn't understand why it was going so wrong.

'I'm sorry,' she mumbled eventually. 'I didn't . . .' She stopped as her interrogator stood up abruptly.

'I beg your pardon.' The temperature of Sister Morris's voice dropped another few degrees.

Katy blinked. What had she done now?

Sister Morris drew herself to her full height which to Katy's horrified eyes looked about six foot five. 'Miss Parsons, I don't know your background or why you have been foisted on me as you have, but I would like to make one thing quite clear. When you are addressing a senior nursing Sister in this hospital you will address her as Sister. Is that quite understood?'

Katy felt herself flush. 'Yes, er . . . Sister.'

Sister Morris barely paused in her diatribe. 'If in the unlikely event you are called upon to speak to a doctor, you will address him as Doctor. Junior nurses you will address as Nurse, staff nurses as Staff.'

Katy nodded meekly. 'Yes, Sister.' She was getting the hang of it now.

Sister frowned. 'You will of course appreciate that as an untrained probationer, you are the lowest of the low. In general, therefore, you will not be expected to speak at all unless specifically asked to do so.'

'Yes, Sister.' It was out before Katy had time to stop it and she cringed as the ice-blue eyes bored into her once more. She prayed Sister Morris wouldn't think she was being facetious.

'Thank you, Nurse, that will do,' Sister Morris said dangerously. She saw Katy's start of surprise and pursed her lips. 'You are not a nurse, of course, yet, but for the benefit of the patients you will be referred to as such. Now, I am going to ask Staff Hicks to come in. She is a qualified State Registered Nurse and she will be in charge of you. You will do as she tells you quickly and efficiently and without question.'

She went to the door and glanced out. Staff Nurse Hicks was clearly awaiting the summons because at once Katy could hear the rapid click of heels approaching Sister's office.

Before she arrived Sister Morris turned to Katy. 'I have three rules on my ward, Nurse. Godliness, cleanliness and diligence. I expect you to uphold them at all times.'

'Yes, Sister,' Katy muttered, turning in some relief as the nurse she had spoken to outside stepped into the office.

The introductions were brisk and unemotional. Katy's ingratiating smile was met by a stern nod of the head. Clearly the other nurses, even staff nurses, didn't let their hair down in sister's awe-inspiring presence.

'Is she always like that?' Katy whispered as she was led away.

Staff Hicks blinked in surprise. 'Sister Morris is one of the most respected sisters in this hospital,' she said stiffly. 'We are all proud to be on her ward.' She stopped at the polished table from which Sister had delivered the prayers and frowned at Katy. 'Now, Nurse, I'm going to explain the organisation of the ward. Listen carefully please as I won't have time to go through it again.'

Certainly time seemed to be something generally in short order on Ethel Barnet ward. Katy could not believe how much had to be done in such a short space of time. And if it wasn't finished in the time allocated Sister would come bearing down with a sharp rebuke that left the offending nurse quivering with fear.

Most of what Staff Hicks said passed over her head but she did gather that the ward was divided into three areas: Northside and Southside with twenty beds each, and Centre Aisle, with no beds but most of the medical equipment, the trolleys, the steriliser and Sister's table. Centre Aisle was looked after by one third-year nurse, but Northside and Southside were both under the charge of staff nurses, each of whom had a junior nurse or a probationer to assist with the more menial jobs.

Staff Hicks was responsible for the twenty beds on Northside. She wasted no time in getting Katy to work.

Some of the jobs were better than others. Filling and delivering the stone hot-water bottles and hot dusting the windowsills and lockers wasn't too bad, but bed-making was back-breakingly hard work. Every patient's bed had to be completely stripped and remade with the sheets and blankets folded back and tucked at the top and bottom to some precise formula laid down by Sister. As most of the Ethel Barnet patients were incapacitated, lifting or rolling them to get the sheets under them was a killer. By the twentieth bed Katy thought she was going to crack in two.

But, by any standard, washing out the bed pans was the worst job. Despite the nurses' strict instructions to keep the sluice room clean, the smell in there was quite horrible. Each bed pan had to be emptied into a kind of trough and then swilled, scrubbed with a special long-handled brush, rinsed and dried. If any droplets of water, or anything else, fell on the ward's highly polished floor. Sister was down on the offender like a ton of bricks.

The patients were as terrified of Sister as everyone else and even those in obvious pain were circumspect in their groaning when she was within earshot. Once, as Katy hurried up the ward to fetch a clean duster, she heard one of the patients crying. Not daring to call for help, Katy broke into a run in her haste to find Staff Hicks.

At once a bellow echoed round the walls.

'What do you think you are doing?' Faced with Sister Morris once again advancing towards her, Katy screeched to a standstill. 'I do not allow running on my ward, Nurse, it would be as well to remember that.'

'But that lady was crying,' Katy said uncertainly. 'I think she's in pain, Sister.'

Sister's glare did not waver. 'You would be in pain if you had had your leg removed, Nurse. Mrs James is as comfortable as can be expected.' Her uniform rustled alarmingly. 'Haven't you got anything to do, Nurse?'

Katy nodded dumbly. 'Yes, Sister, I'm meant to be helping Staff Hicks move the screen round Mrs James's bed.'

'Well, I suggest you get on with it, then. I do not tolerate slacking on my ward.'

Meals arrived up in the ward on an enormous trolley from the kitchens wheeled up by hospital porters and were preceded by grace. Once again everyone had to kneel on the floor and this time it didn't occur to Katy to giggle. She was far too exhausted, and in any case she was far too scared of receiving another lashing from Sister's vicious tongue. Oddly it wasn't being told off that she minded, it was being told off in front of the patients and the other nurses.

One of the worst moments of the day came as she queued up in turn to carry a lunch tray to one of the patients.

Noticing Katy standing by the trolley, Sister stopped serving for a moment. Her eyes travelled slowly from the top of Katy's floppy cap to the toes of her new specially purchased black shoes and back to a small stain on her apron. 'Your appearance is a disgrace, Nurse,' she said. 'If you're intending to remain on this ward, you're going to have to tidy yourself up.'

She turned to Staff Hicks who was standing behind her. 'Please see that she remains in the sluice room during the doctors' rounds this afternoon. I can't have her being seen about the place looking like this.'

Katy thought she detected a certain amount of glee in Staff Hicks' expression as she nodded. 'Yes, Sister.'

Katy tried not to mind, but she wished the other nurses would be a bit more friendly. None of them had made any effort to talk to her or make her feel at home. On the contrary she sensed they were all watching and waiting for her next humiliating mistake. One in particular, the Southside probationer, a small pixie-faced girl with beady eyes and a sullen mouth, seemed to take vicarious delight in her discomfort.

And as the long first day wore on, her discomfort was considerable. Quite apart from the repeated reprimands, never in all her life had she felt so utterly and completely exhausted. Everything ached, her back, her legs, her head and, worst of all, her feet.

She had never been so pleased to see anyone as she was to see the six night nurses arrive at eight o'clock in the evening. The final straw was being told five minutes before going off duty that she had to fetch a loaf of bread from the kitchen for their midnight snack. At one point on the walk down the endless corridors to the far distant kitchen Katy thought she was going to collapse. She wondered how long she would be left lying in a little heap at the side of the passage before anyone came to rescue her. Then she remembered what Sister Morris would have to say about it and forced her weary legs to complete the journey.

The only saving grace of the entire day was that no air-raid had yet been signalled, which meant that the buses were still running normally, and for the five-minute ride along Lavender Hill, she was able to sit down for the first time since seven thirty that morning.

It was odd being out of doors in the real world again. Very little sense of the outside world had penetrated the antiseptic, disciplined environment of the Ethel Barnet ward and Katy realised, somewhat to her surprise, as she listened idly to the chat on the bus, that a day of war had passed without her. Normally she spent every possible moment listening to the news broadcasts and yet today, for once, she hadn't given them a thought.

Back at the pub she discovered from her mother that the exiled French General, Charles de Gaulle, had landed in Dakar, Senegal with his Free French forces, the King had broadcast from Buckingham Palace, and eighty-three children had been drowned when the *City of Benares* evacuee ship was torpedoed by German submarines on the way to America.

But for once the news failed to affect her. Nor did her parents' anxious remarks about how pale and tired she looked. Nor did the sirens wailing out just as her mother began to cook her some supper.

All she cared about was tidying up her uniform for tomorrow. Even though her legs and back ached unmercifully, she sat up in the cellar until two in the morning with pins and needles and the light of a candle, trying desperately to get it into some semblance of order.

Chapter Four

Celia Rutherford stood in the bedroom doorway and smiled. 'Is that humming I hear, Mrs Carter?'

Joyce looked up with a guilty start from her polishing and Celia laughed. 'Don't stop. It makes a pleasant change from endless bad news which is all I seem to hear on the wireless these days. That de Gaulle fellow has had to withdraw from Dakar, you know. He didn't last long, did he?'

Joyce shook her head. 'They're hopeless, them French. If they had put up a better fight of it in the beginning we wouldn't be in this mess.'

Celia Rutherford raised her eyebrows. 'A better fight?' she said scornfully. 'They hardly put up a fight at all. Paris wasn't touched, you know. And now they're sitting there all comfy in their nice warm homes watching the guts being bombed out of London.'

'I heard the Fulham hospital caught it last night,' Joyce said. 'Lost a whole wing.' She nodded out of the bedroom window which looked out over Clapham Common. 'And several houses gone over on the other side of the common. It's still cordoned off.'

Mr Lorenz, the pawnbroker, had told her that when she bumped into him earlier. Then he'd given her that funny little bow and raised his hat and walked away down the street. Joyce smiled to herself now. He was a funny chap, Lorenz, tight as a tart's corset, Stanley'd always said, but she'd always found him all right. She felt sorry for him really. Once, in an uncharacteristically forthright moment, he'd told her that he'd lost a lot of friends in the Nazi purges in Poland. God knew what would happen to him if Hitler invaded.

She glanced out of Mrs Rutherford's bedroom window over the common. The beautifully tended playing fields had long gone, the remaining grass was burnt in places from shrapnel and the bomb craters were already filling with leaves from the shedding autumn trees.

'There was one bit of good news,' Celia said suddenly from her chest of drawers. 'They found a boatload of children from that *City of Benares* evacuee ship. They'd been drifting for over a week. They'd kept alive by singing songs.'

'Poor little blighters,' Joyce said. 'Not much cop for the rest of them, though. They'd have been better off staying put.'

'I don't know about that,' Celia said. 'People have started sleeping in the Underground stations now and the conditions are dreadful apparently. The government are beginning to worry about disease.' She shook her head. 'I saw in the paper this morning that the Bishop of Norwich recommends the shelter of God. But as they are saying that seven thousand people have been killed in London during the month of September, it makes you wonder, doesn't it? Seven thousand. And that's not counting the thousands more injured.'

Joyce grimaced. 'You're making me feel guilty for humming now.'

'Oh, I didn't mean to,' Celia said, turning round. 'We've got to keep our spirits up somehow, Mrs Carter. God knows things are bad enough without seeing long faces about everywhere.' She sighed slightly and rolled her eyes towards the door. 'I've got one of those along the passage.'

Joyce smiled sympathetically. 'Miss Louise?' She'd caught a glimpse of her earlier on the landing looking like a bear with a sore paw. Man problems, she had thought. That was usually the cause of Miss fancy-pants Louise Rutherford's bad humour. Not like Jen, whose current sulks were due to the delay in ENSA finding her a suitable concert party to join. The sooner they found one the better, in Joyce's opinion. She was sick of Jen's moods, her snappy retorts, her irritability.

Even Bob's arrival home hadn't cheered Jen up. He'd done Mick and Pete a lot of good with his prison jokes and his teasing and that. Made them smarten themselves up a bit. And there was laughter in the house now and that made a nice change. But, if anything, having Bob around had made Jen worse. Once or twice when he had teased her about something, Jen had looked as if she might burst into tears. And last night when Mick had asked if he could have her bedroom when she went, she had nearly bitten his head off.

Celia lowered her voice. 'I'm quite worried about Louise actually,' she said. 'She's been so jumpy recently. And she really looks quite poorly. She's not eating at all well but she refuses to see the doctor.' She shook her head. 'I don't know if it's the bombing or what that's making her so low.'

Joyce wondered about putting her man theory forward but decided not to. Mrs Rutherford was all very friendly and that these days but you never knew with these classy women. Sometimes they got on their high horse over nothing at all, and Joyce didn't want to fall out of favour. Just for once things seemed to be going pretty well. That was why she'd been humming. What with having Bob home and that, for the first time in ages she had felt almost happy. It would be a shame to rock the boat. If nothing else, she needed her wages.

'Are you going out on the WVS van tonight, Mrs Carter?' Celia asked suddenly.

Joyce nodded. 'Yes.' She hesitated. She knew Mr Rutherford had put his foot down last week. 'Are you?'

Celia smiled. Joyce noticed a certain gritty determination in that smile. 'Oh yes, I wouldn't miss it for the world. In any case, I believe we have to stand up for our principles, don't you, Mrs Carter?'

'Well, yes, I suppose so,' Joyce said doubtfully. Actually she wasn't sure about principles. Principles were a bit of a luxury, she'd always thought. Good in theory but not quite so good in practice. Celia

Rutherford could apparently cope with a bit of displeasure from her husband about the WVS. But then Greville Rutherford, bastard though he was, was hardly likely to stop her housekeeping or start knocking her about. Perhaps principles were easier for the rich. She could feel her employer's eyes on her but luckily the discussion was curtailed by the arrival of a car in the driveway below.

'It's your husband's car,' Joyce said, peering out of the window.

Most people's cars were up on blocks by now, or used only for special occasions, but Mr Rutherford, as owner of the brewery, had special petrol rations.

'Oh yes.' Celia nodded. 'That'll be Mr Wallace. Apparently some parcel arrived for me this morning at Clapham Junction.' She moved to the door. 'I wonder what it is.'

'Whatever it is, he doesn't look very pleased about it,' Joyce remarked. She didn't like Mr Wallace, the Rutherfords' chauffeur, he was a supercilious bastard. Just because he could drive a car he thought he was bloody royalty, whereas in fact he was a jumped-up little git from Peckham. She frowned. 'He seems to be having difficulty getting out of the car.' Then her eyes widened. 'Oh my God, Mrs Rutherford, no wonder he can't get out. He's got some kind of bird in there with him.'

'A bird?' Celia Rutherford looked shocked. Then suddenly she put her hand to her mouth. 'Oh goodness,' she gasped. 'It must be my point-of-lay pullets.'

Joyce blinked. 'Your what?'

Celia giggled. 'My hens. Well, chickens really, they're only six months old. I ordered half a dozen last week. But I had no idea they would come so soon. Oh dear. I haven't mentioned it to Greville yet.'

'Come on, Nurse Parsons, for goodness' sake.' Staff Nurse Hicks tapped her foot impatiently as she waited for Katy to tuck in the foot of the bed. 'We haven't got all day.'

It was nine thirty in the morning and the Ethel Barnet ward was a hive of activity, racing to get ready for the hospital Matron's ward round at ten. Twelve extra beds had been brought into the ward overnight. Four extra on each side and four end to end up the centre aisle. Already they were filled with casualties from collapsed buildings, falling masonry, flying shrapnel. The doctors had been operating all night. The nurses were rushed off their feet. The raids over the weekend had taken their toll on Balham, Clapham and Battersea. What with the Fulham hospital being bombed and St Thomas's and the Bolingbroke now effectively closed to all but emergency cases, the Wilhelmina, with its bomb-proof buildings and its vast reinforced basements, was one of the few fully operational hospitals left in South London.

'I'm sorry,' Katy muttered, 'I don't know what's the matter with me today.'

But she did know. Last night Louise Rutherford had waylaid her on her way home and told her she was pregnant with Stefan Pininski's child.

'I've got to get rid of it,' Louise had added as they stood shivering on the corner of Lavender Road. 'I thought you'd know how to now that you're a nurse.'

Katy had gaped at her in horror. Did she mean 'know how to' in terms of Katy personally locating and disposing of the foetus? She swallowed hard. 'But Louise . . .' She had stopped, groping for the right thing to say. 'I wouldn't have the faintest idea how to go about . . .' She was appalled at the very thought. 'I honestly don't think it's as easy as that. Anyway, I'm on the surgical ward, I haven't heard of anyone needing . . . anything like that. Our patients mostly have broken bones and fractures.'

'Surely you can find out,' Louise said crossly. 'There must be someone who'd know. Someone you could ask.'

For an awful second Katy imagined herself asking Sister Morris, and cringed. It was quite simply out of the question. The very thought made her feel sick.

'I don't think there is,' she had said helplessly. 'I don't know anyone well enough to ask, not about something like that. I've only been there a week.' A week? It seemed like a lifetime. A lifetime of aching feet and continual reprimands. Was it really only a week? She wondered if she would last another. Deep down she wondered if she wanted to.

Louise's eyes suddenly filled with tears. 'Please, Katy.' Her classy BBC voice had choked. 'You must help me. There's nobody else I can turn to.'

'I suppose I could ask Jen,' Katy said doubtfully. 'She might know.'

'Good Lord, no, don't ask her. I don't want her knowing.' Louise looked horrified. 'If her mother found out and told mine, all hell would be let loose.'

'I needn't say it's you,' Katy said mildly. 'I could pretend it's someone at the hospital or something. I think she's our best bet.'

Louise was unconvinced. 'Well, all right,' she said, desperation winning over caution. 'If you think so. But do be careful.'

But Jen, although intrigued, had not been able to help. 'I think it's the sort of thing you get done in the back streets of Balham,' she had said. 'And it hurts like hell. Other than that I haven't a clue.' She eyed Katy with interest. 'So who do you know that's been having some illicit hanky-panky, then?' She grinned. 'It's not you, is it?'

'Me?' Katy had stared at her, astonished. 'Of course not. Anyway,' she opened her hands, belatedly realising that Jen was teasing, 'who on earth would I find to have hanky-panky with?'

'Oh I don't know,' Jen had said airily. 'What about Ward Frazer?'

For a terrible second as the breath caught in her throat, Katy had thought she was going to choke. Don't blush, she told herself sternly, for goodness' sake don't blush or she'll tease about it unmercifully. But it was too late, she could already feel the heat in her neck and the knowing sparkle in Jen's eyes and it was with a heroic effort that she had forced her shoulders into a nonchalant shrug and her mouth into a wry smile.

'If only,' she had said, trying to match Jen's light hearted tone. She was gratified to see the surprise on Jen's face. She had obviously been expecting a heated denial. Seizing the initiative, Katy had raised her eyebrows. 'Anyway he seems much more interested in you than me.'

'In me?' Jen had shaken her head. 'Oh no, definitely not.' She grinned. 'Not that I'd say no, given the chance. No, if anyone, I think he's still interested in Louise Rutherford.'

'Louise?' Katy had repeated faintly.

Jen had nodded. 'He was asking about her the other day. Said he hadn't seen her for a while. A friend of hers had told him she was seeing some glamorous Polish Count. I got the impression he wasn't very happy about it.'

Katy had grimaced. If only he knew. Louise reckoned Ward had ditched her because she was too inexperienced. Well, Louise had certainly rectified that. Her affair with Stefan Pininski had by her own admission been shockingly uninhibited. And now she was paying the price.

To Katy's abject relief, before she could make any response to Jen's remark, the air-raid warning had sounded and she had hurried back across the road to lie tossing and turning on her camp bed in the smoky cellar, dreaming about a man with steel-grey eyes laughing uproariously at the very thought of going out with her.

Now, as she straightened her aching back and glanced ahead down the long line of beds still to be made, she realised she had got no further in solving Louise's problem.

Staff Hicks' irate voice broke suddenly into her thoughts. 'Nurse Parsons, you really are the most ineffective bed-maker I have ever had the misfortune to meet. I've told you a hundred times it's left over right, not right over left.'

Katy jolted. 'I'm sorry, Staff,' she muttered, rectifying the mistake and moving hastily on to the next bed.

As she began to strip it she could feel the ominous tightness in her chest and wished she was less ineffective all round. Half the time she couldn't even breathe properly. She had woken up wheezing in the night and she had been terrified that she wouldn't be fit enough to work this morning.

She glanced at Staff Hicks' sour face at the other end of the bed and steeled herself to go on. The Southside nurses on the other side of the ward had already finished their beds and were getting their patients ready for Matron's round.

She could feel the breath rasping in her throat again now and prayed it wouldn't develop into another full-blown wheezing session. She had been ordered to sit quietly for an hour in Sister's office only last Thursday when she started coughing and gasping in the sluice room. Sister had been remarkably tolerant over that, but the other nurses had obviously thought it was a good excuse to avoid the bed pans.

Just as now they would think it was an excuse if she asked to be let off the rest of the bed-making. Just as Louise would think it was an excuse if she told her there was nobody to ask about her baby. Gritting her teeth she tried to breathe calmly, tried not to think about coughing. If only she was fit and effective she wouldn't need excuses.

Katy sighed. It was no wonder Staff Hicks was impatient with her. She wasn't just an ineffective bed-maker, she had come to realise that she was a pretty ineffective nurse too. Not that she had got on to any real nursing yet, of course. Staff Hicks or Sister dealt with that. Probationer duties mostly entailed an endless round of cleaning, bed-making and bed pan emptying. But she was slow and clumsy at those. And it had taken ages for her to get the hang of taking a temperature, and she still couldn't work the steriliser properly. And she had nearly fainted when she had watched some stitches being removed from a leg wound on Friday. Luckily Sister had sent her away before she hit the deck, but she had felt a complete idiot nevertheless, particularly when she had noticed the pixie-faced probationer smirking in the background.

The only thing she had apparently managed to get right was her uniform. After that first awful day there had been fewer comments about her appearance. Despite her debilitating exhaustion, she had made a huge effort to keep clean and tidy and had finally learnt how to fold and pin her cap. And thank God she had because that morning Matron decided to inspect all the nurses on the ward before beginning her round.

Sister Morris had a reputation of being strict, but Matron was considered to be a complete tartar. Katy had only met her once. She had been summoned to Matron's office on her second day and had prayed never to have to go again. Matron was renowned for her eagle eyes and her unerring ability to find fault.

But it wasn't Katy's uniform she found fault with today, it was her health.

'What is the meaning of this, Nurse?' she asked crisply, as she heard Katy's laboured breathing. 'Why haven't you reported yourself sick?'

'I . . . I'm not really sick,' Katy stammered, flushing. 'It's just the bed-making, it seems to make me short of breath.'

Ignoring Katy, Matron turned to Sister Morris. 'Keep an eye on this nurse. If she's not fit to be on duty she must be sent home.'

Then before Sister Morris could respond, Matron had raised her voice and was addressing the ward. 'In this hospital we pride ourselves on our attention to detail,' she said crisply. 'In the circumstances in which we find ourselves it is all too easy to let standards slip. For the benefit of our great city and its inhabitants in this difficult time we must continue to strive for excellence. We must do our duty with courage and patience, nurses and patients alike. It is only by pulling together and giving our all that the tyrant in Germany will be defeated. And defeated he will be, you mark my words.'

She stopped and glared around as though someone was about to dare to argue. Then she smiled thinly and relaxed slightly.

'Does anyone have any questions?'

Yes, Katy thought. How does one go about getting an abortion? But she shook her head along with the others. 'No, Matron,' she murmured meekly.

'They'll have to go in the coal bunker,' Celia Rutherford said. She saw Joyce's start of surprise. 'Only temporarily of course,' she added quickly. 'Just until I've had time to find them some kind of hutch.'

'But they'll get all dirty in the coal bunker,' Joyce said, peering into the crate at the five sleek copper-coloured birds. The sixth bird was still in the car, having somehow extricated itself from the crate on the way back from Clapham Junction and subsequently, to Joyce's secret glee, evaded all Mr Wallace's red-faced efforts to recapture it. It was nice to see the chauffeur brought down a peg or two by a chicken.

'Wouldn't they be happier in the greenhouse?' she suggested. 'Or what about your husband's tool shed?'

'Now that's a good idea.' Celia turned to the chauffeur. 'Could you take them down to the tool shed, please, Mr Wallace? And do try not to let any more escape.'

It was clear from Mr Wallace's expression that if he had his way the hens would swiftly be consigned to the cooking pot. But mindful of his wages, he shouldered the crate. 'What about that one?' he growled nodding towards the wily bird in the car.

Celia smiled. 'Oh, Mrs Carter will deal with that.'

Joyce blinked at her. 'Will I?'

'I will entice it with some food and once it is eating you will catch it and hold it.'

Joyce took a quick glance to make sure Mr Wallace was out of earshot. 'I don't know how to hold a hen,' she said. 'Let alone catch it.'

Celia laughed. 'Well, we can't make any more of a mess of it than Mr Wallace, that's for certain.'

If it was a challenge it had the desired effect. Joyce was aware that catching the bird had suddenly became very important, a matter of female pride.

And in fact with the aid of a tasty piece of fruit cake she managed to grab it on the third attempt. After a short struggle she got it in a firm grip round the wings and breast. It was surprisingly light and bony and its feathers were cool to the touch and smooth.

'The poor thing's scared witless,' she remarked as she carried it triumphantly down the garden. 'I can feel his little heart going like the clappers.'

'I hope he's a her.' Mrs Rutherford smiled. 'Or we're not going to get many eggs.'

Joyce chuckled. 'Might get a few more chickens though.'

Mr Wallace was quite clearly not pleased that Joyce had succeeded where he had failed. 'Used to handling poultry, are you, Mrs Carter?' he asked with his customary sneer as she gently lowered her charge to the shed's wooden floor and watched her scuttle to join her more retiring travelling companions behind the lawn mower. 'No different from street pigeons, I suppose.'

Joyce bristled. 'We don't eat street pigeons in Clapham, Mr Wallace,' she said. 'I think it's only in the slums of Peckham that they do that.'

'It just needed a delicate touch,' Celia cut in placatingly.

'Which you obviously haven't got, Mr Wallace,' Joyce added sweetly. She saw Mrs Rutherford turn away quickly to hide her amusement and felt a strange kick of pleasure. She enjoyed needling Mr Wallace. But more importantly she loved making Mrs Rutherford laugh. Poor woman hadn't much to laugh about what with her poker-faced husband and that son of hers being a conchie and that and banished to Shropshire. As for her sulky little madam of a daughter, why wasn't she helping with the hens? Why was she sitting nice and warm indoors while her poor mother tramped about in the vegetable patch looking for some cabbage leaves for them to peck at?

'Poor darlings must be starving if they've been travelling all night,' Celia said, peering in to see if the hens liked her offering. They didn't and stood awkwardly at the back of the shed looking thoroughly miserable. Celia looked concerned. 'I'll need to get them some proper hen food, balancer meal I think they call it. I believe if you give up your egg ration you get an allocation.'

'What about something for them to sit on?' Joyce said. 'That floor looks a bit uncomfortable. I wouldn't want to lay an egg on that.'

Celia chuckled. 'Yes, they'll need some straw.' She turned to the chauffeur. 'Mr Wallace, I wonder if you would run the car down to the brewery and bring me back some straw from the stables and some oats or corn or whatever the dray horses eat.'

'Straw?' Mr Wallace looked appalled. 'In the car? Are you sure, madam? It will make a dreadful mess. I don't think your husband . . .'

Celia frowned. 'I will telephone my husband,' she said stiffly, 'and ask him to arrange for someone to put the straw in a box so it doesn't dirty the car.'

Mr Wallace shook his head. 'The hens have made enough mess as it is.'

Celia flushed slightly. 'Well I'm sorry about that, Mr Wallace, but you may have noticed we have a war on and we can't be quite as fussy as we used to be.'

Mr Wallace sniffed at the rebuke. 'Well, I don't think Mr Rutherford is going to like it.'

'Well, Mr Rutherford is going to have to lump it,' Joyce cut in violently. 'Mrs Rutherford has only ordered these chickens so as he can have his boiled egg for breakfast and he ought to be grateful.'

Mr Wallace didn't deign to respond to Joyce's outburst. Instead he addressed Celia stiffly. 'And where will I put the straw on my return, madam?'

'Oh, just leave it outside the shed, please, Mr Wallace,' Celia said meekly. 'I'll see to it later.'

'I could have told him where to put it,' Joyce muttered darkly as he strutted away up the garden path. 'And the box and all. He wouldn't be smirking like that if he had a few splinters up his arse.'

She was startled by Celia's snort of laughter.

'Well, I mean, honestly . . .' Joyce said indignantly. 'He shouldn't talk to you like that. He's only a bloody chauffeur, after all.'

Celia shook her head. 'He's a man. They're all the same.'

'Well, it's not right,' Joyce said stoutly. 'I mean, what do they think we are?'

Celia smiled wryly. 'Second best, I'm afraid, Mrs Carter. Second best.'

As Katy had failed to come up with a means to dispose of her baby, Louise had in desperation turned to Aaref Hoch. Aaref had changed a lot in the year since he had first arrived in London with his two younger brothers. He had been seventeen when Louise first started teaching him English, thin as a reed with wary eyes sunk deep in his pinched, pallid face.

In those days he had been difficult to talk to, spiky and suspicious, a strange mixture of fierce pride and intense shyness. But gradually, as the terror of the previous few years in Austria receded and the fear of persecution faded, he had become more confident, more relaxed and assured.

To her astonishment, when she had put her predicament to him, his first reaction had been to offer to marry her.

'I could make you happy, Louise. If you were my wife I would love you very much.'

'Don't be absurd, Aaref,' Louise said. 'I can't possibly marry you. You're far too young and, anyway, Daddy would have a fit.'

'Because I am Jewish?'

Louise shifted uneasily. 'Well, yes, partly because of that, but also because you haven't got any money or anything.'

Aaref shrugged. 'I will make money. Already I have ideas for business. I think in a few years I will make your father swallow his words.'

'Eat his words,' Louise corrected automatically. 'No, but seriously, Aaref, I wouldn't dream of it. Anyway where would we live?'

Aaref smiled. 'You could come to live with us. Lael wouldn't mind.'

Aaref and his brothers lived with Lael d'Arcy Billière, the strange, rather exotic woman who owned the house on the other side of the road from the Rutherfords. It was in Mrs d'Arcy Billière's house that Louise had met Stefan Pininski too and even though their subsequent affair had been carried out in complete secrecy, Louise still felt awkward in the other woman's company. The thought of living in the odd, unconventional household made Louise feel distinctly uneasy.

'No, Aaref,' she said firmly. 'You're very nice and everything but you're just not the right type for me. Anyway making money in a few years won't do. It's now I'm worried about. If Daddy finds out about this blasted baby, he'll kill me. Or he'll throw me out and then what would I do? Nobody would marry me then.'

'I would look after you,' Aaref said. 'Even if you wouldn't marry me, I would look after you.'

Louise grimaced. 'Oh for goodness' sake, Aaref,' she'd said irritably in rising panic, 'be serious for a minute. Now, look, will you help me or not?'

And he had helped her. Even though he said he didn't like it, that life was sacred, and any child should have the right to live, he had promised to do what he could.

Since he had been interned earlier in the year, he had made contact with a network of Jewish émigrés all over London and it was from one of these a week or so later that he had elicited the address of a man who carried out abortions just off Balham High Road.

'Apparently it is clean and hygienic,' he said, handing over the scrap of paper reluctantly as they strolled across Clapham Common one afternoon.

It was early October and the autumn rain had given way to a

fragile sunlight that glittered on the wet grass. The ground was littered with shrapnel after last night's heavy raid. Aaref watched a woman with a pram negotiate a crater that had damaged the path. Quickly he turned back to Louise. 'I was careful to ask that. This man used to be some kind of hospital surgeon so he must have correct instruments and equipment.'

'Instruments and equipment?' Louise frowned. She stirred a pile of leaves with her toe. 'What do you mean? Don't they just give you medicine or pills or something? Something that makes it fall out? Stefan said it was quite simple.' She looked up at Aaref again and was shocked by the expression on his face.

'It's not so easy,' he said awkwardly. 'Didn't you know? It is operation. A surgery.'

Louise paled and sat down quickly on a nearby bench. 'You mean they cut you open?'

If anything Aaref looked even more distressed as he sat down beside her and shook his head slowly. 'I don't think they cut you,' he said. He flushed as he groped for the right words and Louise began to feel very sick. Sick and scared.

'I think they . . . how would you say? Go up from below,' he suggested at last. 'And pull it out that way.'

For a dreadful second as his words sank in, Louise thought she was going to faint. How could Stefan have misled her so badly? And then the gorge rose in her throat and she struggled to her feet clasping her hand to her mouth.

She was sick under a tree and afterwards leaned weakly against the trunk, sobbing as Aaref awkwardly offered her his handkerchief.

'I'm sorry,' he said. 'I thought you knew.' He touched her arm. 'Don't do it, Louise. Think again. Please. Have the baby. I will take care of you.'

For the moment as she stared at him, Louise was tempted. She hated pain, the very thought of it made her feel faint. And Aaref's stumbling description had sounded like the worst kind of torture. But then it was painful having a baby too. Agony, they said.

'No.' She spoke through gritted teeth. 'No, I can't have a baby. I can't ruin my life. I don't want to live in poverty and misery. I'm too young.'

She swallowed hard as the tears threatened again. She put her hand to her eyes and sobbed pitifully. 'I want to have fun.'

Chapter Five

Shivering, Katy pressed herself back against the shop window and closed her eyes.

She had been on her way home from the hospital when the sirens had started blaring, but there had been no sound of planes so she had hurried on. It was only when she heard the thumping roar of the guns up on the common that she had hesitated in the entrance to Arding & Hobbs department store at the crossroads on Lavender Hill. The shop was shut of course, but the recessed doorway gave a little shelter and Katy had been glad of it as a bomb exploded somewhere down in Battersea by the river. They were aiming at the gas works most likely, or the bridges, or the armament factories by the railway line. Nowhere was safe any more. Not at night. By day the valiant RAF could just about keep the Luftwaffe at bay, but once it got dark the Germans seemed able to drop their bombs just where they pleased. They'd already damaged Number 10 Downing Street, Buckingham Palace and Broadcasting House. Last night the high altar at St Paul's had been destroyed.

Now, as the immediate danger seemed to have passed, Katy opened her eyes and peered cautiously out at the empty road. It was a clear night. Above the darkened buildings the stars were bright and she could see the white trails of the German planes. Absurdly it was almost pretty. Even as she watched, half a dozen flares exploded to the north and began to float down over Chelsea, lighting the sky with bright phosphorescence. Overhead a small formation of fat-bellied bombers showed up suddenly against the light, growling across the sky, and at once the anti-aircraft barrage sprung into action again, the shells bursting in red and orange puffs of smoke. Had she not seen first-hand the pain and suffering caused by those planes she might almost have enjoyed the spectacle.

Flinching back again as some flak fell with a clatter on the road, her heart sank as an ARP warden appeared from St John's Road and ran across the road towards her clutching his white hat.

'You ought to be in a shelter,' he shouted.

'I only live round the corner,' Katy said, raising her voice over the sound of the guns. 'I was hoping to get home.'

As usual she was desperate to sleep. In the last three weeks she had done little else than work and sleep. Or try to sleep. It wasn't that easy in the smoke-filled pub cellar with a crowd of men laughing and joking just the other side of her screen of crates. And if it wasn't the men, it was her parents fussing and worrying about her. Was she warm enough? Was she sure the nursing wasn't too much for her? What about a hot drink? And hadn't she met any nice doctors yet? They'd heard of quite a few nurses marrying doctors.

Katy sighed. Working the hours she did there was no time to meet anybody. Let alone doctors who in any case seemed to treat the nurses like dirt. Less than dirt. Like invisible dirt. She didn't care. She didn't want to marry a doctor. She didn't want to marry anybody. All she wanted to do was sleep.

Still, she was starting night duty tomorrow. And that meant that she had a full day off tomorrow. The first in three weeks. She was intending to sleep the whole day.

As a plane roared suddenly low overhead Katy jumped nervously.

'Junker,' the ARP warden said. 'You can tell by the engine.'

Katy nodded silently. She had a cloak now, as part of her uniform, a sweeping navy affair with red trim. She huddled it round her as the wind blew a cloud of dirty acrid smoke towards them.

The man glanced at her. 'You a nurse? Marvellous job for a girl, nursing. Nice and ladylike, not like these factory girls in trousers and that.'

Katy smiled thinly. If only he knew. This morning she had dropped a bed pan. It just slipped out of her hand and the mess splashed and spread all over the ward floor. Sister Morris had been apoplectic and Katy had spent a painful and humiliating hour and a half on her hands and knees scrubbing the floorboards until you could have eaten your dinner off them. Twice Sister inspected it and twice she said it wasn't good enough. By the third time Katy was in tears and Sister told her to pull herself together and apologise to the adjacent patients whose beds had been pulled to one side for the disruption she had caused them.

The patients were all terribly nice about it, many of them looking quite embarrassed themselves, and she almost cried again when one of them, an old lady whose leg had been amputated the day before, said if she'd still had her other foot she would have got out and helped her.

'Don't you let her get you down, duck,' she whispered, reaching out a bony arthritic hand to pat Katy's arm. 'You're a good girl and you deserve better than being shouted at all day long.'

It was only the patients that made her struggle on day after day. Mostly lucky to be alive, their appreciation of the nurses' efforts was gratifying. Katy found their stoic courage in face of abominable pain and discomfort humbling. And the occasional pleasure of making one of them a little more comfortable seemed to make the whole ordeal worthwhile. If she could somehow bring a smile to their faces it was even better. Not that she often had a chance to try. Sister didn't encourage fraternisation with the patients.

'I hope you're not going to start getting emotional, Nurse,' she snapped at Katy when a young woman Katy had helped prepare for theatre failed to return from the operation.

'She told me she had young children, Sister. What will become of them?'

71

'That's not our problem, Nurse,' Sister had replied firmly. 'We are here to nurse our patients, not worry about their families.'

Katy turned suddenly to her companion in the Arding & Hobbs doorway. 'Do you think it's safe to go now?' she asked.

The ARP man looked dubious. 'Wait for the next blast and then run for it,' he said. 'But hug the buildings, mind.' He nodded to the sky. 'Some of them Jerry buggers aren't above machine-gunning if they see anyone about.'

Five minutes later, panting, Katy let herself into the pub.

For once it was only her parents in the cellar. And she was shocked as she ran down the steps to see her father sitting with his head in his hands.

'What's happened? What's the matter?' she asked, stopping abruptly. Her heart, already beating fast from the run, now jerked into overdrive and thumped painfully in her chest. Had someone been hurt? Someone in the street? Someone she knew?

Her father looked up wearily. 'Phil Dunn's going.'

Katy blinked. Phil Dunn was the barman. 'Going? You mean dying?'

'Dying?' Her father looked surprised. 'No, he's leaving, he's decided to enlist. He'll be joining the London Regiment in a month or two.'

Katy stared. 'Is that all? Is that why you both look so depressed? Because Phil Dunn's joining up?'

Her father frowned, but it was her mother who answered. 'It may not mean much to you, love, but it's a terrible blow to your father. Phil's been with us for years. Goodness knows how we'll manage without him.'

Katy shrugged off her cloak. 'But there must be masses of people you could get to replace him.'

Her father shook his head. 'All the good men have joined up. I don't want some halfwit or cripple working here.'

For a second she wondered if he was being funny, but his face was solemn, he obviously didn't see the irony. The fact that he himself only had one leg was clearly immaterial.

'I'll help,' Katy said suddenly. 'I'll give up nursing and come and work here.' Surely this was just the excuse she needed. A means of giving up while retaining her pride. Sister Morris's angry face swam before her eyes, followed by a stream of bed pans, and she cringed inwardly. The thought of standing behind the bar smiling at customers suddenly seemed extraordinarily appealing. But her father was already shaking his head.

'*You* work *here*?' He laughed. 'You must be joking. You wouldn't last five minutes, love. It's hard, dirty work running a pub, you know.'

Katy bit her lip. 'It's hard, dirty work nursing, too,' she said. But she could see in his eyes it was no good. He didn't want her. He didn't think she was up to it. Even though her parents had warned her that nursing was hard work, they didn't really believe it. Like the ARP warden they thought it was nice and ladylike. And that when she said she was tired it was because she was weak and feeble, not because she had put in a day's hard physical labour among the injured and dying. Dully she sat down on her camp bed and began to unlace her shoes.

'No,' her father sighed heavily, 'I dare say we'll muddle through. In any case what with Barry Fish out of action and the bloody air-raids, the takings are so badly down just now I doubt we could afford a new man.'

Katy looked up. Barry Fish was the entertainer who came into the pub on Wednesdays and at weekends. Katy didn't like him, she found him smarmy and ingratiating, but she knew the pub was always pretty crowded when he was in. He was a good pianist. 'What's that matter with Barry Fish?' she asked.

'He's broken his arm,' her father said. He shook his head sadly. 'I was hoping for a good crowd tomorrow night, but now they'll all have one pint and slope off to the Windmill.'

His shoulders slumped and suddenly, despite her earlier irritation, Katy felt sorry for him. He was usually so strong, so confident. She hated to see him like this, weary and down. She wished there was some way she could help him. A way he might accept. Then suddenly realised there was.

'I'm sure if I asked Jen, she would do a few turns for you,' she said. Surely Jen would help her. After all, what were friends for? 'She's really good. They'd stay and listen to her. And she knows how to do singalongs too. She did them in the cinema that time.'

For a moment her father didn't reply. But her mother looked quite excited. 'That's a good idea, love, if she'd do it. Do you think she would?'

Katy nodded eagerly. 'I'm sure she would.' She smiled at her father. 'What do you think, Daddy? I'm starting nights tomorrow night so I've got the day off. I could ask her first thing?'

To her delight he smiled back. 'Well, there's no harm in asking, is there?' he said and leaned over to pat her on the hand. 'You're a good girl, Katy.' He winked and ruffled her hair. 'I didn't mean no harm before. We're very proud of you doing your nursing. I was only saying to your mother earlier how pretty you look in your uniform.'

Pam was sitting at the kitchen table, yawning over a cup of weak tea when Alan came in after a night on duty with the Home Guard. There was a new fear of German paratroopers landing under cover of the bombing and Alan had spent much of the last few nights patrolling the streets looking for signs of airborne infiltrators.

'I just bumped into Sheila,' he said, taking off his jacket and sitting down. 'She looks like death.'

Pam winced. She had hardly seen Sheila Whitehead since she had stormed out of their air-raid shelter a couple of weeks before. What with getting to and from work each day and trying to keep food on the table for Alan, Pam had simply not had time to do anything about making peace with her friend. That didn't stop her worrying about her, though. And about little George.

Pam knew Sheila had pretty much taken up residence in Clapham South Underground station where a 6d ticket guaranteed safety for the night. Unfortunately with the crowds of people now flocking there each evening, the 6d also guaranteed increasingly insanitary and unhygienic sleeping conditions and Pam wished she could persuade Sheila either to use her own cellar or to go to her relatives in the country instead.

'She doesn't like them,' Alan said. 'They bully her and keep trying to discipline George.' He reached for the teapot. 'Is this drinkable?'

Pam grimaced. 'It's drinkable, but there's not much of it. I haven't managed to get hold of this week's ration yet. I was just steeling myself to go out and do a bit of queuing when you came back.' She watched Alan pour the almost colourless dregs into his cup and drink them with apparent relish. She felt a sudden spurt of affection for him. There weren't many men who would still be smiling after a cold tiring night out on the streets of Clapham.

As he put down the cup he caught her eye and looked away again. Pam knew that look and her heart sank slightly. She knew he had something on his mind and she knew what it was.

She took a deep breath. 'You want to have Sheila back here, don't you?'

He avoided her eyes. 'It's George,' he said. 'If they're here I feel we can at least give him a little bit of family life. A bit of normality. God knows he doesn't get it from her.'

Alan loved children. Pam knew it grieved him deeply that they hadn't yet managed to have any. She knew he would do anything to help a child, to help anyone come to that. It was Alan who had risked his life taking his little boat to Dunkirk to save the troops trapped there, it was Alan who had taken young Mick Carter under his wing last year when Joyce threw him out, Alan who had let Sean Byrne, their sexy Irish lodger, stay longer than necessary, even though he suspected he was IRA, because he thought he was making Pam happy. And now he was prepared to open his doors once again to Sheila and George. Pam bit her lip wishing she had an equally generous nature.

'I think we should at least offer,' Alan said mildly. 'The conditions in those Tube stations really are dreadful.'

Pam sighed. 'OK, OK, you don't have to rub it in.' She stood up briskly and pulled their ration books out of the sideboard drawer. 'I'll go over and ask her now, on my way to the shops.'

'Oh.' Alan looked slightly taken aback.

'What?' Pam stared at him. 'Did you think it would be better if you asked her, then?'

Alan shook his head. 'No, I think it would be better if you asked her.' He hesitated, leaning back in his chair to look up at her. 'But I wondered if we might leave asking her until a little bit later.'

Pam frowned. 'Later? What do you mean?'

Alan ran his hands through his hair. 'Well,' he said seriously, 'it strikes me that this is the first time for a long time that we have been alone in the house together. And Adolf Hitler permitting, we might just manage a couple of hours' peace and quiet.' He grinned suddenly. 'So I wondered . . .' He raised his eyebrows questioningly and Pam's eyes widened.

'Alan!' she said. 'But you've been up all night. You must be exhausted. I can't believe you want to . . .'

His face fell. 'Don't you?'

She blinked. 'Well, I don't . . . I mean, it's the middle of the morning.' She flapped the ration books helplessly. 'What about our rations?'

He stood up and took her in his arms and kissed her. 'There's only one ration I'm interested in just now, my love, and I think the government have been selling me a bit short recently.'

Jen refused to sing in the pub. 'No fear,' she said. 'I'm a professional now, you know. I'm not going to sing to a lot of drunks in a bar.'

Katy didn't know what to say. She knew Jen was often spiky and irritable, but she had never dreamed she would refuse such a small favour. She was bitterly disappointed and it obviously showed.

'Look, I'm going off on tour first thing in the morning,' Jen said with a sigh. 'First stop some armaments factory in Birmingham. It's my first professional engagement. I can't afford to wear my voice out in a noisy pub. I'm sorry but it's too much of a risk.' She shrugged. 'Anyway the Miss Taylors are having a little party for me tonight, bombing permitting.'

A little party? Not only would Jen not sing a few songs in her parents' pub, she hadn't even asked her to her leaving party. Katy bit her lip.

'Don't look so miserable,' Jen laughed. 'You're invited. About eight o'clock. I meant to ask you in the week but you're never around these days.'

'I'm starting nights tonight,' Katy said. 'I go on duty at eight.'

Jen frowned. 'Well, can't you be late for once? It is my last night after all.'

Katy gaped at her. 'I couldn't possibly be late. It's dreadfully strict. You have no idea.'

'It sounds like my idea of hell,' Jen said. 'Almost as bad as going on tour with half a dozen strangers.' She shrugged. 'Well, if you can't, you can't.' She glanced at Katy. 'By the way, did you find an abortionist?'

'No,' Katy said dully. I failed Louise over that, she thought, and now I've got to tell my father I've failed on Jen. Suddenly she felt very weary. Quickly she smiled at Jen. 'Good luck with the tour. I'd better go and get some more sleep in. I'm sure you'll be great. I'll miss you.'

To her horror sudden tears filled Jen's eyes.

'I'm sorry, Katy,' she said abruptly. 'I'm sorry for being such a cow. But now the moment has come, I really don't want to go.'

Katy stared at her. 'I had no idea. I thought you were looking forward to it.'

Jen bit her lip. 'I'm scared to death. I'm not like you. You're so brave, Katy, you take everything in your stride. Like the nursing. It sounds ghastly and you're being so brave about it.'

Katy blinked. 'I'm not,' she said. 'I spend most of the time in tears.' She was crying now.

She was still crying a few minutes later when she walked out into the street and bumped straight into Ward Frazer.

If only the stupid Carters hadn't let their front hedge grow so tall, she would have seen him in time and perhaps managed to avoid him. As it was, she pushed open the rickety gate and practically fell into his arms.

'Katy, hi.' He greeted her cheerfully, steadying her easily, as though he was quite used to women throwing themselves at him out of concealed gateways. 'How are you? How's the nursing?'

For a short stolen moment she allowed herself to revel in the feel of his hands grasping her upper arms, then she stepped back abruptly out of his range and immediately wished she hadn't because now he would surely be able to see the hideous evidence of her tears. Why hadn't she stayed with Jen another five minutes, she asked herself. Why hadn't one of those lazy Carter boys taken the trouble to trim their beastly hedge?

'Hey, what's up? Are you OK?' Sure enough he was looking at her now. She could feel those grey eyes on her face, cool and assessing, and she wished the pavement would open at her feet and swallow her whole. When actresses cried they looked pretty and vulnerable – even Jen hadn't looked too bad just now, so why when she cried, Katy wondered, did her nose run and her skin go blotchy?

'I'm sorry.' His voice was gentle. He held up his hands and took a half step back. 'Was it me? I didn't mean to hurt you.'

Katy looked up at him astonished. 'You didn't,' she stammered, trying not to notice his lovely mouth, the crisp dark hair, the slight frown on his forehead. 'It wasn't you, I mean, it wasn't your fault. I was already crying . . .' She stopped abruptly, cringing. Why, oh why, did she become completely incoherent every time she got within six feet of Ward Frazer?

She glanced at him again. Because he is quite the most attractive man you have ever clapped eyes on, she told herself crossly, and felt the colour creeping up her neck. Oh God, she groaned inwardly, looking away quickly, now I'll be blotchy and red.

'Thank God for that,' he said and grimaced slightly at her startled look. 'I didn't mean thank God you were crying, I mean thank God I haven't done you any lasting damage.'

It occurred to Katy that she would be more than happy for Ward Frazer to do her some lasting damage if it involved physical contact, but she obligingly shook her head. 'No, honestly, I'm fine. I'm tougher than I look.' She even managed a small smile. He'd go now. And she would be able to go and beat her brains out in the privacy of her bedroom.

'Are you?' For a second a wry smile curved his lips, then the concern was back in his voice.

'So what about the tears? Is there anything I can do about those?'

He wasn't going. He was standing there, hands in his pockets now, completely relaxed, looking as though he was prepared to stand there all day.

Trying to get a grip on herself, Katy smiled wanly. 'Not unless you're prepared to commit murder on my behalf.'

He grinned. 'Sure, no problem, who's it to be?'

That easy charm was irresistible. To her surprise, Katy felt herself smile back. 'A lady called Miss Morris. She's one of the nursing sisters at the Wilhelmina.'

'And do you want it quick and clean, or slow and lingering?'

Katy giggled. 'Oh, slow and lingering, definitely. And if you could use a bed pan as the murder weapon I'd be really grateful.'

'A bed pan?' He was still smiling but his eyes were thoughtful. He shook his head slightly, watching her. 'It's that bad, huh?'

To her horror Katy felt her lip tremble. Why did he have to be so damn understanding? Why couldn't he be brash and unconcerned?

'I hate it,' she said, swallowing hard. 'I hate everything about it. Most of all I hate the other nurses. They're so smug and efficient and . . . well, just beastly. That's the only way to describe them.'

Ward accepted that without comment. 'What about the patients?' he asked.

Katy blinked. 'Oh, I like the patients.' She tried to smile and didn't quite succeed. 'Except when they die of course. I hate it when they die.'

He looked away up the street. 'Death and sorrow will be the companions of our journey,' he murmured softly, 'hardship our garment; constancy and valour our only shield.'

Katy stared at him. For a second then, just before he turned away, there had been something cold and flat in his eyes. 'Who said that?' she asked uncertainly.

He turned back to her. 'Winston Churchill.'

'Well, it's all very well for him to talk about constancy and valour,' Katy said crossly. 'He doesn't have to work for Sister Morris.'

Ward chuckled. 'That's true enough. But then on the other hand, nor do you.' He saw her expression and shrugged. 'You may not want to throw in the towel just yet. But you could. After all, there are plenty of other useful things a bright kid like you could do.'

Kid? Had she heard him correctly? The smile froze on her lips as her brain sorted out the implication of that one word. Kid? Ward Frazer thought she was a kid. A child. A juvenile. And there she had been, thinking, wondering, hoping that he might, given the right circumstances, might just find her the tiniest bit interesting. After all, he had stopped to talk to her.

But no. She was wrong. He thought she was a child.

She glanced at him quickly and caught a sympathetic expression on his face. At that moment she almost hated him. How dare he pretend to be concerned about her? He didn't care. Not in the way she wanted him to care at any rate. Not in the way she cared about him.

Hoping her lips wouldn't crack, she widened her smile and shrugged her shoulders negligently. 'Oh well, I dare say I'll stick at it a bit longer,' she said grittily. She looked at her watch. 'I'd better go. I promised I'd be back by opening time.'

Ward looked surprised. 'You help out in the pub as well?'

'No.' Katy sighed. 'No, I don't. But I promised to be back anyway.' If only to give them the bad news about Jen, she thought with a sigh.

'Are you coming to Jen's leaving party this evening?' Ward asked suddenly as she turned to cross the road.

'I can't. I start my week's night duty tonight.' It sounded abrupt and offhand. She couldn't help it. She knew he didn't care two hoots whether she was at the party or not.

But he didn't seem to notice her rudeness. He merely inclined his head politely. 'Then I guess I'd better say goodbye now because I probably won't see you for a while. I've got to go away.'

Katy stopped and turned back towards him. She knew what 'going away' meant in Ward Frazer's line of business. No wonder he had had that cold, remote look in his eyes when he had quoted Churchill's portentous words.

'Oh.' She swallowed, wishing she could apologise. Wishing she could express her fear for him, but knowing it would only embarrass him and make her look even more stupid, and childish. 'Well, be careful, won't you,' she said inadequately. It was the best she could do, and even that made her flush like a schoolgirl.

He smiled. 'I'll try.' Then he nodded her a quick farewell, and walked away down the street.

At quarter past five on Sunday the thirteenth of October, Princess Elizabeth made her first ever broadcast on the wireless. Joyce listened to it while she prepared the boys' tea and was impressed by the steadiness of the fourteen-year-old Princess's voice as she addressed the Empire's children. She wondered if her two younger children had heard it in Devon, Angie was the same age as the Princess Elizabeth. Joyce shook her head. She hadn't seen Angie or young Paul since they were evacuated to Devon over a year ago. As she turned off the wireless she wondered what they would be having for their tea on the farm.

And now Jen had gone and all. Bob had walked her to Clapham Junction this morning. She was meeting the other members of her concert party somewhere near Paddington and travelling on with them to Birmingham. Well, good luck to her, Joyce thought as she stuck a fork in the boiling cabbage. She couldn't say she was sorry to see her go. It was one less to feed and the boys might get on better without Jen needling them and running them down the whole time.

Joyce took the cabbage off the heat and poured the cloudy water into a bowl. That would come in handy for a soup later in the week. You had to save every bit of nourishment you could nowadays. You never knew when you were going to find your shelves bare and your purse empty. And with winter coming there would soon be the usual problem about fuel. God knew what the coal price would be this winter. Last Christmas they had been saved from freezing by gathering wood blown down in the gales up on the common. Maybe Bob would pick up a job soon and then they'd be home and dry.

Joyce shook her head as she opened the door of the small oven and sniffed appreciatively. Shepherd's pie, even if most of the meat was bread. It was only because of Mr Lorenz they were having meat at all. He'd given her half a pound of mince yesterday. Someone had given it to him in the shop and he didn't know what to do with it, he said.

For a moment she'd thought someone had tried to pawn it, and for about the first time ever she had seen him laugh. It turned out someone had given it to him in part payment, and before she could wonder why he had accepted it if he didn't know what to do with it, he had handed it over.

So she had made two pies: a big one for the boys and a small one for Lorenz. She'd drop it off for him later on her way to the WVS.

She glanced at the clock. When the sirens had wailed last night, it had been the two hundredth alarm of the war. And the bombs had fallen thick and fast. South London had been particularly badly hit. The WVS van had spent most of the night in Garrett Lane where several pubs and a line of houses had been completely wrecked.

The rescue services had been digging for bodies all night. They reckoned tonight would be even worse.

Aware of a tremor of nervous anticipation, Joyce shook her head and set the pie on the table. Before she had put the knives and forks out the boys had come in. They'd been up to see the bomb damage in the City.

'There's a six mile an hour speed limit around St Paul's,' Mick said.

'They reckon the bombs have damaged the foundations,' Bob explained taking a fork out of the drawer. He grinned. 'Imagine, Mum, one rev too many and the whole friggin' cathedral comes tumbling down on top of you.'

Pete and Mick were tucking into the pie greedily and Joyce smiled. It was nice having the boys at home. What with them larking about in the evenings, Mrs Rutherford fussing over those daft hens by day and the excitement of the WVS van at night, Joyce felt for the first time in a long time that she was having a bit of fun. Money was still short, mind, but she was used to that. And it somehow didn't matter so much if you felt if you were doing something worthwhile.

She had barely had the thought when the front door crashed open.

The three boys all stopped eating at once, their forks poised halfway between their plates and their mouths.

'Who is it?' Mick asked as they heard someone lurch over the threshold, swearing as he stumbled on the mat.

From her vantage point at the sink, Joyce could see right up the narrow passage to the front door, and the breath caught in her throat. For a second, the burly, thickset figure was silhouetted in the doorway as he kicked the offending mat out of the way. Then the door slammed and he stood there, swaying slightly, as his eyes accustomed themselves to the dark hallway.

'It's your dad,' she said hoarsely, straightening up and taking off her apron as an awful surge of guilt washed over her.

She had forgotten. She had forgotten that her husband was coming out of jail today. And now here he was. Home. Her Stanley. Staggering drunkenly down the passage towards her. And all she felt was anger that after being locked away for a year, he hadn't even made the effort to come home sober.

Not that she'd say so, mind. She knew better than that. Even after a year she recognised the signs. She could tell by the beady eyes and the flush across the bridge of his nose that he was close to reaching the belligerent stage. And she didn't want a black eye on his first evening home. Something twisted inside her. She didn't want this. Already she could feel the little lump of fear in her chest, the placating smile on her lips.

'Hello, Stanley,' she said. 'Welcome home.' She saw the boys glance at him tentatively and then at each other. They knew as well as she did that he was drunk.

Bob pushed his chair back and stood up. 'Hi, Dad,' he said. 'Long time no see.'

Stanley glanced round the small room. He didn't seem to notice Bob or the boys but he took in the empty pie dish on the table. 'Nice of you to wait,' he said.

'There's another one,' Mick said, nodding to the drainer where Mr Lorenz's pie stood steaming gently.

'That's right,' Joyce agreed hastily, rinsing a plate for him. 'I made you a special one. Didn't know what time you'd be home what with the Sunday trains and that.'

Poor old Lorenz would have to go without, she thought quickly. He wouldn't mind. It was worth the sacrifice. Worth it to see the way Stanley's shoulders relaxed, the nod of satisfaction as he took Bob's place at the table.

Bob took his jacket off the back of the chair and jerked his head to Mick and Pete. 'We'll be off then,' he said with a quick glance at Joyce. 'Maybe see you over at the Flag for a pint later, Dad?'

As Mick and Pete stood up obediently, Joyce realised she didn't want them to go. She didn't want to be left alone with her husband in this mood. But Bob thought he was doing the right thing, and she hadn't the guts to stop him.

Stanley ate the pie greedily, belched, chuckled, and then looked up, wiping his mouth. 'That's more like it. You always was a good cook.'

Joyce smiled tentatively. Perhaps it was going to be all right after all.

'Going out, were you?' he asked suddenly.

The tone was light but she sensed the suspicion behind the question. 'What do you mean?'

'I mean you're all done up, clean and tidy.'

Joyce blinked. Had she really looked so tatty before, that a decent cardigan and a clean skirt made him think she was going out? She had been going to put on a dash of lipstick too, before taking the pie to Lorenz. Thank God Stanley had come in when he did. God knew what would have happened if he'd seen her knocking at Lorenz's door.

'I've got to go out on the WVS mobile canteen,' she said. 'I told you I was doing a bit of voluntary. They reckon things will be bad tonight.'

'Well, you won't be going out on any WVS jaunt tonight,' he said, standing up. 'You'll be staying here where you belong. I'm not having you gallivanting all over London with a load of busybodies.'

Joyce blinked at him. 'They do useful work, Stanley. They're not busybodies.'

'Useful,' he snorted, leaning on the table. 'I know them WVS types. They came in to the nick. Toffee-nosed do-gooders. Poking their noses into everyone's business.'

'It's not like that on the canteen, Stanley. We dole out refreshments to the bomb victims and rescue workers and that.'

'I don't care what you bloody do.' His voice rose slightly. 'I don't want you having anything to do with them, do you hear me?'

Joyce thought it best not to argue. Best broach the subject again when he was sober. After all, she could hardly desert him on his first night home. She tried a smile. 'Well, I dare say they can manage without me for once.' She'd pop down in a moment and let them know. The sirens hadn't gone off yet. With any luck they'd be able to call in a replacement.

Stanley pushed himself off the table and straightened up, looking mollified. 'That's right, Joyce love, you may have been gadding about while I've been inside, but I'm back now and you'll have to remember who's boss again, won't you?'

Joyce swallowed. She didn't like the look of that faint leer as he headed for the back door.

'Aren't you going over to the Flag?' she asked. She needed a few minutes to herself suddenly. To come to terms with his return.

But he shook his head. 'I've been in a boozer all afternoon. I'm going for a piss and then I'm going upstairs.'

She sighed in relief. That meant he was going to sleep. Perhaps things would be better once he'd slept it off. After all, it wasn't surprising if a man wanted a drink after a year without a drop. Particularly a good solid drinker like Stanley. It was a good sign, she thought, that he wasn't heading over the road to the Flag and Garter. Normally he drank until he dropped.

She had put her pinny back on and was washing up when she heard the clank of the flush from the privy in the back yard.

As he came back through the kitchen, Stanley glanced at the pile of dirty dishes. 'Don't be all bloody night doing that,' he said gruffly.

Joyce was surprised. He had never used to bother how long her chores took in the old days. She stopped for a moment with her hands in the water and looked out of the window into the back yard. Maybe this was a chance to start again. They'd get to know each other again. Take it easy. See how it went. Take it a step at a time. He might be better now Jen had gone. Jen had always annoyed him with her fancy ways. Perhaps he'd be able to keep off the booze and find a decent job. Poor bugger hadn't had much luck with jobs over the years. But now with so many men in the services he would be sure to find something. It would be good for him to work. To do something useful. Perhaps then he'd understand better about the WVS and that.

She was drying the dishes when she heard him call, and she went upstairs to see what was wrong. She was surprised to find him sitting awkwardly on the edge of the bed in his vest and pants.

The rest of his clothes were on the floor. She felt odd seeing him like that. It wasn't a pretty sight. The flesh on his arms and legs was white and flabby and there was a sour odour hanging round him, a mixture of sweat and beer that she remembered of old. She felt an unexpected rush of dismay. She'd had the room to herself for the last year and she didn't like the way he was filling it with his clothes and his smells. It was like an invasion of her privacy. She wondered if she dared ask him to sleep in Jen's room. Just until she got used to him again.

She smiled tentatively. 'What was it you wanted, Stanley?'

He looked up sharply. 'There you are. About bloody time too.' He frowned. 'What do you think I want? I'm your husband, damn it. Now get that apron off and let me have a look at you. I'd forgotten what a fine-looking woman you are, especially when you're done up all nice.'

Joyce stepped back abruptly. 'Stanley, I don't think . . .'

He stood up. 'I don't care what you think. You'll do as you're bloody told. I don't know what you've been up to while I've been away, but you're my wife and don't you bloody forget it.'

Joyce flinched back as he lurched towards her. 'I haven't been up to anything,' she said quickly, untying the apron and letting it fall to the ground. 'But don't you think it might be better to wait until . . .'

'Are you saying no?' he interrupted quietly. 'Are you denying your husband his rights after he's been shut away for a year, thinking about nothing else? Well, that's a fine welcome home, isn't it?'

Joyce shivered. She knew that tone and she knew the violence of the temper that usually followed it. 'No,' she shook her head quickly. 'I wasn't saying that. I just thought you might like a bit of a wash first. I've got the kettle on the stove. I could bring you up some hot water.'

'A wash first?' His eyes narrowed. 'Oh, we've got very namby pamby all of a sudden, haven't we?' He reached for her arm, jerked her towards him. 'So who's been washing you, my lovely? Who's been "washing you first"?'

Joyce could feel his hand digging cruelly into her arm, feel his other hand reaching down to pull up her skirt. 'Stanley, you're hurting me,' she mumbled as tears of pain blurred her vision.

He pushed her roughly back on to the bed. 'And whose fault is that?' he grunted, climbing on top of her and fumbling with her underwear. She heard the rip as the lining of her skirt gave way, felt the yanked knicker elastic burn the flesh in her inner thigh.

'Oh yes.' He stopped for a second, smiling salaciously, as he finally managed to expose her. 'This is what I've been missing, my lovely. And you were trying to keep it from me.'

Joyce could feel his fingers on her, hard and probing. She could see the beads of sweat on his forehead as he forced her legs apart with his knee. She closed her mind to the rank odour of his armpits. This isn't happening, she told herself. This is a bad dream. A nightmare.

But it was happening, already he was manoeuvring into position, rubbing himself against her, his face suddenly so close she could smell the shepherd's pie on his breath, see the lust in his eyes. She knew there was no stopping him now, even though she could hear the familiar rising wail of the air-raid sirens starting up. The two hundred and first warning of the war.

'You'll be careful, won't you, Stan?' she muttered. 'I don't want no more babies.'

The slap was unexpected. It was also extremely painful. For a second her ears buzzed unnervingly, drowning out the sirens.

'You shut your mouth.'

So she did. And her eyes.

*   *   *

Louise and Aaref had just arrived in Balham when the warning sounded. They had taken the Tube the one stop from Clapham South and had been shocked by the numbers of people already settling down for the night on the station platforms. It made it almost impossible to get on and off the trains, and the stench of unwashed bodies made Louise feel even more nauseous than she did already. It would be a relief to get up on to street level if only to get some fresh air, even though every step they took brought her closer to her forthcoming ordeal.

She had tried not to think about it, tried to tell herself that by tomorrow morning it would all be over and she would be able to start her life again without this awful debilitating fear hanging over her. She didn't know if it was the fear or the pregnancy that was making her feel so sick but she guessed it was the fear because when they heard the first undulating wails of the sirens, she felt a sharp stab of relief. Now the moment was almost upon her, she was grateful for anything that would delay the inevitable.

Aaref looked at her closely as she hesitated at the bottom of the stairs. 'Should I go and see how bad it is up there?' he said.

'OK, I'll stay here,' she said.

But after he had gone, she realised she couldn't stay on the platform. The atmosphere was too vile and there were more people arriving by the minute. She would have to go up and hope the bombers delayed long enough for Aaref to find a proper shelter with proper sanitation. If she stayed here another moment she really would be sick.

She was about halfway up the stairs, barging through the people coming down, when she heard the explosion. A massive, gut-wrenching crash, followed by a terrible kind of grinding roar.

For a second the ground seemed to move beneath her feet. And then she saw the water. A trickle at first, running past her down the concrete stairs. But then more, and dust, and suddenly the wall beside her crumbled and she was knocked off her feet by an avalanche of masonry.

For a moment she lay winded and badly bruised, then, as the dust settled, she scrambled to her feet, coughing. She stared about frantically. Where was everyone? Below her the tunnel seemed to be blocked, although she could hear people scrabbling and shouting on the other side. Above her the water was flowing more strongly.

Terrified, Louise didn't know which way to go.

The water was pouring now, gushing down the stairs, splashing round the corners in its haste to get to the bottom. Where was all this water coming from, she wondered in sudden alarm, grabbing the dangling stair rail for support. Why the hell didn't someone turn it off?

She had to get down to warn those people on the platform. If they weren't careful they would be trapped down there like unwanted kittens in a bucket. Then she realised if she let go of her rail she would also be hurtling to the bottom as though on some ghastly kind of funfair water slide. Already she could feel it dragging on her clothes as she clung desperately to the loose rail.

'Help me!' she screamed. 'Please help me!' But her voice was drowned by another roar of falling masonry somewhere above her. Where were the rescue workers? The ARP wardens? Aaref? She prayed someone would come for her. She knew she couldn't last long.

Suddenly she could hear screaming below her, as the water broke through the blockage. She guessed people were trying to climb the stairs. But it was hopeless.

The torrent was bringing bricks and rubble down with it now, tossing and rolling past her in the muddy, frothing cascade. She felt something crash into her foot and screamed with pain. For a second she nearly panicked and let go of the rail. A splash of water in the face brought her to her senses. To let go would be the end. She would be swept down to join the helpless victims on the platform. As she spat out the taste of grime and tried to wipe her face on her arm, she realised her only chance was to try to manoeuvre herself a few yards higher up where she would be out of the main force of the current as it swirled round the corner.

She got a few feet, but she simply hadn't the strength left in her arms. Something was wrong with her foot, too, every time she put pressure on it, a crucifying pain shot up her leg. A sudden despair washed over her. The rail was slippery now, and cold, and she could feel the strength ebbing out of her.

Just as her fingers began to go numb, she heard shouting above her, men's voices calling to each other urgently, and she began screaming again, praying they would hear her above the dreadful roar of the water.

Clinging on, Louise felt tears stinging her eyes. Please let it be all right. Please let her be rescued. 'Please hurry,' she whispered.

A length of rope snaked round the corner followed by an arm and then a helmeted man, hugging the wall on the other side of the stairs, lowering himself carefully down the steps. He was nearly at the end of the rope. Louise could see the knotted tail of it flicking wildly in the water like an eel. He didn't seem to have noticed her yet, all his attention was on keeping his balance. The water was waist deep now. Half crouching, half lying as she was, Louise could feel it creeping steadily up her body.

'I'm here,' she cried. 'Please help me.'

He obviously hadn't heard her earlier screams, because he jerked his head round as though stung.

'Hold tight, love, I'll come over.'

But he was on the wrong side of the stair tunnel. Louise knew the power of the cascading water would never let him across.

A moment later he realised it too. 'Can you hold on while I get help?' he shouted, already beginning to work his way hand over hand back up the rope.

'No,' Louise screamed. 'I can't. Please don't leave me.'

She saw him glance at the rising water level and realised there wasn't time for him to get help anyway. Another few inches and her face would be under water and that would be the end of her.

'I'll throw you the end of the rope,' he shouted. 'When you catch it, tuck the knot under your arm and grip with both hands. I'll pull you up. For God's sake don't let go.'

Barely daring to let go of the rail even with one hand, it took three attempts for Louise to catch the rope. It was only just long enough to reach her. Thanking her lucky stars that she had previously edged up those last few feet, she wedged the wet knot under her armpit, grasped the thick, fibrous rope firmly, took a deep breath and launched herself into the current.

She was halfway across, being battered almost to death by the cascading debris when she lost her footing. As she struggled for balance, something heavy swung round the corner and caught her a massive thump across the hip.

She heard the bone crack a second before the pain hit her. Then her scream was lost in the water and everything went black.

Chapter Six

Alone in the corrugated Anderson shelter in the back yard, Pam laid down her knitting and listened to the distant crump of bombs falling. It was difficult to tell, but it sounded as if the explosions were coming from the south tonight. As though the Germans were dropping their deadly load and turning back before having to face the Clapham Common guns. She shuddered and wished she had managed to persuade Sheila to give up her spot on the platform at Clapham South and return to Lavender Road and the relative comfort of the Anderson shelter.

But Sheila had been adamant. It may be dirty and smelly down in the Underground station but at least it was safe. She could relax there, she said. And the people around her were kind to her and had taken quite a shine to little George. Yesterday someone had given him a lovely ham sandwich.

Pam picked up her knitting again and frowned. Sheila's pointed comments had made her feel guilty. As they were meant to do. It wasn't fair. Pam loved little George and would do anything for him. And she was very fond of Sheila too. It was just that having them both living in the house for so long had got on her nerves. Particularly the way they had monopolised the air-raid shelter.

It wouldn't have mattered if she didn't work. Then she could sleep by day like so many people did now. But if she and Alan were ever going to have children of their own they needed to save, and in any case, Pam liked her job. She liked doing something useful, something to help with the war effort, even if it did mean having a few problems at home.

She winced as the sound of another distant explosion echoed off the walls of the house and wondered how many more unfortunate families would be homeless tomorrow.

She could hear planes now, but couldn't tell if they were coming or going. Alan would know. He would be out there now with his platoon of the Home Guard, watching them like a hawk, waiting for the hint of a parachute, longing for the moment when his team might have the chance to foil a German attempt at an airborne invasion, or at very least catch a paratrooper infiltrator.

Pam shook her head. The war had changed Alan. Since his daring escapade rescuing the stranded troops at Dunkirk he had become more confident, more enthusiastic and, recently, more virile.

She smiled and felt a faint heat on her skin as she remembered his passionate love-making yesterday afternoon. For once they had been able to take their time, exploring each other's bodies as they had used to when they were first married, teasing and tantalising and giggling as their mutual arousal became more and more intense. And then, to her surprise, Alan had taken control, encouraging her to accept his intimate caresses without the distraction of responding, driving her to a frenzy of excitement, and only then allowing her the release she craved.

When she asked him coyly afterwards what had come over him he smiled. 'It's you, my darling. You are the sexiest thing this side of Hollywood.'

Pam had laughed, pleased by the absurd compliment, but she knew that wasn't it. She knew his real reason. She knew he wanted a child and he was going to do everything in his power to get one.

And suddenly as she sat alone in the shelter, she hoped this time that it would work. That she would conceive. Perhaps the time was right to have a baby. Despite the war. Life had to go on after all, and if anything did happen to Alan, God forbid, out on those bleak exposed streets, it would be nice to have a little baby to remember him by. Shocked by the thought, quickly she crossed her fingers and was just embarking on a prayer for his safety when she heard the back door of the house open and Alan's quick steps across the back yard.

Pam's welcoming smile died on her lips when she saw the expression on his face.

'What's happened?' she asked.

'Balham Tube's been hit,' he said baldly. 'There's hundreds trapped down there on the platforms and the water main has burst. If they don't get help soon, they'll drown. It's already flooding the tunnels to Clapham South.'

Pam swallowed. 'Sheila?'

Alan nodded. 'That's why I came. They're trying to clear the stations up the line, but you know what she's like. She might refuse to move. If I see her I'll tell her to come back here.'

Pam stared at him. He was talking quickly as though he was in a hurry. And there was something in his expression she didn't like. Something that scared her.

'What are you going to do, Alan?' she asked tentatively. She had a feeling she didn't want to know.

When he hesitated she knew she was right. He was about to do something heroic and probably get himself killed in the process.

'They're fetching the boats off the lake in Battersea Park,' he said. 'If we can launch them off the platform at Clapham South we might be able to get up the tunnel to Balham to get some of those poor sods out. If it's not already too late.'

Pam had a sudden vision of a black tunnel, filling rapidly with water, and a small rowing boat struggling against the flow as the water got higher and higher until it was right up to the roof and there was nowhere for the boat to go, no air for its occupants to breathe. Just water.

'Don't you go, Alan,' she whispered, standing up to hold his arm.

This was going to be like Dunkirk all over again. She remembered the dreadful debilitating fear as she waited for him to come home. 'Let someone else go this time. You've done enough.'

He pulled her into his arms and kissed her gently. 'I dare say there'll be plenty of more willing volunteers,' he said with a reassuring smile.

But she knew there wouldn't be many volunteers. Not for a terrifying task like that. Not who knew about boats. Her heart twisted. She knew Alan would do it. He would step forward when everyone else stepped back. It wasn't that he was fearless, it was just that in his quiet self-effacing way he was extraordinarily brave.

And then he was gone, his boots rattling away across the yard, and she hadn't even had time to say be careful.

Pam knew what she had to do. She pulled her coat on, grabbed the torch and ran into the house to change her shoes. She could hardly tramp across Clapham Common in the slippers she wore in the shelter. Her heart was thumping, partly for Alan, partly for herself. It was madness to go running about in the middle of an air-raid. Even if the Germans didn't get you, the flak from the anti-aircraft guns was just as lethal. But she had to go. She had to do something. She couldn't just sit there worrying. She had to at least go and fetch Sheila and George home.

As she opened the front door, she took a quick steadying breath and crossed her fingers.

Outside it was a bright moonlit night. On the opposite side of the street, the undrawn curtains in Sheila's dark house showed she wasn't there. In the next house along, at the Miss Taylors', the blackout curtains were up but Pam hoped the two old ladies were safely installed in their cellar. Not that there was any sound of planes or guns, but ahead of her three bright parachute flares were descending slowly.

At the top of the road she paused to take stock before crossing on to the common. The big long-muzzled guns to her left were elevated, but quiet, and high above the common a barrage balloon floated flabby and silver in the bright moonlight.

She was just about to cross the road when she heard a vehicle coming up Lavender Road behind her and it occurred to her she might be able to cadge a lift. Peering behind the dimmed headlights she realised it was a van of sorts and she put out her hand to wave it down.

As it stopped she saw it was a WVS canteen van, and to her surprise Mrs Rutherford's head appeared out of the passenger window.

'Is that you, Mrs Nelson? What are you doing out and about? There's an alarm on, you know.'

Mrs Rutherford was Alan's boss's wife and Pam had always felt uneasy in her company. However, it would be much quicker to get round the common by van than cross it by foot.

'I need to get to Clapham South,' she said. 'I don't suppose you're going that way?'

Celia Rutherford nodded and pushed open the door. 'We are indeed. They're in turmoil down there because the Tube line is flooding.'

'All aboard?' Mrs Trewgarth, the verger's wife, was at the wheel, revving impatiently as Pam climbed up awkwardly into the cab next to Mrs Rutherford. 'Chocks away,' she added heartily as she released the clutch, and Pam nearly nose dived into Mrs Rutherford's lap as they swung violently on to Clapham Common Northside.

'Do you come out with the canteen every night?' Pam asked, wishing her thigh wasn't pressed quite so firmly against Mrs Rutherford's.

'We work in teams of three,' Celia Rutherford explained, clinging to the dashboard. 'We're short staffed tonight. Normally we have Mrs Carter with us.'

'Mrs Carter?' Pam gaped. She found it hard to imagine rough and ready Joyce Carter volunteering to work alongside these two classy, overbearing women. To be honest, she found it hard to imagine her volunteering for anything at all come to that. She shook her head. It was amazing what war did to people. Even people like Joyce Carter.

Mrs Trewgarth changed gear noisily. 'She's let us down badly tonight. Just didn't turn up. No word why. That's why we're late going out. It's most disappointing. Makes things very difficult if people don't keep their word.'

Pam winced. She wouldn't want to be in Joyce Carter's shoes tomorrow.

As they approached Clapham South, Mrs Trewgarth braked abruptly and it was only Mrs Rutherford's firm thigh that prevented Pam's bottom from sliding off the narrow bench seat. She peered out of the windscreen. Ahead she could dimly see hordes of people milling about on the corner of the common opposite the Tube station. White-helmeted ARP officials were trying to marshal them into some kind of order, presumably with the aim of directing them to other public shelters, but nobody seemed to be taking much notice. They were far more intent on watching a group of men unloading a number of small boats from the back of a truck.

'Gracious, whatever are they doing?' Mrs Trewgarth exclaimed as the soldiers shouldered two of the boats and disappeared with them into the Tube station.

'They're going to row up the flooded tunnel to rescue the people trapped at Balham,' Pam said.

'Dear me, the things they do.' Mrs Rutherford shuddered. Then she craned forward. 'Good lord, Mrs Nelson, isn't that your husband?'

'Yes it is,' Pam said shortly. She had seen Alan too, holding a gas mask and pulling on a pair of waterproof trousers. She suddenly felt very sick.

Dragging her eyes away, she searched the crowds for a glimpse of Sheila or George. But before she could locate them, Mrs Trewgarth was clapping her hands.

'Come on now, ladies, action stations, we can't sit here all night. Kettles on, Mrs Rutherford, please, there's a queue forming already.'

Thanking them for the lift, Pam jumped out of the cab and began to push through the crowds towards the boat party. She had this terrible premonition of impending disaster. She had to stop him.

But before she had reached him, she felt something tugging at her coat. 'Auntie Pam, Auntie Pam, have you come to save us? Mummy says we'll die if we stay out here.'

It was little George, his face smeared with recent tears. Pam stopped at once and crouched to hug him. 'Yes. I've come to take you home.' She straightened up with the child in her arms and looked around. 'Where is Mummy?'

He pointed towards a nearby bench where Sheila was sobbing hysterically surrounded by a group of women.

In the other direction, out of the corner of her eye Pam could see that Alan was about to move off and her heart sank. In a moment it would be too late. Quickly she set George back on the ground.

'Go and fetch Mummy and wait with her by the WVS van there,' she told him. 'I'll be with you in a moment.' Turning back, she saw Alan had gone.

'Please let me through.' She pushed frantically through the crowd in front of her. She could see him again now, heading for the Tube entrance, in the yellow oilskin trousers.

'Alan!' she shouted. 'Alan, wait, please.'

But he didn't hear her, and by the time she reached the entrance, he had disappeared inside. A policeman stopped her as she went to follow him.

'Sorry, madam, the line's flooded. Only rescue workers allowed in. There's other shelters over on the common.'

'But my husband . . .' Pam panted.

The policeman smiled. 'He'll be all right, love, everyone's out of here now. The main damage is up at Balham anyway.'

'I know.' Pam glared at him. 'That's where he's going . . . in one of the boats . . . in the tunnel.'

The policeman's expression changed subtly. For a moment she thought he was going to let her past, then he shook his head. 'He's only doing his duty, love. And it looks like it's the only chance them poor buggers at Balham have got.' He patted her on the arm. 'Let him go. I don't reckon as they'll get through anyway. Sounds like the whole tunnel's collapsing.'

It was hardly the reassurance she was looking for. 'Exactly,' Pam said crossly. 'What if the tunnel collapses on Alan?'

The policeman shrugged. 'At least you'll know he was doing his duty.'

'Damn his bloody duty,' Pam muttered, turning away. 'Why's he always doing his duty by other people? Why doesn't he do his duty by me for a change?' But even as she said it she knew it was unfair. Alan was a loyal, loving husband. And it wasn't necessarily his fault that they had failed to have children. It might just as well be her inability to conceive. She sighed and headed back to the WVS van, stopping momentarily in shock when she saw the colour of the sky behind it.

To the north, over central London, an ominous red glow was rising from the horizon. Even the distant barrage balloons looked pink. And east towards Streatham the air was full of rose-coloured smoke. Although there was no sign of planes now, they had obviously done significant damage earlier. Pam had heard talk at the Ministry about a new kind of German weapon, a kind of Molotov cocktail that split high in the air to spill fifteen or twenty high-explosive bombs over a large area. By the look of the sky it had been effective this evening. She glanced at her watch. It was only nine o'clock. There would almost certainly be more to come. She just prayed it didn't come anywhere near the Balham to Clapham South Tube line.

Sheila and George were waiting for her by the van. As soon as she saw her, Sheila flung herself on Pam. 'I saw Alan going in there with the boats. He's going to die, isn't he? You should have stopped him. I don't know what I'll do if Alan dies. It's not fair. I've already lost Jo and Ray. Everyone's dying. Think of all those people dying at Balham. Drowning, they say . . .'

Over her shoulder Pam caught Celia Rutherford's eye at the serving hatch. She was leaning forward, holding out a cup of tea. 'Here,' Celia said sympathetically. 'See if this might help.'

Pam nodded and tried to prise Sheila off her neck. 'Come on, Sheila, love,' she said, putting the steaming cup into her hands. 'Please don't give up on us now. We've got to get George home to the shelter.'

As Sheila's sobs gradually subsided, Pam glanced up gratefully at Mrs Rutherford behind the high counter. 'Thank you,' she murmured.

Mrs Rutherford smiled back. 'I've discovered over the last few weeks that tea is a great healer.' She paused for a moment in laying out her cups and her eyes were kindly. 'He's a fine man, your husband, Mrs Nelson.'

Caught off balance, surprised and touched, Pam felt her eyes water. 'I know,' she said.

Mrs Rutherford nodded. 'I'm sure he'll come back safely.'

Katy was in the sluice room washing bed pans with Nurse Coogan, the pixie-faced probationer who worked on the other side of the ward, when the ward telephone rang just outside the door. Since Katy had joined the Ethel Barnet ward, she had scarcely exchanged half a dozen sentences with Nurse Coogan, but she had felt the other girl's beady eyes on her and sensed her dislike. Even now as they shared the most disgusting task on the ward, Katy had failed to illicit any sense of rapport. She didn't know what she had done to alienate her, but there was no doubt she was getting the cold shoulder. However, when they heard Sister answering the phone in her usual abrupt manner, by tacit consent they slowed in their unpleasant duty to listen.

'Yes, she's one of my probationers,' Sister was saying. 'Yes, I'll let her know.'

Katy glanced at Nurse Coogan. 'It must be news for one of us,' she whispered.

Nurse Coogan shrugged indifferently. 'It can't be for me. I haven't got anyone left to worry about.'

Katy stared at her. 'You mean you've lost your whole family?

But . . .' She stopped, sensing from the other girl's closed expression that her interest was not welcome.

'I was an orphan to start with, if you must know,' Nurse Coogan said abruptly. 'But now my step-parents have gone and all.'

'What?' Katy swallowed. 'Recently? In the bombing, you mean?'

Nurse Coogan sneered slightly. 'Oh don't worry. You don't have to feel sorry for me. It was before you arrived on the scene.'

Katy wanted to say she would feel sorry for her whenever it was, but before she could speak Sister Morris loomed in the sluice room doorway.

'Nurse Parsons?'

Sister was looking grave. Katy felt the panic rise. She swallowed hard but couldn't control her anxiety. 'Is it something to do with my family, Sister? My parents?'

'No,' Sister said. 'It's nothing to do with your parents. But there's someone in casualty asking for you. Sister Parkes has asked if you could be spared for a few minutes to go down. I wouldn't normally allow it but it seems the girl's father is on the hospital committee. So I don't have much say in the matter.'

Katy blinked. She had no idea she had such influential friends. 'Who is it, Sister? Do you know her name?'

'Her name is Louise Rutherford. It's most inconvenient, but there's nothing that can be done.' She glared at Katy as though it was her fault, then glanced at her fob watch. 'I'll give you ten minutes, Nurse, and not a moment more. Nurse Coogan will have to finish up for you here.'

As she quickly untied her apron, Katy glanced at Nurse Coogan. 'Sorry about the pans,' she muttered. 'Leave them if you want and I'll do them when I get back.'

Nurse Coogan sniffed. 'Don't worry about me. I'm used to doing everyone's dirty work. You run along and play with your fancy friend.'

It was unfair but Katy didn't have time to argue. Sister's ten minutes were already ticking away.

Casualty was busy, a dozen or so stretchers were waiting at the door and all the chairs lining the corridor outside were occupied. Katy couldn't see Louise anywhere, but mindful of the Wilhelmina etiquette, rather than just barging in, she waited at the door for one of the nurses to notice her.

Eventually a staff nurse spotted her and escorted her to Sister Parkes who was tending to someone in a curtained-off cubicle. She swung round irritably as Katy coughed nervously behind her.

'I'm Nurse Parsons,' Katy introduced herself nervously. 'Sister Morris said you wanted me.'

'Katy!' The voice was barely audible. A croaky whisper. It came from the stretcher in the cubicle.

Peering round Sister Parkes, Katy realised, to her shock, that it was indeed Louise lying there. From a distance Katy never would have recognised her. Her hair was wet and pulled back off her face in a towel, her lips were blue, the only colour in her otherwise sheet-white face, and under the blanket which covered her, her whole body was trembling.

Katy glanced at Sister Parkes for permission, then ran to the bed. 'Louise.' She peered down at her friend in horror. 'What happened?'

It was clear that Louise was in considerable pain. She certainly wasn't up to describing her ordeal, even if she could remember it.

'She was caught in a bomb at Balham Underground station,' Sister Parkes said crisply behind her. 'She is very lucky to be alive. One of the rescue workers just managed to drag her out before the whole place was flooded out. She's got a broken ankle and fractured pelvis.' She pursed her lips. 'She also has a suspected ruptured bladder, she's bleeding heavily. But she insisted on seeing you before we investigate.'

Katy swallowed and looked back at Louise. She didn't know what to say. What to do.

But Louise, despite her injuries, apparently knew exactly what she wanted. 'Tell that fat woman to go away,' she whispered. 'I want to talk to you alone.'

Katy flinched and choked back a shocked giggle. You just didn't say things like that in front of Wilhelmina nursing sisters. But it seemed Mr Rutherford pulled a lot of weight at the Wilhelmina. Sister Parkes withdrew with a sharp meaningful glance at Katy as she tapped her forefinger on her watch.

'What is it, Louise?' Katy whispered. 'What do you want me to do?'

Louise's breathing was laboured. 'It's not a ruptured bladder,' she said painfully. 'It's the baby coming out. I'm sure it is. But I don't want anyone to know.'

Katy blinked at her in horror. 'But they'll find out anyway,' she said. 'As soon as they investigate.'

Louise closed her eyes and for a dreadful moment Katy thought she had lost consciousness. But then the lashes fluttered up again.

'Tell them, then,' Louise croaked. 'But you mustn't let them tell my father. He's on his way here now. When they found out who I was, they telephoned him at home. Mummy wasn't there. I suppose she's out on the WVS.'

Katy gulped. 'I don't know if I can stop them telling him,' she whispered.

'You must,' Louise said, 'otherwise I might as well die.' Her pale, pain-filled eyes fixed Katy's for a second. 'Please, Katy, it's the only thing I ask.'

Joyce leaned on the sink in the cold, dark kitchen and held the damp tea towel to her cheek. Stanley was asleep upstairs and the boys were in the shelter outside. She had heard them come back earlier when the alarm went, Mick shouting his mouth off with some cock and bull story he'd heard from one of the Home Guard boys about a bomb at Balham and some of the men rowing up the tunnel to rescue the people trapped on the platform. If he'd been on duty he'd have volunteered he'd said and Bob had laughed his head off and said that Mick wouldn't have the guts to row across a bath. They were still arguing when the planes came overhead and they fled into the shelter.

For a long time Joyce had lain numbly on the bed listening to Stanley's snores. Then gradually the throb of planes and the occasional crump of an explosion had roused her and very carefully and quietly she eased her feet to the floor, adjusted her clothes and crept down to the kitchen.

It made her sick to think what had just happened. Her whole body ached and her bruised cheekbone was tender to the touch. The cold cloth was helping a bit, but it still hurt to close her eye. But more than the pain and the humiliation, more than anything, she felt a crippling disappointment.

She knew she was stupid to have expected any different. To have wondered if a year in jail might have changed Stanley. Done him good. Made him realise she could manage on her own. That she had her own life, her own ideas, her own way of doing things. But she should have known. It was silly of her to think her life could go on as it had with him away. He was her husband after all and he was entitled to have things as he wanted. And he wanted things as they'd always been. With him in charge and everyone doing what he said. It was understandable. A man should be master in his own home.

Joyce sighed and wetted the cloth again. As she wrung it out and lifted it to her face, she wondered what Mrs Rutherford would say about her missing the WVS tonight. She wouldn't be pleased most likely, nor would that Mrs Trewgarth woman, she was a funny old stick and all with her barked-out orders and her driving as though Adolf Hitler himself was after her. Not that Adolf Hitler would stand a chance against Mrs Trewgarth. She'd flatten him with her sandwich board as soon as look at him.

Hearing a sound behind her Joyce swung round nervously.

But it was only Bob. Standing at the back door. She could just make him out from the odd pinkish moonlight filtering around her new kitchen curtains. She hadn't put up the blackout tonight, what with Stanley coming home, she hadn't had a chance. And the boys never bothered. Dealing with curtains, even blackout curtains, was pansy in their eyes. They preferred to fumble around in semi darkness. Not that she complained. At least it saved on electricity. And tonight she was glad. She didn't want Bob to see her bruised face and blood-shot eyes. Surreptitiously she dropped the cloth in the sink.

Bob was surprised to see her there. 'I thought you was going out on the WVS,' he said.

Joyce shook her head, wincing slightly as something clicked in the back of her neck. 'No, your dad didn't want me to go,' she said.

Bob nodded. 'I didn't think he'd like you doing that. No reason why you should risk them bombs if you don't have to.' He glanced around. 'Where is Dad, then? He never came over the Flag.'

'He's asleep upstairs,' Joyce said shortly.

'Oh.' Bob frowned. 'I reckon you should tell him to come out to the shelter. It's bad out there tonight.'

'You can tell him if you want,' Joyce said. 'I'm not going to.'

Bob grinned. 'Had a bit of a tiff, have you?'

'You could say that.' Her cheek was hurting again now. She wished Bob would go back to the shelter so she could deal with it alone.

A distant flare lit the sky outside. Bob stared at her. 'What are you doing? What's the matter with your face?'

Joyce closed her eyes for a moment. Suddenly she didn't care if Bob knew or not. Maybe it was better if he knew. He was her favourite after all. She might get a bit of moral support. He might even speak to his father.

She reached into the sink and lifted the cloth back to her cheek. Then she turned to face him. 'He hit me, Bob. Quite hard. That's what's the matter with my face.'

'Oh.' Bob looked embarrassed. For a moment she thought he was going to hug her and she stiffened, nervous she might cry if he did.

But he was merely reaching for a cup. 'Well, you must have annoyed him,' he said, pouring himself a drink of water. 'You shouldn't try to argue with him. Just do as he says.' He shrugged as he wiped his mouth. 'I know you've been trying to manage everything while he's been away and that, but he's a man after all. He knows what's best.'

'I thought I said ten minutes, Nurse Parsons. Why are you still here?'

Katy swung round. It was Sister Morris, advancing menacingly across the busy casualty ward. Katy had never been so pleased to see anyone in all her life. Sister Morris might be strict and starchy, but at least Katy knew her, whereas Sister Parkes was a complete stranger and a very unpleasant one at that as far as she could see. And Louise had hardly endeared herself to her with that 'fat' comment. All in all, Sister Morris was a gift from heaven.

'Oh, Sister,' she cried, running towards her mentor in relief. 'Thank goodness you've come. A terrible thing has happened and I need your help.'

Sister Morris looked astonished, but she quickly drew Katy behind a screen and addressed her sharply. 'What are you thinking of, Nurse? Running about and behaving like a hysterical child. I am ashamed of you. Goodness knows what Sister Parkes will think.'

For once Sister's astonishment went over Katy's head. 'Oh, Sister, I'm really sorry. But Louise Rutherford is having a miscarriage and her father mustn't know. Please will you tell Sister Parkes not to tell him?'

Sister Morris looked appalled. 'I will do no such thing. I don't know what you are talking about. I'm quite sure Sister Parkes knows what she's doing.'

'But she doesn't,' Katy insisted, desperately clutching Sister's sleeve as she went to turn away. 'That's the whole point. She thinks it's a ruptured bladder. And Louise was on her way to have an abortion and nobody would have known so it's not fair if they know now. Can't they just be told about the fractures and not about the baby? It was all a terrible mistake anyway. She didn't mean to get pregnant. But she was in love with him and he tricked her by not saying he was married. And he was very sexy and she didn't know about French letters and . . .'

Sensing she might have gone a step too far, Katy stopped suddenly and flushed. She hardly dared to glance at Sister Morris, but when she did she was astonished to find that Sister was slightly pink too. Goodness, she thought, I've made Sister Morris blush. But before she could fully take in this extraordinary phenomenon, Sister was pulling herself up to her full impressive height.

'I've heard quite enough, Nurse,' she said crisply, brushing her sleeves. 'More than enough . . .'

Katy knew she was losing her case. But somewhere behind that fierce façade surely there had been a hint of compassion. Hadn't there? She looked up at Sister's stern face and steeled herself for one final effort. 'If her father finds out it's a miscarriage and not a bladder problem he will kill her,' she said. 'He may be a benefactor of the hospital but at home he's completely ruthless. He'll throw her out and cut her off and her life will be ruined for ever.'

Sister Morris pursed her lips. 'I am not the slightest bit concerned with Mr Rutherford's character, Nurse. However, I am concerned if a misdiagnosis has taken place and I will mention the matter to Sister Parkes.'

Katy blinked at her. 'But will you mention about not saying anything about the baby too?' She tugged at her arm. 'Please, Sister. I promised Louise.'

Sister Morris shook her off. 'Then you were most foolish. As a probationer nurse you had no right to promise any such thing.'

'I only promised to try,' Katy muttered but Sister silenced her with a lift of her hand.

'That's *enough*!' she barked. 'I have never heard such nonsense in all my life. Now go back to the ward at once. And if I hear another word out of you about this matter, I shall not be pleased. Is that quite understood?'

Katy quailed as her last shreds of courage deserted her under Sister's icy stare. 'Yes, Sister.'

So that was it, she thought. She had failed once again. Good old

Katy Parsons. Ask her to do something important and you can guarantee she'll let you down.

At the exit she glanced back into the ward and saw Sister Morris disappearing into Louise's cubicle with Sister Parkes and a white-coated doctor.

A moment later Katy was sent flying as the swing doors were flung open and Greville Rutherford strode into the ward.

Rather than hovering nervously by the door like most hospital visitors did, he marched straight up to a nearby staff nurse. 'My name is Rutherford. I want to see my daughter.'

The staff nurse looked taken aback. 'I'll find Sister for you,' she murmured. 'If you could just wait a moment.'

As she picked herself up off the floor, Katy's heart sank. So this was it. Poor Louise. She was about to slink away when she heard Greville Rutherford's voice again.

'I don't want to see any damn fool Sister,' he said loudly. 'I want to see my daughter and I want to see her now.'

Katy stopped in her tracks and turned round. She realised the whole of casualty ward had suddenly fallen quiet. Most of the nurses had gone white and the doctors had straightened up to see what was going on. Even the porters had momentarily stopped clanking the trolleys about. Everyone was clearly holding their breath, waiting to see how Sister Parkes would react.

Sister Parkes had already emerged from Louise's cubicle and was advancing across the ward. Her face was expressionless but her whole body was rigid with suppressed fury. Any lesser man would have been daunted, but Greville Rutherford seemed quite impervious to the reaction he had provoked.

'Can I help you, sir?' she asked with frosty politeness. She was clearly expecting some kind of apology, but as owner of the Rutherford & Berry brewery and a major benefactor to the Wilhelmina, Greville Rutherford clearly felt himself above such social niceties.

'Yes,' he said. 'I want to see my daughter, Louise Rutherford. I gather she was brought in earlier.'

Noticing Sister Morris and the doctor tactfully withdrawing from Louise's cubicle, Katy slid behind a screen. If Sister Morris noticed her still lurking around, she would hit the roof. But there was no way Katy could leave, not until she knew what was going to happen.

In any case she was interested to see Louise's father in action. She had heard so much about him from her own father, who lived in constant fear of him withdrawing the lease of the Flag and Garter, and she had seen him in church of course, tall and upright in the front pew, leading the responses in his hard confident voice, but she had never witnessed his terrifying personality herself.

'I'll want the best treatment,' he was saying as Sister Parkes led him to Louise's cubicle. 'The best doctors. The best nurses.' He glanced around disparagingly at the wide-eyed casualty nurses. 'And a private room.'

Peeping out from behind her screen Katy could see Sister Parkes bristling visibly. 'I can assure you that the Wilhelmina nurses are the best you'll find anywhere, Mr Rutherford,' she said, her voice becoming more arctic by the moment. 'Now, here's your daughter. She's very poorly and suffering from considerable shock so I would be grateful if you would refrain from upsetting her.'

Out of the corner of her eye, Katy suddenly spotted Sister Morris heading rapidly in her direction. With a gasp of horror she retreated further into the screened off area in search of somewhere to hide. She was just considering climbing on to the empty stretcher trolley and covering herself with a blanket, when the screen was jerked back. Katy closed her eyes in sudden hope that if she prayed hard enough God might take pity on her and momentarily render her invisible.

'Nurse Parsons. What, may I ask, are you doing?'

Katy opened her eyes again. God apparently had not obliged and Sister Morris clearly was not amused. Or was she? Her lip was twitching slightly but it was difficult to tell if she was holding back a smile or a snarl of fury. Assuming the snarl was more likely, Katy dropped her eyes meekly waiting for the tirade.

When it didn't come, Katy looked up again in surprise.

Sister Morris was tapping her foot in that ominous way she had. 'I am waiting for an explanation, Nurse,' she said tightly.

Katy swallowed nervously. This was probably the end of her nursing career. Consoling herself that she hadn't liked it anyway, she took a deep breath and thought quickly.

'Well, Sister,' she said, crossing her fingers behind her back. 'I was just leaving the ward when Mr Rutherford came in rather, er . . . violently and I wasn't looking and the swing door caught me and knocked me over and I actually think it must have knocked me out for a minute, Sister, because when I stood up I felt quite faint, but I didn't want to cause any fuss with Mr Rutherford being a benefactor and everything so I thought I'd better lie down in here for a moment, but I feel better now so I'll get back to the ward at once.'

She stopped abruptly and uncrossed her fingers again. Well, it was almost true. She decided to risk a glance at Sister to see if she had swallowed it.

Sister's lip was twitching badly now. So badly she suddenly seemed incapable of speech. But as Katy began edging nervously past her towards the infamous swing doors, she suddenly gave a terrible snort, like an enraged animal, and Katy nearly jumped out of her skin.

'I have never heard such nonsense in all my life,' Sister Morris barked. 'You have made an utter nuisance of yourself tonight, Nurse Parsons, and you will lose your half day off as a result. You will spend it scrubbing out the sluice room from top to bottom.'

Katy blinked. Sister Morris was looking rather red in the face suddenly. She hoped she wasn't going to have a heart attack. She would rather scrub out the sluice room than attempt resuscitation on Sister Morris.

'Yes, Sister,' she murmured.

'Oh, and Nurse Parsons, for your information, Sister Parkes doesn't feel it is necessary to inform Mr Rutherford of the er . . . full extent of his daughter's injuries. The fractured pelvis is quite worrying enough.'

'Yes, Sister,' Katy murmured again and it was not until she was through the swing doors in the passage on the way back to the Ethel Barnet ward that Sister Morris's words finally sunk in.

'I've done it,' she said to herself as a smile of disbelief curled on to her mouth. 'I've actually done it.' She toyed with doing a high kick and decided she'd probably slip and break her leg, but she was still smiling when she pushed through the Ethel Barnet nurses' door.

'You'll be for the high jump,' Nurse Coogan called across gleefully. 'Sister went looking for you hours ago.'

'Yes, I know,' Katy tossed her head airily. 'We've been sorting out a misdiagnosis on casualty ward.'

Chapter Seven

The all-clear had long sounded when Alan finally came home. Lying in bed, unable to sleep, Pam recognised his step on the path before he had even opened the front door and a wave of relief washed over her. He was back. He was safe.

Quickly she got out of bed and pulled her dressing gown round her. If he'd been struggling around in the flooded Tube line all this time he would be bound to be wet and cold and she had kept the fire going in the sitting-room grate especially, to make sure the water in the back boiler was piping hot for his return.

'Oh, Alan,' she breathed, pausing at the top of the stairs. 'Thank God you're back.' She was so pleased to see him there in the hallway below her that it was a moment before she took in the expression in his eyes, the defeated slump to his shoulders as he shrugged off his jacket.

'Alan?' She hurried down to him. 'What happened?'

He ran his hands wearily over his face and through his hair. 'Nothing happened,' he said. 'We were too late. The water was too high. We tried to push the boats along with our feet on the roof of the tunnel but it was no good, there was too much rubble. Too much water. We couldn't get through.'

Pam shivered, less at the words themselves than at the awful blank tone in which he spoke them. She patted his arm. 'At least you got back safely,' she said gently. 'That's the main thing. And Sheila and

George are back too, safe and sound. And the best news is that after tonight Sheila has decided they'd be safer in the country after all. She says they'll go as soon as they can.'

But he didn't seem to hear her. 'We could hear them shouting,' he went on in the same chilling monotone. 'Screaming. At least that's what it sounded like. It seemed to come down the tunnel carried on the water. This awful noise.' He stopped abruptly and put his hands to his face.

He turned away so quickly, it was a second before Pam realised he was crying.

As his shoulders heaved suddenly on a choked word, Pam stared at him blankly. She had never seen a grown man cry. Not properly with tears and sobs and shaking shoulders. She had vaguely thought crying was something men just didn't do. However upset they were. Certainly Alan had been upset over things before without crying. In all the years they had been married she had never known him cry. But now, suddenly he was crying as though he would never stop and she didn't know what on earth to do.

'Alan.' She touched him tentatively. 'Alan, please don't cry.'

At first he tried to shrug her off but she knew she couldn't just leave him there in the hall, dripping wet and sobbing his guts out, so with more force than persuasion she led him into the warm sitting-room.

'Oh God, I'm sorry,' he muttered incoherently as she stood him in front of the fire and began to strip his clothes as though he was a recalcitrant child. He didn't struggle exactly but he didn't help either. His determination to keep his hands over his face made it hard to get his shirt and vest off. She knew, even in his distress, he was ashamed and deeply embarrassed that she should see him cry, but she sensed the quicker she got him warm and dry, the quicker he would recover.

She left him standing in his underpants while she went to set the bath running and fetch a blanket. He was still there when she came back, still sobbing, the tears running between his fingers and dripping down his chest. As she wrapped the blanket round him she shook him slightly.

'Alan, please,' she said. 'Please. Talk to me. Tell me what's on your mind.'

But although he did try to stop by taking several shuddering breaths, he was quite incapable of speech and it was only when she led him to the bath that he finally managed to strip off his own underpants and get in unaided.

Pam watched him slide under the water. She had filled the bath fuller than usual. Fuller than was really allowed these days, but it still didn't cover him. She took a flannel and squeezed it repeatedly over his goose pimpled shoulders. It was a long time since she had seen him in the bath, even longer since she had bathed him.

In the early years of their marriage they had often romped in the bath together, but gradually the novelty had worn off. In any case, having other people permanently in the house had limited their love-making to the bedroom and what with the war and water restrictions as well, the old arousing baths had gone by the board.

Not that she was aroused now, of course. Pam sighed as she sluiced the water over his raised thighs. Nor, quite clearly, was he.

And yet as she dried him off thoroughly and led him to bed he seemed to want her to hold him in her arms, to stroke him, to entwine her limbs with his. For a long time they lay stiffly in the silent darkness but very gradually, almost imperceptibly, as her fingers trailed gently over his back and the natural warmth came back into his skin, Pam felt something stirring inside her and found her fingers straying further and further afield, hoping for some kind of response.

She guessed that he was utterly mortified by his emotional outburst and thought that if she could persuade him to make love it might block out thoughts of his humiliating loss of control. She had been shocked by it too. And deep down she realised she wanted reassurance. Reassurance that despite the girlish tears her husband was still a man, the same man who had made such powerful love to her at the weekend.

Languidly she moved against him, her lips dotting little kisses up his neck and chin until she found his mouth. But despite Alan's valiant efforts to respond, and her increasingly desperate attempts to arouse him, the will was not there and at last he drew away from her with a groan.

'I'm sorry,' he whispered in the darkness. 'I'm so, so sorry.'

Pam bit her lip. Suddenly she was close to tears herself. 'It doesn't matter,' she muttered. 'Honestly, Alan, it doesn't matter.'

'It does matter,' he said. 'It's my fault. I failed to rescue those poor drowning people and now I've failed you too.'

Pam felt a shudder of guilt. She had been so worried about him she had scarcely given a thought to the people he was trying to rescue. 'You haven't failed,' she said. 'You could only do your best for those poor people. And as for me, it was stupid of me to try after what you'd been through tonight.'

She felt him shake his head. 'I'm no good as a husband to you. And now I've kept you awake all night for no purpose and you'll be dead beat at work again tomorrow.'

Unexpectedly Pam felt her temper rise. Suddenly she knew what this was all about. 'You're the best husband anyone could want,' she snapped. 'Just because we haven't managed to have any children doesn't make you a bad husband. It's probably not even your fault. Women can be infertile too, you know. It's just as likely to be my fault. In any case,' she added suddenly, 'whoever's fault it is, crying about it won't help.'

For a long moment Alan didn't respond. Then he sighed deeply. 'I'm sorry, Pam. I'm truly sorry. I was upset about those people trapped like rats in a cage at Balham, and then everything sort of got on top of me and I couldn't stop. What must you think of me? It's just that sometimes I long for children so much it hurts.'

Louise knew she was lucky to be alive. Everyone kept telling her.

In fact if anyone else told her she would probably scream. Because she didn't feel lucky to be alive. Even when she lay still as a corpse, her whole body throbbed and ached and if she so much as moved a muscle, or worse if anyone moved her or the sandbags wedged against her hips, red-hot pain shot through her limbs like liquid agony. The mere touch of a sheet brought tears to her eyes and she would willingly have killed the doctor who tried to manipulate her broken pelvis. Sadly, before she could summon the strength to sit up and stab him with his vicious long-needled syringe, she had fainted, right in the middle of a scream.

But above all the pain and discomfort, lying over her like a black shroud was a terrible sense of loss, an aching void that no amount of painkilling injections could touch.

She knew it was the baby, of course. And it infuriated her that the baby she had never wanted, that had made her moody and miserable for weeks, was still affecting her now, even though she had finally lost it.

If there had been someone she could have confided in, it might have helped. If she could have stormed about and kicked things and possibly even cried, she might have got it out of her system. But trapped immobile on a hospital bed with even the tiniest sob feeling like a hot poker applied to her nerve endings, the only way she could express her misery was in temper.

She knew the nurses hated her for it. She didn't care. She hated them too with their brisk, meaningless smiles and bland words of reassurance. It was a pleasure to shout at them, to refuse their requests for co-operation, to insist on different food and then to say it was disgusting and push it away. Some of the younger ones gave in, ran about to her beck and call, but some of the older, more senior ones were tougher and refused to back down even when she threatened to report them to her father and the board of governors.

It was the six-hourly back rubs that she railed against most of all. 'It's for your own good,' they would say through gritted teeth as they manoeuvred her into position, ruthlessly ignoring her screams and threats. 'We can't have you getting bedsores, now, can we?' or they'd laugh off her tantrum with the bracing, 'Chin up, Miss Rutherford, a few broken bones aren't worth shouting about.' Or more irritating still, the inevitable, 'Look on the bright side, it could have been worse.'

They didn't know about the baby, of course. The worst of the bleeding had stopped soon after she had been brought in, and as far as the nurses were concerned she'd been having her monthly at the time of the accident. Thanks to Katy Parsons the only people who knew the truth were the casualty doctor and the two grim-faced nursing Sisters, Parkes and Morris.

Even her mother didn't know, though in the face of her initial white-faced anxiety, Louise had almost been overcome by an overwhelming urge to tell her. She had had no idea how much her mother's tender concern would affect her. This morning, a week after the accident, it was still as much as she could do to stop herself from sobbing out the whole sordid story. Instead she turned her head away and interrupted her irritably when for want of other conversation her mother had rustled in her handbag and started to read out a letter from Bertie.

'I don't want to hear about stupid Bertie,' Louise snapped after the first sentence. 'It's all right for him safe and sound up in Shropshire.'

'But that's the whole point, darling,' her mother said. 'He wants to come back.' She glanced at the letter and Louise noticed her hand was shaking slightly. 'He says he's lonely up there and Aunt Delia is beginning to get on his nerves.'

'Well, it serves him right,' Louise said crossly. 'It's his own fault for being so wet. If he'd joined up like everyone else, he wouldn't be lonely, would he? He ought to try lying on his own in screeching agony for hours on end. He wouldn't complain about being lonely then.'

'Oh, my poor darling,' Celia said, reaching over to touch Louise's hand. 'Is it really so painful?'

'Yes,' Louise said. 'It is. Although not as bad as when I was first brought in.'

Her mother looked stricken. 'I feel so awful I wasn't able to be with you that night. I was out on the WVS van and they couldn't track us down.' She shook her head ruefully. 'I can't tell you how angry Daddy was about that.'

Louise sniffed. She could imagine how angry her father had been. He'd been moaning on about her mother's WVS work for weeks and now he had been proved right. Her mother should have been at home when she was needed. Ready to come and hold her daughter's hand in her hour of need. As it was, Louise had had to suffer alone and if it hadn't been for Katy Parsons, the whole thing could have been a complete and utter disaster.

It was pretty bad as it was, Louise thought, as another wave of self pity washed over her; after all, who was going to come and visit her stuck in the beastly Wilhelmina? Her smart Kensington friends were hardly likely to come trekking down to Clapham every five minutes. Bertie was in Shropshire. Her younger brother Douglas was away at school. Katy Parsons had popped in once or twice, but with that beastly Sister Morris breathing down her neck, she hardly had two minutes to call her own. In any case she had to work such ridiculously long hours that she was usually dead on her feet by the time she came off duty.

Louise sighed. The only person who might have visited her was Aaref Hoch. But as soon as her father had discovered that she had been with Aaref the night of the accident, he had banned Aaref from seeing her. Louise hadn't had the strength to argue. In any case she didn't want to see him. It was his fault she had been at Balham in the first place.

No, she frowned, she was quite clearly going to be bored to death at the Wilhelmina. She wondered suddenly how long she would be stuck here. She hadn't dared ask. In another week it would be the end of October. Surely it couldn't be more than a couple of weeks after that? Still, even a couple of weeks would drag. Maybe her brother should come home after all.

'Bertie is so stupid,' she said suddenly. 'Why doesn't he just tell

119

Daddy he's not a conscientious objector any more? Then he could come home with no problem. After all, he's still too young to get called up.'

'He says it's a matter of principle,' her mother said with a sigh. 'It's not that he's a coward. It's that he doesn't approve of the war.' She shook her head. 'That's what Daddy doesn't understand.'

'Then Daddy is stupid too,' Louise said angrily. 'It's obvious the war's stupid. Hitler is stupid, Mussolini is stupid. Even Churchill is stupid. They're all stupid and dangerous and it's not fair.'

Her mother smiled slightly. 'They're all men, darling. Men do seem a bit stupid sometimes, I know. But they are in charge, I'm afraid, and we haven't got any choice.'

Louise bit her lip. She suddenly felt very close to tears. 'Well, we should have. It's not fair that they should have all the say.'

Her mother stood up and smoothed Louise's brow. 'I'll talk to Daddy about Bertie,' she said placatingly. 'But in the meantime don't you fret. Just concentrate on getting well. The doctor says with any luck you'll be out of hospital and back on your feet again by Christmas.'

The arrival of the Rutherford & Berry delivery dray woke Katy from a deep dreamless sleep. With cotton wool stuffed in her ears and one of her father's black socks tied round her head like a children's blindfold she found she could sleep through the usual noises of the pub day, but the clanking of steel-rimmed barrels as they ran down the ramp into the cellar was too much for her makeshift ear plugs. Pulling them out she peeled the sock off her eyes to glance at the clock on her bedside table.

Four o'clock. She had been asleep nearly seven hours. She smiled and yawned, snuggling back into the warm bed. Unlike many of the nurses, she had little problem in sleeping by day. At least by day she could normally sleep in her own bed in her own room in relative peace and quiet and not in the dingy smoke-filled cellar on an uncomfortable camp bed with half a dozen men coughing and spluttering and her mother jumping out of her skin every time a bomb fell or the guns fired.

In fact, to her surprise, Katy had found that night duty was her salvation. With the bombing of London now in its fiftieth consecutive night, dealing with emergency admissions at night was a full-time job. There was little time for the tedious daytime chores, the endless bed-making and dusting. Instead, she spent much of her time washing and bathing wounds and trying to comfort those in pain. Although it was hard traumatic work, it felt more like the nursing she had expected, and the nights passed quickly.

It also meant that when she came off duty her sleep was undisturbed by bombing and when she woke up she still had a couple of daylight hours to call her own.

She yawned again and listened to the voices outside. They were loading the empties back on the dray now and she could hear Cyril the dray driver shouting at young Mick Carter to pull his weight. Unaware or uncaring of the fact that his voice carried clearly up the street, old Cyril's ritual abuse became increasingly explicit until Katy was giggling in her bed and wishing Jen was still around to witness her cocky, cack-handed younger brother getting his just deserts.

She had only heard once from Jen since she had gone off on her ENSA tour, a rather flat little letter saying she had never been so exhausted in all her life. Her group had apparently done three shows a night for seven nights on the trot, at a different venue each night. The other singer and the two strings players were quite nice but the pianist was ghastly and seemed to delight in playing Jen's music at the wrong tempo.

Katy stretched lazily. There were several things she had promised herself she would do this afternoon before going back on duty at eight, and writing to Jen was one of them. Visiting the Miss Taylors was another. She hadn't seen either of the two old ladies or Mrs Frost for ages and she felt guilty for neglecting them. She could go and give them Jen's news and at the same time tactfully enquire if they had heard if Ward Frazer was safely back yet from his mission.

But an hour later as she sat sipping tea in the Miss Taylors' cluttered sitting-room, Katy found it more difficult than she had thought to bring the conversation round to their nephew. She could feel Mrs Frost's beady eyes on her and she had a nasty feeling that if she mentioned his name she might blush and give the game away. Not that she fancied Ward Frazer, good heavens no; after his reference to her as a kid, she had decided she didn't even like him, but nevertheless she wanted to know if he was still alive.

'I hear Louise Rutherford was injured in that dreadful bomb at Balham,' Esme Taylor said. 'I gather she's quite bad.'

Katy grimaced. She would never forget the night Louise had been brought in to the Wilhelmina, her awful confrontation with Sister Morris and the disgusting job of scrubbing out the sluice room that had followed it as punishment for her insubordination.

'Poor Louise,' she said now. 'She's still in a lot of pain.' And she certainly lets everyone know it, she added silently to herself. Louise's reputation as the worst patient on earth had spread rapidly round the hospital, although to be fair she was always civil to Katy when she popped in to see her each evening before going on duty.

'Poor child must be lonely,' Thelma Taylor said. 'Perhaps we ought to visit her.'

'I doubt she'd want to see us,' Esme chipped in. 'She doesn't have much time for ancients, that Louise Rutherford. What we ought to do is send Ward in when he gets back.'

Katy sighed in relief. The dreaded name had been mentioned at last. 'Is he not back yet?' she asked innocently. 'I thought he was only going away for a couple of weeks.'

The Miss Taylors looked at each other quickly, but it was Mrs Frost who answered. 'He was due back yesterday, but as usual he's late, and as usual Esme and Thelma are already imagining the worst.'

Esme turned to Katy with a frown. 'It wouldn't be so bad if

122

someone would tell us why he is delayed. But it's all so hush-hush and nobody will ever say anything.'

'They're probably not allowed to,' Katy said placatingly. 'For fear of compromising him.'

'Exactly,' Mrs Frost said briskly. 'And he's been late back countless times before so I really don't think we need start worrying yet.'

But it was clear the old ladies were worrying. And even though Katy took the hint from Mrs Frost and tried to divert them with news of Jen, she found as she walked back down Lavender Road half an hour later that she felt angry with Ward Frazer for causing them such anxiety.

Poor old things. There was enough to worry about at the moment without knowing your long lost nephew was risking his life behind enemy lines. What happened if he did get killed? They would probably never know. He just wouldn't come back and that would be that. It wasn't as if he was a proper soldier whose death would have to be notified by the enemy. He was a spy and everyone knew what happened to spies. If they didn't get killed outright, they got captured, then tortured, then disappeared without trace. Katy suddenly felt very sick.

She stopped outside the pub for a moment to recover and jumped as someone spoke softly behind her.

'Miss Parsons?'

It was the Jewish boy, Aaref Hoch, Louise's former pupil.

'I think you are a friend of Miss Louise?' he said. 'I have heard she is in your hospital.'

Katy nodded. Of course. Aaref would have heard about the accident and would want to know how she was.

But it was more than that.

'I think not many people know why she was in Balham that evening,' he said tentatively. 'But I think you know, Miss Parsons, and I know also.'

Katy blinked nervously. She knew all right, but she wasn't sure if anyone else ought to. 'What makes you think you know what her, um . . . purpose was?' she asked suspiciously. Surely Louise wouldn't have confided in her pupil.

But clearly she had. 'It was not her wish to have a child,' Aaref said stiffly. 'She asked me to find someone to help her dispose of it.'

Katy stared at him incredulously. 'Louise asked *you* to find an abortionist?'

He looked hurt. 'I can do many things, Miss Parsons. I know many people. Perhaps one day I will be able to help you.'

Katy swallowed hard. 'Perhaps you will,' she said faintly, unable to imagine any scenario in which she could possibly be helped by an eighteen-year-old Jewish refugee.

'You do not believe me,' he said. 'You are laughing at me.'

She shook her head hastily. 'No, I'm not laughing, honestly. I was thinking of something else. Something completely different.' She sobered abruptly and wondered what to say next. Presumably if Louise had trusted him sufficiently to ask him to arrange the abortion, she wouldn't mind him knowing about the miscarriage. She eyed him doubtfully, suddenly seeing him through new eyes. Aaref was no longer a rather pathetic, displaced youth but a sharp, streetwise young man. And yet oddly she trusted him.

'She lost the baby,' she said. 'The accident caused her to miscarry. Nobody knows,' she went on quickly. 'Not even her parents.'

For an odd second she could have sworn he looked angry but then he nodded and looked away. 'It is for the best,' he said. Then his eyes came back to Katy again, very intent and dark. 'How is she? Is she in very much pain?'

Katy nodded reluctantly. 'Yes, she is still in some pain. They've operated on her broken ankle and that's in plaster now, but there's not much they can do for her fractured pelvis except keep her completely still.'

To her surprise Aaref touched her on the arm. 'Will you be kind to send her my regards?' he said.

'Of course,' Katy said. 'But you could visit her in hospital, you know. I'm sure she would be pleased to see you.'

A pulse flickered suddenly in his cheek. 'It is not possible. Her father will not permit it. Already I have asked for permission and I have been told to go away.'

Katy stared at him, appalled. So Louise's father was more than a tyrant, he was clearly anti-Semitic as well. She didn't know what to say. She could see the fierce pride in Aaref's thin face as he fought to conceal his hurt, but in the struggle he let something else through, a wistful longing that made Katy's eyes widen. 'You're really fond of her, aren't you?' she asked suddenly.

For a moment she thought he was going to deny it, but then he shrugged. 'Yes,' he said simply. 'I love her.'

To her surprise Katy felt tears in her eyes and looked away. Once again she couldn't think of anything to say. 'I'll give her your message,' she said at last, wishing her voice sounded less gruff.

He didn't seem to notice. He inclined his head and clicked his heels politely. 'Thank you,' he said and walked away down the street.

In the pub her father was fretting about his beer. 'They were late delivering. And then that idiot Carter boy nearly dropped the draught,' he said, nodding to the wooden barrel on the counter. 'And now it's not going to have time to settle. If I spike it now it will explode.'

Katy knew nothing about beer. As far as she was concerned it was brown, frothy and disgusting. But she knew from long years of living above the public bar that for her father's customers the nuances of taste and texture were crucially important. She knew that achieving the perfect pint involved a combination of technical expertise and publican's instinct. And she also knew that the customers were fickle. If for any reason the beer wasn't to their liking, they would spend their money elsewhere.

There were loyal regulars of course, but never as many as her father would like. The war hadn't helped in that respect, taking away some of the best local drinkers, replacing them with more transient custom, short-term contractors, drafted in for war work, servicemen in London for training, and foreigners, evacuees, with few local ties and a strange taste in beer.

And now the war had finally taken Phil Dunn the barman too, and watching her father anxiously adjusting the draught on the stillage, Katy realised how much he was feeling that loss. She had often heard him and Phil discussing the spiking of the beer or the best quantity of the finings for the ale. Phil Dunn was a placid, jovial fellow and his willing ear and good humour had tempered her father's more serious nature. But now her father had to make the decisions on his own and the strain was already showing on his face.

'You look tired,' she said suddenly. 'Why don't you sit down for half an hour?'

He looked up at her astonished. 'Sit down? I haven't got time to sit down. I haven't even started fining the new ale.' He waved his hand round the bar rather frantically. 'I haven't cashed up from the lunch trade yet or sorted out the glasses, and I've still got yesterday's empties to crate up downstairs.'

Katy frowned. It sounded a lot to do before opening time. 'Can't you leave the empties till tomorrow?'

Her father shook his head irritably. 'I can't afford to leave them. There's money tied up in empties, you know. And I need all the money I can get at the moment, just to keep the bloody brewers off my back.'

Katy blinked. It was most unlike her father to swear. She looked at him more closely and realised it wasn't just tiredness on his face but strain too. Obviously things were worse than she realised. She knew her father lived in fear of Rutherford & Berry pulling the plug on his lease. Being a tenant for a ruthless brewery was not a peaceful existence. Particularly if profits were down. Three months' notice to vacate and you lost not only your livelihood but also your home.

She shivered. 'Mr Rutherford couldn't throw us out,' she said. 'Surely. Not after you served with his father in the Great War and everything.'

Malcolm Parsons shrugged as he opened the till. He stared at the contents gloomily and closed it again. 'I don't think that counts for much any more. In any case, old man Rutherford's been dead for years. It's profits Greville Rutherford wants, not sentiment. And it's difficult to pull in profits when you're closed half the night because of air-raids.'

'But that's not your fault,' Katy said hotly. 'And it's not your fault if they deliver the beer so late you can't serve it.'

'No,' her father agreed, reaching for the spike and positioning it carefully at the top of the barrel of draught. He picked up his mallet. 'But it's a clever way of keeping up the pressure.'

She watched him hammer in the spike with professional precision. The sudden hiss of gas made her jump. 'You mean they delivered late on purpose?' She had assumed the dray was late because of last night's bomb damage in Wandsworth.

Her father was listening carefully to the escaping gas. At some indefinable moment he tightened the spike with a deft twist and looked up.

'They know I'm strapped after the burglary. They know I can't afford to replace Phil. They know your mother isn't well. I reckon they just want to make sure I know that they know.'

Katy stared at him as a cold finger touched her heart. 'What do you mean Mummy isn't well? What's the matter with her?'

She knew from his closed expression that he had said more than he meant to, and the chill spread to the rest of her body.

He glanced over his shoulder and lowered his voice. 'I don't mean she's ill,' he said with an attempt at a reassuring smile. 'Don't worry yourself. But it's the bombing. Night after night. It's getting to her. It's getting to her nerves.' He shook his head wearily. 'It's draining her energy. She used to do the floors each morning but she can't manage it now. It's as much as she can do to polish the glasses.'

Katy felt a dreadful wash of guilt. He was talking about her own mother and she had no idea. She knew her mother was nervous of course, but she always had been. She had always worried, but gradually Katy had learned to ignore it. She had had to ignore it because if she didn't she found it affected her too, pulling her into an endless downward spiral of anxiety. And that was when her chest tightened and she started to wheeze. She bit her lip. Perhaps she had tried so hard recently to build her own health and confidence, that she had missed the fact that her mother's was waning. And she was meant to be a nurse.

'I had no idea,' she whispered. She looked at her father and knew he was wishing he hadn't mentioned it. She swallowed hard. She knew why they hadn't mentioned it before. As usual her parents were trying to protect her. All her life they had tried to shelter her from the harsh reality of life. Well maybe now was the time for her to show she was up to taking the rough with the smooth.

'Perhaps she should go away for a while,' she said tentatively. 'Away from the bombing. To the country. To build up her strength.'

Her father sighed and dropped his gaze. She knew what he was going to say before he said it. 'I've suggested that but she's worried about leaving us. Worried about what we'd do for food and that. And she's worried about you. Worried that you'll get poorly when she's away.'

Katy frowned crossly. 'I won't get poorly,' she said. 'And if I do, so what? A few wheezes never killed anyone. And as for food, I can easily manage that.' It surely couldn't be too hard to shop and cook for two.

Or could it? She had no idea. Quickly squashing a niggle of unease, she smiled bravely at her father. 'And what's more I'll help with the chores here. You certainly won't be able to manage the whole pub on your own.'

Her father looked taken aback, stunned into silence by her uncharacteristic show of confidence. 'But what about your nursing?' he asked eventually.

Katy lifted her chin. 'I'll do that as well,' she said.

Chapter Eight

Louise took one mouthful of the rice pudding and nearly retched. Spitting out as much as she could, she flung the spoon down and pushed the bowl away angrily. Of all the million things she hated about the Wilhelmina, the thing she hated most was the food.

If you could call it food. Tonight's effort was a good example. Some kind of grey utterly tasteless stew, over boiled, equally tasteless potatoes and a blob of puréed vegetable that defied recognition. From its consistency Louise suspected it might once have been carrot, but somehow in the cooking process it had contrived to lose both its taste and its colour.

The so-called rice pudding, on the other hand, had gone one step further, transforming itself into a different colour altogether, a distinctly unpleasant shade of khaki which more than matched its taste, and if the nurse who'd brought it to her hadn't been called away on some emergency, Louise would have been tempted to throw the whole lot in her face.

She had complained countless times. So had her mother. Each time they had been promised an improvement. And each time the next meal had arrived just as disgusting as before. It was clear to Louise that the hospital cook or whoever operated the kitchen was a complete moron. Thankfully her mother brought in a few bits and pieces most days, but with reduced supplies in the shops and increased rationing even people with money to spend were having problems getting anything interesting to eat.

Knowing the nurse would shortly return for her tray, when the door of her room opened Louise was ready to launch into a new round of complaints. Instead she stopped abruptly and gaped at her unexpected visitor.

'Bertie!'

Grinning, her eighteen-year-old brother glanced furtively over his shoulder, than slipped into the room and closed the door. 'Well, well. What a sorry sight!'

Louise couldn't believe her eyes. 'Bertie!' she said again. 'What are you doing here? I thought you were still in Shropshire. And how on earth did you get in?'

He laughed. 'I craftily came in by a side entrance and sweet-talked a rather pretty nurse to tell me where you were.' His smile faded slightly as he took in the wince of pain on her face as she levered up on an elbow to look at him. 'You are in a bad way, Sis, aren't you?'

'Yes I am,' Louise said grimly, flopping back on her pillows. 'And so would you be if the whole of beastly Balham Tube station had fallen in on top of you.' She saw his expression and grimaced. 'If you say I'm lucky to be alive, I'll throw that rice pudding at you.'

'Mmm.' He brightened as he glanced at her discarded tray. 'Rice pudding. Don't you want it?'

Louise shook her head and wished she hadn't as a pain shot up her side. 'Have it if you want,' she said. 'But I don't recommend it.'

He picked up the bowl and sniffed it appreciatively. 'Condensed milk, my favourite!'

Looking at him, she realised he had grown up while he had been away. His hair was longer, a bit too long to be honest, and he seemed less lanky than he had in the summer. His clothes left a bit to be desired. The waistcoat under the ostentatiously shabby tweed jacket was too bright, and the arty cravat was a bit wet, but from the neck up he was nice looking, she would give him that.

Despite the effeminate dark wavy hair he had good regular features, clear brown eyes, a straight, thin nose and a mouth that turned up at the corners in a faintly derisive smirk.

In fact if he wasn't her brother she might even quite fancy him herself. Although his cocky self-confidence would get on her nerves. Not that he had anything to be self-confident about. Nobody liked conchies. One or two of the porters in the hospital were objectors and she'd heard them getting a hard time.

She looked at him again as he scraped the plate and wondered why he was so set on his absurd pacifist ideals. There was nothing in his face to show his stubbornness, his *principles*, as her mother had referred to them. On the contrary, apart from his arty clothes he looked like the faintly supercilious well-to-do young man that he was, exactly the sort that joined some smart cavalry regiment and pranced about at fashionable London parties showing off his uniform.

'So how come you've managed to get permission to come home?' she asked. 'Mummy told me that you were still persona non grata as far as Daddy was concerned. Don't tell me he's had a change of heart.'

He shrugged. 'He doesn't know I'm back.'

Louise stared at him. 'You mean you haven't been home yet?'

He grinned. 'I called by but there was only that awful old Mrs Carter there. God, she's a sour old thing, isn't she? And she looks like something the cat sicked up. I can't think why the mater has her in the house. Anyway I managed to get out of her that the parents were both out for the morning, so I thought I'd pop down and see my dear old sis instead. See how the land lay.'

His voice was light but Louise sensed that under his blasé unconcern he was genuinely keen to know. She frowned. 'I don't think it lies very well, Bertie. I doubt whether Daddy will let you stay.'

Bertie looked taken aback. 'He can hardly shut the door in my face, can he? Not now I'm actually here?'

Louise was prevented a reply by the arrival of the nurse to take away the tray. She looked shocked and flustered to find her patient entertaining an unauthorised male visitor and even more so when Bertie stood up and put on his most charming smile.

'Hello there, I'm Bertie Rutherford, Louise's brother. I know, I know,' he said holding up his hands. 'I'm not supposed to be here, but I've just got back to London and I couldn't wait to see my poor ailing sister.'

'Well.' The nurse pursed her lips disapprovingly and glanced nervously towards the door. 'That's as may be. But I don't think it would be wise to let Sister catch you. She'll be doing her round soon.'

Bertie made a grimace of mock terror and Louise was astonished to see the nurse suddenly smile. They never smiled for her. 'Well, if you can cheer up Miss Louise, that's a good thing,' the nurse said, picking up the tray. 'But you'd better make it snappy.' She flashed him a coy look from the door. 'You can always come back at the proper visiting time.'

As the door closed behind her Louise swivelled her eyes to her brother. She had never seen him flirt before. 'Bertie, really. Do you have to?' she said crossly.

He glanced at her, a smile still playing on his lips. 'Don't you just love nurses?' he said. 'All that prudish purity, when underneath they're just as naughty as the next woman.'

'No, I don't love them.' Louise was shocked. This was her brother talking. Her younger brother, who ought to be looking to his older sister for advice on how to deal with women, not eyeing them up as though he knew all too well how to deal with them. 'And I'd be grateful if you didn't make a fool of yourself over them, Bertie. Most of the nurses here are far too old for you in any case. And far too common.'

To her irritation, he laughed. 'Oh, but I like older women, Sis. And as a general rule, I find they like me.' He yawned and stretched lazily, ignoring her appalled glare. 'As for common, who cares? I'm not exactly looking for someone to take to the opera, am I?'

Despite herself, Louise giggled. He was incorrigible and she didn't believe a word of it. As far as she was aware he'd never even taken a girl to the pictures, let alone the opera. 'I don't know what you're looking for, Bertie,' she said. 'And quite honestly I don't care. But I do think you'd better go and look for it somewhere else or Sister will catch you. And I can categorically guarantee you wouldn't want to take her to the opera.'

He held up his hands. 'OK, OK. I'm going. I get the message.' He grinned. 'I'd better go back and face the music anyway.' He blew her a kiss from the door. 'Wish me luck. I've got this feeling I might need it.'

'I've got this feeling you might too,' Louise said to herself after he had gone. Her brother's blasé charm might work on the nurses, but her stubborn, autocratic father was hardly likely to be impressed by it. On the contrary, it seemed to Louise rather more likely that, as far as her father was concerned, anything short of a full-blown apology, a patriotic rendering of 'Onward Christian Soldiers' and immediate enlistment into the Rifle Brigade was likely to be responded to with an uncompromising kick in the teeth.

Joyce was cleaning out Mrs Rutherford's chickens when she heard the car. She hesitated for a second then carried on with her task of scooping out the muck and replacing it with fresh straw. She liked helping with the hens. Especially now they had their own little coop.

Mr Rutherford hadn't been at all pleased to find them in his tool shed that day when they had arrived, and had soon afterwards sent a man over from the brewery to equip them with their own accommodation. Shivering slightly in the late October breeze, Joyce watched them now, scratching about under the apple trees, and shook her head. She'd got quite fond of them over the last few weeks. She particularly liked the rogue hen, the one that had caused them trouble from the start. It had more character than the others and far more guts. Twice she had found it in the house and Mrs Rutherford had told her that it had taken a terrible dislike to her husband, squawking its head off if he so much as set foot in the garden.

'He's awfully annoyed about it,' Mrs Rutherford had said. 'If she wasn't such a good layer I think he'd be tempted to wring her neck.'

'Maybe that's why she does it,' Joyce had replied. 'Probably senses danger.'

She's got her head screwed on, that hen, she thought now, pulling her cardigan closer round her. Men were dangerous. They were bigger and stronger. And the way the world was set up meant they were in charge. That was why she had dropped out of the WVS. Because Stanley didn't want her to do it. Simple as that. She knew Mrs Rutherford was upset about it but there was nothing she could do about it. It wasn't worth fighting about. Because it would hurt and Stanley would win.

Stanley didn't like her cleaning for the Rutherfords either, come to that, but at least he had the brain to realise they needed the money. Especially as he was showing no sign of finding a job.

As she heard the car door slam and steps coming through the house, Joyce straightened up nervously. She had a feeling Mrs Rutherford wasn't going to like what she had to tell her. The news that her son Bertram had come home earlier.

As she had expected, Mrs Rutherford did not take it well. 'Oh my goodness.' She looked around wildly as though the boy was about to jump out of the hen coop. 'Where is he now? If Greville catches him in the house he'll skin him alive.'

'He went down to the hospital,' Joyce said. 'To see your daughter.'

Celia ran her hands over her face. 'It really is too much. I told him not to come back. I told him that his father wouldn't have him in the house until he'd changed his ways.' She had a sudden thought and glanced at Joyce. 'How did he seem, Mrs Carter? Did he look as if he'd changed his ways? Did he look at all repentant?'

'Not really.' Joyce shook her head slowly. 'More on the cocky side, I would have said.'

And that was putting it mildly. As far as she was concerned he looked a right little prig with his drawled vowels and looking down his upper class nose at her as though she was a bit of dog dirt stuck on his shoe.

She knew she didn't look like much but there was no need to make it so obvious. Mr Lorenz hadn't sneered like that when he'd seen her on Lavender Hill the other day. He'd raised his hat politely the way he always did. She would have crossed over to talk to him but she couldn't risk Stanley catching her. In any case she didn't want Lorenz seeing her close up, not in her tatty old coat, all peaky white with dirty hair under her mob cap. But she daren't do herself up much at the moment in case Stanley got the wrong idea again. For some daft reason he'd got it in his head that she'd been dressing up for another man.

Tarting herself up, he called it, and the very thought of it seemed to make him randy. Every night this week he'd had his way with her after the all-clear had gone, as soon as they'd got into bed. A quick, rough grope and a couple of thrusts leaving him satisfied and asleep, and her bruised and wakeful for the rest of the night.

He hadn't hit her again, though. Not since that awful first night. But he was back on the beer. And he'd taken her wages. Needed to repay a debt, he'd said, but she was certain it had gone on the horses. She sighed. There was nothing she could do. Sooner or later he'd find a job. And then they'd be back on the straight and narrow.

In the meantime she wished everyone would leave her alone. Mrs Rutherford had asked her twice yesterday if she was all right. And that Katy Parsons had given her a funny look when she'd seen her in the street.

Of course she was bloody all right. In any case she was hardly going to say if she wasn't, was she? She had her pride, her loyalty. Stanley was her husband for better or worse. And that was all there was to it. Everyone else could just mind their own business.

'I'd better go and tell Greville,' Mrs Rutherford said suddenly and Joyce stared at her blankly.

'What about?' she asked in sudden alarm. She didn't want that dreadful Mr Rutherford poking his nose into her business.

Celia Rutherford looked at her oddly. 'About Bertie coming back from Shropshire. I dread to think what he'll say.' She was looking anxious but she hesitated before moving away. 'Are you sure you're all right, Mrs Carter?' she asked gently. 'You do look very tired.'

'I'm quite all right,' Joyce said crossly, turning away quickly to hide her embarrassment. She felt a complete idiot. For a moment then she had forgotten what they were talking about.

Celia's discussion with her husband didn't last long. Bertie arrived home less than ten minutes later and by the time Joyce went back into the house, she could hear Greville Rutherford's raised voice through his study door.

She could also hear quite clearly what he was saying and the gist of it was that Bertie would not be tolerated in the house, nor allowed to set one foot inside the door until he had given up his pacifist views. He was to go straight back to Shropshire and stay there until he had come to his senses. If he insisted on staying in London, Greville Rutherford would wash his hands of him. He would be given no financial support of any kind and steps would be taken to disinherit him from the family business.

In other words, Joyce said to herself, as she searched in the hall cupboard for the polish, Greville Rutherford is not too happy about having a conscientious objector in the family.

Moments later the study door flew open and the boy came out. Flattening herself awkwardly into the shallow cupboard, Joyce saw him pick up the leather suitcase which still stood in the hall then turn back to his father who stood red faced and menacing, clearly itching for a fight. It was only Celia's presence that seemed to be holding him back.

'I'm going,' Bertie said scornfully. 'Don't worry. I'm glad to go. I would rather sleep rough on the common than spend a night under the same roof as you. I always knew you were pompous and short sighted, blinded by your own absurd form of patriotism, but I had no idea you were so bigoted you would throw out your own son.'

'You're not my son any more,' Greville Rutherford roared. He shook off Celia's clutching fingers and stepped forward to open the front door. 'Get out,' he shouted, pushing the boy roughly down the steps. 'Just get out and don't come back.'

'Bertie, stop, please . . . wait . . .'

Celia ran forward, but as she went to follow the boy, Greville swung her back. 'Leave him, Celia.' His voice was angry. 'Let him go.'

Without waiting for a reply, he slammed the door and went back into his office.

Tears were streaming down Celia's face. Joyce emerged from the cupboard and touched her arm. 'Don't fret yourself, Mrs Rutherford,' she said. 'I threw my Mick out once and it did him a world of good.'

'Oh, Mrs Carter.' For a second Celia tried to control her emotion but the shock was clearly too much for her. She slumped down in the hall chair and put her head in her hands, sobbing violently.

Joyce was just wondering what to do when a hard voice spoke behind her. 'We won't be needing you any more today, Mrs Carter.'

'Oh.' Joyce turned, startled. Greville Rutherford's icy expression brooked no argument even if she had wanted to. 'I'll just get my things then,' she said stiffly.

Greville Rutherford nodded and opened the front door for her when she came back from the pantry with her coat and bag. 'I hope I don't need to ask you to keep what's happened to yourself, Mrs Carter?'

Joyce lifted her chin. 'No, you don't.'

He nodded again. 'Good.'

Good. It was a threat. A veiled one but a threat nevertheless. She knew a threat when she saw one. Men were all the same. From Mr bloody Rutherford to Stanley Carter, they loved their threats. Good. She sniffed as she crunched down the gravel drive.

Then as she turned out of the wide gates she stopped as she caught sight of Bertie Rutherford sitting on a bench on the other side of the road by the entrance to the allotments they'd made on the common.

For a second she hesitated, wondering if she ought to do anything about him. Not for him. She didn't care two hoots about him. But for Mrs Rutherford. The poor woman would be worried to death about him with the bombing and all. Already there was activity around the gun emplacements and it wasn't even dark yet. He certainly wouldn't want to be sitting there in an hour or two.

Joyce watched him fumbling with a cigarette and felt her conscience prick. As he'd been stuck up in Shropshire since the bombing began he probably didn't realise yet that Clapham in October 1940 was not a place in which anyone in their right minds would choose to be homeless.

She was about to cross the road when he glanced up and saw her. At once a cynical smile curled on to his lips. Leaning back he crossed his ankles and blew out smoke lazily, waiting for her approach.

Immediately Joyce changed her mind. Let him stew, she thought. Cocky little sod. Pushing her hands up the sleeves of her coat, she turned abruptly and walked away down Lavender Road. There were plenty of public air-raid shelters after all. He could spend the night in one of those. Like everyone else.

'Word has it your la-di-da friend Miss Rutherford had a rather lovely visitor today,' Nurse Coogan whispered to Katy as they lined up the heavy stone hot-water bottles ready for warming the beds for the night's admissions.

Katy looked up surprised. Since the night of Louise's accident, she and Nurse Coogan had barely exchanged half a dozen sentences. Shocked by the other girl's unexpected revelations about the loss of her family, Katy had made some efforts to be friendly, but it was a slow process. Clearly regretting her moment of indiscretion, Nurse

Coogan had been as spiky and uncommunicative as ever and, in any case, Katy was almost too tired to bother any more.

Already she was beginning to regret her impulsive offer to help in the pub. Her mother had duly gone away to a friend in Didcot and Katy had spent the rest of the week trying to queue for food and cook and clean the pub by day and still keep her eyes open on night duty.

Oddly, from previously letting her do nothing in the pub, her father suddenly seemed to expect her to do everything. Not on the drinks side of course, he wouldn't dream of letting her spike the beer or measure the shorts, but he had been so pleased the first day when she had scrubbed the floors and polished the furniture, that she had gradually taken on more and more until she was spending virtually all her precious off-duty doing apparently crucial domestic chores.

But she knew she wouldn't be able to keep it up much longer. She would have to sleep tomorrow after she had done the floors and her father would just have to manage his own lunch.

Suddenly sensing Nurse Coogan's impatience, she frowned and tried to remember what the other girl had said. Something about Louise's visitor, wasn't it? Typical that Nurse Coogan would choose tonight to start chatting.

'It was probably her brother,' Katy said. The rumour on Lavender Road was that Mr Rutherford had thrown Bertie out of the house without a bean and the poor boy was sleeping rough in the public shelter on the common. Katy didn't know if it was true. She hadn't had time to see Louise yesterday and this evening when she had popped in just before she came on duty Mrs Rutherford was there so she hadn't had a chance to find out what had really happened.

But Nurse Coogan was shaking her head. 'It wasn't the brother. Everyone knows what the brother looks like by now. Not him. Mind you, he's not so bad looking himself. No.' She shook her head. 'This was another man. Taller than the brother. Talked like a Hollywood film star. American, Nurse Kilroy thought. Grey eyes and handsome.

Miss Rutherford was over the moon afterwards, Nurse Kilroy said.' She stopped and stared at Katy. 'What's the matter?' She put her hands quickly to her face. 'Have I got a mark on me or a bogey or something?'

Katy felt herself flush slightly. 'No, no, you look fine.' She swallowed and busied herself checking to see if the water had reached the right temperature for the bottles. But suddenly the preparation of beds for new arrivals seemed less urgent than it had before. So Ward Frazer was back, was he? Safe. And the first person he went to see was Louise Rutherford. She took a breath and glanced up again trying to make her voice casually conversational. 'What else did Nurse Kilroy say?'

Nurse Coogan grinned. 'Lucky Miss Rutherford, is what she said. Oh and Italy has invaded Greece.'

Katy blinked. 'What?'

'Italy has invaded Greece,' Nurse Coogan repeated. 'Nurse Kilroy heard it on the wireless.'

'Oh, the war.' Katy shook her head. It seemed incredible that beyond these reinforced walls the war was going on without her. In the past she had followed every gruesome detail. Now it was as much as she could do to keep track of what day it was, let alone which country Hitler had marched into next.

'Poor old Greece,' Nurse Coogan grimaced. 'They'd been asking for help for days apparently. Or so it said on the wireless.' She frowned and slanted a glance at Katy. 'Are you all right? You look a bit green. Are you feeling sick?'

Katy forced a smile. 'I'm fine.' She shook her head. 'Just a bit tired.'

Louise was quick to confirm the rumour. She was eating her breakfast when Katy called by the following morning, the moment she came off duty.

'Ward Frazer came in yesterday,' she said airily.

Katy nodded as she sat down. 'I heard you'd had a visitor. I guessed that was who it was.'

Louise looked up from buttering her toast and smiled smugly. 'So the nurses are gossiping about him, are they? I thought they would.'

Katy smiled wearily. 'I suppose his aunts had told him you were here.'

'Yes.' Louise giggled. 'Thank God I'd had my hair washed only a couple of hours earlier. Otherwise I'd have looked a complete fright.'

Katy looked around, trying to imagine Ward Frazer in this sterile little room. A vase of flowers stood on the table by the small grilled window. They hadn't been there on her previous visit. It wasn't too hard to imagine who had brought them. But she was wrong.

'Aaref Hoch sent me those,' Louise said, following her gaze. 'One of the porters brought them up this morning.'

'They're lovely,' Katy said, getting up to smell them. 'How sweet of him.'

She felt sorry for Aaref Hoch. He seemed such a nice boy and yet Louise had just laughed when Katy had passed on his good wishes last week. 'Oh, he's nice enough,' she had said when Katy stood up for him. 'But he's hardly husband material, is he?'

Now, as Katy admired his flowers, Louise nodded. 'They're quite pretty, aren't they?' Her voice was dismissive.

Clearly Ward's visit was worth more than poor Aaref's flowers, Katy thought. So how come Ward Frazer was allowed to swan in when Aaref had been refused point blank, she wondered, sitting down again. Probably because Ward Frazer was considered to be 'husband material', she realised with a jolt. Then again, Ward Frazer had probably not even bothered to ask.

'Where did Ward sit?' she asked suddenly.

Louise looked surprised. 'What?'

Katy flushed slightly. 'Where did he sit?' she repeated doggedly.

Louise waved her toast impatiently. 'He sat on the chair, of course. Where you're sitting. You'd hardly expect him to climb into bed

141

with me on his first visit, would you? I know he's got a bit of a reputation, but nobody has ever accused him of being crass.'

Katy bit her lip. 'How did he seem?' she asked. 'I know he's been away for a while. Did he look all right?'

Louise smiled. 'He looked the same as usual. Relaxed, charming, cool.' Her eyes went a bit dreamy. 'He seemed very concerned about my accident. Very solicitous.'

Katy glanced at her friend. I bet he did, she thought. Lying there under the blanket cage, wedged with sandbags, surrounded by pulleys and levers, with her dark hair spread over the white pillow, framing her pale face, Louise looked very small and vulnerable. And very pretty.

In contrast, after a long, unusually busy night, Katy felt gritty-eyed and rather cross. 'Did he ask about me at all?'

Louise chewed a corner of toast and frowned. 'No. Why should he? You hardly know him, do you?'

Katy felt herself colouring. 'Well, I've met him a couple of times at the Miss Taylors',' she said. 'And he knows I nurse here.'

The pique was clear in her voice and Louise was clearly amused by it. 'Well, when he comes this afternoon, I'll tell him you're disappointed he didn't look you up, shall I?'

'No!' In her alarm, Katy almost shouted the word and her flush deepened as Louise giggled. Furious with herself, Katy tried to erase the panic from her voice. 'No, don't say that. I don't particularly want to see him.' She attempted a negligent shrug. 'I don't like him much actually.'

'Don't you?' Louise looked surprise. 'Why on earth not? You must be the only woman I've ever met who doesn't. Even Sister Donaldson got a bit fluttery when she bumped into him in the doorway.'

Katy groaned inwardly. This was unbearable. Now Louise would think she was some kind of asexual freak. She shook her head wearily. She was too tired for this. Why hadn't she contained her impatience and waited to see Louise until after she had slept?

'I don't know,' she said. 'I find him a bit difficult to talk to.'

Louise laughed delightedly. 'You probably fancy him,' she said. 'Men always seem difficult to talk to if you fancy them.'

Katy smiled weakly. 'I haven't got time to fancy anyone at the moment. And I'd be too tired to do anything about it even if I did.' She stood up. 'Talking of which, I must go. I'm needed back at the pub.'

'Goodness.' Louise looked appalled. 'You're not still helping in the pub, are you? Isn't your mother back yet?'

'She's only been gone just over a week,' Katy said. Suddenly she wished she had never told Louise about her mother going away.

'You're mad,' Louise said, pushing away her tray. 'Why don't you just hire someone to do the cleaning? It would be much simpler.'

Katy smiled. Louise lived in a different world. A world of privilege, inhabited by people with plenty of money and plenty of time. It was a far cry from scrubbing spilt beer off the tap room lino or wiping round the urinals.

'I've had a brilliant idea,' Louise said. 'Why doesn't your father ask Bertie to do it? In return for somewhere to live.' She giggled. 'That would serve Bertie right, wouldn't it? And Daddy would be furious. Imagine, his own son having to scrub the floors of one of his pubs for a living.'

Katy felt sick.

'It would be funny, wouldn't it?' Louise was clearly thrilled with the idea.

'It would be hilarious,' Katy said dryly.

And it is completely out of the question, she added silently to herself as she let herself out of the Private Block into the morning drizzle. Coughing slightly as the cold air penetrated her tired lungs, she pulled her cloak round her and headed for home.

Her father might live in terror of Mr Rutherford, but he shared the brewer's views on one thing. Katy knew her father would rather die than have a conscientious objector work for him. Even if he could afford the kind of wages a snooty young man like Bertie Rutherford would demand. Which as things stood at the moment, he clearly couldn't.

★　★　★

'No, Alan. No! You can't be serious. You can't do this to me.' Pam stared at her husband in horror. 'It's so nice having just the two of us here. We've got on so well the last couple of weeks. I really don't want anyone else spoiling it.'

Alan looked crestfallen. 'Oh, come on, Pam, it's nothing. The poor boy just needs somewhere to live. He's been camping out in the air-raid shelter up on the common but they'll only let him in if there's a warning.'

'There's a warning every night,' Pam said crossly.

Alan grimaced. 'But he's got nowhere to go by day. Nothing to do. Nothing to eat. He hasn't had a bath for four days. And you can't imagine a classy boy like that using the public baths, can you?'

Pam looked at him. Something in his voice alerted her to the truth. Her heart sank. 'It's too late, isn't it? You've asked him already.'

For a moment Alan avoided her gaze then he nodded.

Pam sighed. 'And he wants to come?'

Alan brightened. 'Just until he's found his feet. He wasn't expecting old man Rutherford to throw him out penniless.'

Pam frowned suddenly. 'What about old Rutherford, Alan? He'll probably sack you if he finds out.'

Alan shook his head. 'I've asked him.'

Pam stared at him speechlessly.

Alan nodded. 'He said he'd be grateful. He knows people are beginning to talk. It doesn't look good for a pillar of the community to throw out his son even if he is an objector.'

Pam felt her temper rising. 'So just because it doesn't look good for Mr bloody pillar-of-the-community Rutherford, we've got to put up with his toffee-nosed little bastard.' She leaned forward and glared at Alan. 'I don't want him,' she said fiercely, standing up. 'I don't want a bloody conchie here. Why us? It's not fair. Why do we have to have him?'

Alan smiled. 'Because we're warm hospitable people,' he said. He stood up too and kissed Pam on the mouth. Then he shrugged. 'He's not as bad as you make out,' he said. 'He'll be fine. You'll see.'

Pam didn't want to see. She wanted to keep things like they were since Sheila and George had gone. Nice and settled. Just her and Alan. But she knew from her husband's face it was no use arguing.

'When's he coming, then?' she said resignedly. 'Where is he now?'

Alan looked guilty. 'He's waiting outside the front door.'

Pam gaped at him. 'What if I'd said no?'

Alan laughed. 'I knew you'd say no. But I knew you'd change you mind. You're too nice to refuse.'

Pam sighed. 'I don't feel nice,' she said crossly. 'I don't feel nice at all.'

'Where on earth have you been? You said you'd be back by ten thirty to do the floors.'

Katy dropped her baskets on the floor and sat down at one of the bar tables. For a second she thought she was going to cry, then she looked up at her father. 'There was a warning,' she said, trying to rub some warmth back into her hands. She'd forgotten to take her gloves with her and her fingers were numb with cold. 'Didn't you hear it? Some planes came over and everyone rushed for cover and I lost my place in the queue.'

Malcolm Parsons shook his head irritably. 'Well, that's as may be but what about the floors?'

For a moment Katy was tempted to tell him to forget about his blasted floors for once. But she knew she couldn't. Not today.

It was the sixth of November. In any normal year her father would have let off fireworks last night, but the Germans provided quite enough of those already. In any case fireworks were banned. Instead the larger than usual crowd in the Flag and Garter had toasted Guy Fawkes in beer. And they'd toasted the American President Franklin D. Roosevelt for his re-election. And they'd toasted Winston Churchill for his fighting spirit. And the Greeks, who were reported to have pushed back the Italian advance. And the gallant boys in the forces, of course. And the King.

145

And thanks to Barry Fish on the piano they had sung themselves hoarse and drunk themselves sick.

And the floors had paid the price.

'Just let me sit down for two seconds,' Katy said wearily. 'Then I'll do them.'

Her father glanced at the grandfather clock beside the bar. 'Well, don't forget we're opening in half an hour.'

He was heading back towards the cellar steps when Katy remembered something. 'Was Stanley Carter in last night?'

Her father nodded. 'Yes, he was, why?'

'Did he have a lot to drink?'

'He's a good drinker, Stanley,' her father said with satisfaction. 'He had a few pints. Why?'

Katy frowned. 'It's just . . . I saw Mrs Carter down in the market. She looked awful. Really down. And there was a bruise on her face. I think he hits her when he gets drunk.'

Her father looked shocked. Not at Stanley Carter's behaviour, Katy realised suddenly, but at her remarking on it. 'I don't know what you're talking about, Katy. In any case it's none of our business.'

'It's our business if we're serving him the drink,' Katy said doggedly. 'Couldn't you stop serving him when he's obviously had too much?'

Malcolm Parsons was clearly appalled. He came back into the bar and leaned on the table she was sitting at. 'Now you listen to me, young lady. This is a pub we're running. Our job is to sell drink. As much as we can. It is not our job to poke our noses into other people's affairs. What goes on between man and wife is their business.' He was angry now. 'And what's more I will not have you telling me who I should or shouldn't serve. I'm the landlord of this pub and I don't need a useless slip of a girl telling me how to run it. Is that clear?'

Katy closed her eyes. She was too tired to argue. Too tired even to cry. All she wanted to do was lie down and sleep. But even that was impossible. She may be a useless slip of a girl, but she still had her chores to do. And even though she was sorely tempted to throw the floor cloth at her father and tell him to do it himself, she knew she couldn't. She was sure he didn't realise how demanding he was being. How hurtful. He was worried to death about her mother. About the pub. He no longer had room in his brain for worry about her.

'I'm sorry, Daddy,' she said, getting to her feet. 'I was worried about Mrs Carter, that's all.'

But it wasn't just Mrs Carter she was worried about. It was Jen too. The last she had heard was that her group was heading for Coventry, to do the rounds of the munitions factories there. Since when the Midlands had suffered some bad bombing raids.

As she worked the heavy cloth along the floor on her hands and knees, Katy stopped for a moment and leaned her head against the bar. The smooth, well-polished wood was cold and hard and smelled comfortingly of wax. Once again she closed her eyes and this time the tears began to well.

She was trying valiantly to sniff them back when the pub doors opened and Ward Frazer walked in with a draught of cold air.

Chapter Nine

Katy couldn't believe her eyes. I'm hallucinating, she said to herself. Or else he's a mirage, like thirsty people see in the desert, water shimmering in the distance. She blinked and looked again. But there was nothing shimmery about Ward Frazer. With the light from the open doors behind him he was all too unyieldingly real, all six foot two of him from the top of his crisp black hair to the toes of his well-polished brogues, and suddenly Katy wished she was dead.

But sadly she was not dead. She was all too obviously alive, caught in the shaft of light, kneeling bare kneed against the bar like a supplicant of some weird kinky faith, red eyed and white faced with her skirt hitched into her knickers, her beret still on her head and clutching a filthy floor cloth dripping with equally filthy water.

She couldn't look at him. Instead, the image of Louise Rutherford, delicate and immaculate in her pristine hospital bed, flitted across her mind and she gazed in some desperation around her own surroundings. The public bar was not the most salubrious place at the best of times. At night, filled with drinkers with the wall lights on, it had a certain ambience, but in the cold light of day, with the cheap wooden chairs up ended on the tables, the yellowing walls showing their age and the air smelling of old smoke and yesterday's beer, it was not a room to be proud of, and Katy suddenly found herself hating it bitterly.

And hating Ward Frazer too. To her knowledge he'd been back over a week. Not that she'd had sight or sound of him. How dare he march in now as though he owned the blasted place?

As he closed the door and turned back towards her, she stood up abruptly and jerked her skirt out of her knickers with her spare hand.

'We're closed,' she said.

Something, it might have been surprise, flickered across his face and she wished she hadn't been quite so rude. She also wished she hadn't stood up so quickly. She could feel herself swaying unnervingly.

Ward inclined his head. 'I didn't come for a drink. I came to ask a favour. But I guess it's not a good moment.'

You guess right, Katy thought miserably, grasping the counter for support as her head continued to spin. It's just about the worst moment in the whole history of mankind.

'It's OK,' she said ungraciously. She tried to smile but it didn't really work. Still holding the counter carefully, she gestured helplessly with the hand that held her cloth. 'As you see, I'm just doing a bit of cleaning. We've lost our barman and my mother's away so we're short handed.'

He didn't return the smile. 'Louise said you were on night duty.'

Katy nodded and was suddenly conscious of the beret on her head. She thought about taking it off and raised her hand but stopped, remembering there was a cloth in it.

'I am,' she said. He'd just have to think she was eccentric, she decided, it could hardly be worse than he must think already.

'I came home a couple of hours ago,' she added in some desperation when he didn't react. She glanced round at the grandfather clock by the cellar door and frowned in surprise. Bloody Ben's hands were both pointing to twelve. Midnight? Momentarily disoriented, she shook her head. 'No, that can't be right. I came off duty at eight.' For a second she wondered if her eyes were focussing properly. Then finally her tired brain made sense of it. It wasn't night it was

149

day. Midday to be precise. She flushed, hoping he hadn't realised her confusion.

'Four hours ago,' she said turning back to him in some relief. For a moment then she thought she'd lost her mind. She waved the cloth at the clock. 'I came off duty four hours ago.'

But Ward Frazer clearly didn't share her relief. On the contrary he looked decidedly grim. Muttering something that sounded distinctly like an oath, he strode across the bar, took the cloth out of her hand and dropped it on the floor.

Katy stared at him alarmed. 'What are you doing?'

He smiled thinly. 'I'm sending you to bed.'

She recoiled in horror. 'No, I can't go to bed. Not yet. I'm going to do the floors first.'

'Like hell you are,' he said. 'You ought to be asleep. You can't work all night and then all day. I know exhaustion when I see it and you're dead on your feet.'

Katy stared around desperately. 'But I can't leave it. My father will have a fit.'

'I don't care,' he said implacably. Then seeing her expression suddenly he smiled. 'Don't worry. If necessary I'll do it myself.'

Katy gaped at him.

'You can't scrub the floors.'

He looked surprised. 'Why not? I don't have anything else to do right now.'

Katy shook her head then wished she hadn't as the room began to sway again. Suddenly there were tears in her eyes. She was sure there were a million reasons why Ward Frazer couldn't scrub the floors, but none of them sprang to mind.

Ward took her arm and steered her towards the stairs. 'You're beyond arguing,' he said, pushing her gently up the steps in front of him. At the top he looked around with interest at her parents' little sitting-room.

'So this is where you live.'

'Don't look,' Katy said, newly embarrassed. This time by the dreadful purple and beige chair covers, the shiny lilac cushions, the collection of white ornamental dogs on the mantelpiece. 'It's not my taste,' she said frantically, then at once felt guilty as though she had betrayed her mother.

But Ward was smiling. 'It's kind of cute,' he said. 'Homey.' For a second his smiling gaze rested on her face and Katy felt a strange shiver of panic. Then abruptly the smile was gone and he was frowning again. 'You work too hard,' he said sternly. 'And if you're not careful you'll get sick.' He hesitated then glanced towards the small kitchen. 'I'll get you something to eat then you're going to bed.'

Katy stared at him. Was he seriously suggesting he cooked her a meal? Was he seriously suggesting prolonging this agony further? 'No,' she said hastily. 'I'm not hungry, honestly.'

He looked at her closely for a moment as though doubting her word. 'A drink then?' he suggested. 'A cognac?' For some reason he was smiling again. 'Or better still a Guinness?'

That smile unnerved her. She could feel herself heating up even as she shook her head. 'I don't drink,' she said.

'Never?' He was silent for a moment, then he shook his head sadly. 'Damn.' He clicked his fingers. 'How will I ever get to seduce you if you don't drink?'

He was joking. Of course he was joking. She could see from the sparkle in his grey eyes that he was joking. Nevertheless her blood was suddenly hurtling round her veins as though there was no tomorrow and she turned away quickly to hide her tell-tale flush.

Behind her she heard his steps retreating down the stairs and kicked herself for not having the wit to make some equally flirtatious response.

But even as she stood there belatedly wondering what she should have said, he was coming up again. Before she could move he was already at the top of the stairs, a basket of shopping swinging from each hand.

'I guess this is yours?' he said easily as if he had never made the earlier comment.

Katy nodded numbly and stood rooted to the spot as he carried the shopping into the small kitchen, listening in astonishment to the sound of him unpacking it and storing it away.

As he came back through he handed her a glass of milk. 'I thought I told you to go to bed,' he said.

But before she could speak he had gone again. Katy shook her head in wonder. Perhaps she was hallucinating. Perhaps he wasn't really there at all.

But the next minute she heard the sound of voices coming from the cellar as presumably he somehow contrived to explain the situation to her father.

It didn't take long. Even as she drew her curtains and climbed into her bed she could hear Ward whistling softly as he refilled the tin bucket. Then she heard the clank of the handle, a splash of water hitting the floor and a muttered oath. The whistling stopped abruptly.

Katy smiled. It was only as she fell asleep that she realised he had never told her what the favour was that he had come to ask.

Kneeling in her pew on Remembrance Sunday the following weekend, Pam Nelson found herself praying for deliverance. Not like everyone else from the awful threat of the Nazis, but from Bertie Rutherford. He had been in the house for nearly two weeks now, eating their food, sitting in front of their fire, using their coal, their logs, their kindling, with hardly one word of thanks or one penny of payment. Regardless of the fact that Pam and Alan were having to go short. It seemed as though so long as Bertie Rutherford was warm and comfortable, it didn't matter about anyone else.

As the prayers came to an end and the congregation resumed their seats, Pam glanced up to the front pew where Mr and Mrs Rutherford always sat. They were there today. Mr Rutherford had read the lesson earlier in his hard, clipped voice and was now sitting ramrod straight, listening attentively to the vicar's words. Next to him, his wife looked equally stiff in her smart black felt hat.

Pam sighed. Bertie naturally had declined to come to church with her. He'd been reading Alan's *Sunday Express* in his paisley silk dressing gown in front of the sitting-room fire when she left, looking up only to expound some theory about the Church supporting the warmongering establishment in its effort to brainwash the population.

The vicar announced the next hymn, 'Fight the Good Fight', and while the organist launched into her usual dirge-like introduction and the congregation rose to its feet, Pam glanced again at the Rutherford parents up at the front of the church. She didn't blame them for throwing Bertie out. He had barely been in the house five minutes before she had decided he was just about the most obnoxious boy she had ever had the pleasure to meet.

Oddly, Alan didn't mind him, but then he was all right with Alan, civil in his rather supercilious way. But he treated her like a skivvy. As though she was some serving wench. Well, not quite like that, he hadn't put his hand up her skirt or anything. Pam grimaced as she mouthed the words of the hymn. She'd give him what for if he did, toffee-nosed little bastard. But it was quite clear from his attitude that he had been brought up to believe that women were brainless things designed purely and simply to serve and service men.

He'd made no secret of the fact that he thought it was very infra dig that Pam went to work each day; it obviously never occurred to him that she might be doing it for any reason other than the money, and he found it even more incomprehensible that Alan occasionally did the shopping.

Mind you, he wasn't the only person who thought it was odd, Alan helping out with the domestics. Poor old Alan. He didn't mind. Maybe she did take advantage of his good nature sometimes, but she didn't see why men shouldn't do their bit. Particularly as she was working too. In any case it served him right for lumbering her with unwanted house guests all the time. It wouldn't be so bad if he was home more. But at the moment he was spending so much time with the Home Guard that she rarely saw him.

Even today, a Sunday, he was out on some kind of anti-invasion exercise.

The hymn came to an end and she sighed as she sat down again. She was sure Alan wouldn't be so generous with his home and his time if they had a family to keep him busy.

A baby. That was what they needed so badly. Well, Bertie Rutherford's advent had finally forced her to take action. Last week she had finally summoned up the courage to ask the local doctor if she could see a specialist. Someone who would be able to tell once and for all if she was infertile and whether or not they should keep on hoping.

The doctor had been reluctant at first, muttering things about children being a gift from God, but Pam had stood firm and finally he agreed to refer her to the Wilhelmina. She hadn't told Alan. He was so touchy about the baby business that she hadn't dared. Better that she should find out what was wrong with her first. And then, if necessary, she could confess to Alan.

Suddenly the service was over, everyone was filing out of the church, and Pam realised she hadn't heard a word of it. Guiltily she shook hands with the vicar in the porch and then found herself outside in the graveyard face to face with Mrs Rutherford.

'Oh, Mrs Nelson.' Mrs Rutherford affected surprise. She brushed a few specks off her arm and in doing so glanced swiftly at her husband who was deep in conversation with the verger. 'I'm so grateful to you for taking Bertie in.' She spoke rapidly in a low confidential voice. 'Naughty boy, I do hope he's not being a nuisance?'

Caught off guard, Pam found herself shaking her head. 'Oh no, not at all,' she said.

Mrs Rutherford looked relieved. 'I've received his ration book back from Shropshire at last,' she said in the same sepulchral tone. 'I'll drop it in on Monday.' She glanced nervously at her husband again. 'I'd like to give you something for his keep, but Greville won't hear of it. He says Bertie has made his bed and now he must lie on it.'

Pam nodded blankly, only too aware that it was her bed that Bertie was lying on and her food that he was eating. It wouldn't kill that tight-fisted Greville Rutherford to slip them something without Bertie knowing, she thought sourly. But she could hardly say so. Greville Rutherford was Alan's boss at the brewery after all. They couldn't afford to annoy him.

Mrs Rutherford paled suddenly as her husband approached. She turned to him with a nervous, ingratiating smile. 'I was just thanking Mrs Nelson for taking Bertie in,' she said quickly.

Greville Rutherford didn't deign to answer. He didn't even raise his hat. He merely nodded briefly to Pam, then took his wife by the elbow and marched her down the path to the church gates where his car was waiting.

Pam was staring after them in disbelief when she heard behind her the soft shuffling noise that denoted the presence of the Miss Taylors.

'Ungrateful sod,' Thelma Taylor muttered. 'You'd think he'd at least have the courtesy to pass the time of day.'

As Pam gazed at her in amazement, Esme Taylor chipped in. 'Not him. He's far too pleased with himself to worry about pleasing anyone else.'

Her sister nodded. 'And the son's not much better by the looks of him.' She glanced at Pam and winked knowingly.

Pam smiled. The Miss Taylors' house was opposite hers in Lavender Road, next to Sheila's. She'd often seen them sitting in the window. But from the sound of it they saw rather more than anyone realised. Poor old things. They looked very frail today. The relentless bombing was taking its toll on them.

'I must admit I feel sorry for Mrs Rutherford,' Pam said. 'I wouldn't want to be married to him.'

'Goodness no,' Esme Taylor agreed. 'But you're spoilt of course with Mr Nelson.' She smiled. 'We always reckon you've got the best husband in the road, Mrs Nelson.' She nudged her sister. 'We wouldn't mind being married to Mr Nelson, would we, Esme?'

The other old lady shook her head. 'He's a lovely man, your husband. Not many of them about.'

To her astonishment Pam felt herself blushing. She couldn't wait to tell Alan that the Miss Taylors fancied him. 'Oh I don't know,' she said, trying to cover her confusion. 'Your nephew seems pretty lovely.' Certain the old ladies would be pleased with her comment, she was surprised when they didn't respond at once. 'He'll make some lucky girl a lovely husband,' she went on, puzzled by their hesitation. She had never heard anything but good about the handsome Canadian, Ward Frazer. Everyone seemed to like him. Not just the girls either. Alan had only told her yesterday that he'd even helped old Malcolm Parsons out in the Flag and Garter a couple of times last week.

'Oh yes,' Esme said at last, glancing at her sister. 'You can't get better than Ward. But we're rather afraid the lucky girl is going to be that minx Louise Rutherford.'

Pam was surprised. 'I thought it was all over between him and Louise months ago.'

They nodded gloomily. 'So did we. But he doesn't seem to be able to keep away from that blasted hospital nowadays. And it's our fault for suggesting he went to visit her in the first place.'

Katy was ironing her uniform when her father called her down to the bar. Something had gone wrong with the beer pump and he needed to go down to the cellar to sort it out.

'You stand here, right, and when I call, you pull this handle down, like this, steadily, until it stops, then you push it straight back, nice and firm. Got it?'

'I think so,' she said dubiously, looking round the unusually crowded bar. 'But what happens if someone wants serving?'

'You can serve shorts and bottles, I'll shout up the prices, but they'll have to wait for the beer.'

Katy glanced up at the clock. 'You won't be too long, will you? I've got to be at the hospital by quarter to eight.'

Her father frowned. 'I'll be as long as it takes,' he said irritably. 'And mind you're not too generous with the measures.'

A moment later, for the first time ever during opening hours, Katy found herself standing on her own behind the bar.

It was an astonishing record for a publican's daughter, she realised, feeling suddenly absurdly self-conscious. She was eighteen and a half years old and she had never served a single drink.

Behind her on the tall dresser stood the bottles of whisky, gin and other spirits that her father had so painfully had to replace after the burglary. In front of her was the wide wooden counter with its array of soda siphons, beer levers and the old-fashioned till. Below the counter the glasses were ranged neatly on size-related shelves. And on the other side of the counter were the customers.

She could hear a few women's voices coming from the saloon bar, but it was all men in the tap room of course. Sliding a shy glance round she was surprised by how few of them she recognised. Some ARP men in their white arm bands waiting for the sirens to sound, a couple of the stall-holders from Northcote Road market, and the pawnbroker, Mr Lorenz, sitting all alone in the corner.

Her first order came from the saloon bar, a slick-looking man with a full, rather wolfish moustache. 'Two gin and its, love,' he said, offering her the old glasses for a refill.

Katy stared at him blankly. 'Gin and whats?'

'It,' he grinned. 'Italian. Martini, love. Goodness, how long have you been working here?'

'About five minutes.' Katy smiled back, suddenly rather enjoying her new responsibility. But ten minutes later she wasn't smiling any more. She had no idea that standing behind a bar could be so exhausting. People kept asking for drinks and it took her ages to find the right components and the right size glass, then, before she had called down to her father for the prices, let alone worked out the total and calculated the change, the next customer would be drumming on the counter. They mostly wanted ale and she had to keep telling them it was off temporarily. In the middle of it all her father kept shouting up urgently for her to pull the blasted beer pump. And each time she pulled it nothing happened except an empty wheezing noise and then before she had pushed the lever back as instructed, she was being hassled for the next order.

When the gin and it man reappeared for another round, she realised she had been there quite a long time.

'Are you nearly done?' she called anxiously to her father. 'I'm going to have to go in a minute.'

'Not long now,' he called back. 'I think I've found the blockage.'

Katy glanced nervously up at the grandfather clock. Seven thirty. But before she could call down again, there was a polite cough at the bar behind her.

'Good evening, Miss Parsons.'

She turned back at once and smiled. 'Hello, Mr Lorenz. How are you?'

He looked tired, she thought, and wondered how he was coping with the thought of a German invasion. As a Jew he must dread it even more than most. She had heard somewhere that he had had relations in Poland. If it was true, her heart ached for him. She had only seen in the paper that morning that thousands upon thousands of Jews had been confined to some awful ghetto in German-controlled Warsaw. If he'd seen the same report it was no wonder he looked so drawn.

'A small whisky if you would be so kind,' he said, then after a rather furtive look round the bar he lowered his voice and added, 'and a bottle of Guinness.'

Intrigued, but politely trying not to show it, Katy carefully measured the whisky and then looked round in vain for the Guinness.

'Where's the Guinness?' she called down to her father.

'We're short of Guinness, who's it for?'

Glancing over her shoulder, Katy smiled. 'It's for Mr Lorenz.'

There was a moment's pause, then her father's loud, incredulous voice. 'What's old Lorenz want with Guinness?'

Aware that one or two of the men in the bar were chuckling,

Katy cast an agonised glance at the pawnbroker and saw to her horror that he was even more embarrassed than she was.

She didn't know what to do or what to say. All she could do was smile at him reassuringly as the flush gradually subsided on his thin cheeks. 'It's for a friend,' he muttered at last.

'It's for a friend of his,' she relayed down to the cellar.

'A friend?' Her father sounded astonished. For an awful moment she thought he was going to say that Lorenz didn't have any friends. Which as far as she knew was true, but not the sort of thing even an unsociable fellow like Lorenz would want bandied about the local pub. But to her relief her father merely directed her to a small cache of Guinness he had hidden behind the soda siphons. 'He can only have one, mind. Ten pence to him. And make sure he pays for his whisky too.'

Katy cringed and could hardly bear to look at Lorenz as he laid the appropriate coins carefully on the counter. Instead she glanced at the corner where he had been sitting as though hoping some friend might magically have appeared. None had.

Scooping up the coins, too embarrassed to count them, she nodded at the Guinness. 'Do you want it poured out?' she asked hesitantly.

Once again he lowered his voice. 'I wonder if I could take it as it is.'

Certain that was not allowed, she nodded quickly. 'I won't ask my father,' she whispered. 'But you will be sure to bring back the empty, won't you? He gets awfully worried about his empties.'

Lorenz nodded gravely. 'I'll bring back the empty,' he said. Then he suddenly smiled. 'Thank you, Miss Parsons.'

Surprised by the charm in that smile, Katy longed to ask who the Guinness was for, but it was not the sort of question you could ask someone like Lorenz.

But to her astonishment he told her. 'It's for Mrs Carter across the road,' he murmured. 'She doesn't look very well, and I believe Guinness is very health giving.'

'Yes, I believe it is,' Katy mumbled, stunned almost into incoherence. Mr Lorenz, who never bought a drink for anyone, was secretly buying drinks for Mrs Carter. She was completely astonished. She was also intrigued. But more than anything she was immensely touched. She just hoped to God that beastly Stanley Carter didn't find out. Or poor old Lorenz would be for the high jump.

She had barely had the thought when she caught sight of the clock. Quarter to eight. At the same moment she heard the pub doors open behind her and felt a cold breeze on her skin as several newcomers entered the bar.

'Daddy,' she called down frantically. 'I've got to go. I'm going to be late as it is.'

'Try it once more . . .' her father called back. 'Any luck? No? Damn, wait, I'll just try one more thing . . .'

'Daddy, please. I can't . . .' She stopped abruptly as a shiver ran up her spine.

Swinging round, she found Ward Frazer was standing right behind her.

He laughed at her expression. 'You can. You go. I'll hold the fort here.'

Katy stared at him, overwhelmed by relief. She hadn't seen him since the day he had sent her to bed although she knew he had been into the pub once or twice when she had been asleep. She glanced at the clock again. She had to go. She had to go that minute. Even though she suddenly longed more than anything to stay. 'Are you sure?' she asked breathlessly.

He smiled. 'I'm always sure. Now for God's sake go, or that Sister Morris will eat you alive.'

Halfway up the stairs she stopped and looked back. He was still there, hands in his pockets, watching her with a strange expression in his grey eyes. She shook her head. 'How come you always turn up just when I need you?'

For a second he didn't respond, then he laughed lightly. 'Didn't you know? Damsels in distress are my speciality.'

By some miracle, Sister's prayers were delayed by a few minutes that evening because of an emergency with one of the patients, and

Katy was able to take her place with the other night nurses before her absence was noticed. Heart hammering, trying not to pant out loud after her frantic race down Lavender Hill she surreptitiously straightened her uniform and glanced along the line of nurses.

Up at the other end of the ward, the crisis seemed to be over. Sister was already marching down the central aisle and from the look on her face she was not at all pleased by the delay. The two departing day nurses looked extremely chastened as they quickly put on their cloaks and left the ward.

'Where's Nurse Coogan?' Katy whispered urgently to Staff Hicks. 'Has she reported in sick or something?'

Staff Hicks shrugged. 'Not that I know of.' She didn't like Nurse Coogan any more than she liked Katy and clearly relished the thought of the pixie-faced probationer getting it in the neck from Sister.

Sister Morris was only yards away, already reaching for her prayer book, her beady eyes sweeping over the line of nurses, when Katy saw Nurse Coogan's white, anxious face peeping round the nurses' door.

There was only one thing she could possibly do to save the other girl from Sister's rage. Bursting into a violent coughing fit, Katy staggered forward clutching her chest.

Unfortunately in her excitement, she inadvertently trod rather heavily on Staff Hicks's toe and with a shout of pain Staff Hicks leaped into the air, bumped into Sister's table and sent her prayer book flying across the ward.

'I'm so sorry, Sister.' Katy leaned weakly on Sister's table, hoping nobody would see the tears of laughter running down her face as Staff Hicks hopped about squawking like a deranged hen. 'I just can't stop coughing.'

'Somebody get her a glass of water,' Sister snapped as under cover of the general disarray Nurse Coogan slipped unnoticed on to the ward. 'And for goodness' sake pull yourself together, Staff. What are you thinking of?'

'She trod on my foot.' Staff Hicks was clearly in some pain and Katy began to feel rather sorry for her.

But Sister had lost patience. Someone had retrieved her prayer book and opening it now with a glare round the assembled company that immediately silenced the patients' laughter and wiped the smiles off the nurses' faces, she began to pray.

Once the final Amen had been said and Sister had given her report to the senior night nurse, to Katy's relief, she retired to her own quarters with no further comment on the disruption.

Later, on the dot of nine o'clock, she would emerge in her voluminous pink candlewick dressing gown and sweep through the ward for her bath. And God help the nurse responsible if the bathroom wasn't ready for her with all traces of any patient users wiped away and her clean towel and bath cap and special lavender soap waiting on the chair.

It was Katy's turn to prepare the bathroom and it was while she was scrubbing the lavatory bowl that Nurse Coogan slipped into the room on the pretext of bringing her some cleaning soda.

'Here, you'll need this,' she said, plonking the box of crystals down on the chair. She pushed a speck of dirt across the floor with her toe then looked up awkwardly. 'Oh and thanks, by the way, for coughing and that before. I reckon you saved my skin.'

'That's OK.' Katy looked up in surprise. She had been miles away, thinking about Ward Frazer. 'I only just made it in time myself.'

Damsel in distress, he'd said, hadn't he? Yes, she decided, she quite liked that. It certainly sounded much better than kid.

Nurse Coogan eyed her suspiciously. 'What are you smiling about?'

What indeed? One chivalrous comment from a handsome man was hardly enough to build your hopes on. Katy stared down the lavatory bowl as she racked her brain for some other reason for a smile.

'My best friend is coming home for Christmas,' she said. To her relief she had finally heard from Jen that morning. 'I've been worried about her,' she added. 'She's been singing with ENSA in the Midlands.'

Nurse Coogan frowned. 'The Midlands have been hit badly,' she said. 'Coventry Cathedral has copped it completely. They reckon that's why London had the night off the other night. All the Luftwaffe was focussed on Coventry instead.'

'I know.' Katy nodded vaguely. 'Jen said it was unbelievable.' But her mind wasn't really on the devastation of Coventry. It was working out that if Jen came back for Christmas, the Miss Taylors might have a little party. And Ward would be sure to come.

'It's a fellow, isn't it?' Nurse Coogan said sourly. 'You've got some fellow, haven't you? That's why you're looking like a cat that's got the bloody cream.'

Katy stared at her. Surely her infatuation wasn't as obvious as that. Because that's all it was, she was realistic enough to acknowledge that. An infatuation. She sighed. 'I haven't got him,' she said. 'I like him, that's all.'

There, she had admitted it. She liked Ward Frazer. Despite trying not to, she couldn't help it.

'Does he like you?'

Katy grimaced. 'I think he quite likes me but then he likes quite a few other women too.' Damsels, he had said, come to think of it. Not damsel. She didn't like that plural. Presumably Louise was a damsel in distress too. And there may well be others she didn't know about. Certainly he had helped Jen out earlier in the year.

And there was the Jewish girl in Germany before the war. The one that had died. She would have been a damsel in distress all right.

'It's that American,' Nurse Coogan said suddenly. 'Isn't it? That one that visits that fancy piece friend of yours in Private Block.'

'He's Canadian,' Katy said.

Nurse Coogan gave a satisfied sniff, clearly pleased with her powers of deduction. She was about to leave when she stopped and glanced back at Katy. 'You want to watch out for that Louise Rutherford though,' she said gruffly. 'Nurse Kilroy reckons she's got her hooks into him good and proper. She's sweet as pie with him by all accounts. I don't suppose he'll have any idea what a little madam she really is.'

Katy frowned. She knew Louise wasn't popular among the hospital staff. She had behaved very badly at first, it was true. But then she had been in considerable pain. Now she was beginning to get better she seemed much more relaxed and contented. Or was it since Ward Frazer had come back on the scene that she was more relaxed and contented?

Suddenly deflated, Katy stared miserably into the lavatory bowl and was still there five minutes later when Staff Hicks came limping in and tore her off a strip for being not only the clumsiest nurse she had ever had the privilege to work with, but also the slowest.

Louise Rutherford was not the slightest bit relaxed and contented the following morning when Katy called in on her way off duty, but distinctly peevish.

'You said you were going to come in last night,' she said crossly.

'I'm sorry,' Katy said, shutting the door. 'I was going to but we had a problem in the bar. I was late in.'

Louise was silent for a moment then she moved restlessly in the bed. 'Ward said he was going to call in on you. Did you see him?'

Katy nodded. 'For about two seconds. He came in just as I was leaving.' So he had called especially to see her, had he? And not just for a drink. At once her spirits lifted slightly.

Louise shrugged. 'He wants you to persuade his aunts to go to the country. He's worried about them.'

So that was why he'd wanted to see her. Katy felt a flash of disappointment.

She was just mulling morosely over the implications of Ward's request, when the door opened and Bertie Rutherford sauntered in.

Katy had always been rather in awe of Louise's confident, well-spoken brothers. But now she was irritated that he should interrupt, and stood up rather reluctantly.

'Bertie!' Louise glanced at the clock on her bedside table. 'Goodness. You're early.'

He shrugged. 'Don't laugh, Sissy darling. It seems the dear old Wilhelmina might be prepared to take me on as a porter and in a minute I've got to go and impress them with my dedication and charm.'

He glanced round to include Katy in the joke but his grin faltered as he encountered her unsmiling face. With exaggerated concern he raised his hands. 'Oh, I'm sorry, Nurse. Were you in the middle of some crucial medical matter when I so rudely interrupted?'

Before Katy could reply Louise laughed. 'This isn't any old nurse, Bertie. This is Katy Parsons from the pub in Lavender Road. Don't you recognise her?'

He looked at her more closely and then a slow smile spread on to his lips.

'So you're the famous Katy Parsons.' He raised his eyebrows slightly. 'No wonder Sis has been keeping me from you.'

It seemed rude not to smile back.

Apparently satisfied with the effect of his charm, he chuckled complacently and turned back to Louise. 'I think working here might have its compensations after all.'

It was odd, Katy thought afterwards, as she hurried home through the cold, foggy November morning. If Ward Frazer had said something like that she would have blushed scarlet and been unable to speak. But Bertie Rutherford was so absurdly over confident and cocky that she had been able to make some faintly mocking retort and hadn't been the least bit fazed when he asked at once if he could take her out for a drink.

'I live in a pub,' she'd said, laughing. 'Going out for a drink is hardly the most exciting way I could think of spending an evening.'

He had blushed then and she had realised he wasn't quite as confident as he made out. 'What then?' he had asked eagerly. 'What would you like to do instead?'

But Katy had refused to be tricked into a date. 'Nothing,' she had said firmly, drawing on her cloak and moving to the door. 'In any case I'm on nights at the moment so I haven't got any evenings free.'

It occurred to her as she walked up Lavender Hill that soon she would be on days again. Back to that awful routine of nights in the pub cellar and days on the ward and never seeing the light of day. What there was of it. The fog was lying thick up here on the hill. She could barely see the police station. There was a joke going round that the only people who could get around these days were the blind, who could tap along with their white sticks regardless of the fog or the blackout.

Turning into Lavender Road she peered up the shabby road and sighed in relief. It was always a nasty moment when she turned the corner and looked to see if anything had been hit overnight.

This morning, although the buildings seemed intact, there was a lot of glass and debris on the road. A lot of broken windows. The branches of the bare trees were coated with a fine grey dust. A bicycle lay across the gutter outside the pub, either blown there by a distant blast or abandoned by someone rushing for shelter. Either way, coated in the grey November fog it made a dismal scene and Katy felt suddenly tired and very depressed.

The beastly war was spoiling everything. The endless bombing was getting everyone down, driving people away. Her mother had gone. Sheila Whitehead and little George had gone, Jen had gone. And now it seemed the Miss Taylors might go too.

She sighed heavily and was about to go into the pub when she noticed an empty Guinness bottle standing on the corner of the step. Stooping to pick it up she looked at it for a moment and smiled sadly. Then she pushed open the doors and went inside.

It was only a month to Christmas and at this rate, it was going to be a pretty miserable one. But then Adolf Hitler obviously hadn't heard of peace and goodwill.

Chapter Ten

Pam stood in the back yard and cranked the handle of the mangle energetically. It was the first of December and freezing cold and if she didn't get the clothes finished soon she would probably get frostbite.

Behind her in the kitchen she could hear the wireless signal breaking up and made a mental note to ask Alan to get the battery recharged during the week. She didn't mind too much about missing the music, but she hated to miss the news bulletins. Particularly when for once there was good news.

The Greeks had driven the Italians right back across the Albanian border and were now, with the help of the RAF, threatening the Italian position in Albania itself. A couple of days ago the Fleet Air Arm in Sardinia had torpedoed and sunk seven Italian warships and this morning it was rumoured that the American Ambassador to London, Joseph Kennedy, had resigned. Although it wasn't spelt out in so many words Pam guessed the resignation was due to Kennedy's outspoken opposition to the possibility of American involvement in the war. Without his pessimistic reports back to Washington there might be a better chance that President Roosevelt could persuade the American people that the beleaguered Allies deserved their support.

Because it wasn't all good news of course. Liverpool, London and the Midlands had been badly bombed again, and last night Southampton had suffered a seven-hour raid.

Pam shivered and fed some more clothes into the mangle. Bertie Rutherford's clothes. His fancy cotton shirts with double cuffs and pleats down the back that were impossible to iron. He didn't like her mangling them, it crushed the pearl buttons apparently, but she had told him it was the mangle or nothing. There was no other way to get that thick cotton to dry. She had been quite tough about it, and he had been his usual arrogant self, saying that when he started work at the hospital next week he would arrange to have his shirts done at the laundry. Pam gave the mangle an extra ferocious turn. Bloody boy. He'd somehow made it sound as though he was doing her a favour.

As the last shirt plopped into her bowl she sighed in relief and threw the water from the bucket down the drain before hurrying back into the relative warmth of the kitchen. Thankfully Bertie was out, but Alan was due back any moment. Rubbing her hands together to warm her blue fingers, Pam frowned and bit her lip thoughtfully. Yesterday she had received a brisk note from the gynaecologist at the Wilhelmina saying that from the preliminary examination he had carried out there was no obvious reason why she should not conceive. And before embarking on more drastic action he recommended that Alan should come in for some tests.

In some trepidation Pam had broached the subject with Alan last night. After the all-clear had finally gone. After they had made love.

To her surprise Alan had taken it well. Or he had seemed to at the time. In fact what seemed to upset him most about the whole thing was the thought of some strange man poking about in her private parts.

'It was all very matter of fact,' Pam had reassured him. 'And there was a nurse there all the time.'

She didn't say how excruciatingly embarrassing she had found the internal examination. Nor how painful. He didn't need to know how brutally quick and dismissive the doctor had been. How uninterested when his cold probing instruments made her cry out in pain. How she had emerged in tears, convinced by his manner that she was in some way substandard.

Alan had claimed tiredness then and they had gone to sleep, but in the morning he had got up very early and gone out muttering something about the Home Guard, and now Pam had begun wondering if he was more upset than he had let on.

When he finally came in she knew she was right. He looked grey and drawn and she felt her heart sink.

'It's the baby thing, isn't it?' she asked as he ate his meal in silence.

For a moment she thought he would deny it, then he sighed heavily. 'I might have guessed it would turn out to be my fault.'

Pam frowned. 'It's nothing to do with fault,' she said, reaching over to lay her hand over his. 'Please, Alan, don't get funny about it.'

He took his hand away and ran it through his hair. 'I'm not getting funny,' he said. 'But it's not exactly morale boosting to find that some quack has told your wife that your manliness is in some doubt.'

Pam sighed. 'The ability to have children is hardly the only definition of manliness.'

He shrugged. 'It's the only definition that matters if you want a family.'

Pam closed her eyes for a moment. 'Alan, please.' She took a steadying breath. 'It's not worth it. We've got more important things to worry about at the moment: the lack of food, the shortage of coal. And Sheila and George wanting to come for Christmas. In any case it may not be anything to do with you. It might just be a matter of timing. You don't have to have a test. It's not compulsory. For goodness' sake, let's just forget all about it.'

For a long time he was silent, apparently studying his plate. Then finally, just when she was giving up hope, he raised his eyes and shook his head. 'I want to make you happy, Pam. I want to give you a baby. I'll have the test. If it is me, there may be something they can do.'

Pam sighed and stood up to clear their plates. 'Well, don't let's do anything until after Christmas.' Christmas was going to be difficult enough with Bertie being there, let alone with Sheila and George. She didn't want Alan in deep gloom as well.

The Miss Taylors didn't want to go to the country.

'We know it would be safer,' Esme said, while her sister fussed with the tea tray. 'But we wouldn't know anyone there. We'd be so lonely.'

'You'd soon get to know people,' Katy said. 'There are lots of retired people who've gone to the country for the war.' She was trying hard, but she knew she wasn't getting anywhere. Jen's old singing teacher, Mrs Frost, was sitting by the window wearing an expression that said she'd been through it all before. The two old ladies listened and smiled and were grateful for the suggestions, but they just didn't want to go.

'It's not retired people we're worried about.' Thelma looked up from the tea tray suddenly. 'It's young people, like you and Jennifer. We wouldn't be going to see Jennifer next week if we were stuck in the country, would we? And Ward. We'd never know if he was back safely from his . . . trips.'

So that was it. They were worried about Ward.

'He's away again now, isn't he?' Katy asked. She knew he was, because Louise had told her one day last week and Katy had felt ridiculously disappointed that he hadn't bothered to tell her or to say goodbye.

Esme nodded. 'Yes, he is,' she said. Her hand trembled as she passed Katy her cup. 'And I'm afraid this time he won't come back.'

'Nonsense.' Margot Frost spoke up suddenly. 'Of course he'll come back. It was different at the beginning when he didn't know anyone here and was still cut up over the death of his girl in Germany and his family in Canada had cut him off. I'll admit then he might have been happy to die.' She sniffed in faint disdain. 'But now he's got a life here, people he cares for, a reason for staying alive, it's a different matter altogether.'

'Then there's all the more reason for us to stay here,' Thelma said, lifting the smelly old dachshund up on to her knee and feeding it a piece of biscuit. 'Isn't there, Winston? We must make sure he's got something nice to come back to. We don't want him staying alive just for Louise Rutherford.'

Jen came home on the ninth of December. It was a bad moment. The post had just arrived with Bob's call-up papers. And only minutes later the wireless announced that the first major British land offensive had taken place against the Italians in the Western Desert.

Bob paled, and Mick, sensing his fear, had started to taunt him at once.

'I bet General Wavell will be pleased to hear you're joining up. He'll need as much cannon fodder as he can get.'

'Shut up, Micky,' Bob snapped.

'Oooh.' Mick rolled his eyes. 'Touchy. What's the matter? Don't you want to go?'

'No, I don't,' Bob said. 'And nor would you if it was your call-up that had come.'

Mick's eyes widened. 'I would. I can't wait to go. I'd join up tomorrow if they'd have me. Anything would be better than following those bloody brewery horses around.'

Bob stood up. 'Oh, I bet. If an Italian pointed a gun at you, you'd run a mile.'

'I'd shoot him first and then run,' Pete chipped in mildly. 'Otherwise you'd get shot in the back.'

Joyce smiled at Pete, but after a moment's pause the other two ignored him and continued to bicker until Stanley suddenly crashed his fist to the table and roared at them to be quiet. And in the second's shocked silence that ensued, Joyce heard the click of high heels in the passage and then Jen was standing in the door.

She was wearing the most elegant cream-coloured suit Joyce had ever seen, and she wasn't merely standing but posing, hands on

171

slender hips, one elegant stockinged leg slightly in front of the other, a chic little hat on her head and a lipsticked smile on her pretty mouth.

'Well, well, temper temper,' she said loosening her long white gloves finger by finger before pulling them off and slapping them gently on the palm of her hand. 'What's happened?' she asked lightly. 'Don't tell me . . . Mick's broken something?'

'Bob's been called up,' Mick said faintly, his eyes wide open at the apparition of his sister dressed like a film star.

'Oh, poor brave Bob.' Jen stepped forward to kiss her elder brother on the cheek. She then moved round the table kissing them all, even her father, whose lower jaw was almost on the table.

Joyce felt the soft brush of her daughter's skin, the waft of perfume, and waited for the explosion.

It wasn't long in coming. Stanley's face turned from white to red in about three seconds and his fist met the table again in five.

'What in God's name do you think you look like?'

'I don't know.' Jen studied herself with interest in the spotted kitchen mirror. 'What do I look like?'

For a second Stanley was speechless. Then his voice came out hoarse with anger. 'You look like a tart. That's what you look like. And by the look of them clothes I imagine you've been behaving like one and all.'

Jen swung round. 'Oh no I haven't,' she flashed back. 'I don't need men to buy things for me. I'm earning now, remember. Doing an honest job of work. Unlike you presumably.'

He was on his feet at once, but she was too quick for him. 'Oh no,' she said. 'You're not hitting me. It's not my fault if you'd rather sit in the pub all day than work.'

Joyce cringed. It was true. But there was no need for Jen to come prancing in like something off the catwalk and rub it in. She could see the anger pulsing in Stanley's forehead and she prayed it wouldn't be her that paid the price for Jen's lack of tact.

'If you're earning so much why aren't we seeing any of it?' she said suddenly. 'You ought to be sending it home.'

Jen stared at her. 'Send it home? You must be joking. What have you ever done for me? Nothing. Less than nothing. And now, the first time I come home, instead of a bit of a welcome, I get called a tart.' She tossed her head and shrugged her slender shoulders. 'Well, thankfully there are people around here who will be pleased to see me. So if you'll excuse me I'll leave you to your petty squabbles. Oh,' she glanced back from the door, 'just in case you're wondering, the box in the hall has got your Christmas presents in it, so try not to trip over it.'

Then she flounced out of the house.

Katy was delighted to see Jen looking so well and so glamorous.

'Being a star obviously suits you,' she said.

Jen laughed. 'I'm hardly a star,' she said pulling off her gloves. 'But it's better than nothing. I have two solo numbers and a duet, but the audiences seem to like me, even if they are only factory workers on tea break.'

'I bet they do.' Katy smiled enviously. 'You're so lucky, Jen. You're so clever and competent. I wish I could do something that made people take notice of me.'

Jen looked surprised. 'But you're a nurse. Goodness, by the time you're a Sister they'll take notice of you all right.'

Katy's smile faded. 'I don't think I'd ever get that far.' She glanced at her friend, reluctant to admit in words what she secretly knew. 'I'm not very good at it. I'm too clumsy and slow and I get too involved with the patients. There's a woman in there at the moment, who has lost everything, her home, her family, the use of her legs, and Staff Hicks tore me off a strip for sitting on her bed for five minutes.'

Both Katy and the patient had been in tears by the time Staff Hicks had finished. Oddly it had been Nurse Coogan who had cheered her up by muttering that everyone knew Staff Hicks was a heartless bitch, as she passed by with some clean sheets.

Katy wondered what Jen would think of Nurse Coogan. They were quite similar in some ways. They both were tough and neither of them minded saying what they thought. They both despised privilege. And they were both fiercely proud and defensive about their backgrounds. The main difference was that Jen was pretty and Nurse Coogan looked like a garden gnome.

'It's not your fault,' Jen said now. 'You can't help being a nice person. I'd have told the stupid cow to go and jump in the lake weeks ago.'

Katy giggled. 'She wouldn't take any notice,' she said. 'At least not if I said it. Nobody takes any notice of anything I say. I've been trying to help my father in the pub while Mummy's away but he won't listen to any of my ideas. It's even worse in the hospital. I tried to suggest we stacked the bandages in a more logical way and all the senior nurses came down on me like a ton of bricks saying that it had always been done like that, and who was I to presume to change it.'

Jen shrugged. 'That's like my stupid pianist saying we should take the bows together because that's how he's done it before, when it's obvious to me that I should have a separate curtain call.'

Katy smiled to herself. She wondered how long prima donna Jen would last as a probationer on the Ethel Barnet ward and decided that five minutes would be optimistic.

'Will you try to persuade the Miss Taylors to go to the country?' Katy asked her suddenly. 'Ward wanted me to try but needless to say they won't take any notice of me.'

'Ward?' Jen looked up surprised. 'You've seen Ward Frazer?'

'He's called in here a couple of times.' Katy nodded, trying desperately not to blush as she told Jen about him sending her to bed and cleaning the floors himself.

'Maybe he's keen on you.' Jen sounded doubtful.

Katy shook her head. 'No, he's just a nice, kind man. In any case he seems pretty keen on Louise.' Certainly that was the impression Louise gave. There was no doubt she was missing his visits since he'd gone away.

'Pah,' Jen said scornfully. 'Surely he's got more sense.' She eyed Katy closely and grinned. 'But I think we're going to have to pretty you up a bit, Miss Parsons. Men don't wash floors for nothing, you know. And men like Ward Frazer like girls to look like girls, not like drab old floor cloths.'

By some miracle, the following night was a quiet one. For once there were no sirens and for once Katy had a free evening, her night off, prior to starting days again.

She and Jen spent the evening with the Miss Taylors and Mrs Frost and it was just like old times. Mrs Frost played the piano and Jen sang, and for a few precious hours Katy forgot to worry about the pub, about her mother, about resuming the rigours of day duty, about the newly announced action in Libya, about Ward Frazer. Instead, she gave herself over to the pleasure of being among friends, humming along to the music. She hadn't seen the two old ladies enjoy themselves so much for ages. Even hawk-faced Mrs Frost was smiling as she glanced up from the keys at her former pupil.

Whatever Jen said, she had a gift. It wasn't just her voice. It was the force of her personality that made the difference, lifting the spirit, blazing along on her own track, forcing everyone else to follow.

Katy wished she had that ability. It might cause ructions, tantrums, family problems, but it got things done, it made people sit up and take notice, and it meant Jen had a life. A life of her own and not just at the beck and call of everyone else.

And of course Jen effortlessly convinced the Miss Taylors they should go to the country.

'You've got friends near Bristol?' she had exclaimed. 'That sounds nice. You'd love it there and what's more my show's on in Bristol in February. You could come and see me.' She grinned at Katy. 'Maybe you could get Ward to bring you down at the same time and we could all meet up.'

The Miss Taylors looked cautiously interested in the idea. Building on her success, Jen went blithely on to point out how much happier Winston, the dachshund, would be away from the bombing.

'I can't believe you've waited this long,' she said, stroking his ears. 'Poor old thing. He hates bombs. It's cruel to make him stay suffering here when he could be having lovely peaceful country walks in the countryside.'

Katy caught Mrs Frost's eye and smothered a grin. They both knew that Jen loathed the elderly dachshund, but they also knew it was a powerful argument. And they both wished they had thought of it before. Winston was the Miss Taylors' pride and joy and anything that would make him happy was guaranteed to make them happy too.

'Well, perhaps we'll think about it,' Esme said doubtfully.

'It would be nice for Winston,' Thelma said.

Wisely Jen left it at that, but by the time she left the following day to rejoin her ENSA group in Southampton, the old ladies were already beginning to make plans. Plans that they would put to Ward when he came back.

If he came back.

Mr Lorenz touched the lace at the collar of the shirt Joyce had taken out of her bag and then withdrew his hand as though reluctant to investigate it further.

Joyce watched the long fingers retreat to the edge of the counter. He had good hands, Lorenz, delicate hands with clean, nicely trimmed nails. 'It's good quality,' she said. 'My daughter gave it to me. And the skirt.' She realised suddenly what might be bothering him and frowned. 'They haven't been worn. They're brand new.'

He inclined his head. 'They're very pretty,' he said. 'It just seems a shame you can't wear them over the festive period.'

Joyce grimaced. 'It's because of the festive period I've brought them in,' she said bluntly. 'I want to get presents for the kids down in Devon and I'm a bit short of the readies at the moment.' So short, in fact, that at this rate it would be bread and butter for Christmas lunch. So short that she had opened the present from Jen in the hopes of it being something she could pawn.

And it was. Oddly she had been touched that Jen would buy her something so pretty. But she had squashed the desire to try the outfit on and had packed it up again until she had the chance to get over to Northcote Road. Stanley would never notice that she was a present short on Christmas day, nor would Pete or Mick. Bob might have done, but he'd be gone by then, off to some training depot in Wiltshire which he was convinced would be even worse than prison.

'Anyway, it's too small,' she lied, just in case Lorenz refused to take it out of some mistaken sense of chivalry. She already suspected those Guinnesses he sometimes slipped her were bought specially and weren't from a job lot that he'd accepted from someone in part exchange as he claimed.

Not that she'd said anything, mind. She didn't want to embarrass him. In any case she had felt better for them. They'd given her a bit of a lift. And she'd needed all the lift she could find during Jen's visit last week. Stanley hadn't liked having home truths flung in his face by his daughter and had blamed Joyce for letting her run wild during the year he was inside. And if he wasn't screaming at her, Jen was, accusing her of being a doormat and asking why she didn't ever stand up for herself.

Realising Lorenz was looking at her with concern in his eyes she roused a faint smile. 'You've never been married, have you, Mr Lorenz?'

To her surprise he flushed slightly and looked away. 'It has not been my privilege to meet a woman whom I could truly love,' he said.

Joyce blinked. Love? In her experience love didn't have much to do with it. Duty perhaps, or necessity, loyalty even, but not love. It seemed to her that Stanley's ritual abuse and determined coupling had more to do with a jealous sense of possession or possibly punishment than with love. But before she could pursue the thought further, Lorenz was speaking, offering her a price, a good price, his voice formal and stiff again as though his previous remark had never been made.

'Five shillings?' Joyce repeated. 'Are you sure?'

'I will keep it for six months,' he said briskly. 'Interest sixpence a month. If it's not redeemed before that time . . .'

Joyce nodded, she knew the conditions by heart. She would try to make the payments, try to redeem the suit before Jen next came home, but in the meantime five shillings would give her enough for a couple of presents and postage for Angie and Paul. Thank God. She would have hated not to send them anything. Their second Christmas away. She sighed. If she didn't see them soon she would forget what they looked like.

As she left the shop a few minutes later, she glanced back at the pawnbroker. So Lorenz was a romantic, was he? She sighed and buttoned her shabby coat tight against the bitter wind. Once upon a time she had been one too.

In the weeks leading up to Christmas, despite the continued heavy bombing of London and provincial cities, the overseas news was good. In the Middle East thousands of Italians were reported captured by British and Commonwealth troops and the Greeks were having equal success in Albania.

Then suddenly there was talk of invasion again. Apparently the moon and tides would be just right for Hitler on the twenty-third of December.

The news rustled through the hospital, caused a momentary pause in procedure, then was shrugged off as Matron let it be known that the arrangements for Christmas would proceed regardless.

Back on days again, Katy was once more under the eagle eye of Sister Morris, but the determined Christmas spirit seemed to have a beneficial effect on even Sister Morris. She had already produced from her office a box of jolly decorations which traditionally adorned the Ethel Barnet ward, and when one of the porters rang up to the ward to say that someone had brought a box of holly in, she immediately sent Katy along to fetch some with orders to make sure she got a nice big bit with plenty of berries.

Pushing through the swing doors into the main hospital entrance Katy could hardly believe her eyes. The usually pristine and orderly entrance hall had been transformed. Great boxes of holly and mistletoe lay all around, their contents spilling out over the marble floor. Overhead, festoons of homemade streamers looped across the ceiling and half a dozen porters and cleaners were hard at work with stepladders and string, fixing bundles of greenery to every available fixture and fitting.

'It's come from Wimbledon Common,' said one of the porters, grinning at Katy's wide-eyed amazement. 'You can't get much in the way of tinsel or baubles any more but old Mother Nature doesn't know there's a war on, does she?'

Katy giggled. 'I suppose not,' she said. She glanced around. Thankfully Bertie Rutherford was not among the helpers. Since he had joined the staff at the Wilhelmina, she had found it increasingly difficult to turn down his offer of an evening out. She didn't want to go out with Bertie Rutherford. It wasn't that she didn't like him because in a funny way she did, she found his misplaced arrogance quite endearing, but she just didn't have time. There was so much to do at the pub these days, that she had taken to trying to sleep more or less as soon as she went off duty at eight so she could get up early after the raids were over and get some of the cleaning and cooking done in the early hours of the morning before she came back on duty.

Bending down, she began to pick through the nearest box of holly, trying to find a branch that met Sister's description. One or two nurses from other wards were doing the same thing and Katy was just balancing the merits of size of branch over number of berries when the nurse she was talking to suddenly fell silent with a glazed expression on her face.

Turning her head to follow the other's girl's gaze, Katy's face broke into a wide smile and she staggered to her feet clutching a bundle of holly to her chest.

'Ward! You're back.'

Sidestepping a passing ladder, Ward came over to her. 'Hi,' he said, grinning. 'I thought it was you. Although I wasn't sure. In uniform all you nurses look equally gorgeous.'

Aware of the other nurses watching with undisguised interest, Katy tried to edge him out of their earshot. Don't blush, she told herself sternly. Please. Not in public.

'How's the pub?' he asked. 'I'm sorry I haven't been around to help you out for a while.'

Katy was touched by his concern. 'We've survived. Anyway,' she waved the holly about, 'I dare say you've been doing rather more important things than helping me wash the floor.'

He laughed. 'I don't know about that. I reckon it's you who has been doing the important things, like persuading my aunts to take to the country.'

'Oh, that wasn't me,' Katy said. 'That was Jen. I can't take the credit for that.'

'No?' He raised his eyebrows. 'And who enlisted the formidable Jen's support for the plan?'

Katy wriggled uncomfortably behind the bundle of holly. 'Well, me, but . . .'

Ward shook his head. 'No buts. The credit is yours and I'm very grateful. And once I've got them settled I want to take you down to see them for a weekend.'

Katy nearly dropped the holly. Had he just asked her away for the weekend? For a second, in all the surrounding racket of the Christmas decorating, she thought she must have misheard. But he was looking at her with a question in his grey eyes, and a slight frown on his forehead.

She swallowed. 'But surely you don't want to . . . I mean, I couldn't . . .'

'Couldn't you?' He smiled. 'Surely you must be allowed a few days' holiday some time?' He shrugged. 'In any case I've promised them, so there's not much either of us can do about it. And if we can time it so we get to see Jen's show, all the better.' He put his hands in his pockets and went on casually. 'Maybe we can take Louise with us as well. She could do with a break now she's pretty much back on her feet.'

For a dreadful moment Katy thought she was going to be sick. So that was it. What he really wanted was to go away with Louise and merely needed dull sensible little Katy Parsons as a chaperone.

She was just searching for the words to refuse once and for all when one of the workmen leaned down from his ladder and pointed out in a loud voice that they were standing right underneath a bunch of mistletoe.

In the few seconds it took for the hall to fall silent, Katy was aware of an embarrassment so excruciating that her whole body seemed to shudder with it. I'm going to die, she thought. I'm going into a fatal palpitation and in a minute they'll come for me with a stretcher and try to restart my heart.

She glanced at Ward and was astonished to see that he looked completely unfazed. On the contrary he was smiling, and even as she watched, he put out his arm, drawing her towards him. Then he reached over her bundle of holly, cupped her face in his hands and kissed her gently on the lips. At once the audience broke into thunderous applause.

The kiss only lasted a couple of heartbeats, but unfortunately Katy was far more aware of the holly painfully pricking her chest than the feel of his lips. She could tell Ward was aware of it too.

As he released her his mouth curved in amusement. But Katy was mortified. She felt mocked by that smile. She stepped back abruptly, cheeks flaming, and turned to find herself face to face with Sister Morris.

'Nurse Parsons!' Sister's eyes were nearly popping out of her head.

'What are you thinking of? How dare you make a spectacle of yourself. Go back to the ward at once. I will deal with you later.'

Louise couldn't believe her ears. Ward Frazer had kissed Katy Parsons in full view of everyone in the hospital entrance hall. Stopping in mid stride, she leaned forward and rested weakly on her walking frame as tears sprang to her eyes. But Ward Frazer was hers. How dare he kiss another girl?

'Ooh, and by all accounts that Nurse Parsons got a rocket and a half from Sister Morris afterwards,' Nurse Kilroy went on gleefully. 'They could hear it right down in casualty.'

Good, Louise thought furiously as she struggled on a few steps. It served Katy right.

'What on earth was Nurse Parsons doing hanging around in the entrance hall anyway?' she asked.

'Collecting holly,' Nurse Kilroy replied. 'Sister Morris had sent her down for it but she was so long, Sister came to see what had kept her.' She giggled. 'And it was your Mr Frazer what had.'

'Flight Lieutenant Frazer,' Louise corrected her crossly. So at least it hadn't been a prearranged assignation then. She frowned as she mulled over the implications.

By the time she had completed two slow painful lengths of the room, she had convinced herself the kiss meant nothing. Ward was merely being chivalrous. He could hardly refuse to kiss Katy if she was standing under the mistletoe, could he?

No, she wouldn't make a big thing of it, she decided. She would laugh it off. Of course it meant nothing. After all Katy Parsons was hardly a beauty and Ward barely knew her anyway. It worried her that Bertie obviously fancied her though.

She knew Bertie had been pestering Katy to go out with him for an evening. There must be more to mousy little Katy than immediately met the eye, she decided. Even Aaref liked her. Once, ages ago, before the accident, he had told her she was lucky to have such a loyal friend.

Louise sniffed. Stupid Aaref. Little did he know. She glanced at the bracelet on her wrist and grimaced. Aaref had sent it in to her. An early Christmas present. All the nurses had assumed it was from Ward Frazer and she hadn't disillusioned them. It had come with a stilted little note saying he thought of her always and dreamed for the time when he would see her again. She giggled. Well, she dreamed for the time when she would see Ward Frazer again. And this time she'd make damn sure there was mistletoe hanging right over her bed.

When Bertie came up to the ward the following morning and handed Katy a bunch of flowers, she pushed them away crossly. 'Don't you start. I had enough embarrassment yesterday.'

Bertie was peeved. 'They're not from me,' he said.

'Oh,' Katy frowned and quickly opened the accompanying card.

'Katy,' it read. 'Sorry for getting you into trouble. I wish I could apologise in person but I'm heading off again shortly. Hope to see you before I go, if only to say goodbye! Ward.'

Covering her confusion, Katy buried her head in the flowers.

'They're gorgeous,' Nurse Coogan whispered in awe behind her. 'You lucky thing.'

Sister got a bunch too. Katy never discovered what her note said, but she heard her exclamation of surprise.

'Goodness, how absurd. Take them away at once, and give them to some deserving patient.' But although the words were harsh, the tone was forgiving and, to her astonishment, Katy realised that Sister Morris was secretly rather pleased.

Stanley Carter glared at the turkey on the kitchen table. Next to it stood half a dozen brown eggs in a bowl and he glared at those too.

'Where did this lot come from?'

Joyce was busy at the sink. 'I bought them,' she said. 'Christmas isn't the same without a turkey.'

'How much did they cost?'

Joyce licked her lips nervously. It was a trap. She knew it was a trap but she didn't know how to get out of it. Whatever price she said he would accuse her of holding money back. Money that he could have used. He would be angry. Very angry. But he would be even more angry if he knew the truth.

'I don't know,' she said eventually. 'I can't remember.'

'No, I bet you can't remember,' he said, coming round the table menacingly. 'Because you never knew in the first place. Did you?'

'What do you mean?' she asked edging away from him.

'I mean that someone gave them to you, didn't they?' He caught her arm and twisted it painfully. 'And you are going to tell me who, aren't you?'

'Mrs Rutherford,' Joyce said quickly. 'I didn't say at first because I know you don't like charity. But it's not really charity, Stanley. It's like a bonus for me working there and helping with them chickens and that.'

To her relief the pressure on her arm reduced slightly. 'Oh really?' Stanley said. 'Then how come Micky saw that bugger Lorenz walking up Lavender Hill with a ten pound turkey under his arm?'

Joyce froze. She realised he had known all along. That he had just been playing with her like a cat with a mouse. Waiting for the kill. She knew the kill was going to hurt and felt the familiar ball of fear in her stomach. But to her surprise he let her go.

'What are you doing?' she gasped as he picked up the turkey and the bowl of eggs and headed for the front door.

He stopped in the passage and turned back to her, an ugly expression on his face. 'I'm going to get rid of these,' he said. 'And if I ever see any evidence of that filthy Jew in here again I'll break his bloody arms off. And yours.'

A moment later the turkey flew into the street followed by the eggs.

Slamming the door Stanley turned back down the passage. His face was cold, but his eyes were alight with anger. He was rubbing his hands as he advanced towards her. 'Christmas won't be the same without them, eh? I'll give you friggin' Christmas.'

After weeks of persuasion, two days before Christmas, Katy finally agreed to go for a cup of tea in Lyons' with Bertie Rutherford.

She'd bumped into him as she took a patient to theatre and took pity on him when he told her that Pam Nelson had made it clear she didn't want him around that evening because her friend Sheila was coming back from the country with her child.

Poor Bertie, nobody wanted him around. He was unpopular at the hospital. His arrogance and outspoken pacifism hadn't gone down well with the other porters and, despite his looks, the nurses treated him as a bit of a joke.

'Spend the evening with Louise,' Katy had said. 'She needs cheering up.' Louise had been very off the last couple of days. Katy wasn't sure if it was because her discharge from hospital had been delayed or because of the Ward Frazer mistletoe incident. At the time Louise had laughed it off with an airy comment about Ward Frazer's chivalrous nature, but since the flowers had arrived Louise had been distinctly frosty, and relations between them had become rather strained.

'She may need cheering up,' Bertie had said with a shrug. 'But not by me. She's expecting the gorgeous Ward Frazer this evening for a bit of love-play and she made it quite clear that she doesn't want me acting gooseberry.'

'All right then.' Katy had fixed a bright smile on her mouth. 'Sirens permitting, I'll meet you at Lyon's for a cup of tea when I come off duty just after eight.'

Lyon's was surprisingly busy. Bertie was already there and had kept a table. He'd clearly been there for some time. 'What's this Mrs Whitehead woman like, then?' he asked when they'd ordered. 'She sounds a bit of a nutcase.'

Katy grimaced. 'She's really sweet, but since her husband and youngest son were killed she's gone off the rails a bit. She's scared to death that something will happen to little George.'

'So that's why they're going to be sleeping in the air-raid shelter,' Bertie said. 'And I thought it was just because the Nelsons were short of beds. Either way it means there's no room in there for the rest of us.' He made a face. 'Well, let's hope dear Mr Hitler doesn't drop too many on Lavender Road over Christmas or there'll be a few more casualties in the morgue.'

Katy glared at him. 'Bertie, don't. That's an awful thing to say. Anyway you can always come over and spend the night in the pub cellar if things get rough.'

'Oh, Katy,' his eyes widened salaciously, 'now there's an offer I would be crazy to refuse.'

'I didn't mean it like that, as you very well know.'

But he wouldn't be deterred. He reached over and took her hand. 'I wish you did mean it like that,' he said. 'You know how much I want you, Katy darling.'

Jerking her hand away, Katy was annoyed to find she was flushing. 'Stop it, Bertie,' she said crossly, glancing around nervously. 'If you're going to be like this I'm going home. Anyway the sirens will go in a minute and I don't want to be stuck here all night.'

'All right, all right, I promise to be good,' he said quickly as she began to stand up. 'I won't say another word about it.'

But later when he escorted her back to the pub he couldn't resist one more try.

'At least let me kiss you goodnight?' he suggested as they walked up Lavender Road.

'Certainly not,' Katy replied.

'Oh please, Katy,' he pleaded. 'Just one little kiss. After all, it is Christmas. Season of goodwill and all that.'

'No, Bertie. No,' Katy said firmly. She looked up the quiet moonlit street. 'I don't feel that way about you and in any case somebody might see.'

Bertie looked affronted. 'For goodness' sake, you let blasted Ward

Frazer kiss you in full view of the whole hospital. And he's my sister's boyfriend.'

Katy's heart lurched uncomfortably. Was that true? Was Ward Frazer Louise's boyfriend? Was she being stupid to hope that those flowers had meant something more than an apology for that prickly kiss?

Yes, probably she was. After all, where was Ward Frazer now? Here with her? No. He was with Louise, making 'love-play' in her private hospital bedroom.

'All right then,' she said to Bertie crisply. 'You can kiss me, but only a small one.'

She almost laughed at Bertie's expression. She had never previously seen anyone look eager and nervous at the same time. But as his lips met hers she realised she felt nothing. Absolutely nothing.

Bertie was not pleased: 'You could at least pretend you're liking it,' he said crossly.

'I'm not,' Katy said.

He glared at her. 'Well, it's not very flattering for me, is it?'

Taking pity on him she giggled. 'OK, once more and I'll try harder.' She put her hands on his shoulders and closed her eyes. Once again she felt nothing, but this time as he raised his head she sighed deeply. 'Oh Bertie,' she groaned. 'That was so lovely. Have I ever told you you're the best kisser in the whole world?'

A slight tension in his shoulders made her open her eyes.

Somehow, silently, beside them the pub door had opened, and Ward Frazer had emerged on to the street. For a second they all three stood in silence.

Then he inclined his head. 'I'm sorry,' he said. 'I didn't mean to disturb you. I called by earlier. I just wanted to say goodbye.'

Another agonisingly long moment passed in which Katy thought of a million things she could say and said none of them. She couldn't even let go of Bertie's shoulders because she knew if she did she would almost certainly fall over.

She knew Ward was looking at her and finally she dared to meet his eyes. He smiled then. A faint movement of the lips that twisted her heart.

'Happy Christmas, Katy,' he said softly, nodded to Bertie and walked away.

Chapter Eleven

In the event Louise was allowed home on Christmas Day. Perhaps due to the awful weather, the Luftwaffe had kept away for the days leading up to Christmas and, as the supposed date for Hitler's invasion passed, a strange, tentative peace fell over London. For those lucky enough still to have beds to sleep in, it was the first undisturbed rest they had had for nearly four months. Everyone knew it was only a temporary respite, but at least it allowed the immediate repairs and clearing up from previous weeks to continue unabated.

Louise could hardly believe her eyes as Mr Wallace drove along Lavender Hill. Immobilised in her pristine room deep in the reinforced structure of the Wilhelmina since the middle of October, she had been distanced from the damage caused outside by the relentless Nazi bombers. People had told her of course, complained about the wet roads, the severed pipes and amenities, the all-pervasive dust, but it wasn't the same as seeing it for herself.

There was hardly a house without at least one broken or taped-up window. Chimneys and roof slates were missing everywhere and lamp-posts tilted, the glass in their lamps long gone. All the ornamental work in the balustrade of Battersea Town Hall had been brought down and the road outside was pitted and scarred, the tramlines twisted. Along Lavender Hill odd bits of lino and carpet had been used to board up shop fronts and ragged, scrawled signs declared there were still functioning businesses behind. On the corner of one road a bomb blast had sliced off the gable end of two houses, leaving the rooms quite unharmed with beds and furniture still neatly in place on the first and second floors. On the road below, two crumpled cars awaited a tow-away truck.

Louise was glad when Mr Wallace turned up Lavender Road towards the common. Apart from the inevitable chips and scars, Lavender Road itself seemed mostly to be still intact. One of the trees had lost a few branches and its trunk was black from an incendiary device but there were no houses missing, none of the ominous craters and piles of adjacent rubble that adorned some of the nearby streets.

At the top of the road, the common looked bleak and grey. The part opposite her parent's house had been turned into allotments, miserable little patches of unidentifiable root vegetables. The trees were bare of leaves and what grass there was seemed to be coated with ash.

The anti-aircraft guns were silent today and the big searchlights over on the far corner of the common were dark, but behind the Nissen huts a troop of servicewomen seemed to be doing some kind of co-ordinated physical jerks.

Louise shuddered. 'Not much of a Christmas for them,' she remarked.

Her mother looked round from the front of the car. 'Well actually, darling, I didn't like to tell you before, but we've invited a couple of the officers for lunch.'

Louise groaned. 'On my first day home?'

Celia smiled placatingly. 'We didn't know for sure you'd be able to come home today, did we? Anyway they won't stay long.'

The officers turned out to be two thin quiet men from the gun battery and a hearty uniformed woman from the ATS whom Louise disliked on sight.

'I gather you were caught up in the Balham bomb disaster,' the ATS dragon barked over lunch. 'Lucky to get out alive. I was over there last week and they were still digging for bodies. Sixty-four dead so far.'

Louise wondered what the reaction round the table would be if she said she had lost her baby that night. She wondered if that would make the total sixty-five. But perhaps an unborn child wouldn't count in the gruesome statistics.

Thankfully her younger brother Douglas, home from boarding school for the holidays, chipped in with some statistic about national casualties and Louise was saved a response.

'I saw that Jewish boy yesterday out on the common,' Douglas whispered later under cover of some diatribe from her father about the role of the ARP. 'He asked about you.'

Louise feigned surprise. 'Did he?' She glanced at the bracelet on her wrist. It really was very pretty. She couldn't imagine where Aaref had got it from. Perhaps Mrs d'Arcy Billière gave him pocket money or something. And he'd saved up for weeks and weeks.

She smiled at the thought. Poor Aaref. He was a loyal admirer. But sadly for him she had bigger fish to fry. Ward Frazer. He had been so pleased to find she was walking again.

And then he had suggested this idea of her going with him to see his aunts when they moved to Bristol. A weekend away. With Ward Frazer. It was just about the only thing in this dismal war that was worth getting better for.

She grimaced and glanced at her father at the end of the table. It was so important that her parents agreed.

She had intended to ask them when they were mellow during Christmas lunch. Spirit of goodwill and all that. But she couldn't possibly ask in front of these awful army types.

Luckily the military departed soon after the meal. The men had to go on duty and the woman, to Louise and Douglas's delight, had broken her tooth on the silver three penny bit in the Christmas pudding.

'Oh,' Celia had gasped in horror. 'I am so sorry. I had quite forgotten it was in there. The pudding was left over from last year, you see. Luckily, as it turned out, because we couldn't get dried fruit this year for love nor money.'

'Not so lucky for you,' Louise consoled the suddenly silent ATS lady brightly. 'Still, as you got the three penny piece, you'll have to make a wish.'

'Best to wish that there's a dentist open on Christmas Day,' Douglas muttered.

To Louise's relief, Douglas accepted an offer to be shown round the gun placement, leaving her alone with her parents.

She decided it was best to strike while the iron was hot. While she still had the courage. 'You know the Miss Taylors are moving to the country?' She began when they had settled her comfortably by the fire. 'Well, Ward Frazer has asked if I would go with him to visit them some time in February.'

'Well, I don't know about that,' her father said at once.

'You've been seeing quite a lot of him in hospital, haven't you?' Her mother looked up from her knitting.

'Yes, I have,' Louise agreed with a suitably coy smile. Last year when she had first met Ward Frazer, Celia told her that he had only taken her out to be kind to her. Well, now she could eat her words. 'Quite a lot.'

Although she would like to have seen quite a lot more. There was no doubt that Ward Frazer was an extraordinarily attractive man. Not that you could get up to much with a broken pelvis of course. In any case Ward Frazer was very polite and correct. A bit too polite and correct, truth be told. She never knew exactly where she stood with him. He liked her, she knew that. Once he had told her she looked like a girl he had once been in love with. That was a good sign surely. But when she had hinted heavily that she would like a bit less witty conversation and a bit more action, he had always rather annoyingly just laughed it off with some wry comment about not being the right sort of man for her.

She had begun once again to think he was exactly the right sort of man for her. And she suspected her parents secretly did too.

'I thought you approved of him, Daddy?' she ventured.

Her father grunted. 'Seems respectable enough. Nice-looking young man.' He frowned. 'Foreign, of course.'

Louise blinked. 'Canadian? You can hardly call that foreign. They're on our side after all.' She gulped, suddenly emotional. 'Even now he's in France trying to set up a Resistance movement against the Germans. You can hardly be more patriotic than that.'

Her mother looked appalled. 'Good gracious. That sounds rather risky.'

'Very brave though,' Louise said quickly.

'Well yes,' her mother agreed with a frown. 'But I don't think you want to let yourself get too fond of anyone in that line of work, darling.'

'That's why I want to spend time with him when I can,' Louise said pointedly. She picked a thread sadly off her skirt. 'I never know when it might be the last time. And his poor old aunts would be so pleased to see us.'

Her mother glanced doubtfully at her father. 'Well, we'd have to see how you were, darling,' she said gently. 'When the moment came. What the doctors thought.'

Her father was less easily swayed. 'I certainly wouldn't let you go alone with him,' he said crisply. 'Not at all the thing.'

Louise sighed. 'Ward mentioned that Katy Parsons from the Flag and Garter might come too,' she said. Blasted Katy was so fond of his stupid aunts. But she would make a useful chaperone. And she was quite malleable. They could always leave her with the aunts for a few hours. And there wouldn't be any mistletoe around in February.

Her father nodded, 'A nurse, isn't she?'

Louise leaned forward painfully, trying to capitalise on that nod. 'So if she goes, I can go?' She'd force Katy to go if necessary. Insist on it.

'We'll see.' Her father seemed to have lost interest in the discussion and was rather irritatingly fiddling with the wireless. 'Now be quiet, my dears, and listen to the King.'

Pam had dreaded Christmas Day. She had hoped Bertie would be working at the hospital, but for some reason he was given the day off and so she had to face including him in Christmas lunch with Sheila and little George. Knowing it was just over a year ago that Sheila had lost her youngest child, and shortly afterward her husband, Pam had expected her to be very emotional and she was convinced that Bertie's brashness would be the worst antidote to Sheila's inevitable distress.

But as it turned out, Sheila was so pleased to be away from her awful relations in the country that she seemed for once to forget her double bereavement. And George was clearly intrigued by the debonair stranger. After an initial shyness, he kept asking him questions apparently just to hear the lazy, drawling way he spoke.

Bertie, unused to children, was clearly surprised by his success with the little boy and took vicarious delight in teaching him new words which George would then repeat to everyone's amusement in some later conversation.

The food was good too. Sheila had brought a turkey up from the country and on Christmas Eve Mrs Rutherford had surreptitiously dropped off a box of home-grown vegetables and an envelope addressed to Pam containing four pound notes.

'Guilt money,' Pam had said sourly, opening it when she got back from work. 'Still, it's better than nothing I suppose.'

'I can't believe his family won't even have him for Christmas lunch,' Sheila said.

Pam sniffed. 'They've got more sense. I wish we didn't have to have him for ours.'

Sheila looked shocked. 'Oh, don't be mean. Poor boy. He seems nice enough.'

Pam rolled her eyes. 'He's a horror,' she said.

But Sheila had been disposed to feel sorry for Bertie. She was always one for the underdog. Having been an unwanted guest of the Nelsons herself, perhaps she sympathised with him. And nobody could have predicted how well he got on with George.

In any event the net result was much better than Pam had

anticipated. 'I think it's all right,' she whispered to Alan as they cleared the empty plates on to the sideboard. Behind her Sheila was giggling over some scurrilous story Bertie was telling her about the hospital.

'I told you so,' Alan replied. 'You worry too much, my love. They're getting on like a house on fire.'

As Pam turned back to the table, George picked up the salt and pepper pot and frowned at Bertie. 'I can't remember if these are the cutlytree or the candymints,' he announced solemnly.

Breaking off from his story, Bertie laughed. 'Those are the condiments,' he said. 'The knives and forks are the cutlery.'

Pam smiled and glanced at Sheila. Sheila was smiling too, but it wasn't quite the fond, parental smile Pam had expected. It was a completely different smile altogether, fond all right, but not the slightest bit parental, and it was directed not at her six-year-old son but at Bertie Rutherford.

Quickly Pam looked at him and saw his eyes lift from George to Sheila. It was only a quick glance but long enough for Pam's own smile to freeze on her face.

Oh no, she thought. Please no. Her eyes flew to Alan but she knew at once he hadn't noticed anything. He was trying to light the Christmas pudding and nodded gratefully when Bertie offered him his smart gold cigarette lighter.

Suddenly it took and Alan turned round triumphantly. 'Yes! Now quick everyone make a wish before the flame dies.'

Pam had intended to wish for a baby, for Alan not to be proved infertile, for the house not to be bombed or, if she was feeling particularly generous, for world peace. But suddenly as Bertie Rutherford smiled complacently and leaned back in his chair, she found herself revising her plans.

She closed her eyes. Please, please don't let Sheila fall in love with Bertie Rutherford, she wished in silent haste. Then she glanced at the Christmas pudding. The flame had gone, Alan was already reaching for the knife, Bertie was topping up the drinks and Pam had a nasty feeling she hadn't made the wish in time.

'Goodness, Mrs Carter, whatever has happened to you?'

Joyce glared at her employer. She though Mrs Rutherford would have had more tact. 'I fell over the dustbin on Christmas Eve,' she muttered gruffly.

'Oh.' Celia Rutherford took a step back, suddenly looked shocked and embarrassed as a more likely explanation dawned on her. She had obviously asked the question without thinking and was now wishing she had never brought the subject up. 'Oh,' she said awkwardly. 'Oh.' Frowning she raised her arm and then dropped it again and hesitated. 'Is there anything I can do?' she asked quietly. 'Anything at all?'

Joyce wondered what she had in mind. A cold poultice perhaps? Or some help with the heavy jobs for a day or two? Or was she thinking of having a word with Stanley? Telling him politely in her nasal upper-crust voice that it wasn't quite the thing to knock his wife about so obviously, particularly at Christmas.

She shook her head. 'No,' she said stiffly. 'I'm all right.' She sighed and looked away. 'It was my own fault anyway.' She should never have accepted the turkey. Should have given it straight back to Lorenz. She should have known what would happen if she kept it. It was just that it was such a nice, juicy-looking one and she hadn't tasted turkey for so long. And she'd thought it would make a bit of a Christmas for the boys. What with Bob gone and the weather and that, they were all pretty low. But what was done was done. It was no good crying over spilt milk. Some scavenging fox off the common had most likely had a good Christmas dinner. Abruptly she gathered up her dusters and went to leave the room.

'Mrs Carter?' Celia Rutherford's voice was low and concerned.

Joyce sighed and turned back. 'What?' She knew it was ungracious. She couldn't help it. She knew Mrs Rutherford was only trying to be kind. But if everyone had just minded their own business none of this would have happened.

Celia smiled gently. 'Would it help at all if I gave you a couple of days off? Paid of course. Like sick leave?'

Touched despite herself, Joyce hesitated for a second then shook her head. What would she do with a couple of days off? Unless she could go and visit the kids in Devon, and she couldn't afford to do that. Not with the price of train fares what they were. And she didn't want to spend any more time at home than she had to. Stanley was at home.

'I'd rather come in here,' she said abruptly. At least she was safe here. She glanced quickly at her employer as a nasty thought occurred to her. Maybe Celia Rutherford was hinting that she didn't want her around looking like this. 'If you don't mind?' she added gruffly.

'Of course I don't mind,' Mrs Rutherford said warmly. 'I like having you here. You know that.'

Joyce swallowed. Good God, much more of this and she'd burst into tears. She took a few steps towards the door then stopped. She had to say something nice, something friendly. After all, Mrs Rutherford wasn't a bad sort deep down.

'I haven't thanked you for them eggs,' she said at last, looking back with an attempt at a smile.

Celia Rutherford looked pleased. 'They came from the rogue hen. Your favourite,' she said eagerly. 'Did you notice? Hers are always darker than the others. And her shells go crinkly when the guns fire.'

Joyce nodded. She had noticed. The yolks were darker and all. She just hoped Mrs Rutherford hadn't noticed them adorning the tree halfway up Lavender Road.

Katy had never eaten so much turkey in all her life. The Wilhelmina served it roast for lunch on Christmas Day and then in varying forms at lunchtime each of the consecutive days, and her mother, newly back from the country, served it roast for supper on Christmas Day, and then cold in sandwiches for the next four nights.

Had her mother not been away so long, Katy might have tactfully tried to ask for something else but it had been such a struggle persuading her to come home for Christmas at all that she didn't like to hurt her feelings.

It was odd having her mother back. She had forgotten over the last few weeks just how annoying her mother could be with her constant anxiety about the smallest details. But nevertheless it was a relief to hand back the reins of the household, the ration books, the problem of the almost empty larder and the responsibility for the cooking and cleaning.

And her relief was equally matched by her father's obvious and rather touching delight in having his family reunited. He had been a changed man the last few days, laughing and joking with the clientele, humming tunes off the wireless as he polished the glasses and good-naturedly teasing Katy about her attempts to help in the bar.

'I don't know what they're teaching her up at that hospital,' he'd say, winking at her mother. 'But it certainly doesn't include common sense. One day she washed the floor back to front and I caught her trampling about all over the bit she'd already washed.'

Although she tried not to mind, tried to keep smiling, Katy actually found his little digs hurt quite badly. She'd slaved her guts out to keep his blasted pub going while her mother was away. If it hadn't been for Ward Frazer coming to the rescue, she would probably have made herself ill over it.

Ward Frazer. She put her turkey sandwich down on the plate. Suddenly she felt sick.

She had spent most of the Christmas period trying to convince herself that she hadn't made a complete fool of herself that evening when Ward Frazer had stumbled upon her and Bertie outside the pub.

It was a meaningless incident, she told herself, as she made the hospital beds, washed out the bed pans and tossed and turned trying to get some sleep at night. Nothing to get worked up about. Not the end of the world. Surely it didn't matter.

She glared at the sandwich. But it did matter. Deep inside her she had a nasty feeling that it mattered rather a lot.

However much she tried to wrap it up, to change the interpretation, the bald facts were that Ward Frazer had made the effort to come and say goodbye and had found her kissing another man. Not just kissing him but enthusing rather noisily about it. Ward Frazer wasn't to know that the whole thing had been a complete fake, just to boost poor old Bertie Rutherford's morale.

For several days Katy had longed to kill Bertie Rutherford. Her mind had run riot with ways of doing it, her favourite being to strap him on to one of his beastly porter's trolleys and push him down the hill straight into the Thames. By the time he reached the bank he would be travelling at a pretty high speed and the heavy trolley would hopefully skid across the surface far enough to get to the deepest part of the river, before sinking without trace.

An alternative was to accompany him to the hospital morgue and slam him into one of the coffins. But that was rather too gruesome even for her current state of mind and it wasn't really poor Bertie's fault anyway. She hadn't had to kiss him after all. She could have said no. She certainly should have said no.

And she could hardly explain to Ward Frazer that she had merely been trying out Bertie's kiss to see if it was as exciting as the one she had had off Ward under the mistletoe.

Maybe he wouldn't care anyway.

She frowned. That was the rub. She didn't have the faintest clue whether Ward Frazer would care that she was kissing another man or not.

He was far too good at hiding his feelings. If he had any.

Nevertheless, she was left feeling distinctly uneasy about the prospect of his return from France. On the one hand she longed to see him, longed to reassure herself that it had made no difference, and on the other she dreaded his return in case his attitude towards her had changed.

In the event all her planned, carefully phrased explanations were rendered entirely useless, because when she next saw him he was so blindingly angry that he wouldn't have listened to a word she said anyway.

On the twenty-ninth of December, after the Christmas lull, the German bombing had begun again with a vengeance. In that one night alone the Luftwaffe started one thousand five hundred fires in London, mostly concentrated on the City. It was a swift raid designed for maximum destruction and it had the desired effect. The water mains were severed at the outset by high-explosive parachute mines. But when the beleaguered fire crews looked to the river, they found the tide was too low and they hadn't sufficient length of pipes to reach the water. Much of the Guildhall area was utterly destroyed, six churches were gutted and it was only by the extraordinary bravery of the fire fighters that St Paul's itself survived, scathed but intact.

Most of the railway stations were put out of action and several Underground stations and air-raid shelters were hit. As a result, even though there was another lull in the bombing over New Year, the Wilhelmina was bursting to the seams. Once again extra beds had been brought in. There were so many serious burns cases that it was several days before the converted Green Line ambulance buses were able to ship sufficient patients to the outlying hospitals to bring the Wilhelmina wards back to a manageable size.

As well as raising the tempo in the hospital, the raids had made it very difficult for Katy to get home when her day shift ended at eight. Two nights in early January the bombing was so bad she was given permission to sleep in the nurses' basement in the bed of one of the night nurses.

But she didn't like doing that. She spent the whole night worrying about what might be happening in Lavender Road, and she hated not having clean clothes for the next day.

So she got into the habit of waiting for a lull and then running as far as she could towards the next sheltering place before the next wave of fat-bellied bombers came droning overhead.

It didn't always work. On the evening before before the Miss Taylors were due to move, she was still scuttling through the pitch darkness down St John's Hill towards the Arding & Hobbs department store when some red-hot shrapnel hit the road beside her, hissing on the wet surface, and she had just asked herself if having clean underwear was really worth losing her life for, when a high-sided van swerved past her and screeched to a halt a short way in front of her.

As she hadn't even heard it approach, it gave her a terrible shock. Realising she had had a narrow escape, she stopped for a moment in her frantic race to safety and glared at the offending vehicle. Apart from emergency vehicles, traffic usually came to a standstill during bad raids and drivers were meant to head for the nearest air-raid shelter. What with the blackout as well, it was just too dangerous to run the risk of something crashing through the windscreen or bouncing on the road in front of you.

But the driver of this van clearly hadn't read the 'traffic precautions during raids' leaflet. Nor did he show any sign of looking for a shelter. On the contrary, even as two flares exploded overhead, and Katy stood rooted to the spot, he leaped out of the cab and began running back up the road towards her.

Convinced she was about to be confronted by a murderous Nazi infiltrator, or at the very least a mad man, Katy hugged her cloak around her and prepared to flee. But she had only got a couple of yards, when he grabbed her arm and swung her round.

'What the hell are you doing out here?'

Her scream died in her throat as she realised her assailant was none other than Ward Frazer. Ward Frazer as she had never seen him before. Tight lipped and flashing eyes. In the light of the flares overhead he looked murderous, and the grip on her arm as he dragged her back towards the van was punishing.

'You stupid little idiot . . .' he shouted at her furiously, the rest of the sentence, somewhat to Katy's relief, lost under the sudden crack of distant guns.

Suddenly a plane came in low overhead, its engines deafening as it cleared the houses and roared down over the empty street. Before Katy even knew what had happened, practically wrenching her arm out of its socket in the sudden change of direction, Ward had flung her between two of the pillars on the front of Barclays Bank.

For a second all she was aware of was the mouthful of his leather jacket she had taken as he pressed her back painfully against the bank's jutting windowsill, and then, over his shoulder above the sound of the plane, she heard a sudden clatter and the rattling hiss of bullets raking along the road.

And then the plane had gone, and in the second's silence before the big guns up on the common fired again, Katy felt a shudder of belated fear course through her and chill her entire body.

Ward didn't move at once, and for a moment, feeling the weight of him against her, Katy feared he might have been hit. But then she realised he was still breathing, not in pants like her, but steady, regular breaths which stirred the hair on her head and felt pleasantly warm against her left temple.

His heart was beating too, not quite as fast as hers, but in her professional opinion, it was definitely on the quick side for a fit healthy man. Admittedly he had just run a hundred yards in about five seconds and nearly been killed, but nevertheless he was definitely not quite as relaxed as he usually was in her company.

As she tried to disengage her teeth from his collar, the smell of cordite was already mingling with the leathery smell of his jacket and the clean warm scent of his skin. Katy inhaled deeply. It was rather a pleasant experience altogether, she thought dreamily, standing there wrapped in Ward's arms. In fact, if it hadn't been for the Barclays Bank windowsill embedded in her lower spine, she would have been quite happy to stay there for ever.

But it seemed Ward had other ideas, because suddenly he jerked into life, muttered something unintelligible and they were off again running towards the truck.

As they reached it, the moon suddenly sailed out from behind a cloud and they saw clearly the charred holes where the bullets had ripped through the canvas sides.

Katy shivered but Ward swore. 'Let's hope they missed the engine,' he said, shoving Katy rather forcefully into the cab and climbing up behind her.

By his grunt of satisfaction when the engine fired first time it seemed they had. The next moment Katy found herself grovelling in the foot well as the van careered off down the hill.

Reaching over from the steering wheel Ward hauled her unceremoniously back on to the thin rather slippery seat. 'What the hell are you doing?'

Katy glared at him. 'I didn't know you were entering us into the Grand Prix.'

'I want to get out of here before they come back,' he said leaning forward to glance quickly up St John's Road one way and Falcon Road the other before shooting across the junction at Arding & Hobbs. There were no traffic lights at night, of course, or street lamps, and as the van didn't seem to have any lights it was only the light from the moon that showed them the way.

Katy suddenly felt nervous again. How did he know they were coming back? Had they somehow identified him as a dangerous enemy spy? Was the Nazi plane even now circling overhead waiting for the next assault? She swallowed, trying to calm her sudden panic. 'Were they after you specifically, then?' she asked.

'Of course they weren't after me specifically,' he said irritably. 'They were after anything that moved.' He shot her a quick sideways glance. 'You, for example. Not that you were showing much sign of movement when I passed you. Talk about a sitting duck.'

'You nearly ran me over,' she said indignantly, clinging to the dashboard as he swirled round the corner into Lavender Road. 'I was just getting my breath back.'

He shrugged. 'I didn't expect some dimwit nurse to run under my wheels in the middle of an air-raid.'

Seething silently, Katy added 'dimwit nurse' to the list of Ward Frazer's delightful depictions of her. She frowned. There was another one she'd missed. Something he'd yelled at her earlier. 'Stupid little idiot', yes, that was it. Lovely. On balance she'd rather have 'kid', she decided. And 'sitting duck' could almost be considered an endearment.

As he pulled up in front of the pub, it dawned on her that this was probably the last time she would ever see him. Tomorrow, presumably, he would load the Miss Taylors' things into the beastly truck and drive them away for ever. Feeling suddenly rather tearful, she peered across at him, only to find he was staring straight ahead down the dark street, his hands still on the steering wheel as though he couldn't wait to get away.

She began to fumble for the door handle then stopped. She had to say something. Even if it was only goodbye. But she could barely trust herself to speak. She licked her lips and took a deep breath. 'Thanks for the lift,' she said.

He looked across at her then and inclined his head. 'As always it's my pleasure.' He sounded sarcastic, and remembering the number of times he had helped her out, Katy flinched.

'I'm sorry to be such a nuisance,' she said stiffly.

He shook his head and smiled. The first smile she'd seen all evening. 'You're not a nuisance,' he said. 'You're a pain in the backside.'

For some reason Katy didn't find she minded that. In fact there was something about the way he said it that she rather liked. Perhaps it was the smile that went with it. She would have liked to have seen more of that smile, but he was already getting out and coming round to open her door.

He handed her down in silence and escorted her round the truck to the door of the pub. Overhead a flare exploded in a welter of orange lights. Katy shivered and hugged her cloak around her tightly.

For a long second they stood there, looking up at the flare, and then Ward abruptly climbed back into the cab. 'See you soon.'

Katy took a step forward and blinked up at him in surprise. 'Will you?'

'I hope so.' He looked down at her and his eyes narrowed slightly. 'If nothing else we need to discuss the arrangements for the trip to Bristol. I gather Jen will be there at the beginning of February.'

She stared at him astonished. 'You still want me to go, then?'

He reached out to slam the door. 'My aunts will be most disappointed if you don't.'

Chapter Twelve

The following morning Katy got up early to go and say goodbye both to the Miss Taylors and to Mrs Frost who was to accompany them on the journey and stay with them in the cottage Ward had found for them until they were settled in.

Ward was to drive them to Paddington in the truck where the bulk of their belongings would be crated up and put on a freight train in a day or so, troop movements permitting.

He was in the process of loading a box of muddy parsnips when Katy walked up the street. It was still dark and foggy and very cold, but, unshaven and in his shirtsleeves, Ward was already working hard. The truck was half full and around him the pavement was littered with small piles of books and ornaments, a dog basket and half a dozen plant pots each containing a winter cabbage. He straightened up when Katy appeared through the mist and ran his hands through his hair. 'So you survived the night,' he said.

He looked to be in better temper today, but she wasn't going to take any chances. 'Yes, thank you,' she said primly. Avoiding his watchful grey eyes, she glanced away up the grey street.

It had been a bad night. There was a lot of damage. As usual, news of it had spread fast. Two people and a child had been killed when a house collapsed in Clapham Old Town. On Wandsworth Road an ARP warden had been burnt by an incendiary in the street. Up on the common the Rutherfords had had all their windows blown in. Nobody had been hurt because they were all in the cellar, nevertheless the news had made Katy shudder. It seemed only a matter of time before someone on Lavender Road got hit. The Miss Taylors were going at the right time.

She turned back to Ward and made a face at the debris at his feet. 'I'd offer to help but I'm on duty at eight.'

He smiled and flexed his shoulders. 'It's no problem. I dare say we'll get away by the beginning of the next century.'

Even as she laughed, Katy realised she suddenly felt rather short of breath. It was that lazy stretch of his that had done it. That dishevelled look as though he had only just climbed out of bed. She stopped laughing and frowned instead, annoyed by her reaction. OK so he wasn't as fully dressed as usual. But despite the strong bare forearms, he was perfectly decent. Anyone would think he was standing there half naked. Gathering her cloak around her she took a step towards the front door. 'I'll go and say goodbye, then,' she said.

It was a tearful farewell and Katy found herself promising over and over that she would come and see them as soon as possible. She could feel Ward's eyes on her as she said it and her heartbeat increased as she remembered exactly what she was committing herself to.

A few days in the company of Ward Frazer; a man who could raise her pulse rate by the most careless gesture; a man with steely grey eyes and a mocking smile; a man who thought she was a pain in the backside.

She sobered slightly and frowned. Well, she wasn't going for blasted Ward Frazer, she was going for his aunts. And of course Louise would be there as well, pretty, funny, sexy Louise, newly out of hospital and keen to spread her wings again.

Katy sighed. All she had to do was persuade Sister Morris to give her time off. Ward and Louise would organise the rest of the trip between them. She would just go along with what they wanted, a bright smile fixed to her mouth. And when they got there she would spend most of her time with Jen or Mrs Frost or the Miss Taylors. The perfect little chaperone who knew when to make herself scarce.

Closing her eyes wearily, Joyce leaned her head back against the corrugated side of the shelter. She could feel the condensation soaking into the collar of her shabby overcoat, but she didn't mind. All she wanted to do was rest her head for a moment and take advantage of being on her own.

Pete was out fire-watching on some new rota the ARP had set up. She didn't know where Stanley was. Or Mick. She frowned. Frankly she didn't care. All she knew was that for once she had the shelter to herself and she didn't have to listen to Stanley's complaints.

It wasn't her fault the shelter was uncomfortable. Anderson shelters hadn't been designed for comfort. She and Pete had done what they could with the sacking over the door and a few cushions and blankets and that, but it was never going to be the Ritz.

Anyway there weren't so many raids these days. Maybe because of the weather. She'd heard someone say that the fog and sleet made it more difficult for the pilots.

But they were coming through tonight. She'd already heard planes and the occasional crump of a distant explosion.

Lifting her head, she leaned forward suddenly and reached under the slatted bench for the bottle of Guinness Mr Lorenz had given her this morning. She'd been looking forward to it all day. Lifting it to her lips she closed her eyes and took a deep swallow and was about to take another when she heard footsteps in the yard.

Quickly she replaced the bottle under her seat and sat back again as Stanley lurched into the shelter, followed closely by Mick. They brought with them a draught of ice-cold air and a strong smell of alcohol. She could tell instantly that Stanley was very drunk and by the glazed look of him, Mick wasn't far behind.

Slumping down on the bench opposite, Stanley looked around belligerently. 'Where's our dinner?'

Joyce flinched. 'You wasn't here so I didn't bother.'

'You didn't bother?' He turned to Mick. 'Did you hear that? She said she didn't bother. And do you know why she didn't bother?'

Mick shook his head and Stanley leaned over and stabbed an unsteady finger in Joyce's shoulder, his voice slurred and angry. 'Because she was too busy chatting to her fancy man.' He sat back and looked at Mick. 'She can't be bothered with us. Her family. Oh no, she's far more interested in running down to the pawn shop every five minutes.'

Joyce felt Mick's eyes on her, wide with shock. Shock that quickly turned to condemnation as he realised what his father was implying.

But before she could speak, Stanley laughed sourly. 'Oh, it's not her fault, not really. She's only woman, you see. She don't know any better.' He belched and rubbed his stomach as his eyes hardened. 'No, it's his fault. That twisting little Jew's fault. He's doing it on purpose and he's making a laughing stock of me.'

Joyce shook her head. 'He's all right, Stanley. He doesn't mean no harm. He's not my fancy man.'

Stanley looked at her incredulously. 'No?'

Suddenly he leaned forward and grabbed the bottle of Guinness from under her seat. 'No?' he shouted again. 'Well, where did this come from, then?' But before anyone could answer he had hurled it at the end wall of the shelter where it shattered violently.

He looked at the liquid dripping down the corrugated iron for a moment then he turned calmly back to Joyce. 'Now go and get something for us to eat. Young Mick here has put in a hard day's work and he needs his dinner.'

For a while plans for Ward Frazer's trip to Bristol seemed to be progressing well. News came that the Miss Taylors had arrived safely at their cottage, Louise was recovering fast, and Sister Morris agreed to give Katy five days off at the beginning of February.

Even the war news was good. The British and Commonwealth forces were making considerable headway in the desert, Tobruk had been taken, bringing the total of Italian prisoners-of-war to over a hundred thousand.

The Americans had agreed to increase aid to Britain. And Mr Churchill, clearly pleased with developments, promised the world that Britain would not fail mankind 'at this turning point in our fortunes'.

Five days later, on the thirtieth of January, Louise fell down the cellar steps and although she wasn't badly damaged, her father decided it would be unwise for her to risk the journey to Bristol. 'It's a shame,' he said. 'But it's clear now that you're not up to it.'

A cold shiver ran up Louise's spine. 'I am up to it,' she said, trying hard to keep her voice level. 'I'm completely up to it.'

'The doctor says you must take things gently,' her mother chipped in. 'I know you're disappointed but in time you'll realise it's for the best.'

Louise glared at her. 'I will not realise any such thing,' she snapped. 'Because it's not for the best. There's no reason why I shouldn't go. No reason at all. Ward and Katy would help me.'

Celia nodded. 'I'm sure they would,' she said. 'But seriously, darling, is it really fair to ask them to? What with the bombing and everything it's a big responsibility to put on them.'

Louise felt her temper beginning to snap. 'You make me sound like some helpless cripple,' she said angrily, 'when actually I'm perfectly all right.' She threw back the covers suddenly and got out of bed. 'Look,' she hobbled a few painful paces, 'I can walk without crutches.' Reaching the wall she leaned against it gratefully and glared at her parents. 'You want to keep me as an invalid, don't you? You want me to be miserable. You don't want me to get better. To have fun again.' She was shouting now. Furious with her weak legs that even now were trembling beneath her. Furious that there were tears in her eyes.

'Of course we want you to get better,' her mother said placatingly, helping her back to bed. 'And there'll be plenty of other opportunities to have fun.'

'There won't be other opportunities. I want to go this time,' Louise sobbed. It just wasn't fair. She had looked forward to it for so long, worked so hard at her beastly physiotherapy to achieve it. And now it was being snatched from her grasp.

Ward was sympathetic.

'Louise, your mother just told me,' he said, coming into the drawing-room and leaning down to kiss her lightly hello. As he straightened up he touched her cheek gently with the backs of his fingers. 'What a damn shame.'

Louise looked up at him pitifully. 'Can't you persuade her to let me go?'

He spread his hands in faint surprise. 'She said it was the doctor's decision.'

Louise frowned. 'I hate that stupid doctor. He only says what they want to hear. 'She lowered her voice and glared towards the door. 'This fall business is just an excuse. They've never wanted me to go.'

Ward sat down next to her on the sofa. 'They're worried about you, sweetheart. It's not so surprising.'

As usual Louise felt her heart accelerate at his proximity. His knee was almost touching hers. Almost. If she moved a couple of inches it would be. She looked up again and met his grey eyes and her skin prickled. 'Can't we delay the trip?' she murmured. 'I think they'd let me go if it was a couple of weeks later.'

For a long moment as he held her eyes he didn't speak, then he shook his head and looked away. 'We can't.' He sounded genuinely regretful. 'I've got to do some work down there. That's how I've got the petrol. Because it's kind of official business. In any case my aunts are expecting us. And we're fixed to see Jennifer Carter's show,' he shrugged. 'And of course Katy has booked her time off now.'

Of course. Louise grimaced to herself. As though she cared two hoots about Katy Parsons' time off. The only thing she cared about was the thought of Ward and Katy alone in his car for hours on end. And she suddenly found she cared about that rather a lot. To her horror she felt tears prickling at her eyes and she turned her head away, hoping he wouldn't see.

But he did see. Not only did he see, he turned her gently to face him and wiped the tears off her cheeks. 'Don't cry,' he said. 'It's not the end of the world.'

For some reason that made her cry more and with a grimace of pity he drew her into his arms. 'I know you're disappointed,' he murmured into her hair. 'I know how much you want to be well again.'

Louise couldn't have stopped the tears now for love or money. That's not why I'm crying, she wanted to say. I'm crying because I wanted to come with you. I wanted to be with you. I'm in love with you. But she was crying too hard now to say anything. In any case she was enjoying his embrace too much to want to spoil it. She could feel the hard strength of his shoulders and each gasped intake of breath brought with it the warm, clean, masculine scent of his body. The last remnants of longing for Stefan Pininski departed rapidly as she felt Ward's arms tighten around her.

As she felt his fingers smoothing her hair she sighed deeply and moved sensuously against him, the tears finally abating as a more powerful emotion replaced her despair.

At once she felt him stiffen, felt the tension in his shoulders.

'Louise,' he muttered. His voice was low and husky and it sent shivers up her spine. And then he was easing her away from him.

She didn't want to show him her tear-stained face but she had to look up at him. There was a frown on his forehead and a strange expression in his grey eyes. Suddenly she knew he was going to kiss her.

But he didn't kiss her. Instead he swore under his breath and pulled back as he heard footsteps outside the door. Her mother bringing the tea. Before she was through the door, Ward was on his feet.

'Mrs Rutherford. Let me . . .' Courteously, calmly, for all the world as though nothing had happened, he took the tray and set it carefully on the occasional table. 'Mmm, homemade cake. How delicious. Can you still get eggs round here, then?'

It was exactly the right thing to say. Even as her frantic heartbeat subsided a fraction, Louise watched her mother preening with pride. And then she was off, explaining about her chickens, what marvellous layers they were.

Louise groaned inwardly as through a hazy glow, she watched Ward smiling and nodding, suddenly apparently as fascinated with chickens as her mother; she could hardly believe that only moments ago he had been on the verge of making love to her.

Because she was certain that was what would have happened. However hard he tried to hide it. There was no doubt about it. She could hardly wait for tea to be over.

But tea seemed to drag on interminably this afternoon. And to Louise's irritation her mother didn't leave them alone again.

But despite her disappointment, as Ward eventually took his farewell and kissed her chastely on the cheek, she felt a sudden rush of excitement. OK, so let him go away with dull little Katy Parsons. She didn't care. Because when he came back she would be waiting for him. And then she would give him what she knew he wanted.

Katy stared at her mother in disbelief. 'What do you mean Daddy won't let me go?'

Mary Parsons shrugged her thin shoulders as she carefully sliced a piece of bread off the loaf for Katy's supper. 'He says you're not to go. Not alone with that man. Not now that Louise Rutherford isn't going to be going.'

'But Daddy likes Ward Frazer,' Katy said in some desperation. Suddenly all the nervousness that had flooded through her when she heard that Louise had pulled out of the trip had vanished. Replaced by a rapidly mounting sense of frustration. 'And it's not as if we're going away together. He's taking me to visit the

Miss Taylors, for goodness' sake. What could be more respectable than that?'

But her mother was implacable. 'It's your father's decision,' she said.

Katy felt like shaking her. If only for once she would think for herself. Take a decision that hadn't already been decided by her father.

'But why?' Katy asked helplessly.

Mary Parsons looked up from buttering the bread. 'He says you're too young to go jaunting off on your own with a man. He says people will talk.'

Katy felt a jolt of pure anger. 'That's ridiculous,' she said. 'I'm nearly nineteen years old. Anyway, what people?'

'People in the street, of course.' Her mother frowned. 'What would they think you driving off all alone with a handsome man like that? They say he's quite one for the ladies. We've got your reputation to think of.'

'What reputation?' Katy said crossly. But she could see it was hopeless. Her parents were worried about appearances. They were worried full stop. They always had been.

And once again she was paying the price.

And then to everyone's astonishment, out of the blue Mrs Rutherford persuaded Joyce Carter to go with them. She needed a break apparently and this was the ideal opportunity.

It seemed the perfect solution. Katy got a chaperone for the journey and as soon as she had been safely delivered to the Miss Taylors, Joyce would travel on to Devon to see her two younger children at the farm they had been evacuated to at the beginning of the war. Everyone was delighted with the arrangement except Louise.

'Poor old Ward,' she laughed sourly when Katy called in that evening. 'He thought he was taking me away for a romantic few days and now he's lumbered with ghastly Mrs Carter.'

'And with me,' Katy said. Poor old Ward indeed. Her heart bled for him.

'Oh, he likes you,' Louise said lightly. 'He thinks you're sweet.'

★   ★   ★

But Ward didn't show much sign of thinking she was sweet when they set off in the pouring rain at nine o'clock on Saturday morning.

'Who's going to sit in the front?' he asked briskly as he loaded Katy's small suitcase into the boot. He had already installed the small box tied with string, which was the best Joyce could muster, on the back seat alongside two unexplained taped boxes of his own.

'I think you'd better go in the front, Mrs Carter,' Katy said hastily. She felt bad enough about being foisted on Ward for the trip without having to make conversation to him the whole way. And if they stood about much longer they'd all be soaked to the skin. Quickly she hugged her mother who was standing there fussing endlessly that she had her warm underwear and enough cough medicine with her, and climbed thankfully into the back of the small car.

Two minutes later they were under way.

As they worked their way through London towards the Great West Road, Ward tried to engage Joyce in conversation. But Joyce's answers were curt and uninformative and Katy, embarrassed for her and for Ward, wished they had never set off on this awful journey.

She was horribly aware that the wrong people were in the car. Ward had wanted Louise and now, due to Mrs Rutherford's interference, he was stuck not only with Katy but with surly old Mrs Carter as well.

But Ward, apparently unperturbed by Joyce's monosyllabic answers, persevered. At first, when his efforts met with little success, he tried to include Katy with the odd comment over his shoulder. But gradually, amazingly, Joyce began to unbend, and Katy soon found herself left in peace to lean back and stare out of the window.

It wasn't long before wet grey London gave way to green, water-logged fields and moody skies but as they drove on west on the A4 through Maidenhead and Slough, gradually the rain stopped. The clouds lifted, and just beyond Reading some thin shafts of sunlight burst through, touching the surrounding countryside with silver and making Ward and Joyce in the front squint as the wet road reflected the bright morning light.

They were chatting like old friends now and Katy leaned forward curiously to hear what it was that was making Joyce so unusually animated. To her astonishment she found they were talking about hens.

'There's this particular one,' Joyce was saying. 'Mrs Rutherford calls her the rogue hen. Which really knows what's what. She's very partial to porridge. She'll do anything for porridge. But not if a man offers it to her. She won't touch it then. She hates men.'

Ward laughed. 'Perhaps she had a bad experience as a chick.' As he spoke he glanced up and caught Katy's eye in the mirror. For a second his smile widened and then his eyes went back on the road and he was asking Joyce whether Louise had ever had anything to do with the hens.

Quickly, before she could get involved, Katy sat back in her seat. It wasn't hens he was interested in, it was the Rutherfords. And Louise Rutherford in particular.

As Joyce snorted and made some derogatory remark about Louise, Katy found herself watching his reaction. But he seemed more amused than put out. She wished she could see more of his expression. But from her position in the back of the car at best she only got a side view of his face and then only when he occasionally smiled over at Joyce. Even then she only glimpsed the curve of his mouth, the high cheekbones and the crinkles at the side of his eyes.

She could see the back of his head of course, the dark hair, slightly longer than average, cut in fashionably at the nape of his neck. His hair was thick and strong and she guessed his beard would be too if he grew one. She could already see the faint shading of new growth on his jaw. But behind his ear, running down to the top of his collar, was a small expanse of skin that looked smooth and soft. Suddenly she longed to touch that little area. To run her fingertips over it up into his hair.

Abruptly she crossed her arms and turned to stare out of the window again. What was she thinking of? She glanced at her watch. They'd only been on the road two hours. At this rate she'd be craving mad passionate sex with him by the time they arrived in Bristol. To her horror she felt herself blushing and leaned even further towards the window in case Ward caught sight of her in his mirror. Unfortunately in her haste she bumped her nose on the glass.

'Are you OK, Katy?' She felt the small car swerve slightly as he glanced over his shoulder.

'Yes, I'm fine,' she said quickly.

'Not feeling sick?'

'No.' She shook her head violently.

He glanced at his watch. 'Well, I think we'll have a pause in the next town we come to. We've been going a while now.'

A couple of miles later they came into Hungerford and he turned up the wide main street and stopped to let them stretch their legs.

Joyce spotted a public lavatory and hurried off, but Ward held Katy back as she went to follow her.

'What's the matter?' He was looking at her closely.

'Nothing,' Katy said. 'Why?'

'You seem quiet.'

'I'm fine, honestly.' She glared at him. What was this, the Spanish Inquisition?

'Not having second thoughts?'

'What about?'

'About coming on the trip?'

The question was unexpected. She looked at him in surprise. 'No, of course not. Why do you ask that?'

He shrugged slightly and put his hands in his pockets. 'You always gave me the impression you were pretty lukewarm about it.'

'Lukewarm?' Katy gaped at him. 'I wasn't a bit lukewarm. I was desperate to come. I could hardly wait to get away from that beastly hospital. And I've never been to Bristol.' She frowned. 'I've never really been anywhere. And I've been looking forward to spending time with your aunts and Mrs Frost, and I'm dying to see Jen.'

As she stopped and looked up at him eagerly, desperate for him to believe her, something in his expression alerted her to the fact that she perhaps hadn't been a hundred per cent tactful. 'Oh,' she added quickly. 'And I was looking forward to . . . to the journey of course.'

He inclined his head. 'Of course,' he said gravely.

'It's such a shame about Louise, but I'm really glad Mrs Carter could come,' Katy went on hastily. 'Because Daddy would never have let me come on my own.'

Ward smiled. 'So Mrs Rutherford said. But why not? What exactly did your father imagine was going to happen?' he asked, laughing. 'That I'd stop in the first lay-by and leap on you, crazy with lust?'

Katy could feel the heat in her cheeks and prayed he was laughing too much to notice. She tried to smile back but inside she felt more piqued than amused. He needn't make it sound quite so utterly and entirely unlikely.

Eventually Ward managed to control his mirth. He grinned at her and raised his eyebrows. 'Well, hopefully Mrs Carter will make a satisfactory chaperone.'

'I'm sure she will,' Katy said crossly.

Back in London, Alan Nelson was worried about Mick Carter.

Pam sighed. She had about a hundred things far more important to worry about than Mick Carter. She had never much liked the boy at the best of times, although admittedly he had improved in the time they had had him to stay last summer when Joyce refused to have him in her house. Alan had taken him in hand, got him the job on the dray at the brewery, lent him his bicycle and found some sort of role for him with the Home Guard even though he was still under age.

'What's the matter with him?' she asked. For a while after he had gone back to live at home he had called in occasionally for tea, but now she thought about it she hadn't seen him in ages. Certainly not since they'd had Bertie staying.

Alan reached over for the teapot and grimaced slightly when a virtually colourless liquid came out. 'He's stopped coming to the Home Guard,' he said.

Pam shrugged. 'Does that matter so much? I know you put your head on the line and everything to get him in but I can't really believe he's much loss.'

Alan set his cup on the table. 'It wouldn't matter too much if I was sure he didn't still have one of the weapons.'

'A gun?' Pam nearly choked on her tea. 'Oh my God.' Then she frowned. 'What do you mean you're not sure? Surely he's either got one or he hasn't. Haven't you asked him?'

Alan made a face. 'Well, he says he hasn't . . .'

Pam groaned. 'But you don't believe him?'

Alan shrugged. 'I didn't get a chance to talk to him properly. Stanley Carter was there in the background. To be honest I didn't feel awfully welcome.' He sighed. 'I should have asked him at the brewery I suppose, but you never know who might overhear, and if he's innocent I don't want to cause him unnecessary trouble.'

'Of course he's not innocent,' Pam said crossly. 'He's a thoroughly bad lot and if he's back under the influence of that awful father of his, he'll be even worse. I expect Stanley Carter put him up to it. He's probably planning some armed robbery or something. I can't believe anyone was stupid enough to let an adolescent misfit like Mick Carter get his hands on a gun in the first place.'

Alan groaned. 'Don't be angry, Pam. It wasn't my fault. I wasn't even there. It was an exercise on Streatham Common several weeks ago. All I know was that it was a bit of a shambles and in the dark the weapons must have been miscounted.' He tried to smile. 'It may still turn up. And there are plenty of other people who might have taken it. And I can hardly march in and search the Carters' house.'

Pam snorted. 'It wouldn't be the first time they've been searched.'

'Nothing has ever been found,' Alan said reasonably.

'So that means they are innocent?' Pam stared at her husband incredulously. 'Oh come on, Alan. Don't be naive. I know you like to believe the best in people but sometimes I think you go around with your eyes shut. You'll be telling me next you haven't noticed Bertie bloody Rutherford making eyes at Sheila whenever he thinks we're not looking.'

Alan looked surprised. 'I thought you'd be pleased that they are getting on.'

'I think we are talking rather more than just getting on. She's falling for him, Alan, why do you think she's stayed on so long? If the bombing keeps off a bit I honestly wouldn't be surprised if she doesn't suddenly decide to open up her house again. And think what might happen then. That little bastard would have carte blanche.'

'Oh, he's not that bad,' Alan said.

Pam glared at him. 'Can't you see, Alan? He only wants one thing. And he'll drop her flat once he's got it. I don't think Sheila can take many more knocks.' She shook her head crossly. 'Perhaps we could persuade Mick Carter to use that gun on Bertie. At least that would get rid of one of our problems.'

Even as she said the words she regretted them. Because they both knew what the real problem was. Alan's proposed visit to the Wilhelmina. They hadn't talked about it since before Christmas. She hadn't wanted to press him and he hadn't mentioned it. But they were well into January already and Pam was getting impatient. She wanted to know, once and for all, whether they should keep trying to conceive or whether to give up hope. That was why she was so irritable.

'Don't worry,' he said now. 'I've arranged to see the doctor next week.' He tried to smile. 'If the worst comes to the worst I can always get that gun off Mick Carter and use it on myself.'

Chapter Thirteen

Joyce was astonished to see how good Jen was in her show. It was a dreadful place she was singing in, a huge factory canteen down by the Bristol docks with trestle tables and the air so thick with smoke that from the back, where they were sitting, you could hardly see the stage.

But you could see Jen all right in her slinky aquamarine concert dress, and you could hear her too, which was more than could be said for the other girl singer in the show whose low notes disappeared completely in the scraping of chairs, the clearing of throats and the occasional clatter of plates from the kitchen behind them. But Jen was loud and clear and she made the audience laugh too in her comedy number and for the first time Joyce felt a small grudging respect for her daughter.

Losing concentration during the conjuring act, Joyce smoothed the soft material of her skirt over her thighs. She was wearing the outfit Jen had given her for Christmas. She'd bought it back off Lorenz yesterday afternoon with part of the money Mrs Rutherford had lent her. It would go straight back in hock when she got home of course. But she wanted to look nice for Angie and Paul when she travelled on down to Devon tomorrow and she didn't want to feel a complete drab this evening.

She just wished she had something better to wear over it, her old coat let the side down. Particularly as the Miss Taylors had arrived at the factory in smart if rather moth-eaten fur stoles. They'd had their hair done for the occasion too.

Glancing past them along the row, Joyce's restless gaze stopped on Katy Parsons. Katy didn't seem to be particularly absorbed by the conjuror either, although she was pretending to be. But her smiles were a bit late coming. Her mind was obviously somewhere else. Joyce wondered where. Not that she was likely to find out even if she asked. Katy was a quiet little thing at the best of times but she had hardly said a word all day. And now she looked pale and tired after the long journey. She had always been sickly of course. As a child Jen had often complained about Katy being allowed to go home from school early. It was a miracle that she stood up to that nursing she did, Joyce thought. Looking at her now you wouldn't think she'd last five minutes.

Next to Katy was Mrs Frost, looking distinguished in a tasselled silk shawl and at the end of the row was Ward Frazer, leaning forward, his elbows on the table in front of them, squinting through the haze in an attempt to see the conjuror's tricks.

Joyce smiled to herself. Now he was a looker and no mistake. Ten times nicer than that Irish boy, Sean, who Jen had played around with last year. And Sean Byrne hadn't been bad looking himself, even if he had turned out to be IRA. But Ward Frazer was a different kettle of fish. Called a spade a spade. No airs and graces. Charming though, Joyce acknowledged. You had to give him that. She'd got quite flustered herself once or twice when he smiled at her in that steady way he had.

And he had nice hands and all. Competent hands. Long strong fingers. She had noticed them on the steering wheel, those hands, and she could see them now, linked casually at the fingers as they rested on the table.

Katy coughed suddenly and Joyce saw Ward glance along the row in concern. Catching an almost tender look in his eyes, Joyce blinked in surprise. Goodness. Was that the way the land lay then? She stared in amazement. And to think she'd begun to wonder if he might be interested in Jen. Certainly she hoped he wasn't interested in that selfish little madam Louise Rutherford.

Easing forward on her seat for a better look at him, Joyce was disconcerted to find herself meeting his quizzical gaze. And then suddenly the applause broke out and he was clapping and cheering along with the rest of them.

The applause was strong for Jen. She took her curtsy with her pianist. She was smiling, but when the pianist wanted to stay on stage too long, the smile became a little forced and by the time they stepped back into the wings, it was positively rigid.

'Bloody man,' she fumed as they clustered round her afterwards. She had barely waited for their congratulations before launching into a scathing attack on her accompanist. 'He thinks he's got stage presence but honestly he has no idea.' She glanced at Mrs Frost for sympathy. 'He seems to want to stand there grinning like a bloody chimpanzee until the clapping has stopped completely and everyone has gone home. It makes me look a complete idiot. And did you notice how he slowed right up in the Nightingale number?'

Mrs Frost nodded. 'Have you asked him why he does that?'

'He says it keeps me on my toes,' Jen snarled. 'But if he does it again I'll bloody flatten him and he'll find my toes rammed so far down his throat that he chokes on them.'

As Joyce hadn't noticed anything amiss, it seemed to her that Jen was making a fuss about nothing. As usual. 'I thought he looked a nice enough fellow,' she said.

Jen turned on her furiously. 'Oh did you? But then you're not exactly the most experienced theatregoer in the whole world, are you?'

Suddenly Joyce remembered how intensely irritating she found Jen. And now Jen thought she was a prima donna she was even worse.

She was gritting her teeth ready to have a go at Jen, when Ward intervened, suggesting smoothly they all get a bit of fresh air before the next run through.

Katy looked eager but the Miss Taylors and Mrs Frost were more keen to reserve a table closer to the front for the next show.

'Mrs Carter?' Ward glanced at her questioningly. 'What about you? Do you want to take a stroll outside?'

'No. I'm all right here,' she said hastily, glancing from him to Katy and back again. To be honest she wouldn't have minded a breath of fresh air, she was dreading having to sit through the whole damn thing again, but she didn't want to get in his way.

His brows rose slightly. 'Sure?' He was smiling. Suddenly she realised he was amused and she wondered if maybe she had got the wrong end of the stick completely.

It was cold outside. The clouds were low. A stiff wind was blowing up the Avon Gorge from the Severn Estuary and even though it was only five o'clock it was already beginning to get dark.

As Ward and Katy passed through the factory gates, a plane flew low overhead. Katy flinched and Ward smiled. 'It's OK, it's one of ours.'

Feeling stupid as they turned up the road in silence, she frowned. 'I'm sorry, I didn't mean to drag you away.'

He put his hands in his pockets and hunched his shoulders against the wind. 'I seem to recall I made the suggestion.'

'Only because I was coughing.'

He didn't deny it. 'It was smoky in there,' he said mildly. 'I could hardly breathe myself.'

Katy nodded but she knew he was just being kind. Certainly he didn't seem to be having problems breathing now. Whereas she could feel an ominous tightness in her lungs. Cigarette smoke often did that to her, and tiredness, but tonight she had a nasty feeling it was tension that had contributed to it. Tension caused by Ward being nice.

Not just to her. She had watched him being nice to the Miss Taylors, to Mrs Carter, to Mrs Frost and of course to Jen. Nevertheless he had been nice to her too and once or twice since they had arrived at the factory, she had felt his eyes on her. She hadn't dared look back but her muscles had tightened each time and her breathing had suffered.

Now as they started to climb the hill towards the city centre she realised that she was worse than she thought. She raised her head to look up the steep road ahead and knew she wasn't going to make it. Stopping abruptly, she turned as though to look back over the bomb-damaged docks, but she couldn't disguise her short, wheezing breaths and Ward looked at her in concern.

'Katy? Are you OK?'

No, she wasn't OK. But there was no way she could say so. It had come on so quickly. Suddenly it was as much as she could do to breathe at all, let alone speak. Leaning forward with her hands on her thighs, desperately trying to drag some air into her lungs, more than anything, more than her sudden fear, more than the tight constricting pain across her chest, she felt an excruciating embarrassment that Ward Frazer, of all people, should witness her first real asthma attack in over a year.

As she scrabbled in her bag for her medicine, it was a moment before she realised he was crouching beside her. He waited until she had swigged some back, then took the bottle from her and glanced at the label. 'Katy, listen to me. Put your arms round my neck. I'm going to pick you up.'

She tried to cough. She was desperate to cough, desperate to clear the obstruction from her lungs, but she knew it was hopeless. She couldn't get enough air in to cough it out. The cold Bristol air suddenly seemed thin and unsustaining, she longed to be back in London with her mother to look after her, to make her lie down, to bring her steaming water, and if necessary the doctor.

She managed to shake her head. 'Honestly,' she gasped between frightened breaths. 'I'm all right.'

'For God's sake don't be so bloody British,' he said, scooping her off her feet anyway. 'You're far from all right. And this cold wind isn't helping.'

'I'm too heavy,' she muttered. She wanted to struggle but she simply didn't have the energy.

His brisk stride didn't falter. 'Sure you are,' he said. 'I guess it's lucky I've been doing some fitness training.' He glanced down at her as he said it and smiled. She knew he was trying to humour her, to take her mind off her breathing, to make her relax.

She tried to smile back but she couldn't relax. There seemed to be a band of steel round her chest and it was getting tighter by the moment. She longed for the ephedrine to take effect. Even as she gasped for air she prayed she wouldn't black out. It really was frightening when that happened and she didn't know if Ward would know what to do.

An even nastier thought occurred to her. 'I don't want to go back to the factory.' The thought of that smoky canteen filled her with dread. But even as she gasped out the words, she realised they were going uphill, steeply uphill, and despite his joke, Ward was in fact beginning to breathe harder.

He shook his head. 'I know somewhere better,' he said, turning off through a small park. 'Closer.' He hesitated a moment as though deciding the best route then strode on again. 'There's a girl there. She'll look after you.'

A minute later, panting after another steep climb, he stopped outside a tall terraced house and raised a knee to prop Katy up while he hammered on the door.

When there was no response he swore softly under his breath and knocked again, four hard thumps.

A moment later a woman's voice called from inside. 'Who is it?'

Ward glanced quickly up and down the steep, deserted street. 'It's Ward,' he said.

'Are you sure?'

Ward groaned. 'Of course I'm sure.'

The voice giggled. 'Can you prove it?'

Ward had clearly had enough. 'For God's sake, Helen,' he muttered impatiently. 'Stop being so security conscious and let us in.'

'Us?' The door swung open and Katy found herself staring at a classy-looking girl dressed in navy slacks and a chic white sweater. Helen, presumably.

As she took in Katy's condition, the girl's welcoming smile was quickly replaced by an anxious frown. She stepped back quickly to let them in and closed the door behind them. 'What's happened? Has there been a raid? I didn't hear anything.'

Ward shook his head. 'Asthma attack,' he said succinctly. He glanced at the closed door to his right. 'OK to go in here?'

Helen nodded. 'The boys are upstairs.'

Katy felt Ward's quick glance. 'Good. Keep them there. And put some kettles on, Helen, could you? She's had some medicine but a steam inhalation might help. I just wish we had some oxygen.'

To Katy's distracted gaze, the front room seemed rather bleak and unlived in, but she was far too glad to be out of the cold wind to complain about the decor. As Ward deposited her gently on a grey sofa she tried to get enough breath together to apologise. But he shook his head as she rasped and wheezed.

'Don't try and talk. Just lean back and relax. Shut your eyes and try to breathe as slowly and calmly as you can. I'll be back in one minute.'

It was easier said than done, but obediently Katy did as she was told. She knew he was right. She knew from experience that if she could only think about something other than her constricted lungs, sometimes her breathing got easier. She wondered how he knew. But more than anything she wondered about their hostess, the well-spoken Helen. Who was she? And why had Ward never mentioned that he had a friend living in Bristol. A friend?

Katy opened her eyes to cough. Was that all this elegant stranger was? She certainly treated Ward with an enviable familiarity. Katy could hear them now, talking in some distant kitchen.

'Who is she?' the Helen girl was asking curiously. 'Do you know her?'

And Ward's crisp response. 'Of course I know her. She's the girl who travelled down with me. Katy Parsons.'

Helen seemed surprised. 'I thought you were bringing Louise.'

'She wasn't well enough to come in the end.'

'Oh, what a pity.' She sounded disappointed, but Ward's voice was brisk.

'I know. It's a shame. But I couldn't have let Louise come here anyway.'

Katy sensed Helen's smile, 'I'm surprised you've let this Katy person come here,' she said.

Struggling for breath, Katy strained to hear Ward's response. 'It was an emergency. Anyway. Katy doesn't matter. You don't need to worry about her.'

Katy's sudden choking cough drowned out the rest. But she had heard enough in any case. Too much in fact. It seemed quite clear that Ward Frazer was having a secret affair with the glamorous Helen, who by the sound of it was a friend of Louise's.

Katy felt sick. He must have met her while he'd been dating Louise last year and had since installed her in this horrid little house. No wonder he had been so keen to come to Bristol. Business, he had said.

It was odd, Katy thought. Ward had only left her alone for about thirty seconds, a minute at the most, and in that short time all her illusions about him had been shattered.

She coughed again, suddenly hating Ward Frazer with an unaccustomed violence and the band of steel tightened round her chest.

When he came in a second later, she could hardly bring herself to look at him. But she nodded when he crouched in front of her and asked if she was all right.

'As soon as the kettle's boiled we'll try the steam,' he said. 'And if that doesn't help I'll try and find a doctor and some oxygen.'

Then he had gone again and she heard him outside talking to Helen. 'Why the hell doesn't that kettle boil?' And then more softly, 'I'll just nip up and check on the boys.'

The boys? Who could they be, Katy wondered? Children presumably. A cold sweat broke out on her skin as she frowned in concentration. Could it be worse than she thought? Could Ward and Helen be the proud parents of two bouncing boys?

Even in her fuddled state she realised it was unlikely. As far as she knew Ward had only arrived in England eighteen months ago. He would have had to be an awfully quick worker to have produced two children in that time.

Deciding she no longer had the energy to worry about it, Katy closed her eyes again. For once the ephedrine didn't seem to be working and the effect of dragging air into her lungs was exhausting her.

The last thing she heard was Helen's frantic shout. A shout that in normal circumstances would have woken the dead. 'Ward! Quick! I think she's stopped breathing.'

Jen folded her dress carefully and slipped the protective bag over it. 'What do you mean they've disappeared?'

Joyce shrugged helplessly. 'Well, they went out for some fresh air and that's the last we've seen of them.'

Jen swung round and stared at her mother in disbelief. 'But I've done another whole show since then.' She frowned in irritation. 'They must have come in late and been sitting at the back or something.'

She'd been annoyed when her mother came barging into the office she'd been allocated to change in. Now she was annoyed that Ward and Katy had clearly missed the second show. She felt a sudden stab of anxiety that they had found it too excruciating to sit through twice. Then she remembered the enthusiastic applause and felt better.

'They're probably canoodling down on the docks somewhere,' she said carelessly.

Joyce turned her head sharply. 'Do you think so?'

Jen rolled her eyes. 'Of course I don't think so. I was joking.' She groaned inwardly. Sometimes her mother was unbelievably slow. She was about to turn away. But something in her mother's expression made her stop. Surely she didn't think . . .

'Why?' Jen asked suspiciously, suddenly remembering her conversation with Katy before Christmas. 'Do you think that's what they're doing?'

Joyce shifted uneasily. 'Well, I'm not sure.'

Jen stared at her incredulously for a second then she burst out laughing. 'Oh, come off it, Mum. Even if Ward Frazer did have a taste for a bit of how's your father with Katy, he wouldn't be so desperate he had to knock her off down by the docks on an arctic February evening, would he?'

'Don't be crude,' Joyce snapped. Jen laughed but her mother was really angry. 'She's a nice little thing, that Katy Parsons, and if he is interested, I won't have you spoiling it for her.'

Jen raised her eyebrows. 'What? Like you spoiled it for me with Sean Byrne, you mean?'

'I didn't spoil anything with Sean Byrne,' Joyce said sharply. 'If there was anything to spoil, you spoiled it by making a fool of yourself. You let him lead you up the garden path. Let him treat you like a slut. And then you were surprised when he buggered off.'

'He did not treat me like a slut.' Jen's eyes narrowed dangerously. Even now it caused her some pain to think of Sean. Quite often recently, when whiling the time away in lonely digs or on windswept railway stations, she wished she had gone back to Ireland with him. But then she wouldn't have got her career off the ground. Not that a two pound a week tour round munitions factories canteens was exactly the big time. But it was a start and a start was what she had so dearly wanted. A chance to break free. Not that her mother would ever understand that, stuck in her miserable little life in Clapham. Even in the outfit she had given her for Christmas she somehow managed to look drab and downtrodden.

Jen shook her head. 'Anyway, you're hardly one to talk,' she added scornfully. 'Dad doesn't exactly treat you like a lady, does he?' She saw the sudden flash of pain on her mother's face and felt a stab of guilt. 'Oh, forget it,' she said irritably. 'Forget I ever spoke.' She picked up her bag. 'Let's go and find the others. Ward and Katy may have turned up by now.' At the door she stopped and picked a thread fastidiously off her sleeve. 'I just can't understand why you put up with it, that's all,' she said. 'If it was me I'd either kill him or leave him.'

'Come on, Katy, keep breathing,' Ward urged her from the other side of the towel. 'You can do it. In, one . . . two . . . three. Slower. That's it. Now, out, one . . . two . . . three. Good. Again. In . . .'

Inside her little towel tent, Katy stared blindly into the steaming saucepan and felt the pores on her face opening even as the hot wet air eased its way into her lungs.

Under Ward's insistent command she'd been doing five minutes under the towel and two minutes out. Each time now it was becoming fractionally easier to inhale. But increasingly she was beginning to dread the moment when he allowed her to stop. Because then she was going to have to face him. Not only him, but the glamorous Helen too.

But when she finally surfaced, red faced and sweating, but breathing almost normally again, it seemed that Ward was intending leaving her to rest.

'You're over the worst,' he said as he offered her the towel to wipe her face. 'Thank God.' He stood up and flexed his shoulders. 'I'm going to give you another dose of medicine and leave you in peace. I don't know about you, but I'm exhausted.' He grinned. 'I never realised this breathing business was such hard work.'

Somehow Katy couldn't quite bring herself to grin back. Smiling wasn't easy when your heart had been severed by a sharp knife with 'Helen and the boys' expensively engraved on the handle. Instead she buried her face in the towel hoping he would think she was sweating so hard she needed more than a quick rub to sop it all up. Anything was better than letting him see the tears that had suddenly sprang into her eyes.

'Katy? Are you OK?'

She made a supreme effort and looked up. He was watching her with a slightly puzzled look in his grey eyes.

Quickly she looked back at the towel. 'Yes. I'm better now. Thank you.' It sounded flat even to her ears, but it seemed to satisfy him.

After a moment he lifted her feet on to the chair he'd been sitting on. 'Sleep if you can but stay sitting up. It's better for the lungs. I'll get Helen to bring you some blankets and a cup of tea, then I guess I'd better run down to tell my aunts what's happened. The second show will be over by now and they'll be wondering where the hell we've got to.'

It seemed a long time later that Katy next opened her eyes and, to her astonishment, she found herself looking at a thin, wiry-looking man with bright eyes, curly dark hair and an enormous bushy moustache. He looked almost as startled as her. But he recovered quickly and smiled, exposing rather prominent front teeth. 'Mademoiselle.' He bowed slightly. '*Je m'excuse* . . .' A stream of rapid words followed ending in a question and another wide smile.

Bemused, Katy found herself smiling back, but before she could muster enough of her schoolgirl French to explain that she didn't understand a word he was saying, Helen had burst into the room carrying a cup of tea.

She too had suddenly started speaking French. French so fast and fluent that the only word that Katy could understand was '*malade*'. Sick.

Katy blinked. Was she so sick that they had somehow transported her to France without her knowing?

Or was the more likely explanation that Helen had some Frenchman staying with her?

Or two? Already she could hear another voice, a deeper voice outside the room. But, before the second Frenchman could come in, Helen had herded the first one out and shut the door behind him.

'*Merde*,' she muttered under her breath, leaning on the door for a second. Then she turned to Katy, looking flustered.

'I'm so sorry,' she said, suddenly completely English again and plummy with it. She brushed her hands and smiled brightly as though the interruption had never happened. 'Now. How are you feeling? Are you warm enough? Do you need a blanket?'

Katy stared at her. 'Who were those men?'

'Those men?' Helen looked surprised at the question. For a second Katy thought she was going to deny their existence even though they could still be heard muttering to each other outside the door, but then Helen shrugged. 'Pierre and Jean-Luc? Oh, they're just friends.' She was trying to speak lightly, but when she saw Katy's expression she grimaced. 'You don't believe that, do you?' She groaned. 'Damn. Ward's going to kill me. Even though it's his fault for telling them you were here. They never would have come down otherwise.'

It began to occur to Katy that things in this house weren't perhaps quite as she had thought. On the other hand it felt increasingly as though she had stumbled unwittingly into a scene from Alice in Wonderland.

Helen perched on the arm of a chair. 'I think you're aware of what Ward does,' she began tentatively. 'His job, I mean? You know it involves a certain amount of, um . . . secrecy?'

Katy nodded. Yes. Any minute now the Mad Hatter would march in and offer her another cup of tea. 'Those men,' she began tentatively. 'They're what you call the boys, aren't they?'

Helen looked startled. 'You know about the boys?'

'I heard you talk about them,' Katy said. 'But I thought they were your children.'

Helen frowned. 'Mine?'

Katy nodded. 'Yours and Ward's.'

Helen's eyes widened. Then she started laughing. 'Ward and I are colleagues,' she said. 'Not lovers.'

★　★　★

When Ward walked in a few minutes later, fresh from sorting out the Miss Taylors, he was equally amused by Katy's misconception.

'I'm sorry,' he said. 'I should have explained. I guess I was more concerned with keeping you alive.'

While Katy sipped her tea, he explained that he had met Lady Helen de Burrel, as she unnervingly turned out to be, at the same party where he had met Louise. And discovering later that she spoke perfect French and German, had eventually co-opted her to join his department in the War Office.

'Only on the administrative side,' Helen said quickly. 'I leave all the nasty foreign stuff to chaps like Ward.'

Ward made a face. 'Not for much longer. It's getting too difficult for us to get in and out.' He shrugged and glanced at Katy. 'Increasingly we are trying to train up locals. Get them set up with equipment and expertise. That's what Pierre and Jean-Luc are doing here. But obviously it's not something we want to advertise. We don't want the Germans finding out who we've got here and when they're going back.'

Katy tried to stifle a shiver. Helen de Burrel's smiling reference to 'nasty foreign stuff' gave her the creeps, but she was feeling stupid enough already without betraying her chilling anxiety to these two hard-nosed professionals.

'And those boxes in the car,' she said suddenly. 'I suppose I was dozing against a couple of dozen grenades or something?'

Ward had the grace to look apologetic. 'Only a couple of hand-guns,' he said, 'a bit of ammunition, a few wireless parts and some forging equipment.' He smiled. 'Nothing dangerous.'

Helen chuckled. 'I get the feeling from Katy's expression that you and she have a slightly different definition of the term dangerous,' she said. She stood up. 'I think I'd better go and make us all another cup of tea.'

Ward groaned. 'Not tea again. Haven't we got any coffee?'

Helen raised her shoulders. 'Only that disgusting chicory stuff that you hate.'

As she went out Ward leaned back in his chair and grinned at Katy, 'One of the nice things about going over to France occasionally is that they still have decent coffee.'

Katy gaped at him. 'Oh that's great,' she said sarcastically. 'First of all you make me sit next to some deadly weapons all the way from London, then you bring me to some top secret hideout, make me believe I'm being entertained by your common law wife, and now you tell me that the only reason you regularly risk your life on absurd heroic missions to enemy-held territory is because you like the blasted coffee.'

Ward was laughing before she had even finished this tirade. Suddenly he leaned forward. 'Seriously,' he said. 'Is that why you've been acting so weird since we've been here? Because you thought Helen and I . . .?'

He stopped and grinned. 'Now let's just get this straight. Was it the living in sin bit you didn't like? Or the fact that it was me?'

Katy had been asking herself the same question for the last ten minutes but that hadn't made it any easier to answer.

Now, staring into those watchful grey eyes, as the breath caught in her throat, she realised she knew the answer only too well. She had known it all along if she had only admitted it. It wasn't her illusions that had been shattered by the unexpected appearance of Helen de Burrel, but her secret, ridiculous hopes.

Quickly she tried to laugh off his question by claiming that she hadn't been able to breathe, let alone talk. But even as she said it she felt a sense of dismay flooding through her entire body.

Somehow, against her better judgement, against any realistic chance of a response, let alone of future happiness, she had contrived to fall in love with Ward Frazer.

Chapter Fourteen

The train was crowded. Joyce was glad she had let Ward help her find her a seat. She would never have had the gall to barge all through the gaggles of soldiers blocking the passage with their kit bags and helmets and hobnailed boots. They were in the carriages too but one look from Ward had got some young private leaping to his feet and offering his hard won window seat to Joyce. Having stowed her boxes on the luggage rack and made sure she had everything she needed, Ward had retreated from the train and then stood on the platform outside her window to wave her off.

As the train pulled out, Joyce waved rather self-consciously back then settled in her seat with a sigh. Thank God they'd made it.

Even if it had been a bit of a rush. Ward had said he'd bring Katy over to the Miss Taylors' when he came to fetch Joyce to take her to the train and pick up Jen from her digs on the way. But needless to say Jen hadn't been ready, and by the time they'd finally arrived, with Jen irritatingly unrepentant, Joyce had been certain she was going to miss the train.

Now she opened the packet the Miss Taylors had handed her as Ward bundled her into the car and found two rounds of sandwiches, four biscuits and an apple. She shook her head, touched, and looked quickly out of the window in case anyone in the carriage saw the tears in her eyes.

They were funny old birds those Miss Taylors. She hadn't known what to say to them at first last night when she'd had to go back to their little cottage with them in the taxi because of Katy Parsons being ill. Then over a cup of tea they'd got on to the subject of Lavender Road and quite soon they started to have a good old go about Mr Rutherford. It turned out they hated his guts just as much as she did. They thought it was shocking the way he'd thrown the boy out without a bean. Everyone was entitled to their opinion, they reckoned, even if he was an objector.

They'd had a good old gripe about Miss fancy-pants Louise too. Thought she was a right stuck-up little madam. Joyce had agreed readily with that one, but she'd had to put her foot down when they started on Mrs Rutherford.

She was pleased now that she'd stood up for her employer even though it would have been easier to agree. But it was only fair. Mrs Rutherford wasn't a bad sort, even if she was married to that bastard. She meant well. After all, it was her who had suggested she came away. And she'd lent her the money to do it and all.

All in all it was a long time since she'd enjoyed an evening so much. They'd had a sherry before supper and even that sour faced woman Mrs Frost had got a smile on her after that.

And the food had been tasty as well. Joyce felt her stomach rumble embarrassingly at the thought of it. She could hardly remember when she'd last had lamb chops. And it was even longer since anyone had served her with food. And the Miss Taylors had been appalled when she'd offered to do the washing up.

After supper they'd had a round of whist, which Joyce had won. She'd always been quite good at numbers. And at cooking too. That's why she used to dream of combining the two things in running a little cafe. But nothing had ever come of it. Nothing ever would. Helping out on the WVS van had been the closest she had got. And Stanley had put a stop to that.

Quickly Joyce took a biscuit out of the bag and bit into it. She wasn't going to think about Stanley. Or about London. Or about the war. She was away from all that and she was determined to enjoy it. She looked out of the window at the passing green fields dotted with cows grazing contentedly in the watery morning sun, and her spirits lifted. She was on her way to see her two youngest children. She was on holiday.

'So what happened?' Jen asked as soon as Mrs Frost and the Miss Taylors had set off for church. 'Did you sleep with him?'

Katy giggled. 'Of course not. I slept in the same room as his friend's daughter.' This respectable married friend was the story Ward had concocted for the benefit of Jen and his aunts.

What had actually happened was that she had shared Helen de Burrel's bedroom, after a rather delicious dinner cooked by Helen, during which the two Frenchmen drank copious quantities of wine, smoked large numbers of aromatic cigarettes and made a series of flattering comments about Katy, which Ward, much to her embarrassment, delighted in translating.

At first he had offered to stop them smoking but Katy had assured him it didn't matter. 'I live in a pub for goodness' sake,' she said. 'I'm used to it. I'm sure it only affected me this afternoon because I was tired.' It was true, five months of air-raids and four months at the Wilhelmina had taken their toll on her stamina. And two nervous wakeful nights prior to their departure hadn't helped.

Ward had frowned doubtfully. 'I don't want you having a relapse.'

Katy shook her head. 'I won't. I promise.'

'Well, if you're sure . . .' He had slanted her a guilty grin and reached across the table for a cigarette from Pierre's packet. He smiled through the flame of the match as he lit it. 'It was bad enough the first time.'

He's gorgeous, Katy had thought suddenly. Completely gorgeous. Dragging her eyes away she took a gulp of wine in an attempt to restore her equilibrium. 'You seemed to take it pretty calmly.'

He smiled and drew on the cigarette. 'I've been trained to stay calm in a crisis,' he said. 'Even when a pretty girl collapses in my arms.'

Katy had giggled. 'I'm not pretty,' she said.

His brows rose. 'No? How odd.' He blew out smoke. 'I thought you were. Let me just check with the boys.'

Of course Jean-Luc and Pierre had been all too ready to discourse for hours on Katy's beauty. She was scarlet by the time Ward had finished the translation. Then he leaned forward and started telling them something else. Katy could tell from the Frenchmen's expressions that it was something about her and she appealed to Helen. 'What is he saying?'

Helen had laughed as she dished out seconds of the tasty stew. 'He's describing your nurses' uniform,' she said. 'I must say it does sound rather fetching.'

Katy had glared at Ward. 'Stop it,' she said. She had appealed to Helen again. 'Tell him to stop.'

But Ward had merely shrugged and leaned back in his chair. 'It's your own fault. If you will insist on underselling yourself, you just have to be put right.'

She knew he was just being kind, but nevertheless, after nearly twenty-four hours in his company, she had felt a sense of loss when he had dropped her and Jen at the Miss Taylors' the following morning and driven Joyce away to the station.

Now she realised that Jen was looking at her closely. 'You've fallen for him, haven't you?' Jen said. She rolled her eyes dramatically. 'Uh oh. I see a major heartbreak coming up.'

Katy shook her head crossly. 'I haven't fallen for him,' she said.

Jen wasn't taken in. She giggled and put on a pompous expression as she groped for an imaginary stethoscope. 'I'm afraid we'll have to check the symptoms,' she said in a stupid doctor's voice. 'Now let me see, Nurse Parsons. Do you have a sense of malaise when he's out of your sight? Does your heart thump faster the closer he gets? Do you worry about everything you say to him in case he thinks it's stupid? Do you long to see him, then when he turns up you wish you'd waited until you had the money to go to the best beauty parlour?' She stopped and stared over a pair of make-believe

239

half-moon glasses. 'Why, Nurse Parsons, I do believe you've gone a little pink.'

Katy stared at her. 'How do you know all those things?'

Jen shrugged. 'I felt it with Sean.'

Katy frowned. 'I never really knew how you felt about Sean. You were so brave about him going away and everyone saying he was IRA and everything.'

'I felt brave,' Jen said. Her eyes were suddenly distant, gazing out of the Miss Taylors' window over the green countryside. 'I trusted him. I didn't believe he was IRA.'

Katy drew a careful breath. Jen had always avoided this subject before. 'And was he?'

Jen's eyes swung back to hers, and Katy was shocked by the pain in them.

'I don't know,' Jen stood up and went over to the window. 'All I know is that I saw a picture of him in the paper kissing a girl on the steps of the Dublin courthouse after he'd been let off some terrorism charge.'

So that's why Jen had stopped talking about Sean Byrne. That's why she had stopped saying he was waiting for her in Ireland. Aware of the tension in her friend's thin shoulders, the determined set of her chin, Katy realised it was only Jen's fierce pride that had kept her silent. Kept her head above the gossip and the bitter sense of betrayal. Suddenly Katy felt extraordinarily proud of her. And yet desperately sorry for her at the same time. It must have taken a real gritty courage to get her career off the ground with the Sean business undermining her at every turn. Katy wished dearly that she had that sort of courage. It was different, she knew, but even now, even without any of the intimacy Jen had shared with Sean, she knew if anything happened to Ward she would go to pieces.

It seemed Jen's thoughts were running along similar lines. Or perhaps she was just keen to get off the subject of Sean. Either way, she turned away from the window abruptly. 'Katy, I don't know how far down the line you've gone with Ward. But I think you should be careful.' She waved her hands about. 'Somebody like you could get badly hurt. He has a reputation for leading girls up the garden path then backing off at the last minute.' She slanted Katy a quick apologetic glance. 'He did it to Louise, didn't he? Who's to say he wouldn't do it to you?'

Louise. Momentarily Katy had forgotten about Louise waiting impatiently in London for their return. Unnerved she looked away, but Jen continued relentlessly, which somehow was even more unnerving. She couldn't remember when she'd last seen Jen so serious.

Seeing Katy's stricken expression, Jen raised her hands helplessly. 'I'm sorry,' she said. 'But I know how painful it is, and I'm much tougher than you.'

Katy nodded. 'I know. I know you're right. I know it's hopeless. But he's just so . . .' She stopped and flushed. 'So lovely.'

'Lovely?' Jen clutched her stomach. 'Oh yuk. I'll have to ask the Miss Taylors for a sick bowl when they get back.'

Katy was horrified. 'You're not to tell them. Please, Jen. I'd feel such a fool.'

Jen shrugged. 'I expect they've guessed anyway. Mum certainly has.'

Katy stared at her in horror. 'She hasn't?'

Jen grinned. 'It's not that difficult. The way you go green and start ripping your clothes off the moment he appears tends to give the game away.'

'I do not go green,' Katy glared at her. She lifted her chin. 'Anyway, that's not what I want from him.'

'Isn't it?' Jen was surprised. 'That's what I wanted from Sean.'

Katy flushed. 'It's him I like. His personality. Not his body.' Oddly it was true. Jen was wrong about that. The thought of touching him or kissing him completely terrified her. Let alone the rest. He was so male. So gorgeous. The thought of him taking his clothes off appalled her. It would be like an overdose. She would probably faint.

★　★　★

Nevertheless when Ward turned up at the Miss Taylors' little cottage earlier than expected that afternoon, Katy was careful not to show too much obvious pleasure, even though she felt like joining Winston in a paroxysm of excited barking.

Jen and Mrs Frost were at the piano but Katy and his aunts had been arguing about the North African campaign when Ward strolled in, and as soon as they had silenced Winston, the old ladies appealed to Ward for his views.

'We've just been saying that nothing can stop that nice General Wavell taking Libya now,' Thelma said. 'But Katy thinks the Germans might join forces with the Italians.'

Ward lowered himself into a chair. 'Oh, the Germans will turn up all right,' he said grimly. 'And doing well against General Rommel isn't going to be quite as easy as doing well against Marshal Graziano.' He smiled. 'So I'm afraid I tend to side with Katy.'

A sudden giggle from the piano made all eyes swivel in that direction.

But before anyone could speak, Katy jumped to her feet. 'We ought to do the washing up, Jen,' she said with a meaningful glare. 'We did promise.'

In the kitchen she pulled the door to and rounded on Jen angrily. 'That was really mean.'

'What?' Jen was all innocence. 'I didn't say anything.'

'You giggled,' Katy said severely. 'And a giggle is quite enough to give the game away.'

Jen looked aggrieved. 'But I could have been giggling about anything, the way Winston was trying to mount Ward's leg, for example.'

That made Katy giggle. 'He does that to me sometimes,' she said. 'I never know what to do.'

'I just boot him off,' Jen said. 'Although it's a bit tricky if the Miss Taylors are looking.'

A slight noise in the doorway made them both swing round guiltily.

Ward was standing there with his hand on the door handle.

'What are you two giggling about?'

'Nothing.' They both spoke at once and then giggled again.

The faintly speculative look in his eyes showed he wasn't fooled, but he smiled nevertheless. 'My aunts want me to take Winston for a walk. Would either or both of you like to come?'

'Oh, no thanks,' Jen said quickly, rather too quickly for Katy's taste, 'I want to run through some music with Mrs Frost.' She grimaced. 'I'm back on the road tomorrow so this is my last chance.'

He inclined his head and made a wry face at Katy. 'It looks like it's you and me, then.'

Katy racked her brain for an excuse, but oddly it didn't come up with one. 'I'd better get my coat, then,' she said lamely.

As she followed him out into the crisp February afternoon, she glanced back at the house rather desperately. 'Are you sure no one else wants to come?'

Ward was about to shake his head, when he stopped. 'Yes,' he said. 'Winston!' He turned back. 'I'm so excited about going for a walk alone with you that I've forgotten the blasted dog.'

Katy stared at him but before she could ascertain whether he was serious, he had gone back into the house. A moment later he returned with Winston trotting eagerly at his heels and smiled. 'Right, all set? Which way?'

Katy glanced up and down the small village street. In both directions the narrow road led quickly out of the village through rolling farmland with bushy hedgerows and the occasional copse of spiky brown trees. But then she noticed that slightly to the north of them one tree clad hill rose higher than the others and there seemed to be some kind of monument on it.

'Let's go up there,' she said, pointing. 'There's bound to be a track or something, isn't there.'

'Bound to be,' Ward agreed.

Katy glanced at him suspiciously and he made a small apologetic gesture. 'It looks pretty steep,' he said. 'And it might be a bit rough underfoot.'

Katy glared at him. She knew perfectly well it wasn't her footwear he was worried about. 'It's not too steep for me,' she said crossly. 'But if it's too steep for you, say so and we'll go somewhere else.'

Ward laughed. 'It was Winston I was worried about,' he said as they set off along the road. 'I always knew you were tougher than you looked.'

Not believing him for a moment and unsure in any case whether his remark was a compliment or not, Katy gave him a thin little smile and walked briskly on.

Ward was right, it was steeper and rougher than it looked but, to Katy's relief, it was indeed Winston who lagged behind, not her. Behind them the clouds had cleared and the low afternoon sun was suddenly warm on their backs. Then shortly before they reached the trees the ground became muddy where cattle had used the track to cross from one field to another. Aware of Ward's eyes on her, Katy was reluctant to stop but eventually it became impossible to pick her way through and, for the sake of her shoes, she was forced to give up.

'Damn,' she said, peering through the trees. Tantalisingly, just a short way ahead she could see the base of the monument. She looked at Ward in disappointment. 'Another hundred yards and we'd have made it.'

'I could always carry you.'

It seemed he was serious. 'I've done it before, after all,' he said with a slight smile.

Katy felt her heart leap into action. She glanced dubiously at the mud. There was only a few yards of it. Surely she could hold off her impending heart attack that long. And it seemed a shame not to get to the top.

'Well,' she said with a quick glance at him, 'if you don't mind.'

He inclined his head. 'It would be my pleasure,' he replied, bending forward slightly so she could put her arm round his neck.

But if he found it pleasurable he didn't say. In any case, it was only a couple of seconds before he was lowering her to the ground again.

They were just about to walk on when a pathetic little bark made them both turn round.

Katy giggled. 'Oh, poor Winston!' The dachshund, having manfully tried to follow them, was now bogged down completely in the mud.

Ward groaned. 'I suppose I'll have to go back for him now. Or do you think we could leave him there until we come back?'

For once she knew he was joking and sure enough he turned back at once, picking his way once more through the worst of the mud. She heard him murmur something reassuring to the little dog as he reached down to lift him out of the quagmire.

Suddenly she began to feel self-conscious watching him, and by the time he had renegotiated the mud, she was sitting on the base of the monument.

'Come and see the view,' she called as he crouched to wipe his hands on some long grass.

It was spectacular. The tall obelisk, erected in memory of those lost in the Great War, had clearly been sited deliberately so as to be seen from as much as possible of England's green and pleasant land. Even from its base you could see right over the Chew valley and across to the Mendips in Somerset. Just above Katy's head was the date *1914–1918* and the poignant inscription '*Lest We Forget*'.

As though we could avoid forgetting, Katy thought, when for the second time in less than twenty-five years, people were once again dying in defence of the Empire. She wondered if Ward would remark on the irony of it, but although his eyes flicked over the inscription as he came up to her, he didn't make any comment.

Instead he stood with his hands in his trouser pockets, staring out over the undulating countryside for a minute, before coming to sit beside her.

Then he leaned back against the rough stone and crossed his arms. 'Tell me,' he said conversationally, still gazing at the view. 'What's the situation between you and Louise's brother?'

'Bertie?' Katy stared at him incredulously. Had she not been sitting firmly on the wide concrete platform, she almost certainly would have fallen off. Of all the things she thought he might say, that was the last one that would have sprung to mind. 'Nothing,' she said, moving back a fraction in case some further shock was to follow. 'We're just friends. Why?'

He raised his shoulders in a small shrug and smiled slightly. 'I just wondered.'

'Oh.' She looked away wishing she could think of something better to say. But she knew that while the breath was tight in her throat, 'oh' was probably the best she could manage, certainly until she had ascertained whether he really wanted to know about her and Bertie or whether his question had merely been a subtle way to introduce the subject of Louise.

Suddenly he sat up and turned to face her. 'Katy, I . . .' He stopped and swore under his breath.

She glanced at him nervously and found to her dismay his eyes were narrowed. It was a moment before she realised it wasn't her he was frowning at but something behind her. Looking round quickly she saw what it was. Some way below them, toiling up the same way they had come were two small figures. Squinting against the low sun, Katy identified Jen and Mrs Frost.

'Damn,' Ward said. Then, when Katy looked back at him in surprise, he gave a wry smile and ran his hands through his hair. 'I wanted to ask you something,' he said. 'But now the light brigade are coming to your rescue.' He grinned suddenly as he glanced over her shoulder again. 'Or not so light. I hope they've got decent shoes on. I don't mind carrying Jen, but I'm damned if I'm heaving Margot Frost through the mud.'

Katy giggled but it was rather a breathless giggle and when he went to stand up, she put her hand on his arm.

'What was it you were going to ask me?' she asked.

He smiled and shook his head. 'It's too late. I'll ask you another time.'

'No, please,' Katy insisted. 'What sort of thing?' She had to know. She couldn't possibly go through another whole day without knowing. It might be something very important. Or something really romantic. Or it might be something really annoying about Louise. Or it might be something quite innocuous like how long her parents had been running the pub, or whether she thought Mrs Carter was enjoying her time in Devon.

'Ward, please . . .' she said as he stood up. 'What was it?'

He stood looking down at her for a moment then he laughed.

'Don't look so serious,' he said. 'I was only going to ask what you'd say if I told you I wanted to drag you to the ground and make mad passionate love to you.'

This time Katy nearly did fall off the plinth. For an unnerving second as the ground swayed, she thought the obelisk was going to crash down on her head and she clutched frantically at the cold stone. Then she realised it was her that was swaying. I've gone mad, she thought. Either that or I've gone to heaven. Or was he joking? Or teasing? Or both? Or everything? Tentatively she raised her eyes to his, desperate for some clarification before she made a complete idiot of herself.

He was half laughing at her expression, but his eyes were steady. 'Well?'

She gulped. 'Well what?'

'What would you say?'

Katy took a deep breath. It was now or never. Her breath came out in a shaky giggle. 'I'd probably say, yes please,' she said.

For a long second his eyes burnt into hers as though he didn't quite believe her, then he gave a soft laugh. 'Good.'

Good? Katy stared at him aghast. Was that it? Was that all he was going to say?

It seemed so. Already he was moving away. Already she could hear Jen moaning and groaning about the steepness of the climb, Mrs Frost's brisk rejoiner that physical exercise was the best way to expand your lung capacity.

As they ploughed on manfully through the mud, Katy caught Ward's quick complicitous grin of relief and she smiled back. Even though the moment had passed, even though the others were on them and further intimacy was impossible, even though Jen was insisting on going back by a dryer route, Katy could still feel the secret little nugget of excitement inside her.

It stayed with her for the rest of the day, all through Jen's farewell supper and the whole of the night. It was only in the early hours of the morning that she began to wonder exactly what he had meant. Did he mean he actually wanted to throw her to the ground and make mad passionate love to her? Or just that he wondered what she would say if he suggested it? And if he actually wanted to do it, was it something he'd thought about before? Or was it just that precise moment on the top of the hill that he had had a sudden urge?

Joyce woke to the sound of a cock crowing. For a moment she felt the disturbing sense of unease that usually settled on her the moment she opened her eyes, then she suddenly remembered there was no need for her to feel tense today. She was miles away from her worries, warm and snug and alone in Mrs Baxter's enormous spare bedroom.

She had barely had the thought when she heard a tap on the door and a girl's voice, Angie's voice, although she still barely recognised it with its strong West Country burr.

'Are you awake, Mum?'

Quickly rubbing the sleep out of her eyes, Joyce levered herself up on her elbow just as the door opened and her daughter came in with a steaming cup of tea.

'Mrs Baxter says as you looked all done in last night and you're to stay in bed a bit,' Angie said, putting the cup carefully on the bedside table. 'Then when you're ready she'll do you a nice cooked breakfast.' Having delivered this message, she hovered awkwardly by the bed for a moment. 'And then she said I can take you down to show you the threshing.' She stopped when she saw Joyce's blank expression and coloured slightly. 'Only if you'd like to, mind.'

Feeling guilty Joyce nodded hastily. 'I'd like to do that,' she said, sitting up a bit more. 'It's just that I'm not sure what threshing is.'

Angie's eyes widened. 'It's an enormous machine which comes to get the grain off the straw,' she said. 'It's on the next farm now and everyone's down there helping. It'll be here next week and then everyone will come here.' Her eyes sparkled at the thought. 'We're allowed off school when the thresher comes.'

Joyce looked at her eager face. 'But you're not going to school today, are you?' There certainly had been no mention of school last night.

Angie shook her head. 'No. But only because you're here. Otherwise we'd have to go.' She rolled her eyes in a gesture that reminded Joyce of Jen. 'And it's miles to walk. So we're awfully glad you've come.'

'I'm glad I've come too,' Joyce said. It was true. She was glad. Even if the kids were a bit awkward with her, even if they didn't really know how to treat her. It was understandable. They hadn't seen her for eighteen months and letters were hopeless. Big buxom Mrs Baxter had taken her place and although that had been a bit difficult to accept at first, in reality it was a great weight off her mind. Angie and Paul seemed happy and healthy. And if nothing else it meant she could enjoy her holiday.

And she was enjoying it. After the first few minutes of complete terror, she even enjoyed the ride to the neighbouring farm in the pony and trap, once she had got used to the idea of twelve-year-old Paul being in charge of such a sprightly little horse.

She hadn't recognised Paul yesterday. It was only when he walked across the farmyard with a slightly doubtful 'Mum?' that she had realised that in a year and a half her peaky-faced little boy had grown into such a fine-looking young man.

Angie, at fourteen, was an eye-opener and all. Big and bouncy with a rosy complexion and a ready smile, Joyce could hardly believe she was the same underfed spindly child she had sent away.

Yes, Mrs Baxter had worked wonders. The fresh country air had put colour in their cheeks and the fresh country food had put fat on their bones.

She could feel it creeping on to her bones and all. She hadn't seen such food in years. Last night they'd had a great slab of pork, three different vegetables and as many potatoes as you could eat. Lovely crackling. And seconds. And pudding. And bacon and egg for breakfast. And toast and butter. You'd never think there was a war on here.

Joyce ran a cautious hand over her stomach as the trap jolted over the bumps in the track. It wouldn't hurt her to put on a pound or two. But it was lucky she'd decided to give that skirt back to Lorenz when she got home. Because after a day or two of Redlake Farm she'd never get into it anyway.

Somewhat to Katy's dismay, for the next day and a half Ward showed no sign of wanting to drag her to the ground, let alone to make mad passionate love to her. On the two occasions he turned up at the Miss Taylors' cottage he was courteous, charming and thoroughly respectable. He helped the old ladies arrange their furniture, brought them flowers, stacked their logs, fixed the broken hinge on Mrs Frost's window and drove them all into Bristol for a look round the shops. In the evening he played cards, ate and laughed and generally behaved like the perfect nephew.

At first Katy was grateful for the respite. It was so wonderful to be in congenial company away from London and the Wilhelmina that she didn't immediately notice that being the perfect nephew also gave him the perfect excuse to avoid being alone in her company.

Because there was no doubt, she realised suddenly, that his attitude had changed. For no apparent reason, the quick smiles and gentle teasing of the last few days had been replaced by an ominous reluctance to meet her eyes. To anyone else it would have been indiscernible but to her it was as though he had shouted from the rooftops that he had changed his mind. And her misery was impossible to hide.

The Miss Taylors couldn't understand what was wrong and clearly believed that it was her dread of going back to the Wilhelmina that had caused her sudden drop in spirits.

To her horror on the Tuesday afternoon, she overheard them asking Ward to take her out for a walk. Just for ten minutes. To cheer her up. 'It's your last day, after all. And we hate to see her so unhappy.'

Put like that he could hardly refuse and although Katy tried to demur she was overruled: 'In any case a brisk walk will do you good.'

Katy was mortified. She knew Ward didn't want to go and when by some mutual accord they turned left outside the house instead of up towards the hill, she knew she was right.

For a while they walked in silence with Winston trundling at their heels, then as they came out of the village Ward made an obvious effort to rouse himself. 'The boys send their love,' he said. 'You made a big hit there.'

Katy shrugged. 'It wasn't difficult. I think any woman between fifteen and forty would have made a hit with them.' She didn't want to talk about the boys. She wanted to know what was wrong. Why he was acting so strangely.

But if Ward noticed her reluctance he made no sign of it. 'You can't blame them for letting their hair down,' he said. 'Once they go back they'll be in constant danger. There's a lot of betrayal going on in France just now. As it stands at the moment with no proper escape routes set up yet, if the Germans get on to them they won't last ten minutes.'

Katy shivered, shocked by the hard edge to his voice as much by his words. For a moment she forgot her own distress. 'Some of

251

our airmen have got out, haven't they? When they've been shot down.'

He shrugged. 'Uniformed military personnel stand a slightly better chance. If the worst comes to the worst they get taken prisoner-of-war. Resistance fighters just get shot if they won't talk. As do their families and friends.'

Katy thought of those two smiling French faces, Pierre's jaunty moustache and Jean-Luc's soft brown eyes, and sudden tears sprang to her eyes. Getting shot was bad enough but the thought of what might happen to them between getting caught and getting shot was a hundred times worse.

'Hey.' Ward looked appalled at the effect of his words. He stopped and pulled her round to face him. 'Don't take it so hard. It's what war is about. Those guys know the risks and they are prepared to take them.'

Katy swallowed hard. 'I'm sorry,' she said.

He shook his head. 'No, I'm sorry,' he said. 'We're meant to be having a spirit-lifting walk and the first thing I do is make you cry.'

'I'm not crying,' Katy said with a surreptitious sniff. Not about that anyway. But she had been bottling up her emotions for too long and once the tears had started, there suddenly was no stopping them.

And then she really was crying and, with a muffled oath, Ward pulled her against him.

At first he just held her, silently, his body stiff and unyielding and then gradually he eased her away from him and holding her face very gently wiped the tears from her cheeks with his thumbs.

'Don't cry,' he said and to her ears his voice sounded harsh with embarrassment. She couldn't look at him. She couldn't bear to see the rejection in his eyes.

And then one of his hands moved a fraction and instead of smoothing her wet cheeks, suddenly she felt his thumb brush lightly across her mouth. It was like an electric shock.

Her eyes flew open and she nearly gasped aloud at the expression she saw on his face. Because it wasn't embarrassment. Nor was it desire.

It was anger, blazing like a struck match at the back of his eyes.

And then he was kissing her. Not the tender little reassuring peck she might have envisaged, nor the smiling brush of lips she had experienced under the mistletoe that time, but a hard, almost bruising kiss that seemed to invade her whole being, shocking her as much with its devastating effect on her as with its penetrating and unexpected intimacy. She could feel his hands hard on the back of her head, she could taste the salt of her tears on his tongue, and more than anything she could feel a painful, shuddering response course through her entire body.

And then it was over.

And Ward was standing there looking at her. No longer touching her. The anger on his face replaced by a dreadful self-disgust.

'I'm sorry,' he said as she desperately fought to keep her balance. 'I really am. I never meant that to happen. I'm completely out of order.'

Katy stared at him, confused and suddenly very cold. 'But the other day you said . . .'

'I know what I said,' he interrupted irritably. 'I should never have said it.' He tried to smile and failed and thrust his hands into his pockets instead. 'You're a lovely girl, Katy. You deserve better.' He looked away up the road and then back at her. 'We must stop this now. I should never have let it get as far as this.'

As far as what? One angry kiss? Katy felt an icy hand trail slowly up her spine. So this was it. Just as Jen had predicted. They had reached the garden path, but he wasn't even prepared to lead her up it.

'Don't look at me like that,' he said. 'You don't understand. It's not fair on you. You're too sweet. Too young.'

Katy could not believe her ears. Nor could she believe the bitter overwhelming fury that was suddenly erupting all over her body.

'And you are a vicious, beastly, two-faced pig,' she shouted at him. 'And I wish we'd never met.'

She turned then and ran on down the road. She was quick but she wasn't quick enough.

Behind her, even as she ran, she heard his voice, low and rueful. 'I've been wishing that for some time.'

Chapter Fifteen

Joyce knew at once something was wrong between Katy and Ward. If nothing else, the alacrity with which Katy got in the back of the car when they left the station would have alerted her. But it was their studied politeness to each other that gave the game away. Even though Ward asked nicely enough about her journey and her time on the farm, Joyce could almost feel the tension buzzing in the small car.

And partly to fill the uneasy silences, she found herself telling him all about it. All about Angie and Paul, how well they'd settled in there, how they loved the farm, the animals, the chickens and ducks in the farmyard.

'Mrs Rutherford would have liked those chickens,' she said with a glance at Ward. 'They was all different sorts. I wondered about bringing her back a couple of lovely glossy black ones. Mrs Baxter did offer, but I didn't think there'd be room in the car.' Good layers, those black buggers, Mrs Baxter said. Not in so many words of course. The farmer's wife had been pleased to find Joyce was interested in hens. It had broken the ice between them. And Angie and Paul had been impressed with her newfound knowledge and all.

To keep the conversation going she told Ward and Katy about the threshing machine, the noise, the dust and the stooks the size of houses that gradually disappeared into the great machine. And as she talked she frowned, wondering what was the matter with her travelling companions. She had enjoyed her holiday so much, it seemed a shame if something had happened to spoil theirs.

Neither of them seemed to notice when she eventually ran out of steam, and she spent the next few miles staring out of the window, wondering what she could do to cheer them up.

As there were reported to be convoys blocking the roads around Chippenham and Devizes, Ward had decided to take a more southerly route back to London. They had already passed through Bath with its spectacular Georgian terraces but now they were back in open country again, heading for the wide open expanse of Salisbury Plain.

'We pass Stonehenge on this route,' Ward said suddenly. 'Would you like to stop and have a look?'

Joyce glanced over her shoulder to see if Katy would respond, but although she looked up with faint interest in her eyes, she didn't speak. So Joyce nodded instead. 'Oh yes, I'd love to see that,' she said enthusiastically. 'Stones, isn't it? In a circle?'

Ward did smile at that. 'It's pretty spectacular,' he said. 'The stones are enormous. Someone told me the Druids brought them all the way from the Preseli mountains in West Wales.'

Joyce nodded. She didn't particularly care where the stones came from so long as she got a break from the strained atmosphere in the car.

But by the time the stones finally appeared ahead of them, looking curiously small and bleak on the wide expanse of grass, she had decided that it was her presence in the car that was the problem, and most likely all Ward and Katy needed was a few minutes on their own to sort themselves out. In any case it looked rather damp underfoot and she wasn't sure her shoes were up to much more tramping about on wet grass. Reluctant to admit to her shoe problem and suspecting from the look of her that Katy Parsons might take any excuse to avoid being alone with Ward, Joyce decided to stage a small accident. A twisted ankle would do the trick, she decided.

So a few minutes later, as they crossed the road, she duly enacted an elaborate charade of catching her heel in a hole. Having danced around for a bit, squawking, she gingerly lowered her foot to the ground and declared that she had better wait for them in the car.

'I'll take you back,' Ward offered.

Joyce looked at him in horror. 'No, no. It's all right. I mean it's not all right, but I can manage. Look.' And quickly, before they could offer any more assistance, she hobbled hastily away.

Katy watched the retreating figure in dismay. 'Do you think she's really all right?'

'I think so,' Ward said dryly. 'Particularly as she appears to be limping on the wrong foot.'

Katy stared at him and then at Joyce who was almost leaping across the road in her haste to get back to the car. 'You mean she . . .?'

He smiled faintly. 'I mean she's trying to be tactful. She probably has some idea of us being star-crossed lovers who only need a bit of mystical Druid influence to get back on track.'

Katy was nonplussed. Flushing slightly she searched his face for some kind of meaning in his words. But his expression was inscrutable. He gestured politely to the stones. 'So shall we go on? Or is the company of a beastly, two-faced pig simply too unpleasant to contemplate?'

Katy didn't reply but as they walked on in silence and the boulders ahead got bigger and bigger, so did her need to say something. 'I'm sorry,' she said eventually. 'I shouldn't have said that.'

He glanced at her in surprise. 'No, I think you were quite right. I've treated you very badly.' He smiled tentatively as they entered the great ring of stones. 'Will you ever forgive me?'

Katy stopped. That hesitant smile was more unexpected, somehow more shocking than the size of the great boulders all around her. Dragging her eyes from Ward's face, she stared at a stone that must have been nearly three times his height. How on earth had the Druids got them there? You would need a crane to lift one these days and she was certain the Druids didn't have cranes.

She glanced back at Ward and found him watching her with an unnerving expression in his grey eyes. She realised he was waiting for an answer. 'What exactly am I forgiving you for?' she asked.

He spread his hands. 'For behaving so badly.'

Katy glared at him. 'You mean for saying you wanted to make love to me? Or for kissing me? Or for saying you wished you'd never met me?'

For a moment he was silent. Then he looked away and his gaze moved slowly round the ancient site, grey and cold under the cloudy February sky.

'All of it,' he said as his eyes came back to her. 'I should never have said what I did. Done what I did. It was pure self-indulgence. But I badly needed to know how you felt.' He raised his hands in a gesture of irritation. 'That's why I wanted to talk to you on the hill that day.'

Katy frowned. 'But I said . . .'

He shook his head wearily. 'I know what you said. But even then I guess I didn't really believe you. You never showed it. You never showed anything until yesterday and by then it was too late.'

Too late. To Katy's ultra-sensitive ears the words sounded like a death knell. She shivered. 'What do you mean, too late?'

He put his hands in his pockets but his eyes were steady and very grey. 'Katy, I'm going back to France with the boys.'

Something kicked in her chest. 'When?'

He hesitated. 'Soon. Within the next couple of days.'

Katy turned away. She couldn't bear it. Willing herself not to cry, she stared blindly at a great grey slab which lay on the ground a few yards away from her. Dimly she remembered that Tess of the D'Urbervilles went to her death from Stonehenge and shivered again as the cold wind brushed her skin. No wonder it seemed a bleak, lonely place. Then behind her she heard Ward's voice.

'That's why I wanted to distance myself,' he said. 'I thought it would be easier. Safer too, I thought I'd stand a better chance of coming back if I wasn't thinking about you the whole time.'

The words were hard and flat and it was a moment before Katy absorbed their import. Then she swung round, Tess of the D'Urbervilles forgotten, a flicker of hope widening her eyes.

'So you haven't changed your mind?'

Ward looked surprised. 'Of course I haven't changed my mind. God, every time I look at you and think what a mess I've made of it, I feel kind of sick.'

She tried to smile but her voice was shaky. 'Sick with longing or sick with revulsion?'

'Sick at the thought of losing you to someone else.'

For a minute he was silent, apparently studying the ground. Then he swore softly under his breath and looked up. His face was tense.

'Katy, I know I have no right to ask, but if I get back from France this time, would you consider marrying me?'

Katy stared at him, stunned. She had no idea they were talking about marriage. Somehow they had shot up the garden path and were leaping across the threshold before she had even opened the gate.

But why would he want to marry her when there were so many girls he could have had? She eyed him suspiciously as a nasty thought occurred to her. 'You're not asking me because you feel sorry for me, are you? Because of Sister Morris and washing the pub floors and that?'

He shook his head and his eyes were tender. The wind was ruffling his hair making him look suddenly boyish. 'I'm asking you because I love you,' he said. 'I've tried real hard not to but I can't help it.'

'But you've only ever kissed me twice.'

He laughed then. 'I can soon put that right.' He saw her nervous blush and touched her cheek gently. His fingers were cool against her skin. 'It's more than sex, Katy. It's you. What you are. It's what you stand for that I've fallen for. The fact that I find you utterly desirable is just the icing on the cake.'

To her horror Katy suddenly felt very scared. It was all too fast. Too unexpected. She had dreamed for weeks in an abstract rose-tinted way of what might happen between them. A few dates, holding hands in the cinema, walking in the sunshine, perhaps even the occasional illicit kiss and cuddle.

She had dreamed of touching his hair, his skin and his lips. But much as she loved him and longed for him to love her, she had never really dreamed of marrying him, with all the physical intimacy that that entailed. And now here they were on this cold grey day standing among these gloomy windswept stones which had stood here for thousands of years and he was asking her to be his wife.

She jumped as he touched her arm. 'Katy, what's the matter?' His voice was warm but he couldn't disguise the hint of anxiety in his eyes and she felt a stab of pure joy.

'Nothing,' she said nervously. 'It's just that nobody has ever asked me to marry them before and I don't know what to do next'

He laughed softly as he drew her slowly into his arms. 'Three things happen next. First of all you say yes. Then we catch up on that kissing. And then I guess we'd better go tell Mrs Carter the good news.'

Katy had forgotten about Mrs Carter waiting in the car. And a second later she forgot about her again. Ward's kiss was everything she could have asked for. Tender, sweet, and infinitely gentle. Reassured slightly, she smiled when he raised his head and then blinked as she felt his thumb run along the soft curve of her lower lip.

He smiled as her mouth opened slightly and then he was easing back her lower lip gently and lowering his head again. His thumb was still on her lip, she could taste it cold and faintly salty, but she could feel his tongue too, running round her teeth, touching the soft sensitive skin inside her lips.

For a second she was scared by the intimacy of it and then unexpectedly as he moved his hand to pull her closer to him, a jolt of

260

desire shot through her. Their tongues touched and suddenly it was more than a kiss, it was an awakening, a rebirth.

She knew she was clinging to him, she couldn't help it. She wanted to get as close as she could. She wanted to drown in the heady sensation of it. She wanted it to go on for ever.

When he drew back with a low exclamation of surprise she felt she had lost something precious.

He stood staring down at her for a moment with a look of shock on his face. 'That icing is a bit more tasty than I realised,' he said ruefully. 'We'd better go back to Mrs Carter right now. Or God knows what might happen.'

He took her hand and kissed it, then he frowned. 'Did you ever say yes?'

Katy smiled at him. 'Yes. Yes. Yes,' she said, and as she spoke the sun slid out from the clouds and lit the silent stones with a strange ethereal light. For an instant the ancient site did indeed seem magical. And then as quickly as it had come, it had gone again and Ward led her back to the car.

Joyce was cold and bored. When she had tactfully arranged for Katy and Ward to go and see the stones on their own she hadn't meant them to be gone all bloody day. Without the engine on it was just as cold in the car as out of it. She had slammed the door rather pointedly a couple of times as she got out to stamp some warmth back into her body but there had been no sign of either of them since they had disappeared into the distant circle of stones.

She wasn't a fanciful person but she was just beginning to wonder rather nervously if they could have been swept up to heaven, or some other Druid equivalent, when to her relief they suddenly materialised and began walking back over the grass towards her.

She knew at once something had happened. Something nice. For one thing they were holding hands. And for another they were talking. Not the stiff little exchanges they had had earlier in the day, but a laughing, hugging, smiling kind of conversation that made a small tremor of envy pass up Joyce's spine.

It was a long time since she had felt happiness like that. Even on the farm the last couple of days her smiles had been tempered by what waited for her back in London. The notes from poor old Bob saying how much he hated the army life, how he dreaded being sent abroad. Mick's new resentful surliness. And the constant draining worry about Stanley, unemployed, on the bottle and increasingly free with his fist.

Then as Ward and Katy approached she remembered the days when she and Stanley had courted. She had been proud of him then. He'd been a nice-looking lad in his youth. She'd been lucky to get him. Young men had been few and far between in those days after the carnage of the Great War.

She wondered suddenly what had gone wrong. Stanley had treated her all right to start with. He'd always had a rough temper but it was only when it had lost him a couple of jobs that he started turning it on her. He blamed her for losing her looks, for nagging him to find a job, for needing so much money for the children. So much. She sighed. Little did he know how she'd scrimped and saved all these years to keep a roof over their heads and something to eat on the table. It was hardly her fault the marriage had lost its sparkle. And now he was accusing her of fancying poor old Lorenz who wouldn't hurt a flea.

She thought of Jen's scorn, Jen's impatience, her inability to understand why she tolerated the abuse. But then Jen didn't know what it was like being tied to a man year in year out.

Joyce would have liked it to be different. She would have liked it be warm and romantic, but life wasn't like that in her experience.

She got out of the car as they crossed the road, and pretended not to notice as Katy tried to disengage her fingers and Ward wouldn't let her.

They stopped in front of her and he smiled. 'Mrs Carter. I'd like you to be the first to know that Katy has agreed to become my wife.'

Joyce looked from one to the other: Ward, tall and handsome, his dark hair ruffled by the wind, Katy, fragile and flushed with emotion. She saw the mixture of love and fear in their eyes and, before she could summon the words of congratulation, to her complete horror, she burst into tears.

To Katy's relief, Joyce's unexpected emotional outburst didn't last long. By the time Ward had produced a clean white handkerchief and a small silver hip flask from his luggage, her tears were already abating.

Flushing with embarrassment she began to apologise.

But Ward cut her short. 'It's me who should apologise,' he said. 'For keeping you waiting in the cold so long.' He took a swig from the hip flash and offered it to Katy with a wry grin. 'It's just that Katy took a bit of persuading.'

To Katy's surprise, Joyce managed a watery smile. 'I'm really pleased for you both,' she said and she genuinely sounded it, even if her voice was still choked. 'You'll make a lovely couple. I just hope . . .' She stopped abruptly as her eyes filled again and blew her nose.

As the warm brandy slithered down her throat, Katy wondered what it was that Mrs Carter hoped. That she would be invited to the wedding? That they would be happier than her and Mr Carter? That Ward wouldn't get killed in France?

But she never found out because Ward was urging them back into the car.

'We should get going,' he said, drawing her to him for a last brief embrace. 'I'd like to get back to London before the blackout.'

Flushing from his kiss, ignoring Mrs Carter's protests, Katy scrambled hastily into the back seat. She didn't feel up to travelling in the front. She had a feeling Ward might expect her to hold his hand, and much as she craved his attention, Katy had felt absurdly self-conscious at touching him in front of Mrs Carter. To be perfectly honest she felt self-conscious at touching him at all.

But it seemed he had no such inhibitions, indeed several times on the journey he reached back over his seat to stroke her arm, or even with a naughty glint in the mirror, to run his hand over her knee.

By the time they reached London, Katy found she was rather enjoying the illicit caresses. But as they worked their way through the darkening bomb damaged streets of Putney and Wandsworth she realised suddenly the journey was nearly over and she was soon going to have to face the real world again. So much had changed since they had gone away.

There were going to be explanations and arrangements and decisions to be made. She was going to have to face her parents, Sister Morris, Louise.

Her heart sank. Suddenly she wished she could stay in the safe little cocoon of Ward's car for ever.

She realised that Ward and Joyce had fallen quiet as well. She wondered if they were nervous too. Or whether they were just affected by the grey, rubble-filled streets.

It was hard to tell if there had been more damage while they had been away or whether it was just the contrast between the lush green countryside they had driven through and the sad wounded terraces of South London.

Even the people seemed grey in the rapidly fading light, their clothes worn and their faces pale and sunken eyed in comparison to the inhabitants of the small towns and villages they had left behind.

And then they turned into Lavender Road and at once they knew something was wrong.

At first it seemed to be the Flag and Garter which was drawing the attention of the small crowd of people and Katy craned forward in horror, but then as they drew nearer she saw it was Mr Lorenz's house next door that everyone was looking at and she felt guilty for feeling relief.

Several people looked round as Ward brought the car to a standstill. Katy recognised her father in the crowd, and Mr Rutherford.

For a second as Ward turned off the engine the three of them sat still and silent as though in a time capsule and then she met Ward's eyes in the mirror and with one accord they got out.

It wasn't hard to find out what had happened. The fringe members of the crowd were only too happy to tell them.

'Someone heard shots.'

'That Jewish bloke has been shot, they reckon.'

'Anti-Semitic attack.'

'Bleeding like a pig.'

'He won't let anyone in.'

'Blood on the door.'

'Police are on their way.'

Katy was just imagining poor Mr Lorenz lying bleeding to death just inside his front door when suddenly, to her astonishment, Joyce spoke beside her. 'He'll let me in,' she said gruffly and began to push through the crowd.

Drawn by some strange bond of loyalty, Katy followed her.

As they approached they could hear Lorenz's gentle voice from within the house, saying he didn't need the police and please would everyone go away. Nobody moved.

At the gate Joyce stopped and glared at the men on the step. 'He's told you he doesn't want you so why don't you just bugger off?' Before they could move she had raised her voice. 'Mr Lorenz, it's Mrs Carter. I'm just back from the country. Can I come in?'

Lorenz's voice sounded weak but wary. 'I don't want the police.'

'You're not getting the police,' Joyce replied. 'You're getting me and young Katy Parsons.'

She stepped purposefully through the small gate, but as Katy went to follow her father rushed forward. 'Katy, you can't go in there. There's blood everywhere. It's a man's job.'

Already Katy could see the blood on the door. And the gashes in the wood. If someone had really fired at Mr Lorenz they had clearly had several goes at it. The top pane of glass was broken and the blackout curtain behind was torn. She realised suddenly that she was scared about what she might find behind the door, but as she hesitated under the pressure of her father's clutching fingers, she heard Ward's calm voice behind her.

'It's all right, Mr Parsons. Let her go. She's a nurse, remember. She might be able to help.'

The hallway was dark and narrow and Katy almost tripped over a chair as she stepped inside. It was clearly where Mr Lorenz had been sitting. As her eyes accustomed themselves to the gloom, she turned quickly to look at the pawnbroker himself as he carefully relocked the door behind her, but his clothes were so dark she couldn't immediately see the extent of the damage. It was only as he led them slowly along the passage to the small kitchen and turned on the light that she saw that his hands and neck were smeared red and that the top left-hand side of his coat was sodden with blood seeping through a gash in the material on the shoulder.

'Good God,' Joyce said, pulling up a chair for him hastily as his knees gave way. 'You don't need us, you need an ambulance.'

Mr Lorenz shook his head. 'I don't think it's serious. I don't want any fuss.' He was shaking slightly but he looked up and attempted a small smile. 'If you don't mind, Miss Parsons, perhaps you could have a look for me and see what you think?'

'But, Mr Lorenz, I'm not qualified . . .' Katy began nervously. She stopped and tried to sound more definite. 'If you've been shot, you need proper medical attention. And you should talk to the police.'

'Did you see who did it?' Joyce asked suddenly. 'The police will want to know that.'

Lorenz looked at her quickly and then away again. 'It's not necessary to involve the police,' he said carefully. There was a speck of blood on his glasses. 'I don't like hospitals. I quite understand if you can't do anything for me, Miss Parsons. I don't want to cause any trouble.'

He meant it. Katy could see that. He had no intention of seeking professional help. He was quite prepared to sit it out. And yet she could see he was in considerable discomfort. She felt a sudden stab of respect for this proud, lonely little man.

She glanced helplessly at Joyce, but Joyce was leaning on the table almost as white as Lorenz.

Katy suddenly felt sick. 'I'll need scissors and bandages,' she said, 'and dressings and disinfectant and lots of boiling water.' She stopped abruptly, horrified at what she was saying. Then at the same moment she suddenly remembered that outside was someone who was used to dealing with emergencies. Someone she could trust implicitly. A sense of relief flooded through her. She wasn't going to have to deal with this alone.

'We must get Ward in here,' she said to Joyce. 'He'll help us.'

Joyce roused herself at once and straightened up. 'Don't worry,' she said to Mr Lorenz as he began to look anxious. 'He's all right, that Ward Frazer.'

The next minute she was at the front door. 'We need Mr Frazer,' she shouted out. 'Nobody else.'

And then Ward was there, tall and disconcertingly calm, filling the house with a reassuring presence. He greeted Mr Lorenz courteously and listened carefully as Katy quickly explained the situation. She glanced at the pawnbroker. 'I've told Mr Lorenz he ought to go to hospital but he doesn't want to. He doesn't want any fuss. He doesn't want the police involved.'

Ward's brows rose. 'Why not? You've been shot, Mr Lorenz. That's a serious offence. People heard shots, the glass in your door is broken. There's some blood. The police will want to know what happened.'

Lorenz met his gaze. 'Perhaps a car backfired,' he said. 'Perhaps someone threw a stone at the glass.'

Ward's eyes narrowed slightly. Then he pulled his hand out of his pocket and dropped a bullet on the table. 'I picked that up in your hall. It's not a stone, Mr Lorenz. It's a .38 revolver bullet. There are three more embedded in your wallpaper.' He looked steadily at the pawnbroker. 'From the angle and depth I reckon they were fired in quick succession from across the street.'

Katy blinked then shivered. She had forgotten that Ward would know about this kind of thing. Joyce looked startled too. But Mr Lorenz merely flushed slightly. 'I would be most grateful if you would keep that information to yourself, Mr Frazer,' he said. He looked away, his glance skimming Joyce's white face. 'I have my reasons. I assure you it is for the best.'

There was a moment's silence in the small kitchen, then Ward shrugged. 'In that case I'll do what I can.'

Katy looked up at him hopefully. 'And can you find the things I need?'

Ward smiled suddenly and ran his hands through his hair. 'You don't ask much, do you? But I'll try. I have a first aid kit in my car. We'll start off with that'

He drew her into the hall for a moment and touched her face gently. 'Are you sure you want to do this?'

Katy felt choked by his tenderness. By his concern. By his trust in her judgement. 'I don't seem to have much choice,' she said. 'Someone's got to look at him. I just wish I was more qualified.'

Ward frowned. 'He may still have a bullet in him. People heard five shots but there are only three bullet holes.' He nodded down the hall to the scorched, slanting holes in the drab wallpaper. 'Plus the one I picked up. Which leaves one unaccounted for.'

Katy swallowed hard. 'In that case,' she said, 'I'll need tweezers too.'

What followed seemed to Katy to pass in a blur.

Ward was right. There was a bullet in Lorenz's shoulder and it had taken a fair amount of material from his clothes in with it. Unable to get his coat off any other way, she and Joyce ended up cutting it off, and his jacket and his shirt. Afterwards she remembered being surprised by the sinewy strength of the pawnbroker's torso, but at the time she was far more concerned with keeping him warm, wrapping him in grey blankets and towels that Ward produced from upstairs.

Katy hadn't learned much from the Wilhelmina, but one thing she had learned from Sister Morris was the absolute necessity of hygiene, particularly in the treatment of open wounds. It was the only way to prevent infection, and, terrified of doing more harm than good, she made Joyce boil up the makeshift equipment, the scissors and tweezers, before laying them on a clean white cloth she found in the kitchen drawer. Then she rolled up her sleeves, washed her hands until they were raw and tried to recall everything she had learned from her Red Cross exams the previous year.

Ward came and went. He brought her everything she needed. Somehow he got rid of the police and the observers. He got Joyce to make tea and brought sugar from the pub to sweeten it. He boarded up the broken glass in the door. He passed her the clean swabs and took the bloody ones when Joyce reeled away to be sick. And he sponged the blood off the door and the floor.

The shoulder wound was already clotting as Katy tentatively picked out the surrounding debris of material, but amazingly she could already see the base of the bullet protruding. She heard Ward telling Mr Lorenz he was lucky his assailant had been some way away. He was right. A closer shot would have shattered the collarbone.

She didn't need the tweezers. The bullet came out in her fingers with a ghastly sucking noise and another gush of blood. For a moment, as she grabbed a clean swab, Katy thought she was going to faint. Joyce leaned heavily on the kitchen table with a groan, and even Ward paled slightly, but Mr Lorenz, gripping the table with his spare hand, white faced and unflinching, sat throughout the entire procedure in rigid silence.

A little bit later, as she was securing the shoulder dressing with a bandage criss-crossing the chest, Katy realised Ward was once again at her side.

'I've got to go now, Katy,' he murmured. 'I've left your suitcase and Mrs Carter's box at the pub.' Her heart jolted as he touched her arm with warm strong fingers. 'I think you'll be all right now, won't you? The worst is over. You've done a great job.'

He hesitated for a moment, watching her closely. 'By the way,' he added casually, 'I've spoken to your father.'

Bandage poised, Katy stared at him blankly. Then she blushed as the events of the day flooded back to her. It seemed incredible to her that only a few hours ago Ward had proposed to her. She searched his face anxiously for a hint of her father's reaction and found none. 'What did he say?' she asked anxiously. 'Was he surprised?'

Ward smiled. 'He was utterly astonished. At first he said you were too young. But after that he seemed pleased. Anyway he agreed in the end.'

Katy swallowed nervously. 'And you explained about going away?'

'I said I would like a wedding at the beginning of April. We settled on the fifth. I'm sure to be back by then.' He smiled slightly. 'And I don't want to wait too long.'

The fifth of April. Two months. Watching him say goodbye to Mrs Carter and Mr Lorenz, Katy wondered how she would ever survive it. And then at the end of it she would have to marry him. This wonderful, confident, sexy man who sent shivers down her spine by just looking at her. Suddenly the thought filled her with absolute terror.

Seeing the stricken expression in her eyes Ward's own eyes narrowed slightly. Turning to Mrs Carter who was watching them avidly, he smiled lightly.

'Would you mind closing your eyes for a moment, Mrs Carter? And you, Mr Lorenz? Just for a couple of seconds?'

Feeling sudden heat in her cheeks, Katy put the new bandage back on the table as he pulled her into his arms.

Cupping her jaw with his hands he looked deep into her eyes. 'Don't forget I love you,' he murmured. Then he kissed her very gently. 'I'll see you tomorrow evening.'

And then he was gone. She heard his firm tread in the passage and then the click of the front door and then silence.

Flushing wildly Katy picked up the bandage again and found her hand was trembling.

Joyce was blowing her nose noisily and Mr Lorenz cleared his throat. His knuckles were still white on the table edge but his eyes were warm behind the steel-framed spectacles. 'May I be the first to congratulate you?' he said politely.

Katy felt tears in her eyes. But before she could speak, Joyce leaned across the table.

'You can be the second,' she said firmly. 'I was the first.'

Louise couldn't believe her ears. She stared at her father in complete horror.

'I gather young Katy Parsons has got herself engaged to that Ward Frazer fellow.'

That was what he had said. She was certain of it. He had just come in. There had been some commotion in Lavender Road and he had gone to investigate. Someone had taken a pot shot at the Jewish pawnbroker. But as the Jew wouldn't talk to the police there wasn't much anyone could do, so her father had come home. He'd put another log on the fire and settled back in his chair. And then a few minutes later he had looked up from his paper and casually added the bit about Katy and Ward. As an afterthought. As though it was only of minor interest.

'Engaged?' The word came out as a gulp.

Her father nodded. 'Old Parsons is over the moon. Bit unexpected I gather but he's a sound enough chap that Ward Frazer. I doubt the girl could do much better.'

Her mother looked up from her knitting. 'I thought Ward was interested in you, darling.'

Louise felt as though she had been kicked in the stomach. 'He was interested in me,' she said fiercely. 'He is interested in me.' She turned to face her father. 'I don't believe you. You're just saying this to tease me, aren't you?'

He looked surprised. 'I'm only saying what I heard. I didn't know it would upset you.'

'Of course it upsets me,' she shouted. She reached for her crutches and struggled to her feet. 'Ward Frazer was mine. I won't let Katy have him.'

Her mother put down her knitting, 'Louise, please . . .' she said sharply. 'Behave yourself.'

Louise rounded on her. 'It's your fault!' she was almost screaming now. 'You should have let me go to Bristol. I knew something like this would happen.'

Her mother frowned. 'You should try to be generous, Louise. Katy Parsons is a nice little thing. She hasn't had much of a life. She's been through a lot with her health one way and another. She deserves a bit of luck.'

Louise stared at her. 'What do you think I've been through? Don't I deserve a bit of luck?' There were tears streaming down her face now. But she could see they would never understand. They would never understand that Ward Frazer had been hers. She had been certain of it. He had told her he wanted an experienced girl. So she had gone with Stefan. She had lost her virginity, she had lost her baby, and she had almost lost her life. Everything she had done she had done for him. And now it seemed she had lost him too.

As she hobbled painfully to the door she realised the ultimate irony. She had been through all that, and yet in the end she had lost him to Katy Parsons, the sweetest, most innocent little virgin imaginable.

Slamming the drawing-room door behind her, she leaned weakly on her crutches and gritted her teeth. 'I won't let her have him,' she whispered. 'It's not fair.'

Joyce was standing at her bedroom window staring across the road when she heard heavy steps on the landing. She swung round. Stanley was there. In the doorway. Swaying slightly. Anger on his face like a black mask.

'You've made a laughing stock of me tonight,' he said.

She knew better than to answer but as he kicked the door shut behind him with his heel she felt the familiar fear ball in her stomach and tensed ready for flight. But in his fury he was too fast for her.

She missed the first swing but the second caught her on the shoulder. She tried desperately to keep her balance but lost her footing and fell backwards on to the floor. She lay there for a moment, winded, waiting for the feel of his foot.

But he didn't kick her. 'Get up,' he shouted instead, hauling on her arm. 'Get up.'

His eyes glittered as she struggled gratefully to her feet. 'You know what you're going to do now, don't you?'

Joyce shook her head mindlessly. I've been away too long, she thought. This is even worse than usual.

'Oh, yes you do,' he said grimly, rubbing his hands. 'You're going to pay for pandering to that filthy Jew.'

Afterwards she didn't dare move until he was snoring heavily. Then she slid silently off the bed, adjusted her clothes as best she could, licked the blood off her lip, and crept, shivering, along the passage.

Pete was asleep but Mick's bed was empty.

She found him downstairs, white faced, sitting at the kitchen table eating a piece of bread. He jumped nervously when he heard her step in the passage.

'Mum. I didn't know you was home.'

She shut the door.

'Yes, I'm home all right,' she said grimly. 'Where's the gun?'

'What gun?' He tried to look innocent but the sudden colour in his cheeks gave him away.

Joyce walked forward and grabbed his ear. She twisted it hard. 'I said, where's the gun?'

Mick's eyes watered. 'I don't know what you mean.'

'The gun you used to shoot Mr Lorenz. Where is it?'

Mick looked scared. 'How do you know it was me?'

'I worked it out,' she said grimly. 'The bullets had to come from somewhere. It had to be you. Nobody else would be so stupid.' She slapped him hard round the face. 'What the hell did you think you were doing? You damn nearly killed him, you stupid little sod. Luckily for you Lorenz is covering up, otherwise you'd be spending the rest of your life in jail.'

Mick stared at her in horror. 'I didn't mean to hit him. I only wanted to scare him. I wanted to teach him a lesson like Dad said.' Suddenly his face crumpled, there were tears in his eyes. He looked like the child he still was. 'But then the gun went off. I thought he'd run. But he just stood there by his door . . .'

But Joyce didn't want the details, she wanted the gun. 'Where is it?'

Mick sniffed pitifully. 'It's in the air-raid shelter.'

'Get it.'

'What?'

'You heard. Get it and load it.'

Mick stared at her, seriously scared now. 'What are you going to do?'

She laughed sourly. 'I'm going to kill your father.'

Chapter Sixteen

Pam was asleep when she heard someone hammering on the front door.

'What on earth . . .?' She reached over to nudge Alan but he was already half out of bed, groping in the darkness for his old flannel dressing gown.

Pam fumbled for her torch and pointed it at the clock. Eleven thirty.

'It must be Bertie,' she said, frowning. 'He must have got locked out somehow.'

Alan shook his head. 'He was in the living-room when I came up.'

Holding back the blackout curtain he pushed up the sash window and peered out.

'Mr Nelson, is that you?' Mick Carter's anxious shout came into the room with a draught of cold air. 'Please help me, something awful's happened.'

Alan's faint groan was audible only to Pam. 'Calm down, Mick,' he said steadily. 'You don't need to wake the whole street. What exactly has happened?'

'It's Mum,' Mick said. 'She's got a gun and she's going to kill Dad.'

Hastily Pam stuffed the sheet in her mouth to prevent a horrified giggle escaping. It was awful but for some reason she found it completely hilarious. She tried desperately to control herself as, after a second's shocked pause, Alan called down to Mick again.

'Stay there, Mick,' he said with creditable calm 'I'll get some clothes on and come down.'

Then he closed the window and rolled his eyes at Pam. 'Oh my God.' Peering at her more closely as he struggled hastily into his clothes, he frowned. 'It's not funny, you know. I know you think he's a good-for-nothing sod, but if she kills him she'll go to jail for life.'

Pam shook her head guiltily. 'I know, I know. It's awful. You must try and stop her.'

But as he left the room she thought of something else. Leaping out of bed, she ran out on to the landing. 'Alan, for God's sake be careful,' she whispered down the stairs after him. 'Don't do anything heroic. If it's a choice between her shooting him or shooting you, I'd much rather it was him.'

Alan's hand was already on the latch. He paused for a second and looked up at her as she leaned over the banister. 'Really?' He spoke with the faintest hint of sarcasm. 'Oh, darling, that's the nicest thing you've said to me for weeks.'

Shocked, Pam stood rooted to the spot even after the door had closed behind him. Was that true? Had she really been so frugal with her compliments? She had tried so hard to be normal. Not to mind the delay in Alan's results coming back. It had been weeks now since he went for his tests. Once or twice she had even suspected they had come back and he might be keeping them from her.

She wondered suddenly if knowing would really make any difference. Even if he was fine, she still wouldn't be pregnant after all. They would still have to try. Closing her eyes she leaned wearily on the banister. She loved Alan so much. It seemed so unfair that this baby problem should have to come between them.

A sudden shiver reminded her where she was and she was on the point of turning back to her bedroom when to her astonishment the living-room door opened downstairs and with a soft giggle Sheila tiptoed into the hall.

'Sheila!' The exclamation was out of Pam's mouth before she could stop it, and all too late she realised it sounded like an accusation.

There were no lights on in the house but in the faint moonlight filtering through the glass panels on the front door Pam could see that Sheila's hair was in some disarray and her blouse was untucked. Then she saw the defiant expression on her face and the two glasses in her hand and wished she had kept her mouth shut. The last thing in the world she wanted was a midnight confrontation with her volatile friend. Particularly if she had been drinking.

But it seemed Sheila was prepared to brazen it out.

'We heard shouting,' she said, crossing her arms over her chest. 'What's going on?'

Pam looked at her, saw the smudged lipstick, the flush on her delicate cheeks. What indeed, she thought.

'Some problem at the Carters,' she said shortly. 'Where's George?' She hoped to God the poor child wasn't witnessing his mother making a fool of herself with bloody Bertie Rutherford.

Sheila lifted her chin. 'He's in the shelter.'

Pam frowned. 'He doesn't like being in there alone.'

Sheila tossed her head. 'I can't help that. He's got to grow up one day.'

Pam stared at her, appalled. It's you that needs to grow up, she thought. Not poor little George with his broken childhood. He had already lost his father and his brother. Now it seemed as though he was losing his mother. Losing her to an arrogant, selfish young blade who was too much of a coward to come out of the living-room to face her himself.

Standing there, cold and frustrated, Pam wished she could knock some sense into Sheila's pretty head. She wanted to tell her that Bertie was wrong for her. That he was too young for her. Too selfish. That he came from the wrong class. That he would never take her seriously. But she couldn't say any of it. And even if she did, Sheila wouldn't listen. They had been good friends once, but they seemed to be on completely different wavelengths these days.

If only she could persuade Sheila to go back to the country out of harm's way. But every time she tried to bring the subject up she met a blank wall.

As though reading her mind, Sheila shrugged her thin shoulders. 'You might as well be the first to know,' she said. 'I've decided to stay on in London. Oh don't worry,' she added coldly, catching Pam's alarmed expression, 'I'm not going to impose on you any longer. Bertie is going to help me open up my house at the weekend.'

Joyce found she couldn't do it. She'd thought she'd be able to. She thought she'd be able to riddle his fat blubbery body with all six of the bullets she'd forced Mick to load into the gun's revolving chamber. But when the moment came to pull the trigger, she couldn't do it.

She stood at the side of the bed and stared at him as he snored gently, innocently, with one arm hanging off the edge.

In any case it seemed a waste to do it when he was asleep. She wanted to scare him like he scared her and preferably hurt him like he hurt her. She licked the blood of her lip and felt a renewed anger.

'Wake up,' she hissed. She jiggled the bed with her foot. 'Bloody wake up.' Maybe it would be easier when he was awake.

Her arm was shaking and when he didn't immediately wake, she rested it for a moment. The gun was smaller than she had expected, but surprisingly heavy. A revolver, Ward Frazer had thought. She'd have said it was a pistol. But maybe they were one and the same. She smiled to herself as she raised her arm again. Whatever it was, if Mick could hit old Lorenz from across the street with it, surely, even with a trembling hand, she'd be able to hit Stanley from across the bed.

His eyes opened suddenly, red and bleary, and she almost laughed at the incredulous expression that gradually dawned on his face as he took in what he was looking at.

He raised his head slightly. 'What the bloody . . .?'

'Get up,' she snarled at him. She wanted fear not incredulity. She waved the gun. 'Get out of the bed and stand over there by the wall.'

He laughed sourly. 'Don't be . . .'

'Stanley,' Joyce interrupted calmly, 'I don't know if you can see what's in my hand, but it's a gun. A revolver. It's got six bullets loaded in it and in a minute if you don't do as I say one of them is going to be coming your way.'

Somewhat to her surprise he moved then. Levered himself into a sitting position. He seemed reluctant to leave the warmth of the bed and as he slowly pushed back the covers she almost laughed as she realised why.

He was only wearing his vest and socks. In between were his heavy white thighs and the small bundle of genitals he was even now shielding with his crossed hands as he got out of bed and backed away from her towards the wall.

Joyce walked forward a few steps to keep him in range. 'Put your hands up,' she snapped. She was enjoying herself now. If she'd known what power a gun gave you, she'd have got hold of one years ago.

'I *said* put your hands up!' He didn't move and she frowned. 'A couple of hours ago this gun fired a bullet right into Mr Lorenz's shoulder.'

'That wasn't me,' he blustered. He was shivering now, and she hoped it wasn't just from the cold.

'I know it wasn't you,' she said. 'But it will be you that gets the next one if you don't do what you're told.'

As he raised his arms slowly she smiled grimly and adjusted her aim slightly. The gun was shaking again and she tightened her hold on it. 'You know, Stanley,' she said, as her temper flared suddenly, 'I'm tempted to splatter what you've got there between your legs all over the wall.'

She had barely finished speaking when to her astonishment a sudden cracking explosion rocked the room and the gun nearly jumped out of her hand.

'Oh my God!' For a second she thought she had hit him as he crumpled into the corner under the window. Then as the smell of cordite engulfed her, she saw the dust trickling from a deep hole in the chimney breast.

She heard a shout in the street below and footsteps running along the pavement and knew she hadn't got long.

'Get up, Stanley,' she shouted at him. 'I didn't get you then, but I bloody will next time. Now listen to me,' she said as he lumbered to his feet. He was shielding his genitals again but there was real fear in his eyes.

'I want to kill you,' she said. 'I want to kill you for what you've been doing to me for the last few months. But I don't want to spend the rest of my life in jail. So I'm going to bargain with you.' She was shaking now, shaking so much she could barely hold the gun still. She tried to support her arm with the other hand. 'I won't tell the police that you shot Lorenz and you won't lay a hand on me ever again. Ever.'

He stared at her dumbly. 'But I didn't shoot Lorenz.'

She laughed hollowly. 'No? And do you think the police will believe that, if Lorenz says he saw you, and I hand over the gun?' Her eyes glittered dangerously. 'I wonder how long you get for shooting someone, Stanley? Five years? Ten?'

He was white. 'You wouldn't do that. You're my bloody wife.'

She smiled as relief flooded through her. She had got him. Her arm was aching now. But in a minute she would be safe. 'Oh, I bloody would,' she said grittily. 'And if you ever touch me again I will. Ever. Do you hear me?'

She jumped as she heard Alan Nelson's voice outside the door. 'Mrs Carter, are you all right? I heard a shot.'

Just a moment, Mr Nelson,' she said, fighting for calm. 'I'll be with you in a minute.' She turned back to Stanley. It was odd, she was freezing cold but her palms were sweating. The gun was all over the place. 'Well? What do you say?'

He nodded. 'All right. Just for God's sake put the gun down.'

'Say it. Say you won't touch me again.'

'I won't touch you again.'

She waved the gun threateningly. 'Louder.'

'I won't touch you again.'

Joyce glanced at the door. 'Did you hear that, Mr Nelson?'

There was an embarrassed cough. 'Yes, I heard, Mrs Carter.'

She nodded and lowered her arm. 'In that case, Mr Nelson, you can have your gun back.'

Katy had only been back at work a few hours before Nurse Coogan whispered to her that there was a man wanting to see her downstairs.

'One of the porters told me just now,' she said, nodding apologetically at the elderly lady whose hands Katy was washing. 'It's that Canadian chap.' She glanced nervously towards Sister's office. 'He said it was urgent, but Sister Morris will never let you go even if it's life and death.'

Katy felt something twist inside her. She dropped the flannel into the bowl of water and closed her eyes for a second. She hadn't had a chance to tell anyone about her engagement, but if Ward was wanting to see her now it could mean only one thing. That his departure had been brought forward. She could feel Nurse Coogan's curious eyes on her and tried to swallow the sudden lump in her throat. 'I think it probably is life or death,' she said huskily.

Suddenly she felt her patient's hand on her arm. She looked down in surprise at the gnarled arthritic fingers, still wet from their soaping, and then up at the kindly wrinkled face.

'Then you'd best go,' the old lady said. She nodded at Nurse Coogan. 'We'll cover for you, won't we, Nurse? We'll say I knocked the bowl of water over you. Clumsy old codger that I am. And you've gone to change your apron.'

The minute Katy saw Ward leaning against the railings outside the hospital, smoking, she knew her suspicion was correct. He stubbed out his cigarette as she came up to him.

'Thank God,' he said lightly. 'I thought I was going to have to storm the Ethel Barnet ward to get to see you.'

Katy couldn't return his smile. 'You're going, aren't you?'

He nodded. 'I'm sorry. It's the weather. It's threatening to clear and we need the cloud cover.'

He was different, brisker, more remote. She realised he was already distancing himself, turning himself into the tough unemotional fighter he needed to be for the next few weeks. She didn't like it. 'I don't want you to go.'

He looked surprised. 'God, do you think I want to go?' He shook his head. 'But it should be the last time. Then I'll get myself transferred back to the Air Force, back to normal flying duties.'

Flying would be bad enough, but not as bad as him being out of touch in constant danger in France.

He groaned slightly. 'Don't look like that, Katy. I'm coming back this time. I want to get married, remember. And I'm relying on you to fix up a nice wedding.' He smiled suddenly. 'I've already arranged the honeymoon.'

Katy flushed. The less said about the honeymoon the better. 'Is there anything you particularly want?' she asked quickly. 'For the wedding, I mean? Hymns and things?'

He shook his head. 'You are the only thing I particularly want. So long as I get you, I don't mind about anything else.'

'What about Louise?' Katy asked, trying desperately to shake off a sudden terrible sense of foreboding. 'I think you should tell her.' She flushed slightly. 'I think she thought that you and she . . .'

'You are kidding me?' He saw from her expression that she wasn't. 'But I'd made it clear I didn't feel that way about her, so I guess I always assumed her flirting was just a game . . .' He stopped abruptly and made an apologetic face. 'Look, I haven't got time to see her but I promise I'll write to her before I go.' He saw her expression and smiled. 'Sweetheart, don't worry. She'll understand. Maybe she could be a bridesmaid?'

'I suppose I could ask her,' Katy said doubtfully. She had assumed Jen would be her bridesmaid and she couldn't quite imagine Jen and Louise trooping up the St Aldate's aisle side by side. Suddenly she realised she couldn't imagine herself trooping up the aisle either and frowned.

Ward took her hands. 'Shut your eyes a minute.'

'Why?'

He smiled. 'Because I want to kiss you and I don't want you looking at me with that troubled expression.'

Slightly to her surprise he only kissed her gently on the lips before pulling her into his arms, hugging her close, tight and warm. Then he held her at arm's length and studied her face as though he never wanted to forget her.

'You'll be careful, won't you, Katy? No strolling about in the middle of raids?'

She tried to smile. 'The raids seem to have stopped.'

He shrugged. 'For now. The Luftwaffe may have been quiet for the last few weeks while the weather's been bad, but they'll soon be back.' A muscle flickered in his jaw. He glanced over his shoulder and she realised suddenly that someone was waiting for him in a car on the corner.

He touched her cheek with the backs of his fingers. His voice was husky. 'Once, a long time ago, I asked someone else to marry me and she was dead within a few weeks. Don't do that to me, Katy.'

She shivered. 'Then don't you do it to me,' she said fiercely.

★　★　★

It didn't take long for people to notice the difference in Stanley Carter. Where previously he had been argumentative and aggressive, now he seemed unusually quiet and withdrawn, and what was even more odd, he hadn't been in the Flag and Garter for days. Speculation was rife and it didn't take much imagination to link his extraordinary metamorphosis with the Lorenz incident. After all, Stanley had on many an occasion been outspoken in his dislike for the pawnbroker. So the general feeling was that Stanley must have somehow been responsible for the rumoured shots. But as Lorenz refused to comment, and Joyce and Katy kept their mouths shut, nothing was proved, and gradually people began to talk about Katy's engagement instead.

Pam and Alan were the only people who knew the true story and Pam thought it was wonderful. 'Good old Mrs Carter,' she had said when Alan told her what had happened. And she hadn't been able to stop laughing at his description of Stanley Carter standing in terror in the corner of the bedroom clutching his genitals.

For a while it had eased the mounting tension between them. Sheila and George had moved back into their house across the road and, although Pam already missed having little George around and she still had to put up with Bertie, suddenly she felt some of the weight lift from her shoulders.

'We're alone,' she remarked suddenly one evening as she and Alan got up to turn off the wireless after the news. 'Can you believe it? We're alone. Isn't it wonderful?'

Something about Alan's silence made her look up at him sharply. And suddenly she knew. She felt her heart kick in her chest.

'It's the results of the tests, isn't it? You've got the results?'

He was standing very still, very stiff. 'I've had them for a week,' he said. He shrugged. 'I just couldn't bring myself to tell you.' He raised his hands slightly then dropped them again. Pam saw them curl into fists. She swallowed. 'It's bad news, then?' she asked.

Suddenly his veneer of control broke. She watched appalled as his face crumpled in a private agony. 'Oh God, Pam, I'm so sorry.'

'Oh Alan.' She couldn't speak. She stood up but she didn't know what to say. She had had no idea the disappointment would be so intense. She had thought she wouldn't mind. That a baby was a luxury, another mouth to feed, another person to worry about. Oddly she had always thought it mattered to Alan more than to her. But now she stood there in the silent room she realised it mattered a lot. They had both so enjoyed having little George around, now suddenly the prospect of a childless future looked bleak.

She could feel Alan's eyes on her and quickly she turned away to hide her despair.

But it was too late, he had seen the tears welling in her eyes and she felt his hands tentatively on her shoulders. 'Pam,' he spoke into her hair. 'Talk to me, please. I can bear anything except the thought of losing you.'

She swung round then. 'Of course you won't lose me, but . . .'

But he didn't stop to hear. 'We could always adopt.'

Pam blinked in surprise. 'Adopt?'

He grimaced slightly. 'I suppose I've had more time to think about it than you. But I wouldn't mind.' He looked at her eagerly. 'Giving a needy child a home and that. And there must be masses of orphaned bombed-out children wanting homes just now.'

Pam looked into his anxious face and her heart bled for him. He had obviously been working this out for days. Working out a solution to her bitter disappointment. It was a perfect solution. A typically big hearted Alan-type solution. 'Oh Alan,' she said helplessly. 'I love you so much.'

Louise kept Ward's letter for two days, then tore it into tiny pieces and burnt it in her bedroom grate.

As she watched the flames lick at his slanted writing she felt a cold anger envelop her. How dare he write to her, talking of their friendship, his respect for her, his hope that she would soon be fully recovered. How dare he tell her that he had fallen in love with Katy a long time ago and that he had been delighted to discover that she returned his affections. Of course Katy returned his blasted affections. Any girl in their right mind would return Ward Frazer's affections.

She would have returned them herself if only she had had the chance. But she hadn't had the chance, had she? Oh no, she had been spurned in favour of stupid Katy Parsons with her neat little nurse's uniform and her shy little smile.

Louise glared at the fire. She should have known that time when Ward kissed Katy under the mistletoe. She should have seen it coming.

But, locked into her own dream, she hadn't seen it coming. It had knocked her off balance and thanks to Ward's letter she now felt as though she was being kicked in the ribs while she was down.

In the same post had come a letter from Aaref Hoch, asking if she was well enough yet to meet him for a cup of tea, or a drink or a walk or even a cinema if she would care for it. Louise decided to burn his letter for good measure. She didn't want a cup of tea with Aaref bloody Hoch. She wanted a proper boyfriend, a man she could be proud of, someone to take her away from beastly Lavender Road and the miserable people who lived in it. People like Mrs Carter who made no effort to conceal her glee that Katy Parsons had pipped her to the post with Ward Frazer.

Ward Frazer. Louise felt a new wash of misery. How could life be so unfair to her?

Poking the small pile of ash in the grate with her pencil she realised one scrap of Ward's letter had failed to ignite. Crossly she pulled it out and unfolded it. The edges were charred but the writing was clear . . . *sure that one day you will find the same happiness*, it said. *In the meantime I look forward to seeing you when I get back. If not, I guess it will be at the wedding.*

Furiously she struck a match and held it to the paper. She didn't want happiness one day, she wanted it now and she wanted it with him.

If only she had gone to Bristol. If only Katy hadn't gone. If only . . .

She dropped the burning paper as the flames touched her fingers and swore. Bloody Katy Parsons. Bloody Ward Frazer. She didn't want to see either of them ever again.

She certainly wouldn't be going to their beastly wedding.

By the middle of February it had become clear that Hitler wasn't going to let recent Allied successes pass unchallenged. Already he was turning the screws on Vichy France. Even more serious was the news that four hundred thousand German troops had arrived in the Balkans, putting pressure on the non-aligned states of Bulgaria, Turkey and Yugoslavia and threatening the Greek advance in Albania. And most worrying of all was the arrival in Tripoli of General Rommel's desert-trained Afrika Korps, with orders to stop the humiliating rout of Italian troops by Field Marshal Wavell's British army.

And then the bombing started again.

Not every night. But often enough to cause Katy problems on her way home from hospital. Every time she crept home while the warning was on, she guiltily remembered Ward's parting words but short of staying endlessly at the hospital she had little choice. And there was so much to do at home suddenly, so many letters to write, lists to be made.

She hadn't realised how much organisation went into even a small wartime wedding and it was a job in itself to keep her mother from worrying herself to death about it.

Her parents were quite blatantly delighted that she had managed to land herself such a classy, nice looking husband, and they were determined to have the best wedding they could possibly afford. To Katy's dismay, despite the shortages and rationing, they began to talk about printed invitations, flowers, a wedding breakfast and even a white dress.

'It's not every day of the week that your daughter finds herself a husband, is it?' her father said jovially when Katy tried to persuade

287

them that a simple wedding would be quite adequate. 'We want the best for you, love. We always have. And although it's not an easy time for us financially, we're prepared to push the boat out a bit.'

But to her mother's consternation, white wedding dresses were no longer to be found for love nor money. In the end it was Mr Lorenz who solved the problem by shyly offering Katy a bundle of parachute silk one evening when she called to dress his rapidly healing wound.

'I'm afraid it's German,' he murmured as she fingered the strange cold material. 'But there's enough for a dress if it's cut carefully. Even a short train.'

Katy was unbearably touched. 'It's lovely,' she said. 'It's too good. We'd never be able to afford it.'

He looked shocked. 'Oh, I never meant you to pay for it, Miss Parsons. After what you've done for me I hoped you would accept it as a small gift.'

The following day Mrs Carter offered to make a cake. 'It won't be three tiered, mind,' she said. 'But Mrs Rutherford says she's got some old dried fruit we can use and if we put a notice up on the bar I reckon the regulars would donate a bit of sugar for the icing.'

So gradually, painfully, the arrangements for the wedding began to come together and as the cold dark days of February gave way to a marginally warmer March and the banns were read and the printed invitations finally went out, it seemed to Katy that nobody she met ever talked about anything else.

Momentarily they would discuss the German advance on the Greek borders, the sinking of eleven German ships off Norway, the signing of the potentially life-saving American lease lend agreement, but then it was straight back to the wedding.

She didn't mind. She liked it in many ways. At least it made it real. In the continuing absence of Ward she found she needed something to make it real.

He had been gone four weeks now, and although she hadn't said anything to anybody, Katy had gradually become less nervous about actually getting married and more nervous that the dreaded day would arrive and Ward would not be home. She knew any day now her mother would start worrying about it too.

'You can't have a proper wedding without a bridegroom, you know,' she'd say and Katy would almost certainly cry.

Without Jen, the Miss Taylors or Mrs Frost to talk to she was finding it hard to keep up her morale. Bertie was too busy mooning about Sheila Whitehead to listen to Katy's woes, and then to cap it all, one evening she bumped into Louise outside Arding & Hobbs.

She had barely said hello before Louise was hissing at her.

'How could you? It was me he wanted. Me! You knew it too. And you knew I wanted him. You knew I loved him. But it didn't stop you, did it?' Her voice rose. 'You slept with him, didn't you? And then made him feel guilty? That's how you got him, isn't it?'

Katy stared at her in disbelief, terribly aware of the goggled-eyed interest of the passers-by.

'Louise, no,' she whispered. 'I didn't do anything. Honestly. He's barely touched me.'

But Louise seemed oblivious to the interested spectators. 'Well, he's touched me,' she shouted, almost in tears. 'What do you think we were doing all those times he came to visit me in hospital? We weren't talking about the weather.'

Katy felt sick. 'I don't want to talk about it,' she said and stumbled away before she heard any more. She didn't know whether to believe her or not but it rocked her confidence badly.

Bizarrely, it was Nurse Coogan who stopped her from calling the whole thing off.

'Don't talk bloody stupid,' she said when she took over from Katy on fire watch on the roof of the Wilhelmina the following day. Fire-watching was a hated task, cold and lonely and on occasions extremely frightening. Worst of all, from Katy's point of view, it gave her time to think. Time to worry. Time to wonder if Ward wouldn't really be better off with Louise.

'She's a cow, that Louise,' Nurse Coogan went on forcefully. 'Not that I've ever met her of course. But everyone on Private Block says so and you only have to look at that toffee-nosed little git of a brother of hers to know what she'd be like.'

'They're not really toffee nosed,' Katy said, hugging her cloak around her against the cold wind that was blowing across the roof. 'It's just their manner. It's the way they've been brought up. And anyway, it's true what she says. I did know how keen she was on him. What with her accident and everything, maybe she does deserve him much more than I do.'

Nurse Coogan looked at her incredulously. 'Don't be so bloody generous,' she said. 'You're marrying that lovely man whether you like it or not. And who cares what he may or may not have done with that little bitch? It's you he wants now. Most likely it's just sour grapes with her anyway.' She shrugged. 'It's not surprising. He is rather gorgeous. God, even Sister Morris is green with envy. Since he sent her flowers that time she's had the hots for him. I suppose in a minute you're going to say she deserves him too?'

Despite herself Katy giggled. Sister Morris had seemed neither green with envy nor mad with desire for Ward when she had summoned Katy into her office a couple of days earlier. She had been crisp and matter of fact.

'I hear you are getting married, Nurse.'

Katy had nodded meekly. 'Yes, Sister, I hope so.'

Sister Morris had little time for niceties. 'Either you are or you aren't,' she had barked impatiently. 'And if you are, you will have to leave us. You do understand that married nurses are not acceptable in this hospital?'

'Yes, I know.' To her horror Katy had felt tears welling. 'But my . . . my fiancé should have been back by now. I haven't heard from him . . .'

Sister had regarded her for a moment. 'I see,' she had said crisply. 'In that case, Nurse, I suggest you continue with us until such time as he returns.'

That was the end of the interview, but now Katy turned to Nurse Coogan and asked the question she had been longing to ask someone for days. 'What if he doesn't come back?'

Nurse Coogan shrugged. 'Then you'll have to stay on here with me and we can turn into bitter old spinsters like Sister Morris together.'

On the thirtieth of March, the Sunday before the wedding was due to take place, Katy finally took her courage in her hands and telephoned Helen de Burrel from the phone box on Lavender Hill. Helen's polite acceptance of the wedding invitation had come a couple of weeks ago on smart headed notepaper and for days Katy had been wondering if it was presuming on her acquaintance to make use of the neatly embossed telephone number.

To her astonishment she was connected almost straight away, and with a frantic punching of button A, managed to announce herself.

'Katy.' Helen's well-rounded vowels travelled easily down the line from Kensington. 'I'm so glad you called.'

Katy gripped the receiver more tightly. 'Have you heard from Ward, then?'

There was a fractional pause. 'Well, no, actually, not recently,' Helen admitted. 'But on the other hand we haven't heard anything bad either, which is a good sign, if you see what I mean.'

Katy wasn't sure that she did. All she knew was that she felt sick.

'Do you think I should go on with the arrangements for the wedding?' she asked, aware that she had to be careful what she said over the open telephone line. The last thing she wanted was to somehow inadvertently compromise Ward's safety. Even now, right outside the door was an enormous billboard reminding her that Walls had Ears.

'Goodness yes,' Helen said, shocked. 'He'd be awfully miffed if he got back and found you'd called it off.' She hesitated for a second and then went on. 'I'm sure it will be all right, Katy. I really can't say any more than that, but I promise to let you know the moment I hear anything.'

Katy swallowed. 'Even if you hear anything . . . bad . . .?'

Helen's voice was firm, unemotional. 'I promise to let you know that as well.'

Two days later Katy got a letter from Jen saying she wasn't sure she would be able to be bridesmaid after all. *It's the bloody pianist*, she wrote in her usual hasty scrawl. *He's gone and invited some ENSA bigwig to the show the day of the wedding. He's done it on purpose. He knew I was going to be away and he wants to bitch about me behind my back. Katy, much as I long to watch you take the oath to honour and obey the wonderful Ward, I daren't risk being away. Can you find another bridesmaid? Wouldn't that fancy-pants Louise do it? Best of luck anyway. And happy honeymoon!! All love to you both, Jen. P.S. If anything changes on the bigwig front, I'll be there.*

'It's a disaster,' Katy moaned to Nurse Coogan in the sluice room. 'At this rate it'll just be me and Dad in the aisle.'

'And the vicar,' Nurse Coogan said. 'Don't forget him.' She smirked. 'You can't have a wedding without a vicar.'

'Fat lot of good he is,' Katy said sourly. 'He just keeps telling me to pray.'

Nurse Coogan sniffed. 'I used to say my prayers every night but it hasn't done me much good, has it?'

'What did you pray for?' Katy asked, intrigued, then regretted the question when she saw her companion's pointed face turn a blotchy pink. Quickly she looked away, pretending she hadn't noticed.

Nurse Coogan scrubbed harder at her bed pan. 'I prayed that one day my real mother would come and find me,' she said gruffly. 'And I'd suddenly turn out to be rich and beautiful.' She shrugged and glanced at Katy defiantly. 'But I don't care about that any more. When it comes to the crunch, and the bomb falls with your name on it, it doesn't really matter what you look like, does it?' Abruptly she picked up her pile of pans ready to head back on to the ward then stopped abruptly as Staff Hicks came in with a stricken face.

Katy felt a cold chill course through her. 'What is it? What's happened?' she asked urgently. 'Is it a message for me? Is it Ward Frazer?'

Staff Hicks brushed off her alarm with a frown. 'No, it's not Ward Frazer,' she said irritably. 'It's Benghazi. One of the porters just heard on the wireless. We're having to evacuate in the face of Rommel's advance.'

When Katy and Nurse Coogan stared at her blankly she pursed her lips crossly. 'Well, don't just stand there,' she said. 'Get on with the bed pans, you haven't got all day.'

That following evening Katy had just got back from fetching the night nurse's snack tray, when Nurse Coogan screamed down the ward, 'Nurse Parsons, quick! Where on earth have you been? Phone!'

Almost dropping the tray, aware of the sudden shocked silence and of everyone's eyes on her, Katy hurtled up the central aisle, heart hammering, and screeched to a halt by the telephone.

'Who is it?' she gasped, but Nurse Coogan just thrust the receiver into her hand.

'Quick or you'll get cut off. It's a terrible line.'

Expecting Helen de Burrel's plummy tones, Katy nearly died of shock when she heard the accented masculine voice coming through the crackles.

'Katy? Are you there? I've had one hell of a job getting through.'

'Yes,' she croaked, trying desperately to catch her breath. 'Yes, it is. Ward, where are you?'

'I'm at an airfield in Bedfordshire.' Even over the Post Office gurglings she could detect a hint of weariness in his voice. 'Katy, I'm really sorry to have cut it so fine.' Then a slight hesitation. 'Helen tells me you were thinking of cancelling. You haven't changed your mind, have you?'

Something in his voice unsettled her. Just talking to him unsettled her. Suddenly it was all completely unreal again. Was she really intending to marry this disembodied stranger? To give up her nursing career? Everything she had struggled for?

She could feel the expectant hush behind her and glanced round with a sudden stab of emotion at the rigid rows of neatly made beds, the shiny floors, the high pristine white walls, the gleaming trolleys, the well-ordered instruments on their white starched cloth. She had hated it at first, the discipline, the pettiness of it, hated the brisk, immaculate nurses, the meek, white-faced patients, hated the unwavering harshness of the rules.

But now, suddenly, for the first time she felt part of it, no longer an outsider, she had found a role here, a place, albeit a lowly one, but one where she was part of a team, where she knew what she had to do, and did it. Suddenly she appreciated its orderliness, its neatness, the fact that everyone and everything knew its place. Once she left she would be at sea again, thrown back on her own meagre resources, forced to make her own decisions in a cruel, war torn world.

And then she thought of the Miss Taylors already arrived from Bristol, of her parents' excitement, of all Ward's guests preparing to make the journey to St Aldate's Clapham Common on Saturday.

And then suddenly she saw Sister emerging from her office, her skirt rustling starchily as she swept down the central aisle like a battleship in full attack, and five times as fearsome. Private calls were never allowed on the ward telephone. Never.

'Katy.' Ward's voice grated in her ear, urgent now and slightly cracking. 'For God's sake speak to me. Tell me you haven't changed your mind.'

Quickly she turned her back on Sister's advance.

'Have you?' she whispered.

'No.'

And then she heard the Operator interrupting with some query, and Ward's furious shout. 'Get off the line, you stupid woman, I'm trying to get married.'

And then she was laughing, and crying, and the line was crackling and Ward was trying to ask something about the wedding and the Operator was saying his time was up.

She heard Ward swear and the operator's tight-lipped response and then the last thing she heard, before the line went dead, was Ward's strangled shout. 'I'll see you in church.'

Hanging the receiver carefully back on its hook, Katy turned round. She had never seen the Ethel Barnet ward so silent, so still, not even for Sister's prayers. Nobody was talking. Nobody was knitting. Everyone was staring at her. Even Sister had stopped a few yards short.

Overcome, Katy turned to Nurse Coogan, her ally over the long weeks of waiting. 'It looks like I'm going to need a bridesmaid,' she said shyly, touching her arm. 'I don't suppose you . . .?'

And suddenly with one accord all the patients were clapping and cheering. Even the nurses looked pleased. And Sister Morris was almost smiling.

But to Katy's surprise Nurse Coogan's eyes filled with tears. 'Are you sure?' she whispered, her pixie face lighting up in a watery smile of delight. 'I was going to offer before, but I didn't think you'd want me because I'm so ugly.'

Chapter Seventeen

As soon as her father opened the door of the taxi, Katy could hear the organ music, deep and sonorous, making the wicket gate tremble with its long vibrations on the lower notes. To her ears it sounded more suitable for a funeral than a wedding and she shivered, getting a sharp reprimand from her mother who was arranging her veil.

Katy didn't like the veil. It was old and fussy and smelt faintly of mothballs. But her mother had worn it at her wedding and was adamant that it should have another outing even though it looked grey in comparison with the lily-whiteness of the newly finished parachute-silk dress.

Katy was pleased with the dress. It had a few seams in odd places but the overall effect was breathtaking. Even Jen, rushing into the pub just minutes before they left for the church, had approved of it. She had left Southampton at the crack of dawn on the milk train. 'I realised I couldn't miss your happy day even if it meant getting up at four o'clock in the bloody morning,' she'd said, dumping her bag on the floor and slipping off her smart navy coat. 'And with any luck I'll be back in time for the evening shows.'

She had stopped as Katy turned round and smiled slowly as she took in the tight white bodice and the long trailing skirt beneath. 'Oh yes! Virginal but sexy. I like it. Very Snow White. Ward will probably faint with desire at the altar.'

Then Jen had almost fainted herself as Nurse Coogan emerged from Katy's bedroom in a pink pinafore dress with a white sash that made her look rather like one of the seven dwarfs.

'This is Nurse Coogan,' Katy had said quickly. 'I mean Molly Coogan. She was standing in for you.'

Molly Coogan had taken one look at Jen in her chic little peach and white linen suit and flushed. 'You won't want me now.'

Disappointment was so evident in her brusque manner that Katy hadn't the heart to turn her away. 'Of course I want you.'

'But we'll look ridiculous,' Jen had said. 'We clash.'

'I don't care,' Katy had said grittily. 'I want you both.'

The church path was bordered with daffodils. Now as the three of them walked up it together, Jen giggled. 'For goodness sake, Katy, stop trembling. Anyone would think you were going to the gallows.' She peered through the veil. 'Are you still there under that old rag of your mother's? All I can see is a white blur. Ward'll think he's marrying a ghost.'

'She looks lovely,' Molly Coogan said stoutly with a daggers glance at Jen. 'Of course she's nervous. Brides are always nervous. A few butterflies are normal.'

Katy tried to smile. Trust her to end up with two bridesmaids at each other's throats. Molly Coogan was always spiky and Jen had got her back up from the first. Katy had already had to mediate in a wrangle over which of them would hold her flowers during the service. Still, at least their antagonism had taken her mind off her nerves. Nerves that were now crashing around in her stomach more like butter churns than butterflies.

She looked up at the red-brick church in front of her. Through the veil even the sturdy Victorian porch and square tower took on an oddly ethereal guise. It was like a dream. Her dress brushed soft and cold against her legs, the small bouquet of flowers in her hand smelt of spring. For a second she felt she was some mythical princess waiting to be married to her handsome swashbuckling prince from overseas.

And then, on some invisible signal, the organ launched into the wedding march, there was a scraping of feet, and her father was taking her arm.

Katy peered into the porch. It was dark, and dimly beyond she could see people in hats craning round expectantly.

Suddenly as her hazy romantic dream crashed back into harsh terrifying reality, she balked on the step. She was indeed about to marry a man from overseas. A man she hardly knew. A competent, experienced, grown-up man, who would have expectations of his wife. Expectations she wasn't sure she could fulfil. She couldn't even remember exactly what he looked like.

'I can't do it,' she said.

'Yes, you bloody can,' Jen said crudely and gave her a good shove in the back.

Fifty yards away, out on the common, Louise moved out from behind a tree. She was shivering. There was a stiff breeze blowing and she had been there for some time. She had seen the first guests arrive, some RAF boys decked out in smart dress uniform with swords and braid. Then others had come, other uniformed men, Canadians she thought, and then some of the locals, the Nelsons, the awful Carters, her parents, and then to her surprise Bertie had arrived with the Whitehead woman and the little boy. She hadn't seen Bertie for some time. He wasn't allowed to visit her at the house of course and she hadn't ventured out much, partly because she was embarrassed about her limp and partly because she couldn't bear the thought of everyone in Lavender Road laughing behind their hands at the poor jilted rich girl from the big house up on the common.

As she saw some of her friends arrive, Helen de Burrel and Lucinda Veale and Felicity Rowe, girls from Lucie Clayton whom Ward knew through one of their brothers, she suddenly wished she had swallowed her pride and accepted the beastly invitation.

And then Ward Frazer arrived and the thought was gone instantly.

From this distance she couldn't see Ward's expression, but he looked relaxed, smiling and laughing as his friends greeted him with slaps on the arm and hearty handshakes. She saw the way he greeted the other guests who were still milling about outside the church, saw the girls preening as he approached, saw their responsive smiles and eager kisses and her heart twisted.

He should have been hers. There was no doubt about it. He was a man she could have been proud of. A man her friends would have been jealous of.

And then the vicar was drawing Ward inside, the best man was marshalling everyone into the church, Ward was lost to sight, and Louise leaned back weakly against her tree.

More guests trickled in. A surprising number, Louise thought sourly as she swigged back a fortifying mouthful of the brandy she had found in her father's drinks cabinet. After all, who on earth was interested in stupid little Katy Parsons? Louise frowned. It should have been her wedding they were celebrating. Why should Katy Parsons have all the honours?

And then a black taxi drew up and Louise stiffened. At last. She could see the lace veil blowing in the breeze, but until the taxi drew away she couldn't see Katy's full regalia. And even then her parents and the bridesmaids were in the way.

Bridesmaids? Louise's eyes widened in amazement. Were those really the bridesmaids? That awful Jen Carter looked all right, but who on earth was the creature in the pink dress? Suddenly Louise was laughing. She leaned weakly against the tree, lifting the bottle again. Katy Parsons didn't need her to spoil her stupid wedding. It was spoilt already by a pair of absurdly mismatched bridesmaids.

And then, as they lined up outside the porch, just for a second Louise caught a glimpse of Katy. The bride. Anonymous from this distance under the lowered veil, but none the less enviable for that. Sudden tears clouded Louise's vision and she closed her eyes as the rousing strains of the wedding march wafted across the common.

How could she be so unlucky? How could life be so bitterly

unfair? Shivering against the stiff breeze she strengthened her resolve, pushed herself off the tree and began to limp across the damp grass.

St Aldate's wasn't a big church but to Katy, as she stumbled round the font on her father's arm trying to match her steps to his uneven stride, its aisle seemed to stretch to eternity.

And there at the end of it, dressed in smart RAF blue, with his back to her, was Ward.

Suddenly everything else faded. The extraordinary number of people, the muffled whispers, the thumping strains of the organ, the swish of her dress, the click of Jen and Molly's heels behind her, the tension in her father's arm.

Everything became a blur except that tall still figure. Ward Frazer, her husband to be, whom she hadn't seen for two long nerve-racking months.

Suddenly she wished he would look round. Just to remind her. To reassure her. But he didn't and she felt the cold brush of fear on her skin as all her doubts re-assailed her.

And now she was getting closer and closer and her steps were getting slower and slower and she could feel her father almost dragging her on, and she could feel her heart thumping so heavily in her chest that she could barely hear the organ, and still he didn't look round.

And then suddenly she was standing beside him.

And his head was turning and although she knew she wasn't meant to look at him, irresistibly hers turned too. For a moment he looked almost sad and her heart seemed to stop. Then as their eyes met through the barrier of the veil, he gave a muffled groan. And flouting every convention in the book, every tradition, he suddenly drew her into his arms.

'Thank God,' he whispered huskily. 'I was scared you'd changed your mind.'

For a long second there was complete shocked silence in the

church and then as he released her, she heard the faint tutting of disapproval from her mother in the pew behind her. But it was quickly lost in the unmistakable sniffing back of tears from one of her bridesmaids. Molly Coogan, Katy guessed, but she didn't have time to find out because already the vicar was stepping forward, clearing his throat in a flush of embarrassment.

'Dearly beloved,' he began, still blinking in shock, 'we are gathered together here in the sight of God . . .'

Katy didn't hear the words. She didn't hear Jen's slight snigger at the word fornication, she didn't hear Molly Coogan blowing her nose. All she could hear was the soft almost silent breathing of the man standing next to her, the creak of his leather shoes as he turned to face the vicar, the scrape of material as he moved his arm and she crossed her fingers, hoping to God she was doing the right thing. Hoping she would be able to give him the love he deserved. Because just now she didn't seem capable of feeling anything except complete and utter panic.

Louise leaned heavily on the lych-gate and frowned. It had seemed further than she thought from her tree to the gate and now the church path ahead of her was swaying unnervingly. As was the church, come to that. St Aldate's, usually so solid and respectable, was wobbling about all over the place. She was glad she wasn't inside. She was feeling queasy enough as it was without having to sit in a swaying pew. So queasy in fact that she decided she should have another quick sip of brandy to settle her stomach.

But to her astonishment the bottle was empty. She stared at it in dismay. An empty bottle was no good. She couldn't toast Katy and Ward's marriage with an empty bottle.

Katy and Ward's marriage. Suddenly she remembered why she was here and it wasn't to toast Katy and Ward's marriage. Putting the bottle carefully on the wall, she squared her shoulders grimly and pushed open the gate.

Or tried to push it open. Muttering obscenities under her breath she kicked it and shoved it and it was only when she finally, in fury, raised her hand to hit it that she realised the reason it wouldn't open was that there was somebody on the other side.

Aaref Hoch. She hadn't seen him in months but she couldn't fail to recognise that angular face, the dark intensity of his eyes.

'What are you doing here?' she asked rudely and was pleased to see him flush.

'I was invited,' he said.

Louise blinked at him. For some reason he was swaying too. She put a hand on the gate. 'Well, so was I,' she said. 'So let me in.'

He shook his head. 'It's too late,' he said. 'The service has begun.'

Louise frowned. 'Then we'd better hurry.'

But Aaref was still holding the gate. 'No,' he said steadily. 'I can't let you go in, Louise. I can't let you spoil it for her.'

Louise stared at him. How dare this little Jewish pipsqueak get in her way? How dare he stand up for Katy Parsons? Furiously she tried to wrestle the gate out of his grasp, but he was stronger than she had appreciated.

'I'll scream,' she said. And leaned back to take a deep breath. But before she could begin her inhalation, Aaref had wrenched the gate open and was frogmarching her across the road back on to the common.

For a few strides, Louise struggled. Then she suddenly remembered that he was meant to be in love with her and she tried a new tack. 'Please, Aaref,' she wheedled, sagging against him. 'Let me in and I'll do anything you want.' She giggled. 'I'll even go to bed with you if I must.'

'Stop it, Louise.' He let her go at once, sounding annoyed. 'Don't say things you don't mean.'

'I do mean it,' she shouted as she fought to retain her balance. 'Why don't you believe me?'

Aaref's eyes narrowed slightly but his voice was calm. 'Because you are drunk. No, don't deny it. I've been watching you.' He shrugged awkwardly. 'I was going to leave you alone. But when you came to the church I had to stop you.' He shook his head wearily. 'It's not for Katy. It's for yourself, Louise. Everyone would laugh at you. I couldn't allow that to happen.'

Sudden tears filled Louise's eyes. He was right. She would be a laughing stock. She probably was already. She looked up and saw the pity in Aaref's eyes and a sob rose in her throat. Suddenly she saw herself through his eyes, hobbling about on the windswept common, crying for a man who loved someone else. She shuddered convulsively. 'I'm going mad, aren't I?' she said as the tears began to pour down her cheeks. 'I'm going mad.'

Carefully Aaref began to lead her back towards Lavender Road. 'You're not going mad,' he said. 'You've been an invalid too long. You're just bored and lonely.' He hesitated for a second. 'And you've had a bad time. Not so long ago you lost a child. This is a very difficult thing for a girl.'

'But I wanted to lose it,' Louise sobbed. 'And then afterwards I felt so awful. And I couldn't tell anyone. I was so scared what my father would say. I was such a coward.'

Aaref shook his head. 'It is not weak to suffer alone,' he said. 'It is strength.'

Louise suddenly remembered what Aaref and his two younger brothers must have suffered in their flight from Austria eighteen months before. He hadn't just lost a nameless unborn child, he had lost his parents, his home, his friends, his country.

'You have to learn to put the bad things behind you,' he said steadily. 'To look ahead. To the future.'

Louise stopped and looked at him, humbled by the courage in his dark eyes. 'The future is not very bright just at the moment,' she said.

He smiled at her then, a soft smile. 'The future is always brighter for a beautiful girl,' he said.

For a second Louise longed to drown herself in his admiration then she swung away abruptly. 'Don't look at me,' she said curtly.

'Why not?'

She gulped and clutched her mouth. 'Because I'm going to be sick.'

The wedding passed in a blur for Katy. Afterwards all she could really remember were the nerve-racking responses, the sliding on of the ring and the extraordinary emphasis placed on joining of flesh and wifely obedience.

Only this morning her mother had drawn her on one side and given her an awkward little lecture about her wifely duties. 'You have led a sheltered life,' she had said, 'and that's quite as it should be, but now you are going to have to become a wife and that means you are going to belong to Ward. He will look after you, he will provide for you and in return you must do as he tells you.'

She had hesitated for a second, twisting her pinafore nervously. 'There are certain aspects of marriage that aren't always easy or pleasant. You don't know Ward very well and you mustn't mind if he does things . . . if he hurts you.' Seeing Katy's shocked expression, she had hurried on quickly. 'I'm sure he won't mean to, but men are different from women, Katy. They have different desires. Different needs. But whatever happens you can't come running home. You must accept it as part of your wifely duty.'

Even the vicar's sermon concentrated on the necessity of wifely obedience and the joy of children, making all too embarrassingly clear that all she had to do to be a good wife was submit to Ward's carnal desires. It was all right for the vicar to go on about it, she thought. He didn't have a wedding night looming up on him.

And then it was over, her mother's carefully chosen hymns were sung, prayers for procreation made, the blessing given, her veil was lifted, Ward had kissed her briefly on the lips and the register had been signed. The order of it all escaped her, but suddenly the organ was blaring again and she was walking slowly back down the aisle on Ward's arm.

The ceremony was over, but it was only when she saw all the smiling faces lining the aisle, heard the appreciative murmurs, heard the sniffing back of emotion, saw people further back craning to see, the surreptitious wiping of eyes, that the import of it really began to sink in.

She was married. Married to the man walking beside her. Ward Frazer. Not some remote stranger after all, but the man she had longed for ever since she had first met him.

Startled at the thought, she turned her head abruptly to look at him and saw with some surprise that except for the shadows under his eyes, he looked almost exactly the same as he always had. Perhaps it was the dress uniform that had scared her earlier. The stiff formality of it. She had forgotten that it would be the same man inside.

Catching her glance, he smiled at her and a wash of relief flooded through her. It was the same smile too. The warm, faintly quizzical smile that had endeared him to her from the first. She smiled back and felt some of the tension which had built up over the last six weeks ease out of her.

Then they were rounding the font and ahead of her the church doors opened and her eyes widened as she heard a low command, followed by a flash of silver as Ward's RAF colleagues formed a ceremonial arch of swords on the steps of the porch.

Laughing at her astonishment, he took her hand and ducking under the silver arch they emerged blinking into the thin April sunshine.

As the congregation began to shuffle out of the pews after them, Joyce found herself, to her horror, squashed up against Mr Rutherford. For an embarrassing moment as he hastily eased his elbow out of her bosom, she thought he was going to ignore her, but then he glanced at her down his long thin nose and inclined his head.

'Mrs Carter.'

Joyce stared at him as he averted his gaze again. Was that it? Was that all he intended to say? Damn it, she thought, she'd been working for the Rutherfords for well over a year. She'd have thought the snooty bugger could have managed a bit more than her name.

'Lovely wedding,' she said. Surely it wouldn't be too demeaning for him to agree with that? But he seemed too busy peering ahead to see what the blockage was so she nudged him with her hymn book. 'Didn't you think so?'

'What?' He looked round irritably. 'The service? Oh yes. Seemed to go off all right.'

'Oh, it was more than all right,' Joyce said reprovingly. 'It was really romantic. Like a film. I got quite choked when he hugged her like that at the beginning. Didn't you?'

He looked so astonished she almost laughed. 'Certainly not,' he said crisply. 'I thought it was quite unnecessary. Not at all the thing.' He drew himself up to his full height. 'Frankly I wonder sometimes what the world is coming to. I certainly thought that young man would know better.'

Joyce could hardly believe her ears. 'For the last two months that young man has been risking his life on our behalf,' she said grittily. How dare the surly bastard criticise Ward Frazer? The handsome young Canadian was worth a million of him. 'As to what the world is coming to,' she added rudely, wondering if God would mind if she rammed one of the vicar's altar candles down his throat, 'We're at war, Mr Rutherford, in case you haven't noticed. And we all have to make allowances.'

Outside in the churchyard a few minutes later Celia Rutherford came up to her with a friendly smile. 'You're looking very nice today, Mrs Carter,' she said. 'Is that a new outfit?'

Joyce flushed slightly. 'Newish,' she said. 'My daughter gave it to me for Christmas.' She didn't feel it necessary to add that it had lived in Lorenz's pawnshop virtually ever since. Nor that Mr Lorenz had discovered a hat among his unredeemed goods that matched it exactly.

She eyed Mrs Rutherford's smart pale linen belted suit and neat little pillbox hat and grinned. 'You're not looking too bad yourself.'

Celia Rutherford laughed. 'You're feeling better, aren't you, Mrs Carter? I can tell. You've been a different person since you came back from Devon. It was just what you needed, wasn't it? A nice little break like that?'

Joyce nodded. 'Oh yes. It made all the difference.' A nice little break and a nice little gun. Between them she did feel better. Much better. Better too for sleeping in Jen's old room. So far Stanley had kept his word and kept his hands off her. He hadn't said anything but she'd noticed he'd kept off the bottle a bit too. Scared he'd bump into Alan Nelson in the Flag most likely. Not that Alan had said anything to anyone as far as she knew. But neither of them were likely to forget that bedroom scene in a hurry; it made her smile even now to think about it.

It made her smile even more how he had given in over the wedding. He hadn't wanted to come, she knew that, but she was equally determined that he would. And not just come but come clean and tidy and with good grace. And she'd been determined Mick and Pete would turn up and all. She knew Jen would be done up to the nines as bridesmaid and she wasn't going to have the rest of them letting the side down.

And to her astonishment they had agreed. All three of them. Meekly.

She glanced across to the gate where they were standing all clean and tidy, caps in hands, with some of the other men. It was a tonic.

Turning back to Mrs Rutherford, she decided to strike while the iron was hot. Flushing slightly, she steeled herself against a snub. 'I don't suppose there'd be any chance of me coming back on the WVS van at all, would there?'

Celia Rutherford stared at her. 'Oh Mrs Carter! I'm so glad. And Mrs Trewgarth will be thrilled.' Then she frowned and glanced about vaguely. 'But what about your husband? I thought he . . .'

'We're at war,' Joyce said firmly. 'We all have to make sacrifices. In any case,' she added, 'Whatever that bloody vicar might say about wifely obedience and that, I'm damned if I'm going to be a slave to my husband. I have my own life to lead.'

Pam was standing next to Thelma Taylor, watching Ward and Katy pose self-consciously for the photographer from the *Wandsworth Borough News*.

'They make a lovely couple,' Pam said. 'You must be so pleased.'

The old lady smiled at her. 'Best day of our lives,' she said. 'And best of all we got to sit in the Rutherfords' pew.' She giggled naughtily. 'Did you see? They had to sit right at the back with the hoi polloi?'

Pam laughed. 'You should have been listening to the service,' she said. 'Not looking to see where everyone was sitting.'

The old lady winked. 'We like to know what's going on.' She looked around conspiratorially. 'For example we couldn't help noticing that young Louise seems to be absent. Katy told us in her letter that she had taken it badly, but I would have thought she'd have had the grace to turn up.' She glanced at Pam. 'And the boy Bertram seems to be on rather friendly terms suddenly with the poor Whitehead widow. Is that quite wise?'

Pam grimaced. 'It's not at all wise,' she said. 'It's a disaster. There's no future in it. Conscientious objector or not, he's hardly going to marry her, is he? So sooner or later he's going to break her heart, and then I'm going to have to pick up the pieces.'

Thelma Taylor followed her gaze across the churchyard to where Bertie was helping little George balance on the gravestones watched by a smiling Sheila. 'I'm afraid you're right, Mrs Nelson,' she said. 'They're smiling now, but I'm afraid it will end in tears.'

Jen drew Mrs Frost to one side. 'Are you bored with village life yet?'

Mrs Frost looked surprised. 'No, not particularly. Why?'

Jen shrugged. 'I just thought you might be wanting to do more for the war effort and that. After all, walking Winston isn't doing much for the nation's morale, is it?'

Mrs Frost's eyes narrowed beadily. 'And what exactly did you have in mind for me, Jennifer? An Easter Day recital of popular songs in St Paul's cathedral? Or something more daring like a parachute drop into Nazi Germany to steal Hitler's piano?'

Jen grinned. 'Oh no, nothing as exciting as that,' she said. She smiled innocently. 'I was thinking more of you coming on ENSA with me.'

Mrs Frost's eyes widened. 'On ENSA? Don't be absurd. I'm far too old.'

'You're not all that old,' Jen said, then giggled at her former teacher's expression. 'Anyway, age doesn't matter these days. We're all expected to do our bit.'

'And since when are you so keen for us all to do our bit?' Mrs Frost asked, clearly not impressed by Jen's sudden patriotic fervour.

Jen grimaced. 'Since I've been lumbered with that bastard pianist.' She ignored Mrs Frost's disapproving frown and rushed on. 'Honestly, Mrs Frost, he is completely hopeless, worse than hopeless. He delights in making me go wrong. And you'd be so brilliant.' She hesitated then flushed slightly. 'And it would be more fun with you on the team too.'

Mrs Frost didn't respond at once and when Jen glanced at her cautiously she was surprised to see that she looked quite touched. Not that she would admit it of course, but her nose had gone red.

'I'll think about it,' she said gruffly. Then she cleared her throat and glared at Jen. 'But if I did take it on, I'd expect you to behave and to work. And I wouldn't tolerate this prima donna attitude you've adopted. All this tarty make-up, fancy clothes and bad language. You'll be a star when you sing like one and not before.'

Jen folded her hands demurely. 'I'll be an angel,' she said sweetly. 'And, if you're on the piano, I'll sing like one too.'

Mrs Frost just snorted.

★ ★ ★

'Greville?' Celia Rutherford touched her husband's arm. 'You see that man standing over there by the lych-gate? That's Stanley Carter. Mrs Carter's husband.'

Greville Rutherford grunted. 'I know the man you mean. Jailbird, isn't he?'

Celia looked somewhat taken aback. 'Well, yes,' she admitted. 'But I think he's trying to make a fresh start. You already employ his son, Mick. And you were saying the other day that you've lost quite a bit of labour recently . . .' She tailed off under her husband's withering stare.

'Really, my dear, do you honestly think I'm going to take on a fellow like that? Fresh start or not, a criminal is a criminal as far as I'm concerned. I'm not running a charity, you know.'

Celia was about to give up gracefully when someone laughed harshly behind her.

'Generous as always, I see, Dad.' It was Bertie standing there with his hands in his pockets and a sneer on his face. 'Always ready to give someone a helping hand,' he went on sarcastically. 'Always ready to listen to the other fellow's point of view.'

'Bertie!' Celia's eyes darted nervously from her son to her husband.

Greville's face coloured so rapidly that she thought he was about to have a heart attack. She put a hand on his arm but he shook it off impatiently. 'Leave this to me, Celia.' He fixed Bertie with a glacial stare. 'I have nothing to say to you,' he said. 'You're a disgrace. Frankly, I'm surprised you dare show your face here among these serving officers. If I was one of them I would flatten you. In my opinion you should be shot. Now get out of my sight.'

Bertie was as white as his father was red. 'Charming,' he drawled. Then he turned away and walked stiffly back to Sheila who stood quailing a few yards away. 'I was going to introduce you to my delightful parents,' he said. 'But I don't think I'll bother after all.'

Greville Rutherford took a step after him but Celia intervened. 'Greville, please, don't make a scene. It would be too embarrassing. In any case we can leave now. I've said our goodbyes to Mr and

Mrs Parsons. I didn't think you'd want to go back to the pub for the wedding breakfast.'

Greville looked appalled. 'Certainly not,' he said. 'Not at all the thing for people of our position.'

'Why was that man so cross with Bertie?' little George asked Pam, as the Rutherfords swept away across the churchyard.

Pam glanced at Bertie. He was putting a brave face on it, but she could see he was upset. For the first time she felt a sliver of pity for him. After all, he was doing his bit at the hospital now and some of his tasks there sounded pretty gruesome. She smiled down at George. 'That was Bertie's father,' she said. 'He thinks Bertie should join the army.'

George frowned. 'My daddy joined the army,' he said. 'And he died. I don't want Bertie to die.'

Pam looked at the little boy and her heart twisted. She longed to tell George not to get too fond of Bertie. But she couldn't. It wasn't fair.

She sighed. Nothing seemed very fair as far as the Rutherfords were concerned. They're all as selfish as each other, she thought, watching the stiff-backed father marching through the graves.

But at the lych gate to her surprise Greville Rutherford hesitated and glanced at Stanley Carter. 'Carter?' he barked. 'I gather you're looking for work. I might have something for you at the brewery. See my foreman on Monday.'

Most people were walking back to the pub, but Ward and Katy went in the taxi and to delay their arrival by a few minutes, Ward asked the driver to take them the long way round the common.

'So,' he said, sliding the driver's partition closed and collapsing back on the leather seat next to Katy. 'How does it feel to be Mrs Frazer?'

Katy stared at him. She had been preparing herself for a passionate embrace and was rather taken aback by the lazy, smiling question.

'A bit scary,' she admitted.

'Scary?' He sat up again, looking appalled. 'You're not scared of me, are you?'

'Well, no,' she began dubiously, and then, terrified he would guess exactly what she was scared of, she rushed on nervously. 'It's just that it was all so sudden before you went away. And now I suppose I can't really believe it's real. I keep thinking I'll suddenly wake up and find it's all a dream and really you're still in France and I'm in the cellar and there's an air-raid on.'

Ward touched her hand. 'I'm sorry, sweetheart, I really am.' He grimaced. 'I had no idea it would all get so late. I nearly killed myself to get back in time.'

She believed him. The shadows under his eyes told their own story. 'No, I'm sorry,' she said. 'I didn't mean to complain. It's just . . .' She stopped, confused.

He shook his head. 'I know. With everyone around. It's hard to feel anything.' He squeezed her hand reassuringly. 'It'll be easier when we get away later. I've fixed up a nice relaxing place for us to stay.'

Katy blinked. 'What sort of place? On our own?'

He smiled. 'You didn't want me to ask the bridesmaids along, did you?'

'No, of course not.' Katy flushed and realised it might be safer to change the subject. 'Were they all right, the bridesmaids? I'm sorry they didn't match. But Jen had told me she couldn't come so I roped Nurse Coogan in instead. And then when Jen turned up I couldn't let her down.'

Ward laughed. 'She was cute. I just wish she didn't blush every time I looked at her.'

Katy smiled. Poor Molly Coogan. 'I used to do that.'

He smiled and touched her cheek. 'Sometimes you still do. It's one of the things I love about you. I hope you never stop.'

Suddenly she was scarlet. She tried to ignore it. She leaned forward urgently. 'Will you tell her?'

He raised his eyebrows. 'What? That you blush too?'

'No,' Katy giggled as the car drew up. 'Will you tell her she was cute? It's just that she thinks she's so ugly.'

The party was a huge success, mainly due to the large quantity of Canadian beer which had mysteriously made its way behind the bar. Her father had hired Barry Fish to play the piano, and even though Katy didn't like his smarmy comments and insinuations about the wedding night, she had to admit he got the party going with his rousing dance tunes.

Katy danced and chatted and laughed. She had never had a party in her honour before and she found she was enjoying it more than she had anticipated.

As she watched Helen de Burrel dancing with Ward's best man, Katy thought what a shame it was that Louise hadn't come. She would have loved meeting all the handsome Air Force officers.

She said as much to Helen a little bit later as they took sandwiches off the trays Mrs Carter was handing round.

Helen shrugged. 'Louise is touchy,' she said. 'She always has been. Although I don't know what she's so worried about.' She nodded at a pretty girl in a tight little suit who was dancing with Ward. 'Look at Felicity. She and Ward had a bit of a flutter too. But she's here.'

Katy suddenly found she didn't want to look at Felicity, and Helen grimaced. 'Oh God, have I put my foot in it?' She touched Katy's arm. 'I'm sorry but it was ages ago. Nobody thinks anything of it now.'

Nobody except me, Katy thought. And what exactly was a flutter?

Then somewhat to her relief she found Jen at her side. 'Your mother wants to know if you're ready for the speeches?'

This was one of the moments Katy had been dreading. She had a feeling her father's speech was going to be embarrassing. She was right.

Filled with pride, he dwelt in sentimental detail on her childhood, her shyness and her brave acceptance of her poor health. Then he went on to talk about her clearly unsuitable but creditable desire to nurse and ended up with a humorous but, to Katy's mind, extremely unfair description of her attempts to help in the pub while her mother was away. He finished with some welcoming words to Ward and a toast to the bride. 'She's a good little thing, really. I just hope she makes a better wife than she does publican.'

Ward's speech was much more to Katy's taste. Relaxed and smiling, he spoke of how privileged he felt to have met her, how difficult it had been to woo her, how her sense of duty to her family and her job always seemed to get in the way, and how he hoped now at last she might be able to spare him a few minutes of her time.

Through the appreciative laughter he went on to give a vote of thanks to her parents for organising the wedding, to Mrs Carter and other well wishers for the miracle of the cake, to the bridesmaids for their help and support, and finally a special toast to Mr Lorenz for providing the material that helped make Katy the most beautiful bride he had ever seen.

Then he toasted the bridesmaids and kissed Katy on the lips and left his arm round her shoulders all the way through the best man's hilarious speech about Ward's various talents, linguistic, culinary, sporting, flying, rowing, skating, the list seemed endless, and each so-called skill was illustrated with an absurdly humorous example, of course ending up with his ability for attracting the prettiest girls. 'I needn't give an example of that of course,' he said. 'The evidence is all too clear.'

He then called upon Katy and Ward to cut the cake.

Despite the poor ingredients she had to work with, Mrs Carter's cake was a triumph, small admittedly, but thanks to the sugar donated by the Flag and Garter regulars, beautifully iced. They cut it with Ward's ceremonial sword with some difficulty and much hilarity and then Barry Fish launched into a brisk two-step and the dancing started up again.

Katy had never danced so much in all her life. The RAF boys were insatiable and she even managed a stiff little polka with Mr Lorenz and another even stiffer waltz with Jen's brother, Pete.

She was just wondering if she was going to have to take on Mick or, worse, Stanley Carter, when she saw Jen approaching purposefully.

'Your mother wants to know if you want her to help you change,' Jen said. She laughed. 'You always said you wanted to have people at your beck and call,' she added. 'It seems you've achieved your dream.'

Katy shook her head with a wry smile. 'It's not me,' she said, 'It's the wedding. It's tradition. It's being the bride that does it. I could be anyone.'

Then she jumped as Ward spoke behind her. 'Not for me, you couldn't!'

He put his arms round her and pulled her back against his chest. 'I was so glad when you pushed that damned veil back and it really was you underneath.'

Jen grimaced. 'Don't talk about that veil,' she said. 'The sooner it's shoved back into whatever old trunk it came from the better.'

Katy giggled. 'Or preferably the rubbish bin.'

'Don't be too hasty,' Ward murmured against her hair. 'Our daughter may want to wear that veil one day.'

Jen whistled a soft cat-call under her teeth. 'I think you had better go and change,' she said as Katy blushed scarlet. 'I get the impression your husband wants to take you away rather urgently.'

Upstairs Katy rounded on Jen crossly. 'How could you!'

Jen shrugged. 'Well, it's true. He quite obviously can't wait to get his hands on you.' She giggled. 'Don't look like that. It's quite nice, you know. Once you get the hang of it.'

'What do you mean?'

Jen grinned. 'Well, it's bound to be a bit difficult the first time.' She waved her hands expressively towards her groin. 'You know.'

Katy didn't know, but after her mother's lecture this morning she could imagine. As she slipped out of her wedding gown and put on the navy-trimmed going-away suit that her mother had bought her in Arding & Hobbs, she stared at Jen in considerable dismay.

But Jen was smiling. 'I dare say you'll be all right with Ward. I get the impression he'll know what he's doing.'

Katy wondered for a moment if that was quite such a good thing, but before she could say anything her mother had appeared, anxiously wanting to know if Katy was ready because everyone was waiting to wave them off.

Suddenly Katy felt a stab of emotion. This was it. She was leaving home. She looked to her mother for a bit of last minute reassurance, but Mary Parsons was too busy flustering about in the kitchen looking for rice to notice her daughter's sudden attack of nerves.

'Mummy, you can't throw rice,' Katy said helplessly when she reappeared a moment later with a small brown bag. 'It's illegal these days.'

Her mother frowned. 'You can't have a wedding without rice. I'm going to throw it very gently, and then sweep it up afterwards.'

And then she was hurrying Katy downstairs and Ward was taking her hand. As he led her to the car he handed her the bouquet.

'You'd better throw this,' he said, 'or someone will be unhappy.'

So she did, and by some fluke it landed in Molly Coogan's arms.

As Molly stared at it in amazement, Ward stepped forward and kissed her on the cheek. 'Thank you for looking after Katy the last few weeks,' he said. 'And for today.' Then he straightened up and smiled. 'I couldn't have hoped for two more beautiful bridesmaids.'

As everyone cheered and Molly Coogan almost burst with pride, Jen rolled her eyes and grinned at Katy. 'You never told me he was visually impaired,' she whispered. 'Does he carry a white stick?'

And then her mother was crying and kissing her goodbye and the rice was thrown and Katy was in the car and Ward was sitting next to her with his hands resting on the wheel. He grinned at her. 'All set?'

Katy smiled nervously. 'Where are we going?'

He laughed. 'It's a secret. I just hope I've got enough petrol to get there.'

Chapter Eighteen

Ward's mystery honeymoon destination was a small thatched cottage basking in warm evening sunlight.

Opening his door he got out and stretched then came round to let her out. The cottage was on the side of a low hill, behind them trees lined the skyline, in front of them green fields of winter barley stretched away as far as the eye could see.

He glanced at her as though testing her reaction. 'We're not far from Oxford,' he said. 'We can go there if we want some bright lights. But I thought what we both needed right now was some peace and quiet.'

Katy couldn't stop staring at it. 'It's lovely,' she said.

It was. Surrounded by apple trees just coming into blossom and fringed by daffodils, with its low thatched roof and small square windows each side of the front door, it looked like a cottage out of a fairy story.

And it was so quiet.

She looked back at Ward and found his eyes on her. He smiled. 'As it's our home for the next week, I guess I ought to carry you over the doorstep.'

Suddenly Katy felt scared. She followed him meekly up the flagged path and waited while he opened the door then she tensed as he lifted her into his arms. If he noticed he didn't say so, but dropped a quick kiss on her forehead before ducking through the low doorway and lowering her gently to her feet inside.

It was dark inside and looking around she saw they were in a low beamed living-room. To her left, a small curving staircase led away upstairs and through the door at the back she could see a bright little kitchen and a door out into a garden bathed in the evening sun.

It was idyllic. It was also warm and welcoming. Someone had lit the fire and there was an enormous vase of daffodils on the table. Katy wondered if there would be more flowers upstairs beside the honeymoon bed and glanced at the staircase nervously.

Ward touched her arm and she nearly jumped out of her skin. 'Why don't you go up and sort yourself out while I bring the things in?' he said. 'And then I'll get some food going. I don't know about you but I'm starving.'

Katy nodded and was about to go upstairs when he took her arm and turned her back to face him.

'Don't look so scared, sweetheart,' he said softly. 'I know what you're thinking, but I'm not about to rip off your clothes and throw you to the ground, whatever I said before.' He touched her flushed cheek with the backs of his fingers and smiled. 'We don't need to rush it. I can wait. Get to know each other again. Remember, we have all the time in the world now.'

For some reason his words made Katy feel even more embarrassed. Remembering her mother's advice she tried to hide her dismay. 'It's not that I don't want to . . .' she began.

He laughed and hugged her briefly. 'Well, I'm glad about that,' he said. 'But I still think we need something to eat first.'

The regimental cook had provided Ward with a tasty lamb stew and a delicious rhubarb tart. Afterwards he made some bitter black coffee from beans he had brought back with him from France and produced a bottle of brandy from his provisions box and suggested they drank it in front of the fire.

'I'm not a great drinker,' Katy said doubtfully. The coffee was bad enough.

He smiled. 'Think of it as medicinal,' he said, pouring her a small glass. 'You've had a hectic day. It'll help you to sleep.'

She knew it wasn't sleep she needed help with and she knew he knew it too. As bedtime approached she was getting more and more nervous and when Ward took her hand and drew her on to his knee in the armchair, she flinched.

'Just tell me something,' he said, stroking her hair gently. 'Why are you so scared of making love?'

'I don't know,' Katy stammered. 'I suppose it's because everyone makes it sound so difficult.'

'Difficult?' He smiled. 'I've always been under the impression it was quite easy.'

Katy frowned. 'It probably is for you,' she said crossly. 'But I've only ever done kissing before and I've only done that a couple of times.'

To her surprise he burst out laughing at that and hugged her to him, then suddenly he was on his feet with her still in his arms.

'What are you doing?' she asked, wide eyed, as he strode towards the small staircase.

'I'm taking you to bed,' he said.

It was a bit of a squeeze getting up the narrow stairs but he managed it and then he sat her on the edge of the bed. He grinned at her. 'Do you want me to undress you or will you do it yourself?'

She gaped at him. 'I'll do it myself.'

He nodded. 'I thought you'd say that. Well, you've got five minutes, sweetheart. I'm going for a quick wash and then I'll be back.'

Katy had never got undressed so fast in all her life. Dragging on one of the voluminous white lace-collared nightgowns her mother had given her, she climbed into the double bed and then couldn't decide which side to lie on and then whether to lie down or sit up. In the end she bulked up the pillows and half sat up which gave her a perfect view of Ward when he came up the stairs a minute later, naked apart from a towel wrapped round his waist.

'Oh.' Katy's eyes widened as she took in the wide shoulders, the muscular arms, the dark hairs on his chest tapering to a line which ran on under the towel. Then she looked away in embarrassment as he chuckled at her expression.

'I don't seem to have brought my dressing gown,' he said, patting the towel.

'Wh . . . what about your pyjamas?' Katy stammered.

He clicked his fingers. 'Damn. No pyjamas either.' He grinned. 'If my naked body is too much for you, sweetheart, you'd better shut your eyes because I'm about to join you in there.'

And with that he dropped the towel on to the floor and got into the bed.

Katy's eyes were still shut as he drew her into his arms.

'You can look now,' he murmured and she opened them cautiously to find him looking at her tenderly.

He stroked the backs of his fingers down her cheek and gently eased back the collar of the nightgown to kiss her on the neck. She felt his hair against her face, he smelt clean and fresh and lovely and she wished she had the courage to touch him, to kiss him back.

But she didn't, all she could do was lie tense with rigid limbs as he put his hand on her back to bring her closer to him.

She heard him groan slightly as her body came in contact with his. She could feel his legs against hers now through the nightgown, longer and stronger than hers, and she jumped as their toes touched, bare skin against bare skin.

Then very gently he pushed her on to her back and levered himself up on to one elbow to look down at her as she lay there white and trembling.

'Katy,' he said. Then he bent his head and kissed her.

She couldn't respond. She wanted to but she couldn't. It was all too much. The tension of the last few weeks, of the day. The big handsome naked man in the bed with her. The talk of other girls. Suddenly all she wanted to do was cry.

'Oh God,' he said, as the first sob shuddered through her body. 'Oh Katy, I'm sorry. Look,' he moved away from her slightly, 'let's leave it for tonight, huh? We're both tired. It'll be much nicer tomorrow.'

'No, please don't stop,' she cried. 'It'll be worse tomorrow. I'd much rather get it over with.' And then somehow she was back in his arms and the tears were choking out of her.

'Let it go,' he murmured against her hair as she tried to control it. 'You'll feel better for a good cry. You've been strung up like an over tuned fiddle all day.'

Afterwards she didn't remember how long she cried for, all she remembered was Ward reaching out and turning off the lamp and holding her in the silent darkness, uncomplaining, until gradually a strange new awareness of his body next to her broke through her agonised distress.

Suddenly, almost for the first time that day, she felt warm. And as his hand rhythmically smoothed down her back, even through the thick nightgown she could feel the effect of his touch on her skin.

Surreptitiously she sniffed back her tears and moved her head away from the damp pillow, resting it on his chest instead. Now she could feel his cool skin under her cheek, the tickle of his chest hairs against her chin and she could feel the rise and fall of his breathing and the steady beat of his heart. When his hand stopped stroking her back she thought he had gone to sleep and she moved against him regretfully.

But to her surprise he moved too, a lazy stretch which brought her back in full-length contact with him. Certain he was half asleep she tried to ease the nightgown up a fraction so she could feel the texture of his legs, and then with a leap of her heart she realised he was helping her, pulling it up much further than she had intended. For a second she tensed again but his movements were so languid, so unthreatening, and the feel of his strong, hairy legs against hers was so nice that she didn't fight him, even when his hand began to smooth up over her bare thigh, sliding under the bunched material to run gently over the curve of her hip.

Her heart was beating so fast now it took her a moment to realise that his had accelerated too, but still his hands were calm and cool on her skin and this time when he rolled her on to her back she lay quietly as he kissed her ear, her cheeks, her forehead and finally her mouth.

And then as she raised her head for more, he was unbuttoning the front of her nightgown, pulling it back as far as he could, kissing her collarbone with lazy trailing kisses and his fingers were reaching down, curving round her breast, making her gulp and clutch his head as his mouth followed the course of his hands.

'No,' she gasped, but it was too late. She could feel his lips on the sensitive skin, feel the sudden thrill of excitement shudder down her body.

As her fingers grasped his hair, half relishing the thick strength of it, half pushing him away, he tried to reach the other breast but the nightgown was too restricting and with a muffled oath he reached down to her knees and yanked it right up her body, scooping her to him for a second while he drew it over her arms and head and flung it across the room.

The sudden chill on her skin made her feel very exposed, despite the darkness, and when he rolled her back again she tried to cling to him, partly for warmth, partly as a means of evading the shocking effect of his fingers and tongue. But he pushed her away, holding her flat on the bed with a hand on her stomach while he gently kissed each breast in turn. At least she thought that was what he was doing. She couldn't really tell, but anything else was unimaginable and in any case the dreadful pleasure of it was so intense she almost didn't care. It was as much as she could do not to moan out loud.

And then the hand on her stomach was moving, smoothing lower and lower and before she could cry out in renewed shock he was kissing her hard on the mouth and she was desperately trying to pull his hand away from between her legs. But she didn't seem to have any strength in her any more and then she realised she was shaking all over and her body was moving of its own accord, her legs were parting and she couldn't stop them and she was almost crying in mortification.

'Don't cry, darling,' he murmured. 'It's going to be all right.'

'Is it?' she tried to ask, but no noise came out, only a soft whimper as he manoeuvred himself over her.

'I'll try not to hurt you,' he said. 'Just relax, sweetheart.'

But relaxing was impossible. She could feel the scratch of his chest against her breasts, she could taste her tears on his lips as he kissed her gently again.

She was waiting for the pain to begin but the probing pressure she could feel, although desperately embarrassing, wasn't too bad and she had begun to think the worst was over when Ward reached down to kiss her breast again.

At first it was the same as before, thrilling in its gentleness but then the feeling changed, became more intense, more exquisitely painful and suddenly, involuntarily, violently, she arched against him, and cried out in shock as a sheet of flame seemed to burn through her groin.

And then it was gone and through the dull pain it left behind, she could feel his own shock, feel him filling her, feel his muscles tense and pulsing as he lay still on top of her, feel his heart thudding against hers.

And then he moved, very gently at first, and she flinched. But the pain was going and it was being replaced by a new sensation, a kind of pulsing of her own which made her want to hold him, to move with him, but terrified of getting it wrong and scared of inducing more pain, she lay rigidly still, clenching her knuckles as he eased himself up and down, kissing her fleetingly on the lips, his breath warm on her face now, his skin hot to the touch.

She sensed from his shallow breathing that he was controlling himself, sensed that there was something she was meant to do, but she didn't know what it was, all she knew was that a strange tension was spreading through her, emanating from her groin and making

324

her shiver all over as though she had a fever. Fiercely she fought it, but Ward was shaking too now and his movements were more powerful, more insistent and she suddenly felt an overwhelming panic as her whole body seemed to suddenly seize up. And then, just as something exploded inside her, Ward groaned, hesitated, shuddered convulsively and then collapsed on top of her.

He lay like that for a moment, then he groaned again, less violently this time, and rolled off her. For a second she felt abandoned and then he drew her into his arms.

For a long time he held her in silence, then he murmured her name. 'Katy. Are you OK?'

Was she OK? It was an interesting question. She certainly felt most peculiar. Her heart was hammering. Her insides still seemed to be pulsing and her legs felt as though they had turned into jelly and even though for some reason she suddenly felt extraordinarily happy, she also wanted to cry again. Quite badly.

'I think so,' she muttered, biting her lip in an attempt to control the emotion that was threatening to overwhelm her.

He moved slightly then, a languid settling of his limbs as he brought her even closer into his embrace. 'I'm sorry,' he said softly, but before she could ask what exactly he was sorry about, he was asleep.

The garden was surprisingly warm in the morning sun. There was a breeze but it was kept at bay by a thick hedge at the edge of the little patch of lawn where clumps of soft yellow and pink primroses vied for space with the more strident daffodils. From there, sitting on the tartan rug she had brought from the car, Katy could see nearly the whole of the garden and the orchard that bordered it. She could also see the back of the cottage and more specifically the small upstairs window behind which Ward still slept.

She'd been back upstairs twice since she first eased her way out of bed. Once to fetch something warmer to wear, and once to check he wasn't dead.

He wasn't dead. He was so deeply asleep that even when she lifted the blackout curtain a few inches he wasn't woken by the sudden sunlight streaming into the room.

For a second, before she dropped it again, Katy allowed herself to look at him. He was turned away from her, his face buried in the pillow, but she could see his smooth powerful shoulders, the steady rise and fall of his breathing, the arm thrown over her side of the bed and the long, strong shape of him under the bedclothes.

This was her husband. The man who last night had touched her in ways and places she blushed to think about. No wonder her mother had warned her not to complain. The only odd, rather shocking thing about it was that now that it was over, all she could think about was when it might happen again. Even now, as she looked at his sleeping body, she felt a quiver of anticipation deep inside her and she quickly dropped the curtain and went back downstairs.

When he eventually emerged, it was eleven o'clock and Katy, cross-legged on her rug, was intent on watching two robins courting in the apple blossom. They flew away, clicking anxiously when the back door opened and turning her head slowly to face him, Katy felt a similar feeling of panic.

Then, as she saw his expression, she suddenly realised, to her astonishment, that for the first time since she had met him, he looked even more uncomfortable than her.

As he advanced slowly across the grass, he could hardly meet her eyes and when he crouched in front of her she could see the tension in him, the nervous flick of his thick black lashes, the uneasy smile on his beautiful mouth.

'Hello,' she said.

For a moment he seemed intent on studying the grass at his feet but then he looked up at her. 'Katy.' His voice sounded agonised. 'I'm so sorry.'

Katy frowned. 'What about?' she asked.

His eyes flicked briefly to her and then away again. 'Everything,' he said. Slumping down on the lawn, he ran his hands over his face and sighed. 'I wanted everything to be so nice, so good for you, and then I go and mess it up completely.'

He sounded almost angry and Katy blinked nervously. 'What do you mean?'

'What do you think I mean?' He raised his hand impatiently. 'I promised you we didn't have to rush it, and then I go and rush it. I promised you it wouldn't hurt, and then it bloody hurts like hell, and then, having satisfied myself, when you're upset afterwards, what do I do? I fall asleep.' He shook his head in disgust and glanced at Katy. 'I suppose you woke up hours ago?'

She nodded. 'The birds woke me,' she said.

'The birds?' He closed his eyes and groaned. 'Oh God, don't tell me you've been sitting sadly out here since the blasted dawn chorus?'

Katy bit her lip to stop the giggle she could feel in her throat. She had never seen him like this. And it gave her a heady sense of power that it was because of her that he was so brought down.

She crossed her hands primly in her lap. 'It was nice sitting out here,' she said. 'It gave me time to think.'

'To think what a terrible mistake you've made?'

'Not exactly,' she said slowly, tracing the pattern of the rug with her fingertip. 'More along the lines of thinking I was actually rather lucky in my choice of husband.'

He blinked at her. 'Lucky? What do . . .?' He stopped abruptly and looked at her more closely. 'Katy, I do believe you're blushing.'

Caught out, she glared at him. 'Of course I'm blushing after all those awful things you did last night.' She dropped her eyes again and went on gruffly, 'All I'm saying is I don't think it was all quite as bad as you thought.'

He didn't speak at once and when she looked up cautiously she was surprised to find him frowning. 'You don't have to be polite, Katy,' he said at last. 'I would much rather you were honest with me.'

'I am being honest,' she said, surprised. She didn't think she had been particularly polite.

His eyes narrowed. 'You mean the pain wasn't too bad?'

She shook her head. 'No, I mean none of it was too bad.'

He smiled then. The first real smile she had seen that morning and she found herself irresistibly smiling back. He was just so gorgeous. She couldn't help it.

He reached over to take her hand and laughed softly as she quivered to his touch. 'Katy,' he murmured slowly. 'I need to get this straight. Are you trying to tell me you actually quite liked all those awful things I did last night?'

She shook her head, but her flaming colour betrayed her and she gasped in horror as he pulled her into his arms then lay back on the grass with her on top of him.

He smiled up at her shocked face. 'Kiss me.'

Her eyes widened. 'What?'

'Kiss me.'

'I can't.' But then she saw the glint of amusement in his eyes and taking her courage in her hands she traced the rough line of his jaw with her finger. He didn't say anything but she could feel the sudden tension in the warm strong body beneath her, and, emboldened, she wriggled her own body into a more comfortable position and dipped her head.

His lips were cool and she felt a tremor pass through him as they parted slightly under her gentle pressure. Carefully, delicately, she put a line of small kisses along his bottom lip and then jerked her head back abruptly as he groaned.

'Oh my God.'

She tensed. 'What have I done wrong?'

'Nothing.' He closed his eyes for a second. 'You've just done a bit too much right, that's all.' He hesitated, then smiled. 'I don't suppose I could tempt you back to bed, could I?'

Katy stared down at him. 'But it's nearly lunchtime.'

He moved his shoulders. 'We can have sandwiches in bed if you want.' He grinned and ran a hand slowly down her spine. 'But there are one or two more awful things I want to do to you first.'

Realising she had got rather more than she bargained for, Katy felt her heart jump nervously. She suddenly remembered how grateful she had been last night for the cover of darkness. 'But it's light now,' she said rather desperately.

He laughed and rolled her up into a sitting position. 'All the better,' he said standing up and pulling her to her feet. 'This time I'll be able to make damn sure you're enjoying it every inch of the way.'

Despite her qualms she did enjoy it. And each time they did it subsequently she enjoyed it even more. The combination of Ward's delight in her body and the immense attraction she felt for him made it impossible for her not to respond to his caresses, not to show her pleasure.

Gradually one by one her inhibitions faded and she quickly became addicted to his skilful touch, his sudden passion, his soft moans of pleasure, his ability to take her up the spiralling, shocking path of excitement to the moment of perfect exquisite agony when despite her best efforts at restraint, she inevitably lost all control and clung to him half laughing, half crying, half screaming as the intense liquid pleasure crashed over her wave after wave.

But it wasn't just in bed that he satisfied her. He was good company out of bed too. She liked his wry, irreverent sense of humour, his sense of fun, his disregard for convention.

'We're grown-ups. We can do what we like,' he said when she was shocked at his suggestion that they made love in the garden. After living with her parents for eighteen years it was amazing to Katy to find someone able to be so spontaneous, so independent spirited.

'Goodness,' he said. 'You only live once, there isn't time to worry too much about what people might or might not think. That's about the only good thing about this war, it's breaking down the barriers, making people realise they can do things they never thought they could or should do before.'

One evening they had spent so much of the day in bed, they went for a long walk in the dark. In the distance they could hear the ominous rumble of bombers but overhead a large owl was circling in the bright moonlight. 'I wish I could fly,' Katy said, watching its effortless glide back and forth across the lane.

Ward smiled. 'One day I'll teach you to fly,' he said. 'No reason why being a girl should stop you. You'd make a good pilot.'

Katy laughed, but his absurd faith in her abilities was extraordinarily inspiring. With him at her side urging her on she felt she could almost do anything. Somehow by treating her as his equal, as his playmate, his friend and lover, he made her feel liberated, a person in her own right.

But it wasn't just his attitude she liked. It was him. She liked the feel of him, the look of him, the smell of him and the taste of him. She liked the way he made her feel a hundred per cent alive. She even developed a taste for his coffee. She couldn't get enough of him. Nor he of her. It was only with considerable effort over the next couple of days that they dragged themselves away from the cottage and took the bus to Oxford.

There, they walked in the deer park, punted with much hilarity on the Cherwell, danced in the assembly rooms at Carfax. Another day they strolled through water meadows filled with tiny spring flowers for a drink at the celebrated Trout Inn.

It was like a dream, and when Ward bought a newspaper, even the news of devastating bombing in Coventry, fifty per cent taxation and the German invasion of Yugoslavia and Greece didn't seem able to spoil it.

It seemed incredible they had only been away four days. And it seemed equally incredible that they had another four to go, and then the whole of their lives after that.

They talked endlessly, in bed, over delicious meals that Ward cooked, lazing in the garden or the blossom-filled University parks, about their future, how soon Ward could rejoin the Air Force, where he was likely to be posted. They discussed where to live, agreed to take up the Miss Taylors' offer of their house in Lavender Road until they could find somewhere for themselves.

One afternoon in bed they talked about what Katy might do for the war effort now she could no longer nurse. 'The problem is that I'm so hopeless at everything,' she said.

Ward grinned wickedly and slid his hand under the covers. 'I could name quite a few things you're good at.'

She laughed. 'I'd better become a prostitute, then.'

He glared at her, suddenly serious. 'If you ever look at another man, I'll kill him.'

Katy was silent for a second, then she looked away. She thought about Louise, Helen de Burrel, Felicity Rowe, all the other glamorous women Ward had known or might yet meet and she felt a sudden stab of fear.

'What about other women?' she asked tentatively.

'What about them?'

'Will you look at them?'

He turned her to face him and touched her cheek gently. 'Katy, haven't you realised yet that I love you? Completely and utterly?'

The following day he took her into a smart little jeweller's and bought her an engagement ring. Three diamonds in the prettiest setting Katy had ever seen.

'I'm sorry it's a bit late,' he said slipping it on her finger outside the shop. 'I know material things don't prove anything, but perhaps you could think of it as a small token of my affection.'

As she looked up at him through tear-filled eyes, Katy felt the emotion squeezing her heart. She loved him. And by some miracle, that love was returned.

★   ★   ★

331

And then the sword of Damocles fell.

It fell in the form of a car pulling up outside the cottage while Katy was making an early morning cup of tea.

Aware that she wasn't very decently dressed and that it wasn't quite as early as she had thought, Katy ran across the living-room to peep through the blackout curtain to see who it was.

'Who is it?' Ward called from upstairs.

'It's a taxi,' Katy replied. 'There's a man getting out and . . .' She stopped abruptly as the other passenger got out slowly on the other side, and suddenly the implication of who it was crashed into her brain.

'Oh no,' she whispered. 'Oh please no.'

'Katy? What's the matter?' Ward was halfway down the stairs, wearing only a towel round his waist.

She could hardly bear to look at him. When she did, she saw the tousled hair, the broad shoulders, the steady grey eyes as though for the last time. 'It's Helen de Burrel,' she said numbly. 'And another man.'

As soon as she said the name, she knew she was right to worry. For a second he was still, then, swearing under his breath, still in the towel, he marched out of the front door.

'What the hell are you doing here?' he shouted at them. 'For God's sake, this is my sodding honeymoon.'

As the door slammed behind him, Katy sank into a chair. She could hear their voices outside but not what they were saying. All she knew was that for them to come and disturb him here it must be important.

It was important. When he came back in he took her in his arms and told her that one of his agents was injured and compromised in Nazi controlled France.

'I have to get him out,' he said gently. 'It's an act of faith.'

Katy pressed her cheek against his bare chest. 'Why can't someone else go?' But she knew it was useless. Already she could feel him steeling himself for the separation, for the ordeal that lay ahead.

'Nobody else knows him,' he said. 'I can't really explain, sweetheart. But he's crucial to our operation.'

'But you said it was over.'

He groaned softly. 'I thought it was.' Then seeing her expression, he smiled reassuringly and kissed her gently on the lips. 'But this is easy. In and out. I'll hardly even leave the plane.'

She wanted to make a fuss. She wanted to make him feel guilty. She wanted to remind him that it was Easter Day on Sunday, her birthday the following week, that she couldn't bear either without him. But she could see from the tension in his jaw that this parting was no easier for him than it was for her. So she said none of it.

And half an hour later he was dressed and gone.

As the sound of the taxi's engine faded, Helen touched Katy's arm. 'I'll help you pack up,' she said. 'And then I'll drive you back to London.'

Chapter Nineteen

Louise was arranging flowers in the hall when her younger brother Douglas arrived home for the Easter holidays.

'Hello Sis,' he greeted her cheerily, clicking his fingers at Mr Wallace to leave his suitcase at the foot of the stairs. 'I hear you lost your fancy man to that girl at the pub.'

Caught with her guard down, Louise allowed her eyes to fill with tears and then, catching Douglas's gleeful smirk, immediately kicked herself for showing her emotion.

Douglas was like a terrier, once he got on to something he never let it go. At Christmas he had taken delight in teasing her about Ward's visits to the hospital, and now she could see from the gleam in his eye that he was going to spend the whole of Easter needling her about his defection.

'And I hear your school report leaves something to be desired,' she snapped back.

'Oh, touchy, touchy,' he grinned. 'I hardly think good marks in Classics are a prerequisite for becoming a brewer, do you?'

Louise frowned. 'What do you mean?'

Douglas shrugged negligently. 'I mean that if Bertie gets disinherited for being a conchie, I stand to inherit the business. Let's face it, Sis, Dad's hardly likely to leave it to you, is he, a mere girl?' he smirked. 'Particularly one on the shelf.'

For a second Louise toyed with ramming the remaining flowers down his throat, but prudently opted for ramming them into the vase instead. She wiped her hands on her skirt and took her beret off the peg. 'I'm going out,' she said. 'Tell Mummy I won't be in for tea.'

'Where are you going?'

Louise lifted her chin. 'Mind your own business.'

But the truth was she didn't know. In the old days she would have walked down Lavender Road to the pub and moaned to Katy Parsons, but that was out of the question. In any case the stupid girl was still away on her beastly honeymoon. As she hesitated at the end of the drive, Louise gritted her teeth, then she glanced at Mrs d'Arcy Billière's house on the opposite corner and made up her mind. She would call on Aaref Hoch.

Aaref greeted her with evident pleasure and gracefully waved away her gruff thanks for rescuing her on the afternoon of Katy's wedding.

'I'm afraid I wasn't very grateful at the time,' Louise said. It was only much later that she had realised what a complete fool of herself she might have made. If nothing else she had almost certainly splattered his trousers with vomit.

But he merely smiled forgivingly and stood back to let her into the dark hallway. 'And your parents have not noticed the missing brandy?'

Louise flushed slightly. 'My father is notoriously mean with drink,' she said. 'By the time he next offers anyone a brandy, hopefully he'll have forgotten how much he had.'

Aaref smiled and ushered her into Mrs d'Arcy Billière's sitting-room. 'Lael is not at home,' he said. 'But I can make you some tea perhaps?'

Louise nodded. 'But with milk please, not lemon,' she said, remembering how disgusting Lael d'Arcy Billière's tea had always been. Although come to think of it it was unlikely they'd be using lemon now. The only way you could get lemons these days was on the black market.

As Aaref went off, Louise looked around her. It was a long time since she had been to the house and she remembered how uncomfortable she had felt the first time she had been shown into this room. In those days she had found the vibrant decor unnervingly foreign and exotic but now it just reminded her of Count Stefan Pininski, whom she had met here for the first time, and suddenly she wished she hadn't come.

And then she remembered that the alternative was Douglas's gloating at home and she slumped into an armchair draped with a red and black tasselled shawl and looked up with some relief as Aaref came back into the room carrying a small brass tray.

To her surprise, as well as the milk jug there was a generous slice of lemon sitting on a saucer. For a second she toyed with remarking on it but there were more pressing things on her mind.

'I want to get a job, but I don't know what I can do,' she said. 'My whole education has been designed to make me into a perfect wife. I can't imagine being any good at anything else.' She made a sad face. 'At this rate I won't even get the chance to be good at that.'

Aaref poured the tea and dropped the lemon into his cup. 'You were good at teaching English to me and my brothers,' he said mildly.

Louise snorted. 'I wasn't good at it, you were. I don't think your brothers ever learnt a word from me.'

He smiled. 'You would be surprised. Lael has arranged for them to go to school. Thanks to you they will have an education. When the war is over they will become lawyers or doctors. They will be able to take their places in the world. '

Louise laughed, mocking his ambition for his two silent brothers. 'What about you, Aaref, what place will you take in the world?'

He shrugged. 'It is too late for me. I am listed as an enemy alien. Everything is closed to me. But I will make money instead.'

Louise was about to laugh again but something in his expression

336

stopped her. Aaref had changed so much in the last year. A year ago she would definitely have laughed but now the thought of him making money didn't seem quite so absurd. There was a gritty determination about him, a quiet confidence in his manner that suddenly made him seem older than her, even though he was actually a year younger.

'I cannot ask Lael to keep us for ever,' he said. 'I will have to take responsibility for my brothers. There are many others who now need her help more than we do.'

Louise groaned inwardly. The trouble with blasted Aaref these days was that he was so intense, so worthy. Maybe it was a Jewish trait. Whatever it was, it made her feel flippant and insincere and she was glad when he smiled again.

'You will have to work soon, Louise, in any case. You will be registered. Did you not see the papers today? Mobilisation of women for the war effort?'

Louise shook her head. 'I won't have to do it. Daddy will pull strings to get me out of it. He doesn't approve of women working, not our class, even for the war effort. He thinks it will give them ideas.'

Aaref looked surprised. 'Why shouldn't women have ideas? Half the population is women.'

Louise frowned. Looking at it like that, it did seem a bit unfair. 'I suppose he thinks that if women have their own money, they will think they are as clever as men.'

'Women are as clever as men,' Aaref said. 'Look at you. I am sure you are as clever as your brothers, no?'

Louise laughed, she was feeling better already. 'I'm certainly cleverer than Bertie,' she said. 'He's about to make a complete mess of his life with this idiotic conchie business and this crush he's got on that awful common Whitehead woman.' Then she sobered suddenly. 'Mind you, I've made a pretty good mess of my life too, come to think of it.' She groaned. 'If only someone would marry me, all my problems would be solved.'

Aaref looked at his hands for a moment. When he looked up

he was serious again. 'I know I have said it before, but it would be a great honour if you would marry me, Louise.'

Louise groaned. 'Oh, Aaref, don't start that again. I couldn't possibly marry you.' She finished her tea and stood up, watching him colour slightly as she slowly smoothed her skirt over her knees. She smiled to herself. Ridiculous as his proposal was, it was nice to be wanted.

'I like having you as a friend,' she said kindly. 'But anything else is out of the question.'

'That Katy Parsons came back today,' Mick Carter said at tea. 'On her own.'

'What?' Joyce stared at him.

'He got called away, the bloke,' Mick went on through a mouthful of bread. 'One of them girls who was at the wedding brought her back. She looked really sad when she got out of the car.'

'What a bloody shame,' Joyce said. Marriage was no bed of roses, she knew that, but if anyone had struck lucky it was that Katy Parsons and it seemed cruel that the rug should be pulled out from under her feet so soon.

Mick looked surprised to see her so angry. 'He's only going to be gone a day or two,' he said. He chewed thoughtfully for a moment. 'Unless the Germans get him, I suppose.' He grinned. 'Then he might be a bit longer.'

Joyce was not amused. 'I wish the bloody Germans would get you,' she said.

Knotting her fingers nervously in her lap, Pam leaned forward eagerly as the tweedy woman behind the desk finally looked up from her papers.

'I'm sorry, Mrs Nelson,' she said briskly. 'I'm afraid I'm not going to be able to help you.'

Pam stared at her. 'But you said yourself a moment ago that you had hundreds of children looking for new homes.'

The woman nodded. 'Oh, yes we do. We're crying out for people to take them in.'

Pam blinked, wondering if she was going mad. 'Well, that's just what I'm offering to do.'

The woman gathered Pam's application papers together into a neat pile. 'I'm sorry, Mrs Nelson,' she said sliding them back across the desk. 'But you do not meet our criteria.'

Meeting Pam's astonished gaze, she sighed heavily, clearly bored with the whole proceeding. 'Our criteria state that we prefer a home with other children. That adoptive parents should be under thirty. That adoptive mothers should not work.'

Pam swallowed. 'I'd give up my job.'

The woman shrugged. 'In that case you wouldn't meet our marital income criteria.'

Biting back her irritation and disappointment, Pam tried to keep her voice reasonable. She was beginning to dislike her interviewer rather intensely. 'But thousands of people bring up families on less than my husband earns.'

With an exaggerated air of patient resignation the woman glanced at the application form again. 'It says here that your husband only earns seven pounds ten shillings a week and it states quite clearly in our criteria,' she shuffled the papers again and pushed one towards Pam, 'that eight pounds a week is the minimum.'

For a second Pam managed to control herself then she stood up abruptly. 'Thank you for your time,' she said stiffly.

The woman inclined her head. She waved her hand graciously. 'Perhaps you would like to take a copy of our criteria away with you for reference.'

Pam waved her hand not quite so graciously. 'As far as I'm concerned,' she said, 'you can stuff your bloody criteria.'

At the Flag and Garter, Katy's premature homecoming wasn't greeted with quite as much sympathy as she had expected. She could tell from her mother's expression that she wasn't completely convinced that she hadn't fled the marital bed, and her father was gloomily preoccupied with his accounts.

'That's the bloody war for you,' he said when Katy tried to impress upon him her disappointment that her honeymoon had been curtailed. 'It's not easy for any of us at the moment. Let's hope things pick up over Easter.'

Staring at him resentfully, Katy suddenly noticed the lines of strain around his mouth, the weary droop of his shoulders, and felt a stab of guilt. At least she had had a break, she thought, even it was shorter than expected. Her father hadn't had a holiday since war broke out. And not many before that either. In fact now she came to think of it she couldn't even remember him having a day off.

'When Ward comes back, he and I could look after the pub for a night or two,' she suggested suddenly. 'And you and Mum could have a weekend away.'

Her father looked astonished. 'Don't be absurd. Goodness, a couple of nights under your jurisdiction and what small profits I've got would have gone down the drain. And the customers too most likely.'

Katy frowned, but before she could object her mother was drawing her away. 'Leave him, Katy, he's busy.'

'I was only trying to help,' Katy said peevishly as they went upstairs.

Her mother nodded. 'I know, but really, dear, you shouldn't be offering things like that without asking your husband first.'

Katy looked at her mother's anxious subservient face and sighed. 'Ward wouldn't mind,' she said. But she knew it was hopeless. Her parents would never understand. They were a different generation. And as far as they were concerned she was now Ward's property and her duty was to honour and obey him. The wonderful, easy going unity she had experienced with Ward over the last few days was beyond their comprehension. She found it sad.

But her mother was already worrying about the practicalities.

'Well, when's he coming back? Have you thought about where to live? I don't think we've got room for him here.'

'The Miss Taylors are lending us their house,' Katy said. 'We'll stay there until we know where Ward's going to be posted.' She shook her head, trying not to think about the possibility of Ward being posted to Greece or North Africa.

'Well, you'd best stay here until he comes back,' her mother said. 'I don't think you ought to be alone in that house. Not with the air-raids and that. You'll be safer here.' She looked down at her shopping list. 'Now, do you think I should try and get him an Easter egg for Sunday?'

'Yes,' Katy said firmly. 'He'll definitely be back by then. And if he's not, I'll kill him.'

Joyce was pleased to be back on the WVS canteen van. It was nice to be out and about again of an evening. She was even more pleased that Stanley had been taken on by Rutherford & Berry. Suddenly things were looking up. She was humming as she made up the sandwiches, her knife spreading the marge and the dab of Marmite cleanly and efficiently across the bread.

'You like doing this, don't you?' Mrs Rutherford said suddenly and Joyce looked up, surprised.

'Yes, I do. I like being around food. I always have.'

Mrs Rutherford nodded. 'Good.'

Joyce was about to return to her task when it occurred to her that 'good' was rather an odd response. Putting down the knife, she wiped her hand on her apron.

'Why do you say "good" like that?' she asked, peering at Mrs Rutherford suspiciously. 'You've got something up your sleeve, haven't you?'

Celia Rutherford hesitated for a second and Joyce wondered what on earth was coming. What did come nearly made her fall out of the van.

'I'm thinking of opening a little café,' Celia Rutherford said. 'And I wondered if you would be interested in helping me?'

'A cafe?' Joyce felt a trickle of excitement course through her veins. 'But where? And what about the expense? And the licences and that. Isn't there lots of red tape?'

Mrs Rutherford smiled. 'One of the WVS ladies works at the Ministry of Food. I gather all you need is a catering licence, which isn't too hard to get these days. The government is quite keen on communal catering. Saves on fuel consumption. And there's nothing much round here. Lyon's is the nearest but that's right down at Clapham Junction.'

Joyce stared at her. 'You're serious, aren't you? You've looked into it?' She felt another surge of excitement and quickly tried to quash it. Better to be cautious, she thought, than to be disappointed when it went wrong. 'It may not be easy to find a good premises, mind. With a decent kitchen and that.' She hesitated as another problem presented itself. 'What does your husband think about it?'

Celia hesitated. 'I haven't mentioned it yet.'

'Oh.' Joyce's face fell. That was that then. Mr bloody Rutherford would stick a spanner in the works as sure as eggs were eggs.

Celia saw her dismay and smiled grittily. 'There's a war on, Mrs Carter. As you said yourself only the other day, we have our own lives to lead. And I do have a little money of my own.'

Louise chose Easter lunch to tell her father that she wanted to get a job. She thought after reading the lesson during the service of resurrection at St Aldate's he might be in a more sympathetic mood than usual.

She was wrong.

'A job?' he grunted incredulously. 'Don't be absurd. A girl in your position isn't expected to work. What you need, young lady, is a husband. You let that Ward Frazer fellow slip through your fingers. You'd better start looking out for someone else.' He winked at

Douglas and laughed heartily. 'We don't want you ending up an old maid, do we?'

Louise gritted her teeth. 'If I could find a husband I would, Daddy. But in the meantime, I'd like to do something worthwhile.'

'Nothing more worthwhile than looking after a husband,' he said and peered at her over his glasses. 'I don't know what's the matter with you. When your mother was your age she had hundreds of men dancing attendance on her.'

'Then why did she choose you?' Louise muttered.

At once her mother leaped nervously into the fray. 'Louise!'

Her father put down his knife and fork, a dangerous look on his face. 'What did you say?'

Louise felt her heart hammering. 'Nothing, Daddy, honestly.'

Her mother was not taken in for a moment. 'Apologise to your father at once.'

'I'm sorry, Daddy,' she said quickly. 'I didn't mean to be rude.'

For a second she thought he was going to send her to her room and she clenched her fists under the table preparing for the ignominy. She could see Douglas grinning like a Cheshire cat on the other side of the table and wished her legs were strong enough to kick him hard on the shin.

But then to her relief her father picked up his knife and fork again and speared a piece of cabbage. Before putting it in his mouth he glanced coldly at Louise. 'You need to watch your tongue, young lady,' he said, 'Or you'll never find a man to take you on.'

By Easter Sunday afternoon Katy was like a cat on hot bricks. In and out, he had said. No problem. I'll hardly even get out of the plane. So where was he, she wondered, as she paced the flat above the pub, running to the stairs each time someone passed the door, hoping it would be a telegram saying he was landed safely at some regional airport and would be in London that evening.

She had the Miss Taylors' house all ready for him with flowers on the hall table and clean sheets on the spare room bed. She had even taken some cushions down to the cellar in case there was a raid on when he arrived. She had blushed as she carried them down but she couldn't help it. Even after four days she missed the feel of his body. His absence had left a physical ache and she could hardly think of anything except when she would be in his arms again.

'For goodness' sake, Katy.' Her mother looked up from her knitting. 'Do stop marching about like that. Haven't you got anything to do? What about your thank-you letters? Or did you get those written in Oxford?'

'No, of course I didn't,' Katy said. 'I was on my honeymoon, Mummy. I didn't want to waste time writing letters.'

Her mother pursed her lips. 'Well, you'd better sit down and do it now. If people have been kind enough to give you gifts, the least you can do is thank them.'

'That's right.' Her father put down his newspaper. 'You're a married woman now, you have to take on your responsibilities for yourself. You can't expect us to do everything for you.'

'I don't expect you to do everything for me,' Katy said through gritted teeth. 'I don't expect you to do anything for me. I'm perfectly happy to stand on my own feet.' She saw their hurt expressions and stopped, mortified. These were her parents. She loved them dearly. But she loved Ward too and the waiting was driving her mad.

'I'm sorry,' she said, reaching for her jacket. 'You're quite right. I ought to do the letters. But I'll just pop up to the house first to check nothing has arrived there.'

As Easter Monday was a bank holiday, the Employment Exchange was busy on Tuesday morning and Louise had to wait for some time before anyone would see her.

Then at last she was shown into a cubicle where a stern-looking man eyed her chic little suit and stylish hat with some surprise over a pair of half-moon spectacles. 'And what can I do for you?' he asked as she sat down and took off her gloves.

Considering where she was, Louise would have thought it rather obvious what he could do for her, but she smiled winningly nevertheless. 'I want a job,' she said.

'I see,' he said and glanced briefly at the form she had filled out while she was waiting. 'There's been a good response to the Ministry of Labour's advertisements. A lot of women have come forward.' He leaned back in his chair and scratched his chin. 'I don't know that we have anything very suitable for someone like you, however. Have you considered joining the services? Or the land-army? A lot of girls with your kind of background seem to go for those. Or nursing perhaps? That's very worthwhile and more ladylike than factory work.'

Louise shuddered. After her incarceration in the Wilhelmina she never wanted to see another hospital again. And as for nursing, she failed to see why anyone should think it was ladylike, all those bed pans and vomit and blood. And all that gruelling hard work and beastly Sisters. No thank you.

'I don't think I'd be fit enough for nursing,' she said. 'As you'll see on my form I was injured in a bombing incident and my legs still aren't awfully strong.' She smiled bravely. 'I think I'd need a job where I was sitting down.'

'I see.' Clearly touched, her interviewer cleared his throat. 'Well, unfortunately most employers are rather fussy about physical fitness . . .'

But Louise interrupted. 'Oh, please do try and help me,' she said pitifully. 'I do so want to do my bit.' And the thought of another week in the house with Douglas was completely unbearable. And now Katy Parsons was back and everyone was saying what a shame it was that her honeymoon had been cut short. Privately Louise thought it served her right for snitching her man, but the thought of bumping into her made her feel sick. Let alone Ward.

'How dextrous are you?' the man asked suddenly.

Louise blinked. 'I'm quite good at arranging flowers,' she said.

'Ah.' For a moment he looked dubious, then he took a card out of his drawer and wrote on it. 'Gregg Bros,' he said. 'Down by Morgan Crucible on the river. They're looking for tool operators. Delicate work.'

Louise felt a flicker of excitement. Delicate sounded all right. She nodded eagerly and took the card. 'When do I start?'

He smiled and stood up. 'You'll have to persuade them to take you on first.' He held out his hand. 'Good luck, Miss Rutherford. Do come back and see me if you don't have any joy. I'm sure we'll find something for you sooner or later.'

The following day, the sixteenth of April, was Katy's nineteenth birthday.

She had never spent a more miserable day in her life. She couldn't settle. She couldn't relax. Even a letter from Jen saying that Mrs Frost was joining her ENSA group didn't cheer her. She spent the day trundling between the pub and the Miss Taylors' house, terrified a telegram would arrive at whichever location she wasn't at.

She was in the Miss Taylors' house when the sirens started to wail. Reluctantly she turned off the lights, shut the doors according to ARP procedure and let herself out into the street. She would have preferred to stay there, she preferred the silence of the Miss Taylors' cellar to the enquiries that always greeted her at the pub. They were kindly meant, she knew that, but until she heard something from Helen de Burrel or from Ward himself, there was little she could say in response. But her parents had made her promise to come home if there was a warning and she felt she'd upset them enough over the last few days without causing them any more unnecessary anxiety.

At the Miss Taylors' front gate, she bumped into Bertie Rutherford on his way into Sheila's house next door. He peered at her through the dusk, looking a bit sheepish. 'Just checking Sheila's OK,' he said.

Katy smiled. She knew perfectly well that Bertie was doing rather more than checking on Sheila these days. She also knew it was only because of him that Sheila was prepared to sit out the raids in her cellar instead of running to the supposed greater safety of the public shelter or the Nelsons' Anderson shelter on the other side of the road.

She realised Bertie was looking at her with a certain sympathy. 'Still no news?' he asked. 'I saw a post girl go into the pub with a telegram just now. I thought . . .'

But she had gone, running down the street as though wolves were after her.

Left behind, Bertie heard an ominous grumbling in the distance and turning round quickly he saw a number of orange flares lighting the sky in the south. Already there was the sound of distant gunfire and then suddenly in the light of the circling searchlights he caught sight of a formation of bombers heading right towards him. 'Oh bugger,' he said.

As usual just after a warning, the bar of the Flag and Garter was in chaos with people frantically downing their drinks or ordering more in preparation for a long wait in the cellar.

Moments before Katy rushed in, someone had reported the approaching planes, and at once her father started shouting for everyone to go home if they could.

'Katy, thank God,' he said. 'There's planes on their way. Go downstairs quick, love, your mother's there already.'

'Bertie said there's a telegram,' she said breathlessly.

Her father scrabbled under the counter. 'It's from that Helen de Burrel girl,' he said. 'Asking you to phone her. I was just about to come and tell you when the siren went.' He looked up as she headed back to the door. 'Katy? Katy? Where are you going?' He tried to blunder round the bar and knocked a bottle off the end. 'You can't phone now,' he shouted. 'There's planes coming. Stop her, someone.'

But before anyone could stop her, Katy was out of the door and running down the road.

Bombs or no bombs, there was no way she was going to sit in that miserable cellar all night knowing that Helen had news of Ward.

By the time she reached the phone kiosk on Lavender Hill, the planes were overhead. Darting into a shop doorway she could feel the ground under her feet tremble as they roared past. The guns up on the common were firing and the ones in Battersea Park too by the sound of it, but still the formation thundered on, she could see the planes clearly, ominously fat bellied and grey in the waving beams of the searchlights. More than she had ever seen before.

After they had passed she waited a moment before darting into the phone kiosk, praying it was in working order. Hastily she went through the routine, cringing as she heard a violent explosion somewhere behind her. Swinging round, she couldn't see anything, but almost at once a policeman materialised from nowhere and began running in the direction of the blast.

And then the planes were overhead again and she heard a strange screaming roar followed a second later by another juddering explosion, and then suddenly she got her connection and the phone was ringing. Even as someone answered, a fire engine roared past her and as she frantically pressed button A and asked to speak to Helen she realised the glass in the telephone box had broken and was tinkling to the ground around her.

And then Helen was on the phone.

'Katy? Is that you? It's a terrible line.'

'It's not the line, it's bombing,' Katy shouted over the thumping reports of the guns. She realised her hands were clammy on the receiver and gripped it harder.

For a ghastly second she thought she had been cut off, then she heard Helen's voice again. 'Katy, I'm afraid something must have gone wrong. The plane didn't come back. We don't know what's happened. We're still waiting for news.'

Katy closed her eyes. She felt quite calm. Calm and cold and completely bloodless as though someone had just ripped her heart out.

Then she realised they had, and a sudden icy anger shivered through her. 'It was a trap,' she said. 'You sent him into a trap.'

'We don't know what happened,' Helen repeated steadily. 'Katy, I honestly don't think it was a trap. The boys were there. They wouldn't have led Ward into a trap.'

Katy thought briefly of Jean-Luc and Pierre, somehow so tied up in her relationship with Ward, and knew Helen was right. Those men might be unreliable where women were concerned, but they would not deliberately betray Ward Frazer. She had seen the way they looked at him. There was mutual respect there. And trust. And loyalty.

Helen's voice buzzed in her ear. 'Katy, I don't think you should give up hope. We are trying to make contact. Sooner or later we will find out what happened. For all we know, Ward may be perfectly all right.'

He may be all right, Katy thought numbly. Or he may be dead. Or worst of all he may be being tortured by the Gestapo. Suddenly she felt sick but there was one more thing she had to know.

'Helen,' she whispered. 'Do you know if he was in uniform?'

There was a slight pause, then Helen's plummy voice. 'No, I'm afraid he wasn't.'

Katy stayed in the phone kiosk for a long time after she had put down the receiver. She wished she could cry. She wished she could shout. She wished she could do virtually anything but stand there in this terrible icy shock.

And then, suddenly smelling sulphur filtering through the broken glass, she opened her eyes and realised she was in some considerable danger herself. The whole area was suddenly alight with flares. German chandelier flares, yellow, white and orange. She could see them floating down over the river, and with them other parachutes drifting down diagonally on the breeze. For a second she thought it must be the invasion, but then as she took in the bulky shapes hanging beneath the flapping silk she saw they were bombs, mines. And she knew that this was going to be worse than other nights.

Swinging round as something clattered on the road a few yards from the kiosk, she saw the billowing smoke further up the hill and suddenly she felt a new fear. Even as she looked, an ambulance rattled past her and with a chill she saw it turn into Lavender Road.

Or was it the next road? She couldn't quite see, but it forced her numb limbs into action and, hugging the buildings, she began to run back up the hill.

Chapter Twenty

As she turned the corner into Lavender Road, Katy stopped in shock and put her hands to her mouth.

'Oh no,' she said. 'Oh, please God, no.'

It was darker now, but there was enough light from distant flares to see the cluster of people outside the Flag and Garter, the fire engine, the ambulance already pulling away, its wheels crunching through the broken glass.

Stumbling on through the debris on the pavement, Katy felt a sinking sense of dread. Ahead of her she could hear the helmeted rescue workers shouting, instructions being issued. Absurdly a tangled mess of bicycle hung from a lamp post with its wheel gently turning.

And then she saw the black, smoking hole in the side of the pub, the stream of silver water directed from the fireman's hose through the shattered first-floor windows, the pall of smoke above.

Over the engine noise and the shouting, she could hear the water hissing on hot surfaces and she could smell the orange scent of cordite and the faint odour of beer.

For a second she stood and stared. She didn't know what to do. Where to begin. She could hardly believe such devastation could have been caused in such a short time.

An ARP man was erecting a makeshift cordon. He tried to shoo her away. 'You best get underground,' he said briskly. 'Jerry will be back in a minute.'

Katy shook her head. Suddenly her voice seemed a long way away. 'Were there any casualties?'

He shrugged. 'Just the landlord. Blown straight across the bar. Dead before they knew what hit him, I reckon.' He stopped and peered at her through the smoky darkness. 'Who are you anyway?'

Katy stared at him blankly. She knew what he'd said but she couldn't take it in. It's my birthday, she thought numbly. This can't happen on my birthday.

She thought suddenly of all the times she had come home from the hospital expecting to see and hear what she was seeing and hearing now. And yet now that it had happened, she couldn't believe it. She looked again at the jagged, black cave that only half an hour ago had been the Flag and Garter's public bar and then back at the ARP man.

'I'm the landlord's daughter,' she said.

The ARP man looked appalled. 'Oh, my gawd. I'm sorry, love. I didn't know.' To cover his confusion he consulted a list on a clipboard. 'Then your mum's injured and all. Broken leg, they reckon. They've taken her to the Wilhelmina.'

For a second as the blood left her brain, Katy thought she was going to faint. The ARP man clearly thought so too because through a hazy blur she heard him shouting for help. 'Oi, I've got the daughter here. Does anyone know her?'

'It's all right,' Katy said quickly. 'I'm all right. '

But already people were crowding round her. She could hear their voices, their awkward sympathy, their hushed discussions about what to do with her. Someone pushed a cup of tea into her hand and she heard someone else telling her to drink it. It would make her feel better. But she didn't want to feel better. She didn't want to feel anything. She wanted to stay in this strange numb isolation for ever, where nothing could get to her. Nothing else could hurt her.

But someone already had his hand under her elbow.

For a second as she stared at the smoke-blackened face she couldn't think who it was then his mouth opened and she recognised the crooked teeth and slightly leering smile of Barry Fish, the pub pianist.

'Katy, love. What a terrible thing,' he said, drawing her to one side. 'What a terrible thing. Your poor old dad, eh?'

Katy shivered convulsively. 'What happened?' she whispered. 'Why wasn't he in the cellar?'

The pianist shrugged. 'It was too quick,' he said and she realised she could smell the sweat seeping from his clothes. The smell of fear. 'The warning had only just gone. Your mum was down there. Half the lads fell down the steps on top of her. But your dad was still at the bar. He was always last down.' He gave his toothy smile again. 'Worried someone would half inch his bottles while his back was turned.'

Katy felt a stab of anger. Her poor father. How dare Barry Fish mock him. Of course he had been worried about his bottles. Ever since the burglary at the beginning of the Blitz he had been worried about them. They were his livelihood. Even in the cellar he had always sat right by the door, listening.

And now he wouldn't listen any more because he was dead.

Dead.

And then suddenly a shout went up and moments later a plane roared deafeningly overhead. Katy heard the rattle of machine-guns, and some slates from somewhere clattered to the ground. She smelt cordite. And she saw the panic in Barry Fish's eyes as he dragged her down behind the cover of the fire engine.

The ARP man was swearing as he crouched beside them. 'They've done their dirty work. Why can't they bleedin' leave us alone?'

'They see the smoke,' one of the firemen grunted as he swiftly rolled in his hose. 'If they see flames or smoke they know there'll be rescue people around, get more casualties.'

Watching the firemen packing the hoses back on to the grey van, Katy realised their job was finished. The fires were out. They were hurrying to the next emergency.

Most of the survivors had already gone. Several men patted

her arm as they walked past. The spectacle was over. The damage done. She saw the ARP man check his watch and sign off some kind of form.

'That's all we can do here for the time being,' he said, tearing off a slip and handing it to her. 'Will you be all right, love?'

Katy nodded automatically, but her mind was blank. Was that it? Was that all they were going to do? Just leave her with a taped-off, smoking ruin?

Then as the fire engine pulled away, she heard an explosion down towards Clapham Junction and she realised that even as she crouched here other people were losing their homes and loved ones too. It wasn't just her. It was the whole of London. Already the smoke clouds that hung above them were pink with the reflection of distant fires.

Then Barry Fish was pulling her to her feet. 'You come home with me, Katy. I'll take care of you.'

She shook her head. 'I don't need looking after, Mr Fish, thank you.'

He stroked her hair. 'Course you do. Pretty little thing like you. Shocked, that's all. What with your old dad dead and that husband gone off and left you. You need a man to look after you. You come with me. I'll see you all right.'

'No.' Realising they were already halfway across the road, Katy suddenly came to her senses and tried to disengage her arm. 'No, I must go to the hospital. I must go and find my mother . . .' But his grip was tight and she almost lost her footing on the wet surface.

Using her slip to hold her closer, Barry Fish frowned. 'Now you do what you're told, little Katy. Your dad would want me to look after you.'

Suddenly on top of everything else Katy felt angry. Angry and frightened. She didn't want to be looked after by Barry Fish. She had never liked him and she didn't like him now. Nor did she trust him.

'Let me go,' she screamed at him, digging in her heels and skidding on some broken roof slates. 'I don't want to go with you.'

And then to her relief she saw the WVS van bumping down the street towards them.

'Stop,' she shouted, waving her spare arm. 'Please stop.'

For a horrible second, as the van drew up beside them, she thought Barry Fish was going to hit her but then he shrugged. 'Suit yourself,' he said. Then he straightened his clothes. 'You always was a sniffy little bit.' He laughed then, a cold calculating chuckle. 'But you'll soon be singing a different tune. You wait and see.'

As he stalked away Katy found she was trembling. At first she thought it was the cold but then she realised it was shock. She had seen it often enough in patients at the Wilhelmina. Taking a deep breath and hugging her arms round her body, she turned round and found herself looking at Mrs Carter.

'You don't want to have nothing to do with him,' Mrs Carter said, pushing her into the van and climbing in beside her. 'He's a nasty bugger.'

Mrs Rutherford was in the van. She moved over to make room for Katy. 'You poor child,' she said quietly. 'We heard what happened. We'll take you down to the hospital. You'll want to see your mother.'

Casualty was crowded. Extra doctors and nurses had been called back on duty to cope with the influx of wounded. Ambulances were arriving every few minutes, disgorging their bloody cargoes of filthy dust-covered victims. Some were already dead on arrival, others were dying.

At first as she stared round in horrified disbelief Katy thought the Wilhelmina itself had been bombed and then she realised that the smell of burning came from the stretchers by the door. Even as she took in the dreadful sight of three bodies burnt beyond recognition a nurse quickly covered them over with a sheet.

Straightening up, the nurse signalled a porter over. 'These should have been taken straight to the morgue,' she said crisply. 'There's nothing we can do for them here.'

The porter shook his head. 'There's no more trolleys,' he said. 'They'll have to wait.'

The nurse frowned. 'Well, get them moved as soon as you can. Sister doesn't want them here.'

Katy suddenly felt sick. It seemed incredible that it was less than two weeks since she had been working here. Two weeks ago, inured by the endless months of dealing with pain and suffering, she might have said the same thing. But now once again the lack of emotion appalled her.

For all anyone knew, one of those bodies might belong to her. Might be her father. The father who had loved her so much that it had almost annoyed her.

Forcing back a sudden desire to run away and cry, she looked around for someone she knew. But apart from Sister Parkes over on the other side there was no one, and in desperation she accosted a passing nurse and asked if she knew what had happened to Mrs Parsons.

Consulting a clipboard, the nurse told her that Mrs Mary Parsons was already on her way to the operating theatre. 'Fractured femur and broken arm,' the nurse said briskly. 'She was lucky to be one of the first they brought in. Otherwise she'd have had to wait.'

Lucky? Katy shook her head wearily. Lucky to be alive perhaps, but not much more than that. She wondered if her mother would even appreciate that. 'Can I see her?' she asked.

The nurse looked astonished. 'Good lord, no. You'll have to come back tomorrow.' She checked her list again. 'She'll be on the Ethel Barnet ward. Visiting hours are four to six.'

On her way back to Lavender Road, Katy suddenly wished she had argued. After all, she had worked in the blasted Wilhelmina for long enough. She could have just pushed through the swing doors and gone down to theatre herself. She might have been in time to see her mother before they put her under. She could have reassured her. She could have checked which surgeon was operating. She could have done a million useful things but she had done nothing. She had turned on her heel and walked away. Back into the night.

There was no sign of planes now. The guns were quiet. But everywhere she could see the effect of the raid. The sky over central London was red. Against the glow she could see the flabby pink-tinged barrage balloons hanging over the devastated city. The air was thick with dust and smuts. She could hear the distant crackle of fires, the occasional cracking roar of a building collapsing. From the top of Latchmere Road she could see the flames down by the river. Underfoot, debris and glass littered the road. Overhead, smoke hung like a cloud.

It was the worst she had seen it. She wondered how much more London could take. A few more nights like this and there would be nothing left. Just a million burnt-out buildings and the few remaining hospitals full of the dead and dying. Then, as the weary tears stung her eyes, she wondered how much more she could take.

At the moment she felt numb, numb and cold. But deep inside her she could feel something else simmering, she wasn't sure what. Fear perhaps, or panic or anger. Or just a terrible sense of loss. Whatever it was she didn't want it.

'I must stay calm,' she murmured to herself as she rounded the corner into Lavender Road once again. 'It's very important to stay calm.'

Expecting the road to be deserted she was surprised to hear voices ahead, hushed furtive voices interspersed with an incongruous gleeful chuckle. She could see a van with figures moving purposefully around it, the occasional flash of a torch quickly doused. Then suddenly she heard the familiar thump of a barrel hitting the ground and at once with a surge of incredulous anger she knew what was happening.

She'd heard of looters. Looters in the bombed West End shops. Looters in banks and offices. Like everyone else she had shivered with horror at the story of looters picking the jewellery of the dead and dying at the Café Royale even as the rescue teams worked to save the lives of the victims. But never in a million years had she thought she would see looters here. In Clapham. In her father's pub.

'No,' she whispered. 'No. No! NO!'

It never occurred to her that she was one girl against several men. She didn't think about the consequences. She didn't think of getting help. She quite simply didn't think. She just grabbed a piece of metal guttering that was lying in the road and rushed headlong into battle.

The first man didn't know what had hit him. She flayed him with a swing of her gutter as he stepped out of the gaping hole in the side of the pub. The crash of the drinks crate he was carrying hitting the ground alerted the other two and at once Katy realised her mistake. Two against one wasn't good odds. But her anger gave her strength and she had landed one of them a hard crack on the shoulder before the other caught hold of the gutter and tried to wrest it from her.

'It's only a bleedin' girl,' he grunted as she plunged the gutter hard into his stomach. 'Don't just stand there, man, get her arms.'

Screaming for him to keep away from her, Katy let go of the gutter and swung round, fists flailing as he approached. But it was hopeless. She made him scream with a punch to the arm she had damaged before, but then the gutter man had her and was twisting her arms cruelly behind her. And she could smell the odour of him, the whisky on his breath as he clamped a hand over her mouth.

'Shut your mouth, darling. Or you won't have a mouth to shut.'

Kicking and struggling as they slipped and slid about, ankle deep in glass, she caught him hard on the shin with her heel and his grip slipped for a second. Screaming again, Katy suddenly heard someone running up the street towards them.

And then she heard a shout, and the first man was getting to his feet and diving for the van and the man who was holding her was hesitating. Taking advantage of his lapse in concentration, she kicked him hard again and he swore and let her go and the van was firing into life and the shoulder man was getting in. A moment later the van was moving and her assailant was stumbling after it, shouting for them to wait.

But they didn't wait, and the last thing Katy saw was the van accelerating away, scattering drinks crates, with the gutter man hobbling after them in hot pursuit. She laughed once, a strange shriek of hysteria, as he slipped on a Guinness bottle and fell sprawling headlong in the road.

And then she fainted.

When she came round someone was trickling whisky into her mouth. As she coughed and groaned her rescuer sighed in relief. '*Gott sei dank.*'

Opening her eyes in astonishment, Katy found Aaref Hoch peering at her anxiously.

He smiled tentatively. 'Are you alive?'

As the events of the evening rushed back, Katy closed her eyes. Oblivion was suddenly more appealing. But it was too late. The whisky had revived her. Quickly, clinically, she told him what had happened. About Ward. About her mother. About her father. About the looters.

Then suddenly she was crying. Crying as though she would never stop. 'They took his silver goblets,' she sobbed. 'He loved those goblets.'

Aaref didn't try to answer. Nor did he try to stop her tears. He just sat quietly beside her on a piece of circular wood that had once been a tabletop.

'I'm sorry.' Katy tried to wipe her eyes, but the tears would keep coming. 'I'm so sorry.'

Aaref offered her the whisky bottle. 'You should not be sorry,' he said. 'It is good to cry. You have lost someone you love. Perhaps two people. It is no shame to be sad.'

Katy shook her head. 'But it's so pathetic. So many people have lost their loved ones in this beastly war. Look at you. And all the other refugees. And all the widows and orphans.'

Aaref shrugged. 'So let them cry too.' Then he touched her arm. 'You are not pathetic, Miss Katy. It is not pathetic to attack three men when there is just one of you.' He smiled. 'And quite a small one too if you do not mind me saying so.'

Katy took a shaky breath. 'That was just stupid.'

'No, no,' he disagreed. 'Not stupid. Brave.' He smiled again. 'You have courage. And that courage will help you through the difficult weeks ahead.' He stood up and flexed his shoulders. 'And now we must move your things from here to a safe place before those vulture birds come back for the rest.'

It took them three hours.

Aaref fetched a wheelbarrow from Mrs d'Arcy Billière's garden and they trundled it back and forth up the street to the Miss Taylors' house. There was more salvageable than Katy had realised. Although almost everything upstairs was wet from the firemen's hoses, it wasn't burnt, and by the end of it the Miss Taylors' front room looked like a jumble sale, with piles of damp clothes and shoes and ornaments all jumbled up with bottles of drink, barrels of beer, optics, the till and even some surviving chairs. The only thing they couldn't take was glasses. Every single glass in the whole pub was broken.

A policeman helped them for a while, on his way home after the all-clear eventually sounded.

It was five thirty in the morning and already getting light when Katy finally thanked Aaref for the last time and closed the Miss Taylors' front door.

In a daze she stumbled upstairs.

As she walked into the bedroom she had prepared for Ward's homecoming, suddenly she felt a terrible, aching loneliness. She would have given anything to have him there just now. Anything at all to have his arms round her just for one minute. One second.

But he wasn't there and as a shudder of tiredness and emotion coursed through her she feared he would never be there again.

Closing her mind to the awful thought, she knelt like a child at the end of the bed and prayed for his safety.

Then, too tired to move, she dropped her head on to the counterpane and slept.

It had been the heaviest raid of the war, and the following morning London was counting the cost. Five hundred German planes had wreaked havoc right across the capital. Scarcely an area had been unaffected. Over a thousand people had been killed in the one night with tens of thousands more injured.

The thought of all the dead and dying made Louise feel quite sick as she picked her way through the rubble down towards the river to Gregg Bros. But ironically it was the fact of the casualties that got her the job.

Moments before Louise arrived for her interview, Larry Gregg had just been informed that three of his operators had failed to report to work. And although a cocky little madam like her was the last kind of girl he wanted, he took her on in desperation. In any case, women were cheaper than men.

'You'll have to work, mind,' he told her. 'If you don't work you'll be out. We've got government quotas to meet and we're behind already.'

Louise had smiled sweetly. 'I'll work,' she said. 'That's what I'm here for, after all. Just tell me what to do and I'll do it.'

He had eyed her with misgiving. 'Well, you'll have to get them clothes off for a start.'

Louise's eyes widened. 'I beg your pardon?'

He laughed sourly. 'Unless you want your fancy gear covered in grease you'd better get yourself some overalls. I'll find someone to kit you out. Come with me.'

He led her out of his office and across a courtyard stacked with crates. Then he opened a steel door in a large building on the far side and ushered her inside.

The first thing Louise noticed was the noise. It hit her like a moving train and for a moment she reeled back, aghast. It was the machinery, she realised, row after row of dirty, dusty, greasy machines, each squeaking and clunking and grinding louder than the next. She had never seen or heard anything like it and by the time she had followed Mr Gregg across the floor to a line of people operating some kind of ear-piercing drill, Louise felt not only deafened but physically bruised by the noise.

Realising Mr Gregg was attempting to introduce her to a fat woman in voluminous grey overalls and a white mob cap, she tried to smile but her facial muscles were rigid with the effort of blocking out the din, and not only did she fail to hear the woman's name, but she also failed to hear what it was she was supposed to do.

A moment later the fat woman reached under her work bench and shoved what looked like a grey sack into her hands. 'Overalls,' she yelled and jerked her head towards a distant door. 'You best change in the lavvy.'

Aaref was right when he told Katy the days ahead would be difficult. And they were made more difficult by the inability of her mother to come to terms with the situation, and even worse by her inability to make a decision about anything.

It felt odd to be a visitor on the Ethel Barnet ward. It felt even odder trying to force her mother to take some responsibility for their future.

The first day it was understandable. She was in shock. And she was in pain after the operation. She was also weepy despite the heavy sedation the doctor had given her. But the following day it was the same.

'I don't know what to say,' she would murmur helplessly, when Katy asked her tentatively what to do about the funeral arrangements. 'I don't know what's for the best.'

'What about boarding up the pub?' Katy asked. 'The windows and that? Should I get in touch with the brewery? All the big furniture is still in there. And the carpets. What happens if it rains?'

Her mother shook her head. 'I don't know,' she said. 'Your father would have known what to do.' And then she would start crying, slow, silent tears that would drip unhindered down her puckered face.

Once again it was Nurse Coogan who came to her rescue.

'Don't worry her with all that,' she whispered as she passed by with some clean towels. 'You make the decisions and tell her what you've done. It's easier that way.'

It might be easier for her mother, Katy thought later as she sat in the undertaker's grim office on Northcote Road, but it wasn't easier for her. She had no idea about coffins or bearers. Let alone death certificates and obituaries.

But she quickly learned. Just as she learned that damp clothes very quickly went mouldy. That the pub till had been cleared by the looters. That her father's bank account stood at ten pounds ten shillings and four pence.

'Is that all?' She stared at the long-faced bank manager in horror. 'The funeral is costing five pounds. That only leaves us just over five pounds in the world. He must have had some savings.'

The bank manager shook his head regretfully. 'You may not have realised it, Miss er Mrs Frazer, but your father was under considerable financial pressure. The Blitz has taken its toll on a number of businesses. Your father's was no exception. And he had had some unforeseen expenditure to meet of course. There was a robbery, I believe, some months ago? All that stock had to be replaced.' He smiled thinly. 'And there was your wedding, of course . . .'

Of course. Katy shook her head wearily. It was her fault. Her wedding. She thought suddenly of the beautiful leather suitcase her parents had given her, the going-away clothes, the dressmaking, the flowers, the drinks and sandwiches afterwards. It all added up.

And now thanks to her and her five days of married bliss, there was only five pounds left in her father's account.

Five pounds wasn't going to last very long.

And then things got even worse.

The funeral was on the Saturday afternoon. Two weeks to the day since she had walked up the same aisle on her father's arm.

It was a suitably grey day. The news was bleak too. Yugoslavia had fallen. The Allied line in Greece was being hard pressed. There was heavy fighting on the Egyptian border.

The coffin was barely in the ground before Barry Fish touched her arm.

'We need to have a little talk,' he said.

Katy flinched. She had noticed Barry Fish among the other mourners in the church. She had felt his eyes on her from the other side of the aisle as she desperately tried to keep back the tears. Desperately tried to stop herself thinking of her poor dead father lying there right in front of her in the simple coffin she had chosen for him.

And now, just as she wanted to get away, to make sure the tea and sandwiches Mrs Carter had arranged for her in the vestry were ready, here he was, tugging at her sleeve, murmuring about a little bit of business they had to discuss.

'I haven't anything to discuss with you, Mr Fish,' she said bravely.

'Oh, I think you have.' He smiled his leering smile. 'It's a little matter of money. Your old dad owed me, you see.' He tucked an envelope into her pocket. 'I won't worry you with it now,' he said. 'But that's his IOUs. I'd be grateful for early settlement.'

Katy swallowed hard. 'I'll look into it,' she said stiffly. 'Now if you'll excuse me . . .'

Katy was touched by the number of mourners. Many of them were customers. People she didn't know and barely recognised. She was touched by their awkward sympathy. By their offers of help. But kind though they were, there was nothing they could do to bring back her father. Nor could they do anything about the financial situation she found herself in.

Not that she would dream of asking anyone for help. She wanted people to remember her father as the loyal husband and loving father the vicar had talked about, the man of steady faith and determined patriotism. She didn't want them remembering him as poor old peg-leg Parsons who left his wife and daughter with five quid to live on.

She could have told Jen perhaps. Or the Miss Taylors. Or Ward. But none of her real friends were there. And as she smiled bravely through the funeral tea, accepting condolences on behalf of her absent mother, she suddenly felt terribly alone.

Then she saw Mr and Mrs Rutherford approaching to say good-bye. She knew she would have to ask what to do about the pub and her heart quailed.

Mrs Rutherford touched her arm. 'You've borne up awfully well, Katy,' she said. 'Your father would have been proud of you.'

'Terrible thing to happen,' Mr Rutherford said. 'Fine man your father. Served with my father during the Great War, you know.'

Katy nodded and took a quick breath. 'About the pub, Mr Rutherford. I don't know if I ought . . .?'

He brushed aside her question with an imperious wave of his hand as he moved away. 'I'm sure my manager has it in hand.'

Behind her Joyce Carter snorted. 'I'll bloody bet he's sure. Especially if there's money in it.' She smiled grimly as Katy turned round in surprise. 'Don't you let him do you down,' she said, nodding after the departing Rutherfords. 'She's all right, but he's a right bastard and if you're not careful he'll trample all over you.'

Katy watched the Rutherfords climbing into their chauffeur-driven car which was waiting outside the church. 'I'm sure he's not that bad,' she said. 'I'm sure he'll treat us fairly. After all, Daddy's been a tenant of his for years.'

⋆　　⋆　　⋆

Mr Rutherford's manager did indeed have the matter in hand. When Katy got home she found a brown envelope pushed through the Miss Taylors' letterbox.

Opening it, she found a sheet of Rutherford & Berry headed notepaper. For a moment she stared at it uncomprehendingly. And then she realised what it was. It was a bill. Addressed to her mother. A bill for forty-one pounds. For two months' rent and dilapidations in arrears. *Settlement at your earliest convenience.*

Numbly she drew out of her pocket Mr Fish's IOUs. There were three. Together they totalled seven pounds eight shillings.

Leaning back against the door, she closed her eyes. 'Oh Daddy,' she whispered. 'What have you done to us?'

Chapter Twenty-One

To her complete astonishment, after her initial horror of the factory, Louise found she was quite enjoying her job. Oddly, she didn't mind getting her hands greasy. She didn't even mind the hideous grey overalls and mob cap. By the end of the first day she no longer felt self-conscious. On the contrary, she enjoyed the anonymity. Nobody bothered her. Nobody told her off for her manners or her choice of clothes. She no longer had to worry about being ladylike. About her limp. The freedom from parental nagging and concern was liberating.

And she was good at the job. Quick. Nimble fingered with her drill. She enjoyed the sense of making something, the sense of achievement, as one by one the small bolts fell into her hands from the parting tool. And she gained a strange satisfaction from the mindless repetitive task. It calmed her. For the first time in ages she felt almost contented. She didn't even know for sure what they were making the bolts for. She wondered if anyone did. There was minimal chat. The noise on the factory floor was too intense for conversation. Over meal breaks in the grim little canteen, the fat woman, Doris, would occasionally make a few remarks, but most of the men looked at the papers, or smoked, or wandered outside for some fresh air.

Aware that her accent and sex cut her off from the horde, generally Louise kept her mouth shut. She didn't want to draw attention to herself. She didn't want to make friends. In any case, as people mostly seemed to talk in glottal stops and lost vowels, half the time she couldn't understand what they were saying anyway.

Best of all she enjoyed the fact that her father disapproved. His disapproval was liberating too. Because she didn't care. She didn't have the time or the energy to care.

After working a ten-hour day she didn't have the time or the energy to care about anything else either.

She no longer lay awake at night wishing she had a boyfriend. She even felt more forgiving towards Katy Parsons. Not so forgiving that she would actually forgive her, but she did feel sorry for her about losing her father. And if she had had time she might have called to tell her so.

But she didn't have time. All her time was spent striving to perfect her skill. She wanted to be as fast as Doris, whose fat deft fingers turned out a hundred and sixty bolts on a good day. So far Louise could only achieve a hundred. But that was better than the rat-faced man on her other side who only managed ninety. Less than eighty and you got sacked.

At the end of her first week Louise was given one pound eighteen shillings. It was the first wages she had ever had and she was fingering it with relish until it occurred to her that it wasn't very much. One pound eighteen shillings wouldn't even begin to buy a new dress.

She looked at the line of men still waiting to be paid and frowned. 'How does anyone live on one pound eighteen shillings?' she asked the fat woman.

Doris laughed sourly. 'They don't. That's a woman's wage packet you got there.'

Louise glanced at her wage packet, half expecting it to have a pink trim or something, but it looked the same as the rest. 'What do you mean?'

Doris rolled her eyes. 'What I mean is, love, men get more.' She glanced at the rat-faced man who was standing beside them. 'What's it you get, Ken? Three pound odd, ain't it?'

Ken nodded. 'Give or take,' he said with a ratty smile.

Louise stared at him. 'But we do the same job.'

He shrugged. 'Men have families to support.'

'So do some women,' Louise said with a doubtful glance at her mentor. 'Don't they?'

Doris rolled her copious shoulders. 'It's the same everywhere, love. No point in making a fuss about it. Not if you want to keep your job.'

'But it's not fair.'

Rat-faced Ken chuckled complacently. 'Life ain't fair, love. Haven't you noticed?' He winked at Doris. 'No, come to think on it, don't suppose you would, a toff like you.'

Louise lifted her chin. 'I may be a toff,' she snapped, 'but I'm a damned sight better at making bolts than you are.'

At last Katy felt she was making progress. On Molly Coogan's advice she resisted being pressured into any rash decisions about her debts and responsibilities and instead had gone to the Town Hall.

'There's all sorts of help they'll give you,' Molly said. 'When we were bombed right at the beginning it was a shambles, all different forms and people to see. But they're meant to be better now. God knows they've had enough practice.'

She was partly right. It was no longer a shambles, but there were still a welter of different forms to fill out and people to see. There were also, after the recent devastating raids, a huge number of people milling about.

But despite the endless queues, the officers were helpful. Katy found herself directed to the Engineer's Department in respect of bomb damage, the Assistance Board for lost household effects, the Public Assistance Officer for help-in-kind. She was given coupons for food and clothes, forms for the National Registration Officer for replacement food cards and best of all £10 from the Lord Mayor's National Air Raid distress fund for bomb victims.

The allocating officer smiled at her delight and slid yet more forms across his desk. 'You can apply for other grants too,' he said. 'If you're desperate. Household effects, furniture removal, funeral expenses, re-establishment of small businesses.'

Katy smiled weakly. If only there was a grant for repayment of mounting debt. 'I think this will do me for now,' she said.

Feeling she had done a good day's work, she made her way to the Wilhelmina where to her horror she found Barry Fish sitting solicitously by her mother's bed.

'Ah, here she is,' he said as Katy approached. 'I was just telling your mother how you saw off them looters on the night of the bomb. Quite the little heroine, weren't you?'

Katy blinked in surprise. 'Where did you hear that?' She certainly hadn't told anyone, and she very much doubted if Aaref had. In fact the policeman had specifically recommended they kept it quiet. No point in advertising that there was valuable stock left intact in the Miss Taylors' house.

But Barry Fish winked at her mother. 'Oh, you know Clapham. You can't keep a secret for five minutes round here.'

Forcing herself not to recoil from his smarmy smile, Katy stared him steadily in the eye. Suddenly she realised she wanted to hit him. To hurt him. To wipe that shifty, supercilious smile off his beastly mouth. But instead she raised her eyebrows disdainfully. 'So it seems,' she said coldly. 'Now, if you wouldn't mind, Mr Fish, my mother looks rather tired.'

At once Barry Fish's eyes hardened. 'Now now, little Miss Katy. Not so fast.' He glanced at her mother with an ingratiating smile. 'She's always trying to get rid of me, Mary. She doesn't seem to appreciate all I've done for you over the years.'

Seeing her mother was rousing herself to make some placating remark, Katy intervened quickly. 'I do appreciate it,' she said grittily, standing back to let him past. 'You have left us in no doubt that we are in your debt.'

'Ah yes,' he smiled complacently. 'About those IOUs . . .?'

Katy nodded. 'We'll pay you as soon as we can,' she said. 'It's just that things are a bit difficult at the moment.'

He smiled again and let his eyes flicker down her body. 'I'm sure we can come to some kind of agreement.'

Katy felt her skin creep. 'We'll pay you as soon as we can.'

After he had gone she asked her mother irritably why she had let him in.

Mary Parsons looked surprised. 'He only wants to help us, Katy. We need a man.' Tears welled suddenly in her eyes. 'With Malcolm gone and your Ward too. How will we manage otherwise? We need someone to look after us.'

'We may need someone to look after us,' Katy said grimly, surreptitiously wiping the sweat off her palms, 'but I'm damned if it's going to be Barry Fish.'

She couldn't bear to think of Ward gone. The thought that she might never see or hear of him again was too awful to contemplate. At least with her father, she knew he was dead. She had asked to see his body at the undertaker's and although they were reluctant, when she explained she was a nurse, they'd let her see him. Just his face. His face wasn't burnt. It was pale and waxy. Dead. But peaceful.

It had helped. He was dead and that was that. It was sad. Dreadfully sad. The night of the funeral she had cried so hard she had barely noticed the bombing. He was dead and she would never see him again. But she could come to terms with it. Accept it.

But Ward was a different matter.

She had had so little of him. And yet it had meant so much. So incredibly much.

During the day she tried hard to keep herself busy but at night she couldn't keep the memories at bay. The way his grey eyes sparkled when he laughed. The tenderness of his touch. The warmth of his voice as he spoke her name. The feel of his cold bare chest against her face as she had clung to him on that last afternoon.

And the smell of him. That warm clean masculine smell. And the feel of him lying against her, his long strong limbs, the weight of him, the warmth of him. The strong regular pumping of his heart. She felt a sudden panic shuddering through her and clamped it down fiercely. He had been so alive. She refused to believe he might be dead.

And then Helen de Burrel turned up. Out of the blue. Katy saw her from the window.

She had just been pleading for a breathing space with the Rutherford & Berry rent collector on the grounds that her mother was still too ill to deal with financial matters.

But he didn't care two hoots about the health of her mother. 'In that case I will call again next week when I will expect you to have next month's rent ready as well,' he said.

Katy stared at him appalled. 'You mean there's more?' she gasped. 'You mean we'll have to keep paying it?'

He seemed impervious to her distress. 'Your parents signed the lease,' he said. 'Unless another tenant can be found to take it on, I'm afraid your mother is liable.'

Katy saw a ray of hope. 'But if another tenant could be found . . .?' She stopped abruptly when she saw his expression.

'Mr Rutherford is most particular about who he offers his leases to,' he said. 'And currently most suitable men are in the Forces.'

'I see,' Katy said flatly.

He inclined his head. 'So I strongly suggest your mother finds the money she owes us,' he said pointedly. 'I'm sure you appreciate that we cannot allow debts like this to run on.'

As he left he briefly raised his hat. In any other man it would have been a gesture of courtesy. In the rent collector it seemed more like a threat and Katy found she was shivering violently as she closed the door.

'I'm not up to this,' she had whispered to herself. 'I'm too much of a coward. I'm not cut out to fight.'

Earlier she had hidden from Barry Fish, cowering behind a chair as he prowled around outside, peering through the taped-up windows, even trying the front door which mercifully she had locked.

And now she almost wished she could hide from Helen de Burrel. She had spoken to her on the phone only a couple of days before. Told her what had happened to the pub and to her father, listened to her polite commiserations.

She could see the solemn look on the other girl's face now as she pushed open the front gate and suddenly Katy found she didn't want to know. She wanted to carry on living in hope.

But she opened the door. She had no choice. 'It's bad news,' she said baldly. 'Isn't it?'

Helen hesitated, then saw Katy's look of agony and groaned. 'I'm sorry, Katy. We still don't know for sure. But I had to come. I had to keep you in the picture.'

She felt a flash of anger. 'What picture?'

'We've heard what happened to the plane,' Helen said quietly.

Realising Helen was looking at her in concern, Katy dug her nails into the palms of her hands and tried to calm her voice. 'What did happen? Who have you heard from?'

Helen edged towards the sitting-room door. 'I think we should sit down.'

She looked around at the clutter of bottles and crates and barrels and tried to smile. 'If there's room.'

Katy did not want to smile, she wanted the story.

And to her credit once they had sat down, Helen gave it to her. Jean-Luc had eventually managed to radio in a report. The mission hadn't been a trap. But by an unlucky chance a German field unit had shot at the plane as it came into the appointed rendez-vous. It crashed on landing. The pilot was killed. Ward was alive but injured. He couldn't walk.

Helen glanced at Katy anxiously as the colour left her face but then ploughed doggedly on. 'Jean-Luc and Pierre didn't know what to do,' she said. 'They could hear the German vehicles approaching. Ward was telling them to go and leave him. He knew there was no chance of him getting away. But they also had with them the sick man Ward had come to fetch. And then suddenly they were under fire.'

She took a slow breath. 'They knew that if they became encircled they would have had it, so they fired back while they worked out a plan. They realised they couldn't get Ward away. Not without backup . . .'

As Helen tailed off, Katy closed her eyes. She could feel the ominous tightening of her chest. She wanted to scream. She wanted to kill Helen de Burrel. She wanted to kill Jean-Luc and Pierre. She also badly wanted to be sick. But she forced herself to breathe, to stop her voice cracking. 'Is that it?'

Helen shook her head. 'Not quite. There was only one thing they could do, and while Jean-Luc and the sick Resistance fighter held off the Germans, Pierre did it.'

'What?'

'He swopped Ward's clothes with the dead pilot's.'

Katy stared at her blankly as the dreadful meaning of her words sank in.

'They left him,' she whispered. 'Didn't they?' Her voice rose. 'They left Ward there.'

Helen frowned. 'They left him, yes.' She leaned forward urgently. 'But don't you see? They did the best they could for him. They may have given him a chance. If they'd tried to take him with them, they'd all have been killed.'

But Katy couldn't see. All she could see was Ward being left on his own in agony to face the Germans. The Gestapo.

And the thought crucified her.

'They left him,' she repeated. 'They left him.'

'He wanted them to go,' Helen said. 'He insisted on it.' She bit her lip. 'He covered their escape, Katy. If it wasn't for him, they would certainly have been captured.'

She touched Katy's arm and, looking up sharply, Katy saw that there were tears in her eyes. 'Whatever happens to him, he's a hero, Katy. You should feel very proud.'

Katy shook off her hand. She didn't feel proud, she felt angry. Furiously angry.

'What about the other man?' she hissed. 'The beastly sick man who caused this fiasco? What happened to him? I suppose he escaped too?'

Helen shook her head. 'He died,' she said. 'One of the German bullets got him. There was nothing they could do.'

Katy couldn't speak. Nor could she breathe. She could feel the emotion strangling her throat just as she could feel the tension strangling her lungs. So the whole thing had been pointless. Utterly pointless.

Helen was watching her anxiously. 'I shouldn't have told you,' she said. 'I thought it would help.'

But it didn't help. It made everything worse. Much worse. Because she now had an image. An image of Ward Frazer lying injured and in intense pain next to a crashed plane, knowing that sooner or later his bullets would run out.

'Katy, are you all right?' She heard Helen's voice from a long way away. And then more urgently. 'Katy? Speak to me. Are you all right?'

Katy was crying now, the tears pouring unhindered down her face and the breath was rasping in her throat.

She heard Helen's voice again. Heard her swear. Heard her feet on the stairs.

And then the medicine bottle was at her lips and she was trying to swallow. Trying to swallow and breathe and cry and shout and scream.

'Oh God,' Helen muttered to herself in horror. Running to the kitchen she filled the kettle and put it on the stove. 'Steam,' she muttered. 'She needs steam.' But she couldn't get the gas to light and then she realised there was no gas. Nor any electricity.

'Try and relax,' she called to Katy as she ran back down the passage to the front door. 'Try to breathe slowly. I'm going to get help.'

*   *   *

Katy's collapse was the talk of the road. Everyone agreed that it was only the prompt action of Helen de Burrel and Joyce Carter that had saved her life.

'If she'd been on her own, she'd have been a goner.'

But she wasn't a goner. Running down the road, Helen had seen Joyce emerging from her house. Recognising her from Katy's wedding, she immediately enlisted her help. And thanks to Helen's knowledge of Katy's asthma from Bristol, and Joyce's bright idea of fetching the primus stove from the WVS van at the school, she was saved.

Not that it made much difference to Katy. For the first couple of days, as the black despair cloaked her mind completely, she might just as well have been dead.

Sometimes she almost wished she was dead. After all, she thought, what was there to live for? She had lost her father, her husband, her home. She was facing spiralling debt. No, all she wanted to do was stay in the darkness of her bedroom and forget about everything.

But gradually the real world crept back in. She began to hear snatches of conversation downstairs.

She heard Joyce talking to Bertie Rutherford on the doorstep. 'You're the last person she'd want to see,' she said. 'Don't you understand? The sodding Germans have killed her father. Her husband is missing. She doesn't want to hear any of your conchie be-nice-to-the-Germans nonsense.'

The following evening she heard Molly Coogan seeing off Louise. 'So you reckon you're a friend of hers, do you?' She heard Molly's incredulous laugh, the brutal tone in her voice. 'Well, I know exactly who you are. And a fat lot of help you've been to her over the last few weeks. No, you can't bloody come in. You upset her enough before her wedding. It's all added up, you know, all the upsets. That's why she's so bad now. So you can bugger off and take your bloody flowers with you.'

Other people sent gifts. Mrs Rutherford sent three eggs and a lettuce. Aaref Hoch sent a bag of tasty little cakes, two tins of salmon and a pot of plum jam. Mr Lorenz sent a small lamb chop.

'Good God.' Molly Coogan held it up incredulously. 'Who's this from? A puff of wind and it would blow away.'

Joyce frowned. She wasn't sure about Molly Coogan. She was a bit too much like Jen for her liking. Not as pretty of course, but a bit too big for her boots nevertheless. She glanced at the offending chop and felt touched that old Lorenz had bothered at all. 'It's a kind gesture,' she said stiffly.

Molly giggled. 'That's just about all it is,' she said. 'A gesture. Because there's just about enough meat on this to keep a flea alive.'

Luckily there was plenty of drink. Remembering how much Lorenz's Guinnesses had helped her over a bad time, Joyce had decided that Katy should drink a bottle a day. 'It'll build you up a bit,' she said, bringing it into the dark bedroom. 'Full of nourishment.'

But Katy didn't want to be built up. She didn't want to get better. She didn't want to face Barry Fish and the Rutherford & Berry rent collector. She didn't want to face anybody.

It didn't take Joyce long to realise that there was more to Katy's collapse than mere grief. So when Mrs Rutherford asked after Katy the following morning, Joyce told her the truth.

'Not much better for being hounded by your husband's rent collector,' she said sourly. 'I'd have thought he'd have had the grace to hold off a bit. Let them get over their grief.'

Celia looked shocked. 'I had no idea,' she said. 'I wonder if my husband knows about this.'

Joyce stared at her. She was on the verge of saying that as Greville Rutherford owned the blasted brewery, it was pretty likely he knew what was going on, but she bit back the words. No point in ruffling more feathers than she had to. 'Perhaps you could have a quiet word with him,' she suggested. 'See if he can't find somebody to take over the lease of the pub.'

Celia seemed surprised. 'But would anyone want to take it on? Isn't the building completely wrecked?'

Joyce shrugged. 'I don't reckon it's as bad as it looks. My Pete's in the building trade and he says it's not all that big a job.' Although she had to admit she'd been surprised at the time. Not at what he'd said, but that he'd said it at all. Usually poor old Pete kept his mouth well shut. God knew there was enough noise in the house with Mick gabbing off the whole time, but this time Pete had spoken up and to everyone's surprise he had seemed to know what he was talking about.

'In any case,' Joyce said now, passing on Pete's unexpected wisdom, 'the government help towards the war damage. Grants and that.' She shrugged. 'So I reckon as your husband could get it put back together if he wanted. And then someone else might take it on. OK, Katy and her mother would lose their home, but at least they wouldn't have to keep on shelling out rent for a place they can't use.'

She stopped, realising Celia was looking at her oddly, and wondered if she had gone too far. You never knew with toffs. Even ones like Celia Rutherford. Mostly they were all right but then suddenly they'd turn and start treating you all sniffy and disdainful again.

But Celia looked more excited than angry. 'I wonder,' she started and stopped again. Then she smiled. 'I've just thought of the perfect tenant, Mrs Carter.'

Joyce blinked. 'Who?'

Celia clapped her hands. 'Us.'

'Us?' Joyce stared at her employer, wondering if she had gone mad. 'Us?' Joyce shook her head. 'We couldn't run a pub,' she said.

'Not a pub, a café,' Celia chuckled. 'Don't you see, Mrs Carter? It's the perfect place. It's the perfect solution. And we could let Katy and her mother carry on living upstairs. At a lower rent of course.'

Joyce felt a smile curving her mouth. It did indeed seem the perfect solution. But then she sobered. She knew only too well that nothing was quite as good as it seemed. There was bound to be a hitch.

But it was Celia who thought of it. 'Of course we'll have to approach it carefully,' she said with a frown. 'We'd better not raise their hopes too soon, because my husband doesn't approve of women in business.'

★　★　★

Katy was lying in bed when Sister Morris arrived. Pam Nelson let her in on her way out and the first Katy knew of her arrival was when she burst into her bedroom and swept back the curtains with one flick of her powerful wrist.

Then she swung round and fixed Katy with a beady eye as she levered herself up in the bed, blinking against the unexpected light.

'What is the meaning of this?' Sister Morris barked, waving her hand round the dusty, untidy bedroom. 'What are you doing moping about in bed? The last time you saw your poor mother was over a week ago.'

Caught in the glare from the windows, Katy felt curiously naked. Quailing, she pulled the sheet up to her throat.

'Well?' Sister Morris barked again. 'Speak up.'

'My husband is missing,' Katy mumbled.

Sister Morris crossed her arms across her impressive chest. 'A lot of people are missing, young lady,' she said. 'Haven't you been listening to the news? Thousands of our Forces have been cut off in the Middle East and in Greece.'

Katy swallowed. 'But it's different with Ward.'

Sister Morris snorted impatiently. 'All that's different is the fuss you are making about it. Now pull yourself together at once. I will not have a nurse of mine carrying on like this.'

Katy didn't like to say she was no longer a nurse of Sister Morris's, or of anyone else come to that. Once again she was nothing. Like she always had been. Poor little Katy Parsons, no use to anyone.

'And the first thing you can do is clean up this disgusting mess. How do you expect to get better living in a pigsty?'

'I'm sorry, Sister,' Katy muttered.

'No good being sorry. You need to do something about it. Now get washed and get dressed. Now.'

Ten minutes later Katy presented herself meekly downstairs.

Sister Morris inspected her carefully. 'That's better. Now get this room tidied up. It's not at all suitable for you to live among all

379

this alcohol. I suggest you push it all to one side until such time as you can get rid of it.'

'Yes, Sister.'

'Now what are you going to do with yourself? Your husband may be missing, but you can't just sit around waiting. That's just self-indulgent. You must keep yourself busy. If necessary you could consider coming back to the hospital.'

Katy could hardly believe her ears. 'You'd have me back?' she asked incredulously.

Sister Morris snorted. 'Not in your present state I wouldn't. Certainly not. But if you pull yourself together, I expect I could find something for you to do.'

Katy stared at her. 'But I was so useless.'

'You were inexperienced,' Sister Morris said crisply. 'But you had the making of a good little nurse.'

Katy blinked. 'Did I? Did I really?'

But before Sister Morris could reiterate her confidence in Katy's nursing ability, someone knocked at the door.

Seeing Katy jump nervously, Sister Morris went to open it.

Peering nervously past her great bulk, to her astonishment, Katy saw Jen standing on the step.

She was about to come into the house but Sister Morris was barring her way. 'Who are you?'

'I'm Jennifer Carter,' Jen said. 'Who are you?'

As Sister Morris drew herself up to her full height, Katy felt her lips curve for the first time in days.

'This is Sister Morris,' she said, stepping forward hastily and frowning pointedly at Jen. 'She was my ward Sister at the Wilhelmina.'

But Jen was oblivious to Katy's reproof. 'Good God,' she said, doing a double take round Sister Morris's bosoms. 'No wonder Mum wrote to me. You look like death.'

Sister Morris's eyes were popping out of her head. 'I don't know who you are or what you are doing here, but I'd be grateful if you would refrain from taking Our Lord's name in vain.'

Jen grinned. 'I'm on an errand of mercy,' she said. 'I've come to stay with Katy.' She raised her finely plucked eyebrows at Katy. 'I hope that's all right? I've got a week off. And I can't stay at home.' She saw Katy's surprise and shrugged. 'It seems my mother has finally come to her senses and thrown my dad out of her bed. Unfortunately that means he's sleeping in mine. And I don't want to share.' She grimaced. 'Not with him.'

Sister Morris was clearly appalled. She turned to Katy and fixed her with a baleful glare. 'Is this person a friend of yours?'

Katy nodded nervously. 'She's an actress,' she explained. 'She doesn't mean to be rude.'

'An actress,' Sister Morris repeated. 'I see.' And it was clear from her frigid tone what she thought of the acting profession. Not much.

Seeing Jen bristle, Katy quickly intervened. 'Sister, thank you so much for coming round. I really am grateful.'

Sister Morris looked disdainfully down her nose. 'I will expect to see you with your mother at visiting time this afternoon.' Then she swung round to Jen. 'As for you, actress or not, if you are intending to stay here, I would ask you to refrain from blasphemy and to assist in keeping the house clean. Godliness and hygiene are the best remedy for the sick.' With that she gathered her cloak around her and swept out.

As the door closed behind her, Jen turned round to Katy in amazement.

'I'm not surprised you've been having a nervous breakdown if you've had to put up with that old dragon throwing her bosoms around.'

Katy giggled. 'It's the first time she's been.'

Jen rolled her eyes. 'Thank God for that. Because if she comes again, we'll have to get the building reinforced.'

Having Jen back was a tonic. Despite the fact that her arrival put Molly Coogan's nose out of joint, her presence in the house did

Katy a power of good. In fact the combination of Sister Morris's strict pull-yourself-together tactics and Jen's happy-go-lucky irreverence had the effect of lifting her out of her lethargy.

Jen told endless stories about ENSA. How dear Mrs Frost had tripped coming on to the stage on her first evening in the show, exposing not only her petticoat but a pair of long pink knickers to the audience who seemed to think it was part of the act.

She was also intrigued by her mother's sudden unexplained dominance in the Carter household and speculated wildly about what could have brought it about. Eventually she had wheedled the truth, or part of it, out of the much chastened Mick.

'She held a gun on Dad,' she told Katy later. 'Good old Mum. I never thought she had it in her.' She grinned. 'Pity she didn't pull the trigger and all while she had the chance.'

Jen's other new discovery was about Bertie Rutherford's so-called romance with Sheila Whitehead next door. She claimed that their over-enthusiastic love-making kept her awake at night.

'I had to bang on the bloody wall in the end,' she said. 'And then there was this scream because Sheila thought it was a bomb landing.' She grinned at Katy's face. 'Ruined their fun for the night anyway!'

Suddenly, to Katy's surprise, she found she could laugh again. The pain was still there. The sense of loss. The dread of uncertainty. But they were no longer all encompassing. They were in a different part of her mind now. A private part that she visited only when she was on her own, like a shrine.

Her financial problems remained of course, but somehow Jen even managed to make light of those.

'If that bloody Fish man comes sniffing round while I'm here,' she said one lunchtime, 'He'll get a stiletto where he won't like it.'

'But I'll have to pay him sooner or later,' Katy said. 'I'll have to get some money from somewhere.'

Jen waved her arms around. 'Then why don't you sell all this drink? It's like a bloody taproom in here.'

Katy frowned. 'But who can I sell it to? The brewery have already told me they won't have it back.'

'Let's ask that Aaref Hoch,' Jen said. 'He looks like he might know.'

To Katy's surprise, Aaref did know. And the following afternoon he arrived with a smiling publican from Balham and a small truck and supervised the loading. Then he solemnly handed over twenty pounds which Katy and Jen had agreed was a fair price.

Katy lost no time in paying off Barry Fish. The next time he called, she almost threw the money at him before he'd even opened his mealy mouth.

'There are you,' she said. 'There's your money. You'd better count it,' she added, sharply sarcastic. 'Just to be sure I haven't cheated you.'

To her astonishment he did. 'It's all in order,' he said, looking almost disappointed that his excuse for hassling her had been removed. 'That's that then, is it?'

'Yes,' Katy said, closing the door in his face. 'That's that.'

They were just celebrating with a bottle of brandy that Jen had cannily kept back when Mrs Rutherford arrived with her proposal to take over the lease in order to run a café from the Flag and Garter.

'You'll have to ask your mother of course,' she said as Katy stared at her in wide-eyed astonishment. 'And I'll have to talk to my husband. But in principle how does it sound?'

'In principle it sounds wonderful,' Katy stammered, promising to ask her mother just as soon as she could.

It did indeed seem like a gift from heaven.

But later, as she and Jen talked it over, she began to wonder. 'It's always been a pub,' she said, suddenly feeling a stab of nostalgia for the old place. 'It seems a shame to turn it into something else.'

Jen stared at her. 'Good God,' she said. 'Talk about looking a gift horse in the mouth. I don't like those Rutherfords but you're not likely to get a better offer. And what on earth else are you going to do with the bloody place? Run it yourself?' She began to laugh and then suddenly stopped when she saw the expression on Katy's face. For a moment Jen was poised still, her glass halfway to her mouth, then she slowly put it down and her eyes widened. 'Katy?'

For a second Katy stared back, then she sat back in her chair. 'No, of course not. I wouldn't know where to begin.'

Jen hadn't missed that slight hesitation. 'Seriously, Katy,' she said, leaning forward. 'Could you? I mean you never seemed to take any interest in it before.'

'Dad never let me,' Katy said. She recalled her father's speech at her wedding, 'Let's hope she makes a better wife than she does publican,' and frowned. Her father had never had any faith in her. She had never had much faith in herself. Ward was the only person who had faith in her. Suddenly she knew what Ward would say. He'd tell her to go for it. But Ward wasn't here. Ward might never be here again. She swallowed hard and shook her head.

'No,' she said. 'It's a stupid idea.'

Jen frowned. 'I think you ought at least to go and talk to Mr Rutherford.'

Katy gaped. 'Don't be ridiculous.' Then she pushed back her chair. 'Jen, I don't want to talk about it. The whole idea makes me feel sick.'

Jen laughed. 'I'm not surprised. I can't exactly imagine you pulling pints and heaving beer barrels around. No, if I was you, I'd let Mrs Rutherford have it and be grateful.'

And that's what I will do, Katy thought. But I won't tell her straight away. I'll let her stew a bit first. There was no rush after all.

She smiled to herself. The thought of holding out on the Rutherfords was suddenly rather appealing. It gave her a small sense of power. She knew Ward would approve. The very thought of it cheered her up.

Pam stood under one of the budding chestnuts on the common and prayed that George wouldn't fall out of the tree and break his neck.

'Don't go too high,' she called up anxiously as his little legs began to disappear from sight among the new growth. She knew Sheila didn't let him climb trees at all, but Sheila wasn't there. Sheila was at the cinema with Bertie Rutherford, and for the third time that week Pam had found herself babysitting as soon as she got home from work.

She didn't really mind. She loved George dearly. She just wished Sheila would spend more time with him and less with Bertie Rutherford. Unless he was on night shift at the hospital, Bertie spent most nights over there now and Pam could see Sheila getting more and more involved. And George was paying the price.

She could hear his voice now high above her but she couldn't quite hear what he was saying. Then she did hear and her heart sank.

'Auntie Pam, I'm stuck.'

Craning her neck to peer up into the tree all she could see was one small arm clutching what looked like a very insubstantial bough. 'Oh God,' she murmured. Then more loudly, 'Are you sure?'

'Yes, I'm sure.' Then a little sob. 'I'm scared, Auntie Pam.'

Frantically she glanced round for help, but it was getting quite late and apart from a few distant and rather geriatric gardeners on the allotments and the even more distant soldiers on the searchlight and gun emplacements, the common was deserted.

'I think I'm going to fall.'

'If you fall, I'll bloody kill you,' she muttered. 'And Sheila will certainly kill me.'

A whimper from above. 'I can't hear you . . .'

'I said hold tight,' she said, tucking her skirt into her knickers. There was only one thing for it. 'I'm coming up to get you.'

But it wasn't quite as easy as she had thought. In her youth she had been quite a dab hand at tree climbing but now suddenly the branches seemed more slippery than she remembered, more widely spaced. In fact she had only just managed to get off the ground into the first fork when she heard a faint giggle a few branches above her.

'Auntie Pam?'

'Yes?' She hardly dared look up for danger of falling off herself.

'I'm not really stuck.'

Stifling a sudden urge to climb on up and wring his pretty little neck, she dropped awkwardly to the ground and quickly un-tucked her skirt from her knickers. A minute later a small pair of legs appeared above her, waving about frantically as he tried to find a foothold. Holding her breath, Pam hovered underneath him, praying he would arrive safely.

'You're a wicked boy,' she said severely as he finally slithered to the ground beside her.

'I know,' he said happily.

Pam knew she should be more cross but it was hard to berate a child who smiled so rarely. Instead she hugged him to her and discovered he was shivering.

'We ought to go back,' she said. 'It's a cold wind. The last thing we need is you catching a chill. We got our electricity back today so you can have a hot bath before bed.'

A hot bath. She was looking forward to having one herself later. One with Alan perhaps if Bertie wasn't there. A hot bath. She smiled. One thing the war had done was turn simple things back into luxuries.

'You're smiling, Auntie Pam,' George said, slipping his hand into hers as they crossed the road that circled the common and began to walk down Lavender Road. 'I like it when you smile. It makes you pretty. Almost as pretty as Mummy.'

Pam blinked. Goodness, she thought, what a compliment. Then she laughed and hugged him to her. 'I've just realised there are things to smile about,' she said. 'Like having you to play with, and hot water at last, and no bombing for two weeks.' And having more or less come to terms with the fact that she and Alan were clearly destined not to have children. And then as she spoke some drops of rain began to fall and she groaned. 'All we need now is some sun. I've had enough of these blasted April showers.'

And then to everyone's relief as May got under way, the weather did cheer up. Suddenly it was almost summer. And despite the dreadful damage everywhere, despite the lack of food in the shops, despite the loss of the Greek mainland and the gloomy news from Egypt, people's spirits lifted.

Even the determined Tube-dwellers had begun to lose that ghastly Blitz look, the yellow skin and the sunken eyes, red rimmed from fright and sleepless nights.

'London can take it,' had been the slogan. And London had taken it. Taken it hard. Three hundred thousand homes had been made uninhabitable, twenty thousand civilians had been killed. But gradually those remaining were beginning to believe the end of their ordeal was in sight. Since the two dreadful raids in the middle of April, there had been plenty of warnings, but, apart from a few isolated incidents, the Luftwaffe had kept away.

People were smiling again. There was a feeling that if they could survive the last six months they could survive anything.

Even Winston Churchill seemed to believe it. When he spoke in the House of Commons at the end of the first week of May, his words were greeted with a patriotic cheer: 'When I look on the perils that have been overcome, upon the great mountain waves in which the gallant ship had driven; when I remember all that has gone wrong and remember all that has gone right, I feel sure we have no need to fear the tempest. Let it roar, let it rage. We shall come through.'

Three days later the Luftwaffe carried out their most vicious raid of the war. Five hundred and fifty planes dropped one hundred thousand incendiaries. A German pilot shot down and captured later that night said that he had been able to see the the fires burning at London's Elephant and Castle even as he flew over Rouen, a hundred and sixty miles away in France.

In the cellar of the Miss Taylors' house, Jen and Katy were playing cards. They never heard the bomb. All they heard was a strange moaning noise, followed by the cracking of masonry as the house collapsed on top of them.

Chapter Twenty-Two

Pam and Alan heard the strange grumbling roar from their Anderson shelter. It was nothing like anything they had ever heard before and at first they thought it was their house that had gone.

Emerging tentatively from the shelter once the noise had stopped, Alan found the air filled with a fine dust that swirled eerily around the beam of his torch, making it difficult to see anything at all. It also made him cough and he retreated back into the shelter to tie a handkerchief over his mouth.

'We seem to be OK,' he said to Pam. 'I'm just going over to check on Sheila.'

Pam took one look at the white dust already coating his hair and clothes and grabbed her scarf. 'I'm coming with you,' she said grimly. 'I just know something awful has happened and you're going to need help.'

As they stumbled through the dark house, the smell of cordite was so strong Pam could almost taste it. They met their front door halfway up the hall passage, and yet bizarrely most of the furniture from the front room had ended up in the front garden, presumably sucked out through the broken windows by some vacuum effect caused by the explosion. But it was the sight opposite that stopped them at the front gate. Even in the thin, dust-filled moonlight and the hazy beam of Alan's torch the devastation was obvious.

'Oh my God.' Pam clutched her chest. She couldn't take it in.

Ahead of her, Alan was walking forward carefully, his torch playing urgently over the wreckage of what had once been Sheila's cosy little home. Some of it had tipped forward into the street, but most of it seemed to have been blown to the side, into or onto the Miss Taylors' house next door.

Alan was calling their names now. Over and over. His desperate voice almost drowned by the sudden roar of gunfire up on the common. 'Is anyone there? Sheila? Bertie? Can you hear me? Katy? Jen? George? For God's sake someone answer!'

'Bertie's not there,' Pam shouted. 'He's on night duty tonight.'

Then as she stood there looking at the avalanche of girders and pipes and splintered wood that had once been furniture, an overwhelming hopelessness washed over her and she realised it didn't matter whose name Alan called. He wasn't going to get a reply.

He was still shouting when the ARP warden arrived. Pam saw him talking to Alan, saw Alan put his hand to his head in a gesture of shock.

And then suddenly a strange, muffled, high-pitched howl rent the air. For a moment none of them could believe their ears. But it was definitely coming from the rubble.

Pam stumbled forward. 'That's a dog,' she shouted. 'How can there be a dog in there?'

'That's no dog,' the ARP warden said grimly. 'That's someone screaming. Sounds deep. Still, at least it shows someone's alive in there. Not that we stand much chance of getting them out,' he added. 'Not without the heavy rescue.'

But Alan was already running forward, scrambling over the debris, tearing at the wreckage with his bare hands.

'Alan,' Pam screamed. 'Wait, be careful.'

He paused for a second and looked back. 'Go and get some help,' he shouted back. 'Get the Carter boys, Lorenz, anyone you can find. Anyone with a bit of muscle.'

Even as he spoke, there was a wrenching crash as a huge piece of girder slithered towards him, bringing with it another avalanche of rubble.

Pam felt a scream rising in her throat and then the dust settled and she saw Alan was still there, still moving forward. 'Alan, stop,' she screamed. 'It's too dangerous. We'll have to wait for the emergency services.'

The ARP man was stumbling towards her. 'We won't get no emergency services, love, not tonight. Not for a domestic. Haven't you heard the bombing? Look at the colour of the sky. Half bloody London is on fire. Even the bleedin' House of Commons has copped it this time. And the Elephant is burning like buggery.'

It took Katy a long time to realise she was still alive. And even longer to work out that the reason she couldn't speak was because her mouth and throat were full of dust. She knew inhaling would be a disaster. Instead she turned her head to one side and forced herself to cough out the last remaining air in her lungs to try and clear it. The last thing she wanted was that mouthful of dust in her lungs, she'd heard of too many people coming into the Wilhelmina asphyxiated by plaster dust.

'Katy?' It was Jen's voice, low and shaky in the ominously creaking darkness. 'Are you still alive?'

Katy tried to make saliva in her dry mouth so she could spit again before talking. 'I'm alive,' she whispered eventually. 'But I don't seem to be able to move. What about you?'

'I can move my legs,' Jen said. 'But there's something heavy on my shoulder. I'm scared to try and shift it in case something else comes down. If only it wasn't so bloody dark.'

'There was a torch,' Katy said, reaching out her arm to feel around. It took her some time of sifting through the rubble and plaster dust to find it. But then as she played it round the confined space she almost wished they were still in darkness.

Her position wasn't so bad. Flat on her back at the very edge of the cellar, she was half buried in bricks and rubble but the table they'd been sitting at, despite collapsing, had protected her legs from the worst of the falling masonry and the lower part of the cellar steps behind her had held firm. But Jen, lying half on her side a few feet away, was trapped under some large pieces of furniture, on which, apparently, was balanced the rest of the house.

In silent horror Katy tried to make sense of it.

Mostly it was rubble, splintered planks, floorboards presumably, pipes and chunks of masonry. But there was furniture too. She recognised an upside-down armchair, white with dust, balanced across some mangled piping, and a section of wall, still adorned with the Miss Taylors' paisley wallpaper, and even part of a bed. For a second Katy closed her eyes. It was like a scene from hell. And one false move would bring the whole lot pouring down on Jen's head.

'Jen,' she said softy. 'Don't try and move.'

'Why?' Jen said. 'What does it look like?'

'It looks awful,' Katy said. Even as she spoke they heard the distant rumble of the Clapham Common guns firing and a few bricks broke away and tumbled to the ground inches from Jen's nose, showering her with a new coating of dust as they landed. The smell of plaster and stale wallpaper filled the confined space as the torchlight almost disappeared in the swirl of particles.

Jen swore softly and spat the dust out of her mouth. 'What is it holding me down?' she asked. 'It's on my arm. Can you see?'

Carefully picking the bricks off her legs one by one, eventually Katy was able to move. Very cautiously she crawled over to Jen.

'I think it must be a cupboard or something,' she said. 'Let me just see if I can go round the other side.' Inch by inch she eased her way round, terrified lest she touch or knock some crucial supporting part of the teetering mass of death suspended over them. 'Oh my goodness,' she said with a choked giggle. 'It's the piano.'

The next moment her fingers touched one of the keys and a low note sounded loud in the confined space.

'Oh God, that's bloody great,' Jen said. 'Let's have a singsong, why don't we?'

And then the screaming started. High pitched and continuous, in the confined space it was ear-piercingly loud. It echoed round and round the cellar walls.

'What the hell is that?' Jen muttered.

'It's from next door,' Katy said as a series of shivers ran up her spine. It was a horrible noise. Like an animal caught in a snare. A scream of death.

Horror-struck they waited tensely for it to stop. But it didn't stop. It went on and on. And on.

They tried calling, meaningless words of assurance. But it had no effect. In desperation Katy played her torch towards the sound. With all the mess and debris it was difficult to see but it seemed as though the dividing wall between Sheila Whitehead's cellar and theirs had collapsed in places. That was why the noise was so eerily loud.

'There might be a way through,' she whispered to Jen. 'Do you think I should try and see?'

'How safe is it?'

Katy shone her torch again. The rubble seemed denser on that side. Above the most promising route a great bulging piece of carpet was clearly holding back a multitude of sins. God knew what lay beyond that, but so long as it held she might be able to slither underneath.

'I don't know,' she said nervously. 'But nothing seems to be moving.'

'Then go,' Jen said.

Katy played her torch over the piano again and wondered if there was any way she could possibly get Jen out from under it. 'I can't leave you here,' she said. 'Not in the dark.'

Jen laughed sourly. 'You haven't got much choice. Anyway I'd rather die here than listen to that bloody noise much longer. It's getting on my nerves.'

For a second they were silent and then just as Katy was about to crawl away they heard another noise right above them, a distant scraping, voices, and they both coughed as a trickle of dust dropped on to them. And then they heard something creak and a muffled cry of alarm.

'Oh my God,' Jen muttered. 'They're going to bring the whole lot down on top of us.'

Katy shivered. 'Don't think about it,' she said. 'Just shout. Your voice is louder than mine. But don't pitch it too high. We don't want any vibrations. There's enough already with those bloody guns firing.' She didn't say what they both knew, that one more bomb falling anywhere near would be the end of them.

But even though they could hear the occasional noise from outside it quickly became clear that whoever was on the outside couldn't hear them. And all the time the spine-chilling wail from next door went on.

'I'm going,' Katy said suddenly. 'Keep shouting, and if you make contact tell them to stop digging till I'm back.'

What followed was the most frightening half hour of Katy's life. Afterwards she couldn't remember the details but at the time everything she touched as she eased her way, half crawling, half squirming, across the devastated cellar seemed as though it would be permanently engraved on her brain. The roughness of the bricks, the sharp stab of glass, the cold pipes, the splintering wood, dripping water, and everywhere the grey swirling dust. Twice she met a dead end and had to back up blindly, heart hammering in her chest, unable to turn round.

Behind her she could hear Jen trying different voice pitches in order to attract the attention of their rescuers, in front of her the shrill monotone screaming was gradually getting louder.

And then she began to meet furniture she didn't recognise. 'I think I've arrived next door,' she called back softly to Jen. And then as she groped tentatively forward, she felt something different,

394

something soft and wet, and retrieving her torch from between her teeth she pointed it upwards. And screamed.

'Katy?' She heard Jen's voice, muffled now, but urgent all the same. 'What's happened?'

It was a moment before Katy could speak. 'I've found Sheila,' she said.

On the surface Alan had mustered his helpers into a line. Piece by careful piece they were pulling the debris away and passing it from hand to hand back into the street. It was a slow process but it was the only way. From time to time they stopped to listen. But all they could hear was the awful heart-rending wail going on and on. It was Mick Carter, halfway down the chain, who eventually heard Jen's yell.

'That's Jen,' he said. 'That's her all right.' He cupped his mouth to the wreckage. 'Oi, Jen,' he bellowed back. 'Are you all right?'

'Oh God,' Jen groaned in the darkness. 'That sounds like Mick. Well, there goes our chances of getting out alive.'

'Of course I'm not all right,' she shouted back. 'I've got half a bloody house on top of me.'

'It's the whole house,' Mick's muffled voice came back. 'And quite a bit of next door too.'

Then to her relief she heard Alan Nelson's voice. 'Jen? Can you hear me? Have you got Katy there?'

'She's next door,' Jen called. 'She's looking for George. We can hear him screaming. You'd better stop bashing about up there until she gets back. It's pretty precarious down here.'

There was a slight pause, dimly Jen heard his voice shouting some instruction. Then it was directed at her again. 'What about Sheila? Any sign of her?'

Jen hesitated for a second. 'She's dead,' she called up. 'Katy's already found her.' She swallowed hard as she thought of poor Katy fumbling about next door. If tonight proved nothing else, it proved Katy had guts. It was pretty bad lying trapped under a sodding great piano in pitch darkness, knowing that if something slipped she would be crushed to death, but she would rather be there than groping around next door. She could tell from Katy's voice that Sheila Whitehead had not been a pretty sight. And God only knew what kind of a mangled state poor screaming George would be in.

Katy was wondering the same thing. When she had found Sheila's twisted body crushed and bloody under a metal girder she had thought she was going to faint. Or be sick. Or both. And then something had shifted overhead and she quickly jerked herself back into action. The noise of the screaming was so close now it was impossible to tell where it was coming from as it echoed around the mangled furniture.

'George?' she called. 'George. Where are you?'

And then she saw his hand, poking out from under an upturned armchair.

For a horrible second she thought it was just his hand, detached from the rest of his body, but then she realised that the rest of him was submerged in dust under the chair.

It was the chair which had saved him. By some freak it had fallen over him making a little cave, preventing any of the rest of the falling furniture and masonry above it from hitting him or squashing him.

But getting him out was a different matter. She could only reach him by lying flat on her stomach and wriggling under the overhanging crushed remains of what looked like a wardrobe.

'George.' She touched the hand and found it stone cold and rigid. It felt dead but it couldn't be dead because he was still screaming and the noise was deafening now.

'George,' she called more firmly. 'Stop it.'

But it was only when she shone the torch under the chair, straight into his face, that he stopped. Abruptly. Leaving the echo of sound ringing in her ears. And without the noise of his screaming, she suddenly became more aware of the creaking and groaning of the rubble above her. Quickly she played her torch up and saw a beam just waiting to plummet down on the crumpled chair.

'George, listen to me. It's Katy from the pub. Can you hear me?'

There was a long pause then a small voice said, 'Yes.'

Katy closed her eyes for a second and rested her head on her hands in relief. 'Are you hurt?'

'No.'

'Good.' She tried to keep her voice steady. Steady and crisp. She didn't want him to hear her fear, her certainty that any moment the beam was going to crash down on top of them. 'Now I want you to be very brave. And I want you to be very careful. It's like an obstacle course and I want you to do just what I tell you. OK?'

'Yes.'

Taking a deep breath, Katy turned her head and called softly back over her shoulder to Jen. 'I've found him. I'm bringing him back.' She heard Jen relay the news to Alan Nelson. Then Katy began to explain to George what she wanted him to do.

Up at street level they all stood waiting; Alan, Pam, the ARP warden, Mr Lorenz, Mick and Pete Carter and two other men who had appeared from somewhere. Waiting to hear if Katy and George had managed the return journey through the cellar wall. It seemed a long wait. From time to time Jen called that they were making progress.

And then just as they were sure the next time Jen shouted would be to say that they were reunited, the guns began to fire again and a group of German bombers thundered low overhead. And as soon as they had passed, they heard a wrenching crack as the remaining walls of Sheila's house fell in and the whole great pile of debris sank another few yards.

Jen heard the vibration of the bombers and she heard the shuddering grumble as the load above her began to move and she screamed to Katy to hurry. She knew she had no chance herself, but if only Katy could get George back into the corner under the stairs, the two of them at least might be safe.

Outside they heard Jen's scream and they heard the silence that followed it as the rubble settled again. Later, when Pam Nelson looked at the palms of her hands, she found blood where her nails had pierced the skin and she knew that was that moment that had caused it.

Mick's nerve broke before anyone else's and he started shouting Jen's name. His voice got higher and higher until it too cracked and died.

Alan Nelson put his hand on his shoulder. Cupping his hands to his mouth, he knelt down and called steadily. 'Katy? Jen? George? Can any of you hear me?'

And then he listened. And to everyone's astonishment a small voice came back. 'Uncle Alan? Is that you?'

'Oh God,' Pam whispered and found to her surprise she was holding Mick's hand.

'George?' Alan's voice was choked. 'Are you all right?'

'I'm all right,' the voice came back. 'But the two ladies are crying.'

They were crying with relief.

Somehow as the rubble slipped, it had changed balance and momentarily lifted the pressure on the piano. Feeling it tilt fractionally, with a mammoth effort, Jen was able to wriggle free. At the same moment Katy had shoved George violently into the corner under the stairs and thrown herself across him in a tangle of limbs. As the dust once again settled around them, Katy flashed the torch, and catching Jen's wry, incredulous expression, she burst into tears.

It was a long night. They tried desperately to keep George amused. Jen told him jokes. They even sang. Anything to keep his mind off his mother. Eventually to their relief he slept, curled in a ball on some dusty cushions Katy had dragged out of the rubble. It was only then that Jen asked Katy to have a look at her arm.

'It hurts,' she said.

Jen held the torch with her spare hand while Katy carefully rolled back her sleeve. Probing gently she could feel the bones were in the wrong place. 'It's broken,' she whispered as Jen took a sharp breath. 'I think I'd better try and splint it for you.' She looked around for something to use and giggled. 'At least we're not short of suitable pieces of wood.'

For a binding she used her stockings, which were hanging in threads anyway after her long crawl. And then she wrapped her cardigan round it and tied the sleeves over the top to protect it.

'Thank you, Nurse,' Jen said, relaxing slightly. 'If I ever get out of here I'll go and personally thank Sister Morris for training you so well.'

Katy turned off the torch to save the battery and smiled into the darkness. 'If I ever get out of here,' she said, 'I'm going to go to see Mr Rutherford and ask if he'll let me get the pub going again.'

'Katy!' Jen's start of astonishment nearly woke up George. 'Are you serious?'

'Deadly,' Katy said. 'Well, why not? I reckon I know more about running a pub than Mrs Rutherford knows about running a café. Mind you,' she added softly, 'We've got to get out of here first.'

'We'll get out,' Jen said confidently. 'Old Alan Nelson will get us out. He's good at this sort of thing. Think of Dunkirk. He's tougher than he looks.' She was silent for a moment then she smiled in the darkness. 'You know, you've changed,' she said. 'You wouldn't have been talking about taking on the pub a year ago.'

'I haven't changed,' Katy said. 'I've always wanted to be in charge of something. Why not a pub?'

Jen shook her head slowly. 'It's that Ward Frazer,' she said. 'He changed you. He made you see that things are possible.'

Alan Nelson did get them out even though he nearly lost his own life to do it. Twice Pam's heart almost stopped as falling masonry missed him by inches as he struggled to clear a passage to the Miss

Taylors' cellar. Once, as he clambered delicately over the unstable wreckage searching for a way in, he slipped and slithered several yards before Mick Carter caught his arm and stopped him from crashing to the ground.

Pam had to give them their due, the Carter boys worked hard. And old Lorenz too. Even when the WVS van drew up, they only stopped long enough to down a cup of tea and a few bites of a sandwich.

Joyce Carter was on the van. It was the first she had heard of Jen being trapped and she took it in her stride. 'Good God, I wouldn't hurry to get her out,' she said.

'But there's a danger the next house will fall on top,' Pam explained. 'And we've no means of knowing how protected they are down there.'

Joyce snorted. 'If Jen's down there, they'll be all right,' she said. 'That girl could fall in a sewer and come up smelling of roses.' She saw Pam's shocked expression and shook her head wearily. 'If you'd seen what we've seen tonight, Mrs Nelson, you'd be flippant.' Then she handed Pam down half a dozen sandwiches. 'Here, keep these for when they come out,' she said gruffly. 'If I know Jen she'll be starving. Oh,' she added slightly self-consciously, 'and give this extra cuppa to old Lorenz. He looks like he could use it.'

The all-clear sounded at just before six and, as people began to emerge from their shelters, several more men joined in the rescue attempt. By the time it got light, there were twelve of them struggling to free the captives in the cellar. It was like a massive game of spillikins and they were playing against the clock. And for those like Alan at the front, moving the wrong piece could be fatal.

Bertie Rutherford came off duty that Sunday morning at eight o'clock. It had been the worst night the Wilhelmina had seen, with ambulance after ambulance bringing in casualties. At eight fifteen he turned into Lavender Road looking forward to a few hours in bed.

Pam saw him first. Saw him stop for a second and then start running up the street towards them.

'What's happened?' he shouted to her as he approached. His eyes were rimmed red with tiredness. Suddenly, as he saw Pam's expression, they widened in fear. He looked at the wreck of the two houses, the men still struggling with the debris. 'It's Sheila, isn't it? She's still in there, isn't she?'

Pam bit her lip. 'She's still in there, Bertie,' she said gently. 'But she . . .'

But he was gone. Running forward to the chain of men, trying to get to the front, trying to claw something away.

''Ere.' Mick Carter yanked him back. 'You're that sodding conchie, ain't yer? We don't need your sort of help.' He spat then wiped his mouth with his sleeve. 'She's dead anyway, that Mrs Whitehead. It's the others we're after.'

'Tell him to push off,' another man shouted angrily. 'Ask him if he wants to make his bloody peace with Hitler now.'

Someone else threw a brick at him.

Pam saw Bertie reel away. For a moment he stood stunned, his face white. Then he seemed to crumple. His shoulders sagged and Pam saw tears running down his face.

'Oh God,' Pam whispered. The last thing she wanted to do was comfort Bertie Rutherford. But clearly nobody else was going to do it, so she walked forward slowly and touched his shoulder. 'Bertie? Come away. Come inside. There's nothing you can do here.'

The next moment he was in her arms. 'She's dead,' he kept repeating. 'She's dead.'

'I know,' Pam said gently. 'Katy found her body down there somewhere. They'll dig her out later.' She squeezed his shoulders. 'The others are alive, though. Katy and Jen. And little George. He's all right. They're working to get them out now.'

'They wouldn't let me help,' he said dully.

Pam grimaced. 'They're angry,' she said. 'And tired. They've been working all night. Even with the planes overhead.'

'I loved her,' Bertie said.

Pam closed her eyes. She was tired too. It was too late for poor Sheila, but she was worried about the others. And she was worried about Alan. It was taking longer than he thought. The house next door was leaning badly now. It could fall in at any moment, and if it fell it would certainly crush the rescue workers. She was worried he would do something rash. She didn't want to worry about Bertie bloody Rutherford too. It was his fault Sheila was down there in the first place.

She pushed him off her irritably. 'Then do something useful,' she said. 'Go and make some tea.'

It was nine thirty before Alan was able to make an opening wide enough for a rope of knotted sheets to be lowered into the cellar.

The rescue workers were amazed to hear laughter coming up. 'Hurry up, you buggers,' Jen said. 'We're starving down here.'

To her surprise Alan brought a sandwich down with him. 'From your mum,' he said as he tied the rope carefully round George's waist.

Jen grinned as she bit into it. 'Nicest thing she's ever done for me,' she said.

But Katy took one look at the sandwich and clutched her hand to her mouth.

'It's nerves,' Alan said, patting her shoulder as she retched.

'Nerves?' Jen stopped in mid chew and looked at him incredulously. 'You must be joking,' she said. 'That girl's got nerves of steel.'

Nerves of steel or not, it was two days before Katy felt brave enough to go and see Mr Rutherford. To her embarrassment, Jen had kept her side of the bargain by thanking Sister Morris in a loud voice during visiting time on the Ethel Barnet ward for training Katy so well.

'Not only did she save the life of a small child,' she said, waving her plastered arm around dramatically, 'But she saved my arm. The doctor who set it told me she had done a perfect splint. So, thank you, Sister Morris, and now I would like everyone to join me in a round of applause.'

Everyone did, and Katy was amused to see that Sister Morris looked quite flustered. 'That's quite enough of your theatricals, thank you,' she said, frowning beadily at Jen. 'I think it's high time you went back on the stage, broken arm or not.'

Jen smiled sweetly. 'I rejoin my ENSA group next week,' she said. 'But before I go, I would be most honoured if you would sign my plaster.'

'She's got a cheek, that Jen,' Nurse Coogan muttered grudgingly to Katy. 'I'll give her that.'

Katy glanced at her. 'Molly?' she whispered. 'Do you think I could run a pub?'

Molly Coogan's eyes widened. For a second she hesitated. Then she nodded. 'Course you could,' she said staunchly. 'If you put your mind to it.'

But her mother wasn't at all convinced. In fact when Katy put it to her tentatively, she made it quite clear that she thought Katy had taken complete leave of her senses.

'What, on our own? You and me? And me with a broken leg?'

'You won't have a broken leg for ever, Mummy,' Katy said patiently. 'It's healing well now. Sister says you'll be starting physiotherapy next week.' She leaned forward urgently. 'It's our only chance, Mummy. Now the Miss Taylors' house has gone, we need somewhere to live. After all, the licence is still in your name. And we desperately need some form of income to pay off our debts.'

'The pub isn't as badly wrecked as we thought,' she went on quickly as her mother paled. 'It would only take a month or so to put right. I can live in the cellar in the meantime. Jen and I slept down there last night.' She shrugged as her mother shrank in the bed. 'It's not too bad. The beds are still there. There's no electrics or water of course, but it's nearly summer and there's a standpipe in the yard outside.' She touched her mother's cold hand and smiled encouragingly. 'So what do you think?'

Mary Parsons was trembling with anxiety. 'I don't know,' she mumbled. 'I don't know what to say. It's all such a worry. I really don't know what's for the best.' She looked at her daughter pitifully. 'You'll have to decide.'

'I have decided,' Katy said. 'I'm going to see Mr Rutherford tomorrow.'

But Mr Rutherford said no.

Katy stared at him as he stood up and went to the door of his cold unwelcoming office. She had said her bit. Explained that between her and her mother they had a good knowledge of running the pub. That the government might give them a loan to start them off. That she already had ideas for staff. Two barmen was all they would need. To help with the heavy jobs.

It had come out quite well but when she looked up at him expectantly, he had shaken his head and said. 'No. I'm sorry. It's quite out of the question.'

She smoothed her skirt over her knees. She had dressed carefully for the occasion, in clothes borrowed from Pam Nelson. None of her own clothes had been salvaged from the Miss Taylors' house. In fact nothing at all had yet been salvaged from the Miss Taylors' house. Shortly after they had got out, the empty house next door had collapsed on top. It had taken the heavy rescue boys two days to find Sheila Whitehead's body.

But now, despite her grey, businesslike coat and skirt, Katy didn't know what to do. What to say.

She and Jen had rehearsed her speech endlessly. They had even thought of the arguments Greville Rutherford might put up, and had worked out what Katy should say in response. But it had never occurred to them that he would just say no, out of hand, and show her to the door.

He cleared his throat impatiently. 'Mrs Frazer, if you wouldn't mind, I am rather busy.'

Katy turned her head. The door was open now and he was quite clearly waiting for her to leave. She felt a painful stab of disappointment. She also felt rather sick.

'Could you just tell me why?' she said miserably. 'Why you won't even let us try?'

He sighed and glanced pointedly at his fob watch. 'I haven't time to list the reasons,' he said. 'Suffice it to say that I do not consider women to be suitable tenants for a public house.' He gave her a thin dismissive smile.

'Now if you would excuse me I have some rather important matters to see to.'

'Where was you today?' Mick asked his father at tea. 'They was asking me all day at the brewery.'

Joyce looked up sharply, but Stanley just frowned. 'What did you tell 'em?'

'I said I didn't know where you was,' Mick said, reaching unconcernedly for a slice of bread. 'Same as I didn't know where you was the other night when we dug Jen out.'

Stanley's frown deepened. He wiped his mouth and pushed back his chair. 'You tell them I'm off colour if they ask again,' he said. 'Stomach trouble.'

Joyce looked at him. He didn't look off colour. And he'd just eaten a good meal of tinned meat and potatoes with plenty of bread and marge. Three slices he'd had and complained there was no jam. On the contrary he looked quite healthy. Since she'd held the gun on him, he'd been off the booze a bit, that helped. But it wasn't the lack of booze that was putting the gleam in his eye, the secret little smile on his lips.

She had seen that look before and it meant he was on to something, some scam, some money-making scheme that sooner or later brought the police round for a search of the house.

'You'll lose that job if you're not careful,' she said suddenly. 'That Rutherford's a ruthless bastard. Look how he treated Katy Parsons yesterday.'

'Katy Frazer,' Mick said through a mouthful. 'She's married, don't forget. Even if her bloke is missing.'

Joyce ignored him. She wanted to get to the bottom of this Stanley business. 'Where were you that night, Stanley? And why weren't you at work today?'

But Stanley didn't like being interrogated. 'You mind your own business,' he said sharply. 'I don't need you to tell me what to do.' Then, when he saw her warning glance, he laughed sourly and shrugged. 'It's not much of a job anyway, that brewery job.' He touched the side of his nose and winked at Mick. 'I've got bigger and better things in mind.'

Word got round quickly about Mr Rutherford's refusal to let Katy and her mother have a crack at running the pub.

Jen told as many people as she could find before leaving, regretfully, to go back to ENSA.

Louise heard from Aaref when he walked her down to her work one morning and the more she mulled it over the more angry it made her. She knew if Katy had been a man her father wouldn't have hesitated. Why shouldn't women be given the same chance as men?

As she tidied her position at the end of the day ready for the night shift, she glanced at Ken Ratface who was reading the paper. 'How many bolts have you managed today?' she asked.

He looked up at his board. 'Ninety.'

'Oh?' Louise sniffed. 'Is that all? I did a hundred and twenty-five.'

Ken scratched his head. 'Why is it that you women are always trying to prove yourselves?' he asked, folding his paper. 'You've got the vote. Surely that's enough?' He winked. 'Mind you, I reckon as they only gave you that to keep them bleedin' suffragettes quiet. Chaining themselves to the railings and that.' He chuckled. 'Wouldn't do much good now,' he added humorously, 'Because they're taking all them fancy railings down now for the war effort.'

Louise was not amused. I'd like to chain you to the railings and then drop them in the Thames, she thought sourly.

That evening over supper Louise waited till her father had ranted and raved about the news that Hitler's right hand man, Rudolph Hess, had parachuted into Scotland, and how on no account should the British government make terms with him. Then when he had got that out of his system, she took a fortifying breath, crossed her fingers and spoke.

'I don't see why Katy shouldn't have a go at running that pub,' she said. 'After all, what difference does it make to you?'

For a moment her father was thrown off balance by the surprise attack. Then he put down his knife and fork with ominous precision. His voice was quiet. 'Are you questioning my judgement, Louise?'

Louise swallowed nervously. 'No,' she said hastily. 'Of course not, Daddy. But . . .' She quailed for a moment, then bravely ploughed on. She waved a vague hand towards her mother who was frowning at her from the end of the table. 'But if Mummy and that awful Mrs Carter think they can run a café somewhere, I don't really see why Katy and her mother couldn't manage a pub.'

It was a mistake. Her father's mouth narrowed into a thin line. 'You don't see because you don't know anything about it,' he barked. 'Nor does your mother.' For a moment he turned his cold eyes on Celia, who was looking appalled at the turn the conversation had taken. He frowned at her and lowered his voice slightly. 'I thought I'd made it clear what I thought about this ridiculous café idea. It's quite absurd to think a woman could manage a business like that. Haggling with suppliers? Dealing with the till? Keeping accounts?' He laughed scornfully as he folded his napkin. 'You wouldn't know where to begin, my dear. You would soon be a laughing stock. And as for serving every Tom, Dick and Harry who walks in off the street? Good Lord, no. It's quite out of the question.'

Louise stared at her mother. Surely she was going to pursue it. To stand up for herself. Or if not for herself, for women. For Katy. But other than a tight little frown and a baleful glare at Louise, her mother made no response.

Apparently satisfied that his wife's silence denoted compliance, Greville Rutherford reached over and patted her hand. 'Do try and think things through more, Celia,' he said kindly. 'Think of what people would say. Think of your position. It's bad enough having Louise making a fool of herself every day at this dreadful factory she insists on going to.'

'I am not making a fool of myself,' Louise hissed. 'The charge-hand told me yesterday I was one of the quickest drillers they'd got.'

'Well, well, is that so?' To her astonishment he leaned back in his chair and laughed heartily. 'I think that proves my point,' he said. 'Get a pretty girl in a business and the standards go to pot.' He leaned forward and tapped the table with his forefinger. 'It's hard work that counts in business, Louise. Day in day out. Not winning smiles and gossip. That's what women don't understand. That's what that young Katy Frazer doesn't understand. She probably thinks it's all about tittle-tattling with the customers over the bar. She wouldn't last five minutes. She doesn't know what hard work is.'

Louise gaped at him as he picked up his paper and spread it over the table. She couldn't believe her ears. She thought of the long hard hours that the nurses worked at the Wilhelmina. She thought of the time before Christmas when Katy had worked full nights on the Ethel Barnet ward followed by full days in the pub. She thought of the long day she herself had just put in at Gregg Bros. And suddenly she felt her temper rise.

She also felt a surge of panic because she knew what she was going to do and it was a dangerous course of action. Crumpling her napkin, she pushed back her chair and stood up. She knew she couldn't listen to him a moment longer. She knew what he said was wrong. Narrow minded and unfair. She had to put the record straight. Katy had her faults, but nobody could accuse her of not being a hard worker. Nor was she a gossip.

'Daddy?' she began conversationally. 'What would you do if I got pregnant?'

He barely glanced up. 'If you were married I would be pleased.'

'And if I wasn't?'

He looked up then, 'I'd be very angry.'

Louise nodded. 'I know. And you wouldn't want anyone to know, would you? Oh goodness, no, not a pillar of the community like you.' She smiled grimly. 'Think of your position. Mr Rutherford's daughter with an illegitimate bun in the oven. You wouldn't like it, would you? You'd do anything to hush it up.'

She had his full attention now. 'What are you saying, Louise?' he asked dangerously.

Louise took a steadying breath. 'I'm saying that I was pregnant last year.' She didn't dare look at them, but she heard her mother's sharply indrawn breath and hurried on.

'It was a man I met at a party. He's in America now. I was on my way to have an abortion when I was caught in that bomb in Balham. By the time I arrived in the Wilhelmina I was miscarrying. I knew it would upset the apple cart if everyone knew, so I asked Katy to make sure it was hushed up at the hospital.' Louise bit her lip. 'And she did. She hasn't told a soul. Nobody knows.'

Suddenly there were tears in her eyes. She hadn't expected to cry again. She had thought she was over it. She brushed them away angrily as her mother spoke. She could hear the shock in her voice.

'Why didn't you tell us?'

Louise glanced at her. Her face was white. 'I didn't tell you because I was too frightened to tell you.' She turned to her father. 'Do you hear me? Too frightened to tell my own parents.' She squared her shoulders and swallowed the tears. 'Well, I'm not too frightened now. You can throw me out if you want. Like you threw Bertie out.

Sometimes I think he was lucky. Sometimes I'm embarrassed to be your child.'

She turned for the door and then stopped again remembering there was one more thing she had to say. Her final atonement.

'I don't care about my reputation any more,' she said. 'But I know you do.' She lifted her head and met his eyes. 'Katy put her job at the hospital on the line for me. For all of us. The very least you can do is give her a chance. Don't you think she deserves it?'

Aaref Hoch produced a primus stove for Katy and a box of matches. When she asked where he'd got them he dropped his eyes. 'I think it is safer if you do not know.'

'Oh.' Katy stared at him aghast. Then she looked back at the stove and thought how much she longed for some hot food again. She took a quick breath and smiled brightly. 'Then you'd better show me how it works.'

The following day, having climbed precariously up the burnt staircase and unearthed some charred but serviceable crockery from the back of one of the cupboards, she invited Molly Coogan round for a cup of tea during her off duty.

'I want to consult your medical knowledge,' Katy said as they sat down on the upturned crates she used for chairs.

Molly frowned. 'What sort of medical knowledge?'

Katy sipped her tea. 'Gynaecological,' she said.

She saw Molly's surprise and hesitated for a moment. 'I—I haven't had a curse since Ward left. 'What does that mean?'

Molly Coogan stared at her. 'As far as I know it means one of two things,' she said hesitantly. 'Either your cycle has somehow been disrupted by the stress, or you're pregnant.'

Katy nodded. 'That's what I thought.' She smoothed her skirt over her knees quite calmly, but when she looked up at her friend her eyes were anxious. 'I'm pregnant, Molly, I know I am. I've been feeling sick and everything.'

'Don't look like that,' Molly said quickly. 'It's not the end of the world.' She tried to smile. 'Look on the bright side. At least you haven't got to worry about getting the pub going again.'

Katy's eyes widened with horror. 'Goodness, can you imagine?' She shook her head and was about to go on when someone banged on the door upstairs.

She groaned. 'If it's Barry Fish, I'm going to scream.' To her dismay, Barry Fish had come smarming round again only that morning, offering to find her somewhere better to live.

'You can't live in a cellar,' he had said, peering through the crack in the door. 'Not a pretty little thing like you.' He had winked. 'Why don't I find a nice little place for you and your mum? Just to show there's no hard feelings?'

Feeling the revulsion shuddering down her spine, Katy had refused as politely as she could but now she dreaded finding him on the doorstep once again.

But it wasn't Barry Fish, it was the Rutherford & Berry rent collector. 'Mr Rutherford has reconsidered his position,' he said, his voice stiff with disapproval. 'He's prepared to give you until the end of the year to see if you can make a go of it.'

Chapter Twenty-Three

Pam hadn't wanted George to go to Sheila's funeral. She thought he was too young. And she knew the sight of his mother's coffin would upset him even more than he was already. But Sheila's relatives, Mr and Mrs Teacross, insisted he should attend, and the sight of him sitting stiffly between them in the front row in his overlarge Red Cross clothes with his cap clutched in his hands was almost more than she could bear.

He didn't cry. Mr Teacross had told him he would be smacked if he cried.

Pam had hardly been able to believe her ears. 'For goodness' sake,' she objected. 'He's only six. You can't expect a six-year-old not to cry at his mother's funeral.'

Mr Teacross looked at her sternly. 'He's a boy,' he said. 'In my book, boys don't cry. Whatever the circumstances.'

Suddenly Pam had understood why Sheila had preferred to stay in London despite the bombing. 'I've never met a more hateful man in my entire life,' she said to Alan. 'And she's not much better. She told me earlier that I shouldn't let George sit on my knee. That he was quite old enough to sit on his own chair.'

Alan smiled grimly. 'She told me that children should be seen and not heard.' He shook his head. 'Still, thankfully they'll be gone soon. They're taking the four thirty train from Clapham Junction. Let's hope it's running.'

But at quarter to four the bombshell fell. They were intending to take George with them.

Pam was horrified. 'But you can't . . .' she started angrily and stopped again as Alan put his hand on her arm.

'We are more than happy to keep him,' he said to Mrs Teacross. 'We know him so well. We thought it would be less upsetting for him to stay here at least for a while. My wife was going to give up work to look after him . . .'

'That won't be necessary,' Mr Teacross said crisply. 'We appreciate your offer. But in the circumstances we feel we have no choice but to take him with us.'

'In what circumstances?' Pam asked hotly. She couldn't bear the thought of George going with these beastly people. 'What do you mean? Why can't he stay with us? You don't want him.'

Mr Teacross fingered his bristly moustache. 'You don't have children, Mrs Nelson. You seem rather too lenient with him. Too soft. He is our nephew after all. We do want to make sure he's properly brought up.'

'And there is the matter of your lodger,' his wife murmured.

'Our lodger?' Alan said surprised. 'Bertie? He's very fond of George.'

The Teacrosses exchanged a meaningful look but it was Mr Teacross who spoke. 'We understand he has unfortunate views. We are concerned about the influence he might have on George.'

Pam closed her eyes. She could tell from the look that it was hopeless. Their minds were made up. Nothing she or Alan could say would convince them.

Swallowing hard she went out into the passage to find George. She would have to try and make it easy for him. Make the parting quick and painless. As though it didn't matter.

'George,' she called. 'Will you fetch your coat? You're going to go home with your uncle and aunt.'

He was in the kitchen. For a second he just looked at her then

413

he ran. Like a whippet out of a trap. Straight past her up the passage and out into the street.

It took a moment for anyone to realise what had happened. Then as Alan ran after him, Pam swung round to the Teacrosses.

'You see,' she said bitterly. 'He doesn't want to go.'

Mr Teacross seemed unperturbed. 'He'll get used to the idea soon enough. And it'll do him good. He's been thoroughly spoiled all his life. What he needs is a good clip round the ear.'

And when Alan brought him back eventually he got it.

'That'll teach you,' Mr Teacross grunted, jerking the child out of Alan's arms. It didn't make any difference to George, he was screaming anyway, refusing to put on his coat.

'I won't go. Auntie Pam, don't let them take me away.'

But they did take him away. They dragged him screaming and kicking up the street.

Left behind, Pam and Alan could still hear his pitiful cries for help when they turned the corner on to Lavender Hill.

Pam couldn't have felt worse if she had sent a pet lamb to slaughter. The tears were streaming down her own cheeks as she turned back into the house with Alan.

Bertie Rutherford was standing there. His eyes were red. He'd been crying too. He'd cried a lot since Sheila died.

'I'm sorry,' he said awkwardly. 'It's because of me, isn't it? I heard what they said. I'll move out if it would help.'

Even in his funereal black suit Bertie Rutherford contrived to look arrogant. Through swimming eyes Pam took in the unbuttoned jacket, the thin tie, the affectedly long hair flopping over his forehead and suddenly she wanted to hit him. 'If it wasn't for you playing around with her she'd have gone back to the country before and would still be alive.'

Alan took her shoulder. 'Pam, don't, he knows that. He's upset enough already.'

But Pam was beyond caring. 'It serves him right,' she shouted, brushing past him and running upstairs. 'That's what comes of being a coward. If he'd joined up and done his duty to his country none of this would have happened.'

Joyce was surprised to come home one lunchtime to find Bob sitting at the kitchen table in his army uniform, reading the paper.

'What are you doing here?' She stared at him. 'I thought you was sailing for Crete today.'

'I was.' He grinned. 'But I've done my back in. They've sent me home. I've got to rest for a few weeks.'

'A few weeks?' Joyce's eyes narrowed suspiciously. 'What do you mean you've done your back in?'

'I fell over on the assault course a few days ago. It was bloody agony. They reckon I've slipped a disc.'

Joyce frowned. 'It looks all right to me,' she said dubiously. She studied him carefully. There was something in his manner that worried her. 'You haven't gone absent, have you, Bob?'

Bob looked hurt. 'I told you. It's my back. The doctor said I'd got to rest.' He shrugged as he folded the paper. 'I'm not complaining, mind. Looks like Jerry is going to win Crete and all. I'd rather wait here till he's done it.'

Joyce felt a sense of divided loyalty. On the one hand she was pleased that Bob was out of danger for the time being. On the other she didn't like the idea of him shirking his duty. Since that Ward Frazer had disappeared and poor old Malcolm Parsons had been killed in the bombing, she would happily have joined up herself if they'd have had her. That bloody Hitler needed stopping. Even if it did mean sacrifice. Still, if the doctor said Bob wasn't fit to go, there wasn't much she could do about it. And actually now he was standing up she could see he was in a bit of pain, which made her feel better.

'Got any change, Mum?' he asked. 'I could do with a pint. And I'm a bit short of readies at the moment.'

Joyce pursed her lips. She wasn't flush herself. She hadn't seen any of Stanley's brewery wages for the last two weeks and she was worried that if she started giving Bob money she'd be short of housekeeping.

But Bob was smiling at her and she found it hard to resist Bob's smile.

'Oh, come on, Mum.' he wheedled, putting his hand on his back and wincing. 'Surely you've got a couple of bob for a poor injured soldier?'

Joyce sighed. 'Oh, go on then,' she said and opened the drawer of the dresser.

But when she pulled out her housekeeping tin it seemed ominously light. Frowning, she opened it and looked inside. It was empty.

For a moment she couldn't believe it. She even shook it as though there might be some secret compartment. But there was no secret compartment. There was simply no money.

She put it down on the sideboard and looked at Bob. Absurdly she wanted to cry. She wanted to sit down at the table and howl her eyes out. Things had been so good. For the last few weeks she'd thought she'd got everything under control. All the family was in work. Stanley had been behaving himself. For once there'd been enough money.

And now it was all going wrong. She might have known it was too good to last. And the sudden feeling of despair made her want to weep.

But she didn't weep. She just shrugged. 'Someone's had the housekeeping,' she said. 'So if you're really short of cash, you'll have to go and ask Pete. He's over at the Flag and Garter, talking to young Katy about the repairs.'

Katy was amazed by how pleased everyone was that she was going to try and get the pub going again.

The only person who wasn't pleased was her mother, who spent most of every visiting time fretting about the problems and anxiously outlining the reasons it couldn't possibly work.

But apart from her everyone else was extraordinarily supportive. It seemed the whole street was behind her. She received quite a few offers of help, not least from Pete Carter who produced his boss to give her some idea about the cost of rebuilding.

Mr Poole was an elderly, wiry man with very yellow teeth and a pencil behind his ear. 'It'll be a couple of months, love,' he said. 'By the time you've got permissions. The government should pay up for most of the structural stuff. It's war damage fair and square. But I reckon you might have to look to the brewery for the decor and that.'

'What about alterations?' Katy asked tentatively. 'I was thinking it might be nice to build in a little kitchen area somewhere so we could make up sandwiches. And I'd like to make the saloon bar more comfortable, to attract more women in. And if we had a separate entrance for off sales, I think more people might come in there. It puts them off having to come through the public bar.'

Mr Poole had winked at Pete. 'You didn't tell me she was such a little businesswoman,' he said. Then he smiled at Katy. 'I reckon as we could slip in a few extras under the counter,' he said, tapping the side of his nose. 'So long as the brewery gives the all-clear.'

Katy nodded. It seemed to her that if quite a bit of the pub was going to have to be knocked down anyway, it might as well be rebuilt in the best way possible. Even if it did cost a bit more. And since Aaref had told her why Mr Rutherford had changed his mind she reckoned she still had a bit of leeway with the brewery. She wouldn't push her luck but she was going to get as much out of them as she could. She had no qualms about it. According to Alan Nelson who helped her fill out the war damage forms, her father had been paying into the brewery dilapidations fund for years. Well, now she was going to make sure that Rutherford & Berry played fair and paid back their share of the renovations.

The rest of the money she would borrow from Mr Lorenz who had offered to extend her a small loan in return for a stake in the business. Katy didn't know if that was legal or not, but it sounded a good idea and she agreed readily. In any case it was either that or pawning her engagement ring which was the only other alternative. And she didn't want to do that. That ring was one of the few things she still had that reminded her of Ward. Of those happy carefree days in Oxford.

'You still think about him, don't you?' Molly Coogan asked one evening as they sat in the pub cellar with a bowl of water from the standpipe in the yard, scrubbing the pots and pans Katy had retrieved from the burnt out kitchen upstairs.

Katy smiled ruefully. 'All the time. Especially when I'm sick in the mornings.' She shook her head and hesitated for a second. 'And other times too. Like when I have to make a decision about something.' She made a wry face. 'I try and think what Ward would have done and then I do the same.'

Molly Coogan laughed. 'Well, it seems to work,' she said. 'And at least when he comes back he'll feel involved.'

Katy smiled. 'Thanks for saying when,' she said. 'Most people say if.'

Molly's frown was distorted by the flickering candlelight. 'Then most people are stupid.' She was about to say more when they heard someone banging on the makeshift door upstairs.

'That'll be Aaref,' Katy said getting up and reaching for her purse. 'He promised to try and find me a lamp.' Paraffin lamps were like gold dust these days. But somehow Aaref seemed to be able to lay his hands on whatever she needed. At first she had felt uneasy about the provenance of the items he produced. But she had learned not to ask questions. When you needed things as much as she did it didn't pay to be squeamish.

Molly caught her skirt as she headed for the stairs. 'He's not going to come in, is he?' she whispered anxiously, her waving arm casting shadows over the wall as she indicated the old apron she had worn to help with the cleaning. 'I'm not in a fit state to meet a man.'

Katy laughed. 'It's only Aaref,' she said. 'He won't mind. Don't say anything about the baby though,' she added quickly. 'I don't want anyone to know. Not yet.' Definitely not her mother. The poor woman was worried enough as it was. The prospect of having to cope with a brand new baby as well as the pub would probably finish her off altogether.

Upstairs she smiled as Aaref held up his prize. 'Aaref. You're wonderful. No more queuing for blasted candles. Come downstairs and we'll light it and have a cup of tea to celebrate. My friend from the hospital is here, Molly Coogan.'

As she led him downstairs into the cellar, Molly scrambled hastily to her feet.

'Look what I've got,' Katy said to her, brandishing the lamp. But Molly wasn't looking at the lamp, she was too busy trying to shuffle inconspicuously backwards into the shadows.

Laughing, Katy pulled her arm. 'We've been cleaning,' she explained to Aaref. 'So you'll have to excuse our scruffiness.' But as Molly came reluctantly forward it was clear that it was more than her dirty old apron that was bothering her.

'My name is Aaref Hoch. I have heard of you from Katy. I am pleased to meet you.' As he introduced himself, Aaref offered his hand and clicked his heels formally. But poor Molly seemed tongue tied and Katy stared at her in amazement as the truth dawned on her.

In the flickering candlelight Molly's pointed face looked more pixie-like than usual and when Aaref crouched down to light the paraffin lamp Katy could see that she had gone bright red, even to the tips of her sticking-out ears. She fancies him, she thought, as the warm glow of the lantern gradually spread around the dingy cellar. Molly Coogan fancies Aaref Hoch.

As Aaref straightened up Katy looked at him curiously. In her mind she always saw him as he had been when he first arrived with his two younger brothers in England, gaunt and shabby and unable to speak English. More recently she had noticed that he had filled out, lost that gaunt look, and had taken on a new confidence of manner. But now, as she looked at him more closely as he spread his hands in satisfaction at the glow of the lamp and smiled at Molly, she realised she would have to revise her opinion once again. He really was rather nice-looking, in a foreign kind of way, with those long curly lashes, the high cheekbones, the thick brows and dark eyes. No wonder Molly was looking so stunned.

His broken English was attractive too. He was talking to Molly now, seemingly unaware of the startling effect he was having on her. 'She is hard tasking master, this Katy,' he was saying. 'All day at the hospital you work and then she gives you the pans to scrub in the evening time.' He smiled. 'I think she will be a good landlady.'

To Molly's evident relief he didn't stay long. Just long enough to have a cup of tea and to ask Katy if she would be interested in a set of horse-brasses someone had offered him. 'I thought for behind the bar,' he said as he stood up to go. 'It would make an attractive display, yes?'

Katy smiled. 'Yes. But it depends on the price, Aaref. I'm not made of money, you know, and finding glasses is going to be more important than horse-brasses.'

He laughed. 'Trust me,' he said. 'You will have glasses and brasses. And all at the very best price.'

After she had let him out she went back downstairs to the cellar to find Molly Coogan sitting on a crate with her hands clasped round her knees and an agonised expression on her face.

'Why didn't you tell me?' she said. 'Why didn't you tell me you were going to bring some blasted dreamboat down the stairs?'

Katy made an apologetic face. 'I didn't know,' she said. 'I don't really think of him like that.'

Molly sighed deeply. 'He thought I was hideous, didn't he?' she said despondently. 'I know I'm not pretty, but I usually look a bit better than this. And he must have thought I was a complete dimwit into the bargain.'

Katy shook her head. 'I think he liked you. He's not usually as chatty as that.'

Molly brightened at once. 'Do you?' She sat forward eagerly. 'Do you think I might have a chance with him?'

'Well,' Katy felt her heart sink, 'the thing is, Molly, I don't really like to say this but he's rather keen on Louise Rutherford.'

Now, as Molly Coogan exploded in fury at the thought of Aaref being keen on Louise, Katy sighed. Why was life so difficult? So cruel? Why couldn't people simply like the people who liked them? And when it did happen, like with her and Ward, like with her mother and father, like Jen and Sean Byrne, like Bertie Rutherford and Sheila Whitehead, why did one of them always have to be snatched away?

Nobody knew why there had been no more bombing since that dreadful raid on the eleventh of May. Some said it was due to the weather. Some said it was due to a new improved radar deterrent. Some even speculated that it was some kind of secret pact that Rudolph Hess had parachuted into Scotland to negotiate.

But then the Germans mounted an airborne invasion of Crete and a more likely explanation presented itself. The Luftwaffe didn't have enough planes to bomb Crete and London at the same time.

It was an oddly reassuring thought. But it didn't reassure Joyce Carter.

In many ways the bombing had been her salvation. A foolproof, cast-iron excuse to be out at night on the WVS van. Or at least in the Anderson shelter in the garden with Mick and Pete. Without it she felt vulnerable again. She could see the way Stanley was watching her. She could hear the confidence back in his voice, see the dangerous gleam in his eye and she knew her power over him was weakening. Sufficient time had passed that he no longer feared her threat of betrayal to the police over the Lorenz shooting.

Having Bob back at home didn't help. Bob had expected to sleep in Jen's room on his own and was put out to find himself back in with his brothers. Nothing was said but Joyce knew Stanley didn't like it either. Mick and Pete didn't matter. Conjugal rights meant nothing to them. But Bob was a different kettle of fish and, despite a mumbled excuse about snoring, she knew Stanley didn't like Bob knowing they slept in different rooms. It was like a loss of face.

And now Stanley had started taking the money. Two weeks in a row he'd had the boys' housekeeping money out of the tin. By dint of scrimping on her own food, Joyce had managed to buy enough out of her own meagre wages to keep them in basics. But now the small stock of provisions she'd built up over the last few months was running out and she needed cash for the meter, and the rent was due, and when she tried to borrow a bit off Pete he said his dad had had it off him already. That was when she knew she was going to have to talk to Stanley.

She chose her time carefully.

She waited until he had finished his tea, lit up his Woodbine and taken the paper into the front room. Then she told the boys to keep out of the way for a few minutes and went in after him and closed the door.

He'd got the wireless going and through the crackling, Joyce could hear a solemn-voiced announcer reporting that HMS *Hood* had been sunk in the Atlantic by the infamous German ship the *Bismarck* with a loss of fourteen hundred British lives.

For a second she allowed herself to feel sorry for the families of those poor drowned sailors, but then she put them firmly out of her mind and steeled herself to face up to the matter in hand.

'Stanley, I'm a bit short of housekeeping.'

He was sitting where he always sat, slumped in his vest and trousers in the old armchair by the empty grate with his stockinged feet up on the chair opposite. There was a hole in his sock through which a horny yellowing toenail protruded. She made a mental note to get that sock off him later and darn it or it would be ruined.

Slowly he lowered his paper and looked at her. 'Short of house-keeping, are you? Dear, dear. No wonder we've been eating tinned meat and potatoes all week.' He fingered his braces. 'It's not good enough, Joyce. Working men need better than that.'

Joyce frowned. The programme changed on the wireless and Arthur Askey started singing the popular 'Kiss me goodnight, Sergeant Major'.

'There was no money for anything else,' she said.

'Then why didn't you ask me for some?'

'I don't know. I thought it was meant to be in the tin . . .'

'Well, you thought wrong, didn't you?' Stanley said. 'I've decided to look after the money myself. I don't like it sitting idle in that tin. Money has to work, you know. And I've got a nice little scheme going that'll bring us in a tidy bit.'

'Yes, but . . .'

His eyes narrowed. 'You ask me nicely, I'll give you your house-keeping. But I expect you to use it properly, mind. A decent bit of cooking. Me and the boys are sick to the back teeth of bread and marge and tinned bloody stuff.'

'I haven't got time to cook. What with queuing and that.'

'Then you'll have to make time,' he said sharply. Then he leaned back in his chair and laughed softly. 'I reckon as you've got a bit lazy in your old age. You've forgotten your place, my love. You're the woman of the house and your job is to put some decent food on the table for your men.'

He lifted the paper and she frowned. 'Can I have it, then? The housekeeping?'

He looked up surprised. 'Oh, I don't think you quite understand.' He shook his head slowly and his mouth curved in a meaningful smile. 'You'll have to ask me a bit nicer than that.'

Suddenly she did understand. Only too well.

And her heart sank.

He didn't come to her that night. But he did the following night, late after she was asleep. Drunk and randy. And afterwards when she asked about the housekeeping he grunted in satisfaction and laid three ten bob notes out on the bed.

'There's going to be plenty more where that came from, my lovely.'

Joyce looked at the money nervously. 'Where did it come from?' she asked.

'Never you mind that.' He laughed complacently and patted her slightly harder than necessary on the cheek. 'You just keep your mouth shut and your legs open, my lovely, and we'll all be hunky dory.'

The day Katy went to make her peace with Louise was the day the *Bismarck* was sunk. The sinking of the *Hood* a few days before had sparked off the biggest ever naval chase as the Royal Navy vowed to 'pursue and destroy' her attacker. Even the great aircraft carrier *Ark Royal* steamed up from Gibraltar for the action and eventually under the relentless bombardment and a final torpedo strike from HMS *Victorious*, the Germans' newest and fastest battleship sank with all hands.

It was the first successful naval action in days and the newspaper vendors were screaming their heads off about it outside the factory gates as Katy waited for Louise to emerge.

Trying not to think about the kind of world they lived in where the drowning of a thousand men was good news, Katy kept her eyes firmly on the hordes of workers streaming out of Gregg Bros, scared she would miss Louise in the throng.

She needn't have bothered. Among the hurrying workers in their drab workaday clothes and cloth caps, Louise, sauntering out in a jaunty red beret, smart belted jacket and navy slacks, stuck out like a sore thumb.

She was deep in conversation with a very large woman who was waddling along beside her, but when she saw Katy waving at her from the other side of the road she said goodbye at once and crossed over to her.

'Katy.'

'Louise.'

For an awkward second Katy didn't know how to go on. She hadn't seen Louise since the awful day Louise had screamed at her outside Arding & Hobbs. She tried to push the recollection to the back of her mind and smiled instead. 'You're looking great. So chic. I thought you'd be covered in oil or something. And you're hardly limping at all any more.'

Louise looked pleased. 'I do when I'm tired.' She grimaced. 'Which is most of the time. As for chic, we wear overalls, which keeps the worst of the muck off. Apart from the hands.' She help up grease stained hands. 'It doesn't come off skin however much you scrub it. I think I'll have brown fingers for the rest of my life.'

Katy stared at her. Louise had changed. *Overalls?* The old Louise wouldn't have been seen dead in overalls, would never in a million years have laughed about getting her hands dirty. And this new Louise seemed more relaxed. Happier.

It seemed incredible that working in a dingy place like Gregg Bros could effect such a change on anyone. But then Katy remembered how much she herself had changed when she started nursing. Even though she had hated it, it had given her something, a purpose in life, an identity. She wondered suddenly if getting the pub going again would do the same thing for her again. She could certainly do with a lift. As the weeks went by, the pain of Ward's absence seemed if anything to get worse not better. Perhaps running the pub would take her mind off it. And off the nerve-racking thought of his child growing steadily inside her.

'I wanted to thank you for talking to your father,' she said to Louise suddenly as they walked on down the road. 'Aaref told me what you said. It was brave of you. And I'm very grateful.'

Louise shrugged. 'It was the least I could do. I thought it was unfair the way he was treating you.' She cast a quick sideways glance at Katy. 'Things were going badly enough for you as it was. I was really sorry to hear about your father, and your mother being injured.' She hesitated. 'And about Ward of course.' She stopped awkwardly. 'Have you heard anything more?'

'Only that he was last seen badly injured and surrounded by Germans,' Katy said flatly. As usual the thought of it made her feel sick and she had to stop herself saying he was dead. She was so used to seeing him gunned down by Germans in her dreams she was starting to believe it was true.

Louise looked quickly at her white face and shut her eyes for a second. 'Oh, Katy,' she whispered. 'I am so sorry.' She stopped and went on after a moment more strongly. 'I really am. I feel so ashamed about that Ward business. I wasn't myself. I think I was depressed or something.' She grimaced. 'You probably don't know but I nearly ruined your wedding. I got drunk and was all set to come blundering in when Aaref stopped me.'

Katy stared at her appalled. 'He never said.'

Louise shrugged. 'I swore him to secrecy.' She glanced at Katy. 'I feel guilty about him too. He's been so kind to me and I've been so mean to him.' She held up her wrist. 'He sent me this bracelet when I was in hospital and I hardly even thanked him for it.'

Katy smiled. 'Poor Aaref,' she said. 'He's devoted to you, isn't he?' Then she remembered Molly Coogan and added casually, 'What do you feel about him?'

Louise laughed. 'He's sweet, I admit. But honestly, Katy, can you see me with him?' She rolled her eyes. 'I know I haven't been lucky with my choice of men, but really . . .! Surely I can do better than Aaref Hoch.'

It was easy enough for Stanley to say he wanted some decent cooking, Joyce thought, but if there was nothing in the shops it was easier said than done. By the beginning of June the shops and stalls on Northcote Road had more signs saying what they were out of than what they had. *No onions or oranges; No spaghetti; No kippers or herring; No currants, sultanas or raisin; No dried fruit; No fat or dripping; No eggs; No sweets or chocolates; No tomatoes, tinned or fresh; No bananas.*

All there seemed to be were carrots and endless bottles of vinegar. Eventually she tracked down a packet of flour, a piece of stewing steak and a pound of sausages. And she had to queue for half an hour at Dove the Butcher's for those. If she could scrounge an egg off Mrs Rutherford this afternoon she'd make a toad in the hole for tonight and with the fat from the sausages she'd make some pastry for a steak and carrot pie tomorrow.

Somewhat to her surprise, even after picking up the sugar ration and the butter ration, she still had a few shillings left in her pocket. She was reluctant to take it home. She knew Stanley would want it back. But what if his 'little business on the side' went wrong and he lost it all? And his job as well? What would they do then?

On the other hand if he found it hidden in the house somewhere there'd be all hell to pay. And she didn't want him hitting her again. It was a slippery slope, that hitting business. As it stood she could cope with the sex. It was his right after all. But if he started getting violent, she didn't know what she'd do. With a bit of money put aside at least she could get away for a few days, maybe go down to Devon again. To the farm. Without it, her options were nonexistent, she'd have no choice but to stay and put up with him.

What she needed, she realised, was someone else to keep it for her. Someone she could trust. Someone who wouldn't ask questions. Wouldn't tittle-tattle it around.

Looking around to make sure no one was watching her, she crossed the road quickly and pressed the buzzer on the door of Lorenz's pawnshop.

Chapter Twenty-Four

It was cool in the shop after the warm June sun outside. And dark. So dark that it took a moment for Joyce's eyes to adjust sufficiently to see Lorenz behind the counter.

But he could see her apparently because he said her name at once. 'Mrs Carter. This is an unexpected treat.'

As she approached the counter Joyce peered at him suspiciously wondering if he was being sarcastic. But it was difficult to tell. Lorenz's dark eyes were as inscrutable as ever behind those steel-rimmed glasses.

'Yes, well, I haven't had much call to come in,' she said as she put her shopping basket down on the floor. 'What with my husband being in work and that.'

'You don't need any call to come and see me, Mrs Carter,' Mr Lorenz said. 'It's always a pleasure to see you.'

Joyce blinked at him in astonishment. What had come over him? He sounded quite jaunty. Perhaps it was the good weather affecting him. Or maybe the threat of invasion being over for the time being. She had often worried about what Lorenz would do if the Germans invaded. It wouldn't be much fun for anyone. But him being a Jew and that it would be even worse.

'And how is your daughter, Mrs Carter? No ill effects from her ordeal?'

'Her ordeal?' It took a second for Joyce to realise what he was talking about. It wasn't Lorenz's way to make conversation and it threw her rather. 'Oh, the bomb, you mean?' She laughed. 'Oh, good God no. Our Jen's as tough as old boots. A broken arm won't do her any harm.' Then suddenly Joyce recalled that Lorenz had been involved in digging Jen out. He'd been stripped to his vest and braces, covered in grey dust and sweating like the rest of them. 'It was good of you to help get her out,' she said. 'And Katy and that Whitehead child.'

Mr Lorenz raised his hands deprecatingly. 'It was the least I could do. I wish we could have saved that poor Mrs Whitehead too.' He shook his head sadly then smiled. 'Your boys worked hard that night, Mrs Carter, you must have been proud of them.'

Proud of them? Of Mick and Pete? Joyce almost laughed. But Lorenz was looking sincere and she realised with a jolt that it was generous of him to praise her sons. Particularly as it wasn't so very long ago that Mick had tried to shoot him. She frowned. She'd never said anything about that. It had always seemed a bit awkward to mention it. But now she felt duty bound to bring it up. Somehow she felt he had shamed her into it.

'I've never thanked you properly about Mick and that shooting business,' she said gruffly. 'It was good of you to keep quiet.' She shrugged. 'It would have been the end of him if the police had got on to it. Stupid little sod. Thanks to you he seems to have kept his nose clean since then.'

For a moment he hesitated, staring down at his counter. Then as he raised his eyes he flushed slightly. 'I didn't do it for your son, Mrs Carter,' he said. 'I did it for you. I didn't want to cause you any more trouble.'

It was Joyce's turn to flush. 'Oh,' she said. She looked away quickly. And then couldn't think how to go on. Something in his expression had unnerved her. For a second she couldn't think what it was. Then she realised. He cared.

It was an odd thought. Somebody cared about her. Even if it was funny old Lorenz. Not that he was that old. Probably only in his forties. It was that grave manner that made him seem old. Those solemn eyes. Nobody liked him, but he liked her. He cared about her. Absurdly she felt choked. Then to her horror she felt her eyes watering. She sniffed but it was too late. One tear ran out of her eye, down her nose and plopped on the counter.

Hoping he hadn't noticed, she held herself rigid but then another one fell. She couldn't look at him. She couldn't do anything. She just stood there hoping that in a minute she would be able to pull herself together again.

And then she saw his hands move under the counter and the next minute he was pushing a clean white handkerchief over towards her. It was so clean it almost looked new. Either that or it had come straight from the laundry. As she picked it up Joyce wondered what it was doing there under his counter. Perhaps he was used to people crying in his dark little shop. Perhaps he got a lot of people crying in here because he wouldn't give them enough hock for their things. She didn't reckon many people would cry because he was nice to them though. It seemed a bit ridiculous to cry because of that.

Or perhaps he didn't really care; perhaps he just felt sorry for her.

Suddenly she swallowed hard. She blew her nose and dabbed her eyes. She didn't want him to feel sorry for her.

'You don't have to worry about me,' she said crossly. 'I'm all right.'

He looked a bit hurt and she felt guilty. He was only being nice after all. She put the handkerchief on the counter then wondered if she should take it home. She looked at it doubtfully, knowing she'd never get it so crisp and clean again. And then he solved the problem by picking it up and putting it in his pocket.

For a moment she stood there wishing she had put it in her bag, wishing she knew what to say next, how to make him understand that she was sorry for being abrupt. How to explain that she felt all on edge. Uneasy. Cross and sad at the same time. Dreading that he would take the huff, but somehow unable to respond to his concern.

But then, as though nothing untoward had happened, he put his hands flat on the counter and reverted to his normal businesslike mode. 'So what can I do for you today, Mrs Carter? Do you have something for me?'

Joyce blinked, relieved. 'I wondered if you would keep some money for me,' she said.

'Money?'

She flushed. 'It's not much. Just a few shillings.' Suddenly she felt stupid. 'I just . . . I just think it might be handy to keep it out of the way. Where nobody else can get at it.' She saw the understanding dawn on him and again that faint hint of sympathy. And she lifted her chin. 'Me and Mrs Rutherford are thinking of finding a property to rent, you see. For a café. We had our eye on the Flag and Garter but young Katy Frazer is taking it now.' To her horror she felt her lip quiver. All her dreams came to nothing. She swallowed again and looked up at him fiercely. 'I thought if I put a few bob aside now and then, somewhere safe, it would build up a bit.'

Lorenz nodded. He was watching her closely. 'What about a bank, Mrs Carter? Banks are safe.'

She stared at him. 'I don't trust banks. They take your money and never give it back. I want it with someone I can trust.'

'I see.' He smiled slightly, an odd little smile that she couldn't quite make out. Then he inclined his head gravely. 'In that case, Mrs Carter, it would be a pleasure.'

She put the money on the counter and he counted it carefully with his long clean fingers. Then he took out a pen and wrote the amount on a piece of paper. 'Your receipt, Mrs Carter.'

She looked at it doubtfully. 'Could you keep that for me as well?' The last thing she needed was Stanley finding a receipt from Lorenz.

For a second she thought Lorenz was going to insist she took it but then he apparently changed his mind. 'Of course, Mrs Carter,' he said. 'As you wish.'

As he picked up the paper and folded it neatly, she nodded. 'Thank you.'

He looked up at her and held her eyes for a moment. 'I am always happy to be of service, Mrs Carter.'

As she left the shop she felt oddly flustered. She didn't know whether he minded looking after her money or not. Surely it wasn't too much to ask. A few extra bob in his till wasn't going to make much difference. She frowned.

He'd had quite a bit of business off her over the years. He had no cause to complain.

When Sister Morris called her into her office during visiting time, for a moment Katy felt a stab of sheer terror. It was only a second later that she remembered that she no longer had any real need to fear Sister Morris.

Real need or not she could still feel her heart thumping nervously as Sister barked at her to close the door behind her.

'What's this I hear about you opening a public house?' Sister said, waving her to the uncomfortable wooden chair on the other side of her desk.

Katy sat down uneasily. She could tell from the way Sister Morris said the words 'public house' that the licensed trade was not something she was either familiar with or approved of. On the contrary, it sounded as though she was of the opinion that public houses were dens of iniquity and vice and not at all the kind of place one of her ex-nurses should be involved in running.

Hastily Katy tried to reassure her that it wasn't so much a question of opening as reopening, and that she and her mother were intending to keep a thoroughly respectable house which hopefully people from all walks of life would be able to visit with peace of mind.

'But you will be serving alcohol?'

'Well, yes, Sister,' Katy admitted, thanking her lucky stars that nobody else was there to make her giggle. 'But not in excess of course.'

Sister pursed her lips in shock. 'I should think not.' She fixed Katy suddenly with her beady gaze and leaned forward. 'I expect you to run a sober, clean and Godly establishment. Such as befits a nurse trained at this hospital.'

Katy swallowed. 'Yes, Sister,' she murmured gravely.

Sister nodded and sat back again, crossing her arms over her large bosom. 'When do you expect to be ready to open?'

'In August,' Katy said, surprised at Sister's interest. 'Early August.'

'And I expect there is a lot for you to do in the meantime?'

Katy nodded. 'Well, yes but . . .'

'And I gather you are currently living in rather primitive conditions?'

'Yes, Sister, but . . .?'

'In that case I will recommend that your mother is transferred out to one of the cottage hospitals in the sector for her physiotherapy. She is feeling very anxious and unsettled. She needs time in which to come to terms with her situation, time to convalesce, and it will give you a chance to sort out your arrangements. By the time you are ready to open, she will be fully recovered and able to take her place in the business.'

Katy stared at her, astonished by her intuitive grasp of the situation. It hadn't taken Katy long to realise that in her current state her mother was going to be of little help in the new venture. Suddenly she leaned forward and smiled. 'Sister, I don't know if anyone has ever told you, but you are a very wonderful person.'

Sister looked appalled. She got to her feet at once. 'Not at all,' she said firmly. 'I am only doing my duty.' As she spoke she pulled open a drawer in her desk and withdrew a fat leather bound Bible.

'I intended to give you this as a wedding present,' she said as Katy stood up. 'But in the circumstances it wasn't appropriate. Now that you are undertaking another venture I would like you to have it. I would like you to keep it under the counter in your new establishment. You might find it useful to look at it each day before you start work.'

Katy was touched. She fingered the book for a moment and then looked up at her old mentor. 'Thank you,' she said simply. 'Thank you for everything.'

Then at the door she looked back. 'Perhaps you will come to the pub one day. I would like to stand you a drink.' She tried to look suitably grave. 'A soft one of course.'

For the first time Sister permitted herself a small smile. 'I might hold you to that, Mrs Frazer. You may be surprised. I always like to keep an eye on my former nurses. Make sure they are behaving themselves.'

The thought of Sister popping into the Flag and Garter of an evening to check up on her was almost more than Katy could bear without bursting into horrified laughter.

She was still reeling from shock as she left the room a moment later.

Nurse Coogan was waiting for her in the ward, an anxious expression on her pointed face. 'Are you all right?' she whispered. 'What did she want?'

Katy made a rueful face. 'She wants me to pray before opening up each day.'

'To pray?' Molly Coogan looked astonished. 'What on earth for?'

Katy shook her head. 'I don't know.' She glanced back at the door and giggled nervously. 'Good takings, I suppose.'

Louise couldn't believe her bad luck. All these weeks she had been slogging her guts out earning the pathetic woman's wage and just at the moment she had saved up enough to buy some decent new outfit, the government brought in blasted clothes rationing.

That was bad enough, but now she had received a smart little printed invitation from Lucinda Veale, an old finishing-school friend, to her twenty-first birthday party at the Dorchester at the end of June. *Louise Rutherford and partner*, it said. *Dancing to the music of Geraldo. Eight p.m. Carriages midnight. Black tie.*

Louise frowned. She didn't have a partner. And she didn't have anything to wear. And she didn't have a carriage. In the old days she might have asked her father to provide Mr Wallace for the evening. But that was now quite out of the question. Since she had blackmailed her father into giving Katy a chance to run the pub, no more favours in terms of money or goodwill were likely to be forthcoming. Anyway there wasn't enough petrol nowadays for purely social trips.

But she was damned if she was going to refuse. It was the first decent invitation she had had in ages and for the first time in ages she felt up to showing her face in public. For a minute she felt nervous about seeing the Lucie Clayton gang again. She hadn't seen them since her accident and she was scared they'd tease her about her mundane job. She also felt self-conscious about her limp. But then she gritted her teeth and wrote out her acceptance. There was a war on after all. Limps were almost de rigueur these days. And it would make a change from listening to the wireless in her room or fending off Aaref's advances or sitting in Lyon's corner house listening to Bertie droning on about how much he missed Sheila blasted Whitehead.

'Oh for God's sake, Bertie,' she said irritably when he started up again the following evening when they met after work. 'You're not the only person in the world who has lost someone they loved. Look at Katy. She's not whining on about Ward Frazer, is she? She's getting on with her life.' Look at me, she wanted to say. I lost Stefan and Ward. And a baby. And I'm getting on with my life.

Bertie lit a cigarette and inhaled deeply. 'But I feel so guilty,' he groaned. As he blew out the smoke his shoulders slumped. 'It was my fault Sheila died. My fault the Nelsons have lost George. Alan Nelson's been OK about it but I know Mrs Nelson resents me being there. She's never liked me but now she can hardly bring herself to speak to me at all.'

Louise shrugged. 'Well, go out then. You can't sit around feeling guilty all your life. You need some fun. So do something about it.'

Bertie frowned. 'It's not that easy.'

Louise blew out smoke angrily. 'It's not been easy for me either.' Since she had started work against her father's wishes, living in Cedars House had not been a comfortable experience. But her revelation about the baby had made it a hundred times worse. Her father had been even more remote than usual and her mother nervous and uneasy. Conversation had been stilted. Louise knew she had lost the privileged daughter status irrevocably. And any residual sympathy for her broken pelvis had gone with it.

Oddly she didn't care. So long as she notched up a hundred and twenty bolts every day she felt good. She'd done her bit for Katy and she was doing her bit for the war effort. All she needed now was a nice man.

'At least there are plenty of girls around for you to go out with,' she said, watching the Nippy smile at Bertie as he paid the bill. 'But decent men are few and far between these days. They're either dead or serving abroad. I've been asked to a dance in a couple of weeks and I'm going to have to go on my own.'

'It won't be much of a dance, then,' Bertie remarked. 'If there's no men.'

Louise frowned. 'Well, there'll be some men, I suppose. But the ones that are there will be inundated. Otherwise it will be girls dancing together.'

Bertie seemed to brighten slightly. 'So you think your friend is on the look-out for more men to go?'

Louise nodded. 'That's why she put "Louise and partner" on the invitation. Why?'

He lifted his shoulders. 'I'll go with you if you want. I don't mind. As you say, it would do me good to get out a bit more.'

'You?' Louise stared at him. Then she stubbed out her cigarette and laughed. 'Don't be ridiculous. You can't possibly come. Nobody's going to want a bloody conchie hanging around.'

★　★　★

Having written in some trepidation to the Miss Taylors about the destruction of their house, Katy was pleased to gather from their reply that they had taken the news with equanimity. All they seemed worried about was that she was all right. And that she was bearing up to Ward's continuing absence.

We think of you and of him every day, they wrote. *And although neither of us is blessed with psychic or supernatural powers, we do somehow feel, very strongly, that he is still alive and we wonder if you feel the same way?*

I feel that they've gone a bit nutty, Jen wrote back when Katy imparted this information to her. *I also feel very worried about you using my brother Pete to do your repairs. I've always thought he was one sandwich short of a picnic, myself, so do try and make sure he doesn't put windows in the cellar or the entrance up on the first floor. And for God's sake don't be tempted to let Mick loose on it or the whole place will fall down.*

Katy couldn't help laughing when she read this, but for once she thought Jen was wrong. In fact since the renovations had finally begun last week, Pete Carter had proved to be a hard and conscientious worker. Admittedly they were only so far stripping out the rubble and burnt, unstable joists. It was clearly going to be a long job, but nevertheless, two nights in a row he worked later than necessary to reseal the entrance securely, clearly concerned for Katy's safety in her cellar.

For her part Katy found she rather enjoyed having the workmen there. She liked hearing them up on the scaffolding discussing the international news.

'Never heard of that Iraq place what surrendered to our boys last week. Where is that, then?'

'God knows. Lost a lot of poor sods in Crete though. Just like Dunkirk all over again, they said in the paper.'

'Not Frenchies in Crete, are they?'

'No, Greeks, ain't they?'

'All the same. Foreign buggers. I reckon we should bomb the lot of them.'

Katy liked their gratitude when she took them tea. 'Oh, here comes the lovely landlady. Watch your language, lads.'

And she liked the way Mr Poole consulted her about the smallest details. Did she want the same size entrance or would a double door be more welcoming? Or had she thought about what sort of flooring she would be having because it made a difference to how they supported the walls?

'What about this old clock?' he asked one day when the remains of her father's grandfather clock emerged from under the rubble in the bar. 'What do you want me to do with it?'

'I suppose it will have to be chucked out,' Katy said sadly. 'Poor old Big Ben. It was my father's pride and joy.'

Mr Poole frowned. 'You could get young Pete to have a look at it. He's quite interested in things like that.'

'Is he?' Katy was astonished. But when Pete was called down from the scaffolding to inspect the clock, it seemed Mr Poole was right. Pete quickly bared the works, and after a few minutes poking and prodding at the mangled metal, declared shyly that he thought he might be able to make it go again if he could find or make replacements for one or two broken cogs and levers. Eventually it was decided that the clock should be moved down into the cellar, out of the way, so that Pete could tinker about with it in the evenings and on his day off.

It was during one of those tinkering sessions that Pete Carter first came to her aid over Mr Fish.

Barry Fish had called several times over the weeks since she had refused to let him find her somewhere to live. As soon as he heard of her intention to reopen the pub he offered to arrange builders for her and then to help her restock. Convinced that she would find herself buying back her father's looted stock and equipment, Katy refused once again. Then he started angling for a job. 'You'll need help, won't you? Someone who knows the ropes.'

And since the repairs had begun, he had become even more insistent. 'Come on now, Katy love. You'll need a fellow around the place.' He winked at her. 'You and me would make a good team. You'll need someone who knows what's what, slip of a thing like you. Someone the fellows can respect. Someone who knows the business.'

'You were the Saturday night pianist,' Katy said coldly. 'I hardly think that means you know the business.'

Barry Fish's ingratiating smile faded rapidly. 'Oh, we're getting very high and mighty, aren't we?' he said. 'And how often did you spike the beer? How often did you help your dad with his orders? How often did he leave you in charge of the bar?'

Katy frowned. 'He never left you in charge of the bar.'

Barry Fish smirked. 'Oh yes he did. He was always having to pop down to the cellar. Turning the beer on and off. Never knew where we were during all those sirens and raids.'

Katy felt sick. Suddenly she knew for certain why the pub had done so badly those last few months. Because Barry Fish had had his greedy pianist's fingers in the till.

'Thank you, Mr Fish,' she said. 'Thank you for telling me that. It has answered a lot of questions.' She stepped back a pace. 'Now, if you'll excuse me.'

Barry Fish paled slightly. ''Ere. What are you saying?' He took her arm and pulled her close. 'What are you implying?'

'I'm not implying anything,' Katy said nervously. 'I'm just saying that I won't be offering you a job, Mr Fish.'

Barry Fish's eyes narrowed dangerously. 'I'll have to talk to your mother about this.'

Katy was about to say that thankfully her mother was safely out of the way in a cottage hospital in Surrey when suddenly Pete Carter was standing beside her.

'Is this man bothering you, Katy?' he asked quietly as Barry Fish quickly removed his hand from Katy's arm.

Surprised, Katy shook her head. 'No,' she said. 'He's not bothering me. But I think he understands that I don't want him to call again.'

After Barry Fish had gone she found herself telling Pete her suspicions about the pianist. How she suspected that not only had he been cheating her father, but that he was also somehow involved with the looting of the pub. She was rather concerned by how angry it made Pete. 'Don't worry, Pete,' she said quickly as his face darkened. 'I'm sure he's got the message now.'

Unfortunately for Barry Fish, he hadn't. When he called a few days later, a piece of falling scaffolding pipe nearly took his arm off. 'I thought you'd been told to keep clear,' a voice called down as Katy looked on in horror. 'Accidents do happen if people don't do what they are told.'

The next time he wasn't so lucky. He came at the wrong time, when Katy wasn't there.

The following day to her surprise she found three silver tankards at the top of the cellar steps. It only took her a second to realise they were the ones that had disappeared the night of the looting. Looking up in surprise, she caught Pete Carter's eyes on her.

Suddenly she felt a stab of panic. 'Pete,' she whispered. 'What did you do to him?'

Pete Carter shrugged. 'Best if you don't know.'

Katy's eyes widened in horror. 'You didn't kill him?'

He shook his head regretfully. 'No, we didn't kill him. We just frightened him.' He smiled slowly. 'I don't think he'll bother you again in a hurry.'

On the twenty second of June the Germans launched a massive attack on Russia. The same day Stanley got sacked from Rutherford & Berry on suspicion of filching, and his son, Mick was dismissed too.

Mick was surprisingly upset. 'It's not fair,' he said bitterly. 'I never took nothing.'

The following day when she arrived for work at Cedars

House, Joyce overheard the Rutherfords talking about her in Mr Rutherford's study.

'She'll have to go,' Greville Rutherford was saying. 'I've never liked having her here. They're a thoroughly bad lot, those Carters.' Standing, shocked, in the hall Joyce heard Celia begin a counter argument, but he interrupted at once. 'I'm not going to discuss it, Celia. In my opinion she's been a bad influence on you. She looks like something the dog brought in. You've let her get above herself. She's too familiar by half. And I blame her for what happened to Louise. All that WVS business. Absurd. You should have been at home looking after your daughter.'

Joyce frowned. It was hardly her fault that Louise had been caught in the Balham Tube disaster. Then the situation suddenly sunk in. Unless Mrs Rutherford stood up for her more strongly, she was going to be fired. She was about to be cast off. Penniless. With an unemployed husband and son to go with it.

Last night Mick had said he'd join the merchant marine, but that was a joke. He was only sixteen for a start and Bob had nearly wet himself laughing. 'You?' he guffawed. 'They wouldn't want a cack-handed little bastard like you.'

Mick had flushed angrily. 'I may be cack-handed but at least I'm not a coward, not like some people,' and Bob had flared up at once.

'I've got a bad back.'

'Yeah?' Mick had sneered. 'Not so bad you can't get up the West End to see your little fancy piece every five minutes.'

'How do you know about that?'

Mick had shrugged. 'I know more than you might think.' He stood up and kicked his chair in roughly. 'I know where them crates in the Anderson come from and all. And I don't reckon Dad ought to keep them here.'

At the sink Joyce had felt the sudden tension in her shoulders. So Stanley had been filching. Sure enough when she had glanced cautiously into the Anderson shelter later she found several crates of beer. She wondered how he had got them home. There must have been some kind of vehicle. Which meant there were other people involved. Other people to bubble Stanley if the going got rough. And her heart sank.

Now she jumped suddenly as she heard movement behind the study door. Determined not to give Mr Rutherford the satisfaction of catching her eavesdropping, she fled silently into the kitchen and then out into the garden.

She was with the hens when Mrs Rutherford found her. 'Mrs Carter,' she said, her nasal, upper-crust voice crisply unemotional. 'I'm afraid I have some bad news.'

Joyce straightened up slowly. Had she really expected her employer to fight on her behalf? She suddenly realised she had and that she was bitterly disappointed. Stupidly over the last few months she had begun to believe that Mrs Rutherford was on her side.

But clearly she was wrong. 'I'm afraid you'll have to leave us,' Mrs Rutherford was saying firmly. She handed Joyce a small brown envelope. 'Here are the wages for the rest of the week. It's only fair.'

Then just as Joyce was toying with rejecting the envelope out of pride, Celia Rutherford glanced over her shoulder back at the house and lowered her voice.

'There's a month's wages in there,' she whispered under pretence of adjusting the chicken's pop hole. 'That should keep you going. And by then hopefully we'll have found somewhere to open the café. He can't stop me hiring you then.'

Then as Joyce's eyes widened in amazement, she quickly raised her voice again. 'I'm sorry, Mrs Carter,' she said dismissively. 'But there it is. You may take a couple of eggs with you. But other than that I'm afraid there's nothing I can do.'

Joyce felt tears in her eyes. She wanted to thank her, to hug her. To swear eternal loyalty. But all she could do was clutch the envelope and blink. Even when Mrs Rutherford reached into the coop and picked two eggs still warm from the nest and put them into her hands, she could only manage a choked murmur of thanks.

But as Mrs Rutherford steered her swiftly round the house and away down the drive, her mind was already racing. At the corner she hesitated. She didn't want Stanley getting his hands on her month's wages. Damn him. It was his fault she'd been sacked after all.

No. She made up her mind and put the eggs carefully in her pocket. She'd go straight down to Lorenz to give him the money now. Stanley never need know. If he wanted decent food he'd bloody well have to fund it himself.

In the end Louise wore one of last year's dresses to the party, a sleeveless emerald evening gown with a short jacket to top it off. Katy had helped her hem it up to the fashionable mid-calf austerity length and they decided bare legs were preferable to beastly rayon stockings.

Luckily Louise still had the strappy shoes she had bought to go with the dress and although it wasn't the most elegant outfit at the party, it was passable and she was actually rather glad that she hadn't bought anything new. The minute she stepped out of the taxi and entered the smoky ballroom she realised, from the motley selection of outfits on display, that brand new clothes were no longer quite the thing. Some of the girls were even in uniform. As were the men of course. What there were of them. Louise's prediction had been right, men were thin on the ground.

The noise was intense. The band was thumping out some swing. Glasses were chinking and the din of conversation was punctuated by braying laughter and screamed greetings as old friends caught sight of each other across the room.

Everyone was talking about the German invasion of Russia. Minsk had just fallen. 'Good Lord,' someone said. 'That means they're halfway to Moscow already.'

Louise was relieved to find herself quickly absorbed into a group of her old finishing-school chums where the talk was more concerned with the day to day trials and tribulations of war torn London. 'Do you know,' a plummy voiced deb called Marcia Cruickshank announced suddenly, 'I popped into Dickens and Jones yesterday for some bits and pieces and they wouldn't wrap. Can you believe it? And I couldn't find a taxi anywhere so I ended up juggling everything home on the bus.'

Later they all began talking about their war work. Helen de Burrel was in the war office, Lucinda about to join the Wrens. Suddenly Felicity Rowe, a girl Louise had never liked, nudged her and smirked. 'What are you doing for the war effort these days, Louise? Arranging flowers?'

This was the moment she had dreaded. 'No, actually,' she said, calmly. 'I'm working in a factory in Battersea.'

Everyone's brows rose. 'A factory?' Felicity giggled. 'Goodness me, don't you get awfully messy?'

Louise smiled sweetly. 'What do you do, Felicity?'

Felicity swished back her hair. 'I'm a land-girl.'

'Goodness me,' Louise laughed. 'Well, you must know what it's like. At least I only get oil under my fingernails, not cow pats.'

As everyone burst out laughing Louise glanced round in relief and her breath caught in her throat. A sandy-haired man in naval uniform had joined the group and was watching her with a small smile. For a second Louise caught his eye then she looked away. She didn't like fair-haired men. Both Ward Frazer and Stefan Pininski had had dark hair. Thick dark hair and the kind of skin that tanned easily. This man was exactly the opposite. As he moved under the chandelier, his hair seemed almost reddish and although his face was tanned in a rugged, weather beaten kind of way, she guessed that under the smart naval uniform his skin would be pale and freckly.

Nevertheless when he asked her for a dance later she found she felt shy and looked up at him in dismay. It was a long time since she had felt like this.

'I . . . I can't dance,' she stammered. 'I got bombed and it damaged my hip.'

To her surprise his eyes ran appreciatively down her slim figure and he raised his eyebrows mischievously. 'It looks all right to me.' Then seeing her suddenly heightened colour, he laughed. 'Then we'll have to talk instead,' he said easily. 'I'll get you a drink.'

When he came back with two glasses of punch she realised his eyes were piercing blue. As he smiled, the skin around them crinkled appealingly. 'My name is Jack Delmaine,' he said. 'What's yours?'

Louise had to clear her throat before she could speak. Even then it was a moment before she could remember her name. 'Louise,' she said. 'Louise Rutherford.'

Jack Delmaine leaned forward. 'So why have I never seen you before, Louise?'

'I don't know,' Louise stammered. 'I was in hospital over the winter. And since then I've been quite busy.'

'In your factory?'

'Well, yes.' She frowned, thinking he might be mocking her, but he touched her bare arm.

'Don't look like that. If it wasn't for people like you doing the tough dirty jobs, people like me wouldn't have modern well-equipped ships to fight in.' He saw her blink in surprise and smiled again. That same crinkly smile. 'Talking of which, I've got to go up to Liverpool tomorrow for a couple of weeks to supervise a refit. But when I get back perhaps I could take you out to dinner? Or to a show?'

Louise couldn't believe her luck. Already she had forgiven him for his sandy complexion. She tried not to nod too eagerly. 'OK.'

He smiled. 'Are you on the telephone?'

Quickly, before he could change his mind, Louise told him the number and spent the remaining hour of the evening surreptitiously watching him dance with other girls and praying he wouldn't forget it.

★   ★   ★

9th July 1941

Dear Mr Nelson,

I am writing to let you know that we have reconsidered our position about George Whitehead. During the time he has been with us his behaviour has been quite unacceptable. He refuses to respond to discipline and seems quite incapable of doing what he is told. On reflection we are prepared to allow him to come back to London for a while until such time as he learns to behave himself. If you are still willing to take him on I would be pleased if you would let me know and I will then arrange means of transportation. Yours sincerely, Edward Teacross.

Chapter Twenty-Five

Alan looked up from the letter. 'What do you think we should say?'

Pam stared at him incredulously. 'What do you mean?' As far as she was concerned there was no question about it. George was clearly unhappy and must come back. 'Surely we'll say yes,' she said. 'If we send them a telegram this afternoon he could be with us by the weekend.'

But Alan was shaking his head and Pam felt a surge of anxiety. 'Alan? What is it? Surely you're not put off by what they say about his behaviour?' She touched his arm, trying to jolt him out of the strange hesitation he was showing. 'He'd be fine with us. It's only because he's with those awful Teacrosses that he's playing up.' Feeling the reluctance still in him, she stepped back a pace and spread her hands in frustration. 'Alan, it's George. We've got to have him.'

Alan dropped the letter back on the kitchen table and ran a hand through his hair. 'I know it's George. I know we want him. But what we don't want is to have him for a few weeks and then have them whisk him away again. It's not fair on him and it's not fair on us.' He grimaced. 'We've been through too much and so has he. If we get him we keep him for good.'

Pam's breath caught in her throat. 'You mean we should try to adopt him?'

Alan glanced at her and squared his shoulders. 'I mean we should make it a condition of us having him at all.'

Pam was shocked. 'But Alan, what if they say no?'

He folded his arms across his chest. 'Then he'll have to stay with them.'

'Alan!' Pam couldn't believe her ears. Surely Alan wouldn't be so hard. 'But . . .'

But Alan was adamant. 'No, Pam, I'm serious. I'm not prepared to be used as a safety valve for the bloody Teacrosses. We've been through the wringer for the last couple of years and the last thing we need is to be constantly waving goodbye to a child we love. It would be bad enough for us, think what it would do to him?'

Pam looked at him with new respect. He was right but it didn't stop her feeling torn. Much as she longed for George's return, she had to agree that to have him taken away again a few weeks later would be devastating. If nothing else, by then she would have given up her job and might well have problems getting another one as good.

She glanced sadly at the letter lying on the kitchen table. 'So what should we do?'

'I'll write to them now,' he said firmly. 'Explaining our position.'

He picked up the letter and was about to turn away when Pam grabbed his hand. 'Oh Alan,' she said. 'I know you're right. But I want him so much. I can't bear the thought of him staying a moment longer than necessary with those beastly people.'

He grimaced and drew her into his arms. 'I know you want him,' he said steadily. 'I want him too. But this is the only way. I can't bear for you to be disappointed again.'

Suddenly Pam felt choked by emotion. It was her he cared about, her more than anything. 'Alan, whatever happens, I love you.'

He kissed her. 'That's lucky,' he said lightly. 'Because I love you too.'

Katy was sitting on the doorstep in the hot July evening sun when Louise stopped for a chat on the way back from work. 'Do you know,' she said, slumping down beside her crossly, 'I couldn't get any cigarettes tonight. And why not?' She laughed sourly. 'Because they were being kept for men. The shopkeeper had the gall to tell me that the reason cigarettes are short is because of women selfishly smoking them.'

Katy laughed. 'He picked the wrong person to grapple with about women's rights. I bet you gave him a right talking to.'

Louise looked fierce. 'As a matter of fact I did.' Then she saw Katy's amused expression and shrugged. They both knew why Louise was ratty. And it wasn't anything to do with cigarettes.

'No phone call?' Katy asked.

Louise turned her face to the sun and closed her eyes. 'What I can't understand,' she said, 'Is why he said he'd ring if he wasn't going to?'

'I'm sure he will,' Katy said. 'He's probably been delayed up in Liverpool or something.'

'Or something.' Louise lifted her shoulders. 'Exactly. There's always some excuse. Always some reason why women get a raw deal.' She thought about it for a moment and then shrugged sadly. 'Jack Delmaine probably doesn't want a girl who can't dance, anyway.'

Katy stared at her. 'Well, if that's true he's not worth having in the first place,' she said.

But her vehemence didn't cheer Louise and a few minutes later she saw Aaref approaching down the street and groaned. 'Oh no,' she muttered, 'this is all I need.'

But Aaref looked pleased to see Louise and immediately suggested the three of them went for a stroll on the common.

Louise stood up and stretched lazily. 'Not me,' she said carelessly. 'I'm expecting a phone call.'

Katy could see Aaref was disappointed and was cross with Louise for making it so obvious she didn't want to spend time with him.

Katy smiled sympathetically at him. 'I'd like to go but I'm waiting for Molly.' Perhaps this would be Molly's chance.

She looked at him expectantly but he was watching Louise strolling away down the road. 'She's only grumpy because she couldn't find any cigarettes,' Katy said gently. 'But Molly will be here soon. Perhaps she could come with us instead.'

Aaref looked blank. 'Who?' he asked.

Katy grimaced to herself. 'Molly,' she said. Aaref had met Molly Coogan three times now and never seemed to remember her. Mainly, Katy thought, because the little nurse was entirely silent in his company. For a moment she recalled that she had once been like that with Ward and unexpectedly her heart twisted.

She missed him so much.

Everyone said the pain of his absence would lessen over time, but they were wrong, it actually got worse and worse. Sometimes, like the Miss Taylors, she thought she could believe he was still alive. That one day she would see him again. But as time went by she knew that chance became less and less likely.

Quickly, before the pain grew too strong, she looked up at Aaref.

He was frowning. 'Oh, that little nurse, you mean?' He looked doubtful. 'Do you think she'll want to come with us?'

Katy nodded eagerly. 'Oh yes,' she said. 'I'm sure she will.'

Joyce was upstairs turning the boys' beds when she heard Mick shouting from the kitchen. 'Oi, Dad, come out here. There's a friggin' chicken in the yard.'

Running to Jen's old room at the back of the house Joyce looked out of the window and to her horror saw Mick pointing to the roof of the Anderson shelter where a large red hen was watching him with a beady eye.

Desperately trying to open the window, Joyce swore as the sash stuck. Banging it with her fist she finally got it open far enough to lean out. Stanley had joined Mick in the yard now and they were edging cautiously towards the hen.

'Don't!' Joyce shouted down. 'Leave it alone. That's one of Mrs Rutherford's hens. It must have come over the fence.'

Stanley smirked. 'I don't care where it's bloody come from,' he said. 'It's on my property now.'

'No, Stanley, please. Don't kill it.'

Mick looked up, surprised by the emotion in her voice but Stanley just laughed. 'Don't be daft. There'd be a nice meal on that bird.'

Watching in agonised despair as Mick flapped his arms in a vain effort to drive the hen towards Stanley, Joyce felt a stab of relief as the wily bird avoided their first couple of attempts at capture.

As they regrouped, hot and angry now after chasing it round the yard, Joyce ran downstairs, spoiling another attempt as the hen once again slipped out of Mick's grasp and took up its former position on the Anderson shelter, squawking indignantly.

Joyce grabbed Stanley's arm. 'It's a good layer. We'll keep it if you want. But don't kill it.'

'I fancy a nice chicken supper,' Stanley said, shoving her back roughly. 'Don't you, Mick?'

Mick grinned nervously, his eyes darting from Joyce to Stanley.

'Get round the back of the shelter,' Stanley instructed him, wiping the sweat off his face. 'So it can't get back over the fence.'

Joyce could feel tears in her eyes. 'I love that bird. Stanley, please . . .'

But he just laughed and she realised that the more she tried to stop him the more he was determined to kill it. More than the meal it would provide, he wanted to hurt her.

And in that moment she realised she hated him. Any residual feeling of loyalty to him had gone. She didn't care that he was the father of her children. She didn't care that she had married him for better or worse. For richer or poorer. Suddenly she wished she had shot him dead all those weeks ago when she had a chance. A lifetime in prison would have been preferable to a lifetime of hell, living with a man who went out of his way to hurt her. Who enjoyed hurting her.

Mick was beginning to look uneasy. 'Dad, I reckon she's serious,' he mumbled, backing away.

The next moment Stanley had plunged at the hen and caught its wing.

As he jerked it towards him Joyce closed her eyes. She couldn't bear to see the glee on his face. She couldn't bear to see his ugly hands tighten round its beautiful neck. She wished she could block her ears too, to avoid hearing the strangled squawk as the brave bird breathed its last.

But it wasn't a squawk she heard, it was a yell of pain, and opening her eyes in astonishment she saw Stanley reeling back, hands to his face as in a whirl of feathers the hen went for his eyes, its sharp beak pecking at his protecting hands before it fell away and half flew, half scuttled back up on to the Anderson shelter where it stood clucking noisily and ruffled up to twice its size like an angry cat.

'Cor blimey.' Mick emerged warily from the lean-to lavatory where he had retreated during the attack. 'Are you all right, Dad?'

Stanley was flushed and swearing and bleeding copiously from the eyebrow. 'That bird's vicious,' he said angrily, mopping himself up with a grubby handkerchief. 'It ought to be shot.'

If she hadn't been so upset, Joyce might have found it funny. Stanley in all his bullying fury thwarted by a chicken.

'I told you to leave it alone,' she said.

'You didn't say it was vicious,' Mick said.

'It's not vicious,' Joyce said. 'It just doesn't like men.'

Nor do I, she thought. Not any more. Men were so aggressive. So sure they were right. Men spoiled everything. If it wasn't for men there wouldn't be a war. Her air-raid shelter wouldn't be full of stolen goods. And she'd still be working for Mrs Rutherford.

'Get the spade out of the shelter, Mick,' Stanley said. 'See if you can get it with that.'

Mick shook his head and backed off. 'I'm not going near it.'

'Neither of you are going near it,' Joyce said firmly. 'You're both going back in the house and I'm going to catch it and take it back to Mrs Rutherford where it belongs.'

Mick looked at her with new respect. 'You'd better watch out, Mum, in case it goes for you and all.'

Joyce ignored him and glanced at Stanley who was leaning against the mangle dripping blood. 'And you'd better go down the hospital and have someone look at your face,' she said coldly. 'It's a nasty cut. We don't want you getting tetanus.'

Louise was sitting on a bench talking to Doris in her lunch break when Ratface nudged her arm. 'There's a young fellow over there by the gate trying to catch your eye,' he said.

Looking up sharply Louise saw Aaref Hoch standing at the factory gates.

Quickly she got to her feet and went across. 'What are you doing here?'

He smiled, apparently undaunted by her brusqueness. 'Have you time to take a little walk? Perhaps in Battersea Park? It is a very lovely day, no, and it would be nice to talk?'

Louise shook her head. 'I'm due back on shift in a few minutes,' she said. She saw the flicker of disappointment in his dark eyes and groaned inwardly.

'Look, Aaref,' she said. 'I really like you and I really appreciate you being so kind to me when I was ill. But it's awkward for me to be seen with you all the time. People will get the wrong impression. Anyway, I've met someone else . . .' Seeing his suddenly crestfallen expression she stopped in dismay, then grimaced impatiently. 'Can't you find some other girl to be keen on? Then you will forget all about me.'

Squinting slightly against the bright sunshine, Aaref pushed the dark hair off his brow. 'I will never forget you,' he said. 'However many other girls there are, you will always be the one in my heart.'

Disconcerted by the low intensity in his voice, Louise giggled uneasily. 'Aaref, don't. You'll make me feel guilty.' She took a step back and glanced over her shoulder. 'And I've got to go, anyway. The bell will go in a minute.'

Aaref looked at her steadily. 'I understand,' he said. 'You must live your life as you wish. But if you ever need me I will be there waiting for you.' Then as she was about to turn away he handed her a brown paper parcel. 'This is for you.'

Louise frowned warily. 'What is it?'

He shrugged. 'It is only cigarettes. Katy said you were having difficulty finding them.'

Louise blinked. 'Oh. Yes, I was.' She glanced at the parcel in her hands. 'Well, thanks,' she said awkwardly.

Aaref inclined his head. 'It is my pleasure,' he said.

Back in the compound, Louise sighed deeply as she rejoined Doris.

'Who's that? Yer boyfriend?' Doris asked. She smiled appreciatively. 'Nice-looking boy.'

Louise laughed shrilly. 'Of course not.'

'Haven't yer got one, then?' Rat-faced Ken asked. 'A boyfriend?'

Louise sniffed. 'Of course I have.' She crossed her fingers behind her back. 'My boyfriend is an officer in the Royal Navy.'

'Oh really?' Ratty leered. 'What's he like?'

Louise glared at him. 'If you must know he's very handsome with slightly curly dark blonde hair, and beautiful blue eyes with crinkly lines at the corners. And a gorgeous figure. Very fit.'

'Ooh.' Ken looked a bit peeved. 'Aren't you the lucky one.'

'Yes, aren't I?' Louise said sweetly, turning away. Out of sight she frowned. She'd be even more lucky if blasted Jack Delmaine ever rang up. It would be just her luck if he'd got bombed in Liverpool.

In the event Joyce had some considerable problem getting the rogue hen off the Anderson shelter. It seemed understandably reluctant to come down but eventually she lured it down with some particularly tasty breadcrumbs. Once it was on the ground, though, it seemed happy enough to be caught and consigned to a shopping basket for the journey up the road.

Aware that she presented rather an odd sight with a live chicken poking out of her shopping basket, and still trembling slightly, Joyce was disconcerted to find herself face to face with Mr Lorenz.

'That's a fine-looking bird you've got, Mrs Carter,' he said, stopping in front of her and raising his hat.

'It's not mine,' she said. 'It belongs to Mrs Rutherford. It came over the back fence.'

Mr Lorenz nodded gravely. 'I see.' Then to her surprise he glanced somewhat furtively around and lowered his voice.

'I don't know if you are still thinking of opening a small catering establishment, Mrs Carter. But if so, I have heard of a premises that might suit your purpose.'

Joyce stared at him. 'Have you?' she said. 'Where?'

'Mr Cox the ironmonger down at the end of the road,' Lorenz said. 'He can't get the stock he needs any more. So he's thinking of closing down.'

Joyce felt a stab of excitement. She'd never been in Cox's shop but it was certainly a perfect location. At the bottom of Lavender Road, just off Lavender Hill, near the other shops, quite a bit of passing trade, not far from the town hall.

In her glee Joyce hardly spared a thought for poor Mr Cox driven out of a long-standing family business by the trials of war. 'I'll ask Mrs Rutherford now,' she said, moving on eagerly. 'I'm sure she'll be interested.'

Mrs Rutherford was interested. 'It sounds marvellous,' she said as Joyce whispered the news to her as they returned the rogue hen to the coop. 'We must go and see it. Do you think your friend would arrange it for us?'

Joyce made a slight face. 'He's not really my friend,' she said awkwardly. 'He's the pawnbroker from Northcote Road. You know. The Jewish bloke. Lorenz.'

Mrs Rutherford smiled. 'I don't mind who he is. If you say he's all right and if he's found us somewhere to start our business, he's a friend of mine.'

Joyce looked at her in some surprise. Most people weren't too keen on Jews. She'd never discussed it with Mrs Rutherford, but she'd overheard her husband going on about that young Aaref Hoch that Louise hung around with sometimes. 'Lorenz is all right,' she said now, pleased that Mrs Rutherford had such faith in her judgement. 'He's a bit of an odd fellow but he means well.'

'Then let's follow it up,' Celia said.

Joyce glanced nervously at the house. 'What about your husband?' she whispered. She didn't want to get all excited and then find that Greville bloody Rutherford was going to crab the whole thing.

Celia looked surprised. 'Didn't you know? Greville is away. Something to do with the NAAFI. They've asked him to advise them on some brewing issue.' She giggled naughtily. 'So we'd better get moving, Mrs Carter. Now could hardly be a better time.'

George Whitehead came back to Lavender Road on the twentieth of July, the day Winston Churchill first gave the two-fingered V salute and chose the opening chords of Beethoven's Fifth Symphony to be the musical code for the liberation of Europe. Three shorts and a long, the Morse code V. V for Victory.

It was a modified victory for Pam and Alan Nelson. After a rapid exchange of letters, Alan's gritty determination had paid off. In their desperation to get rid of the increasingly rebellious George, the Teacrosses had finally agreed to consider the possibility of adoption. It was in the hands of the lawyers now and Pam and Alan just had to hope that the authorities would view their case favourably and, in due course, issue a court order in their favour. Alan was determined to make it official and this seemed the only way of doing it.

George was delighted to find himself back in Lavender Road. Even the sight of his old home still in ruins on the other side of the street didn't dampen his pleasure. In fact he was intrigued to find a pair of ducks apparently living quite happily in the water-filled crater that had once been his front garden. It seemed he was prepared to put up with virtually anything so long as he was away from the hated Teacrosses.

'Please don't make me go back to those horrid people,' he said to Pam as she tucked him in on his first night. 'Please can I stay with you for ever?'

Pam had felt the tears welling in her eyes and blinked them back determinedly. 'I hope so,' she whispered, kissing him on the top of his blond head. 'I hope so.'

'I just hope to God the Teacrosses don't renege,' Alan said after George had finally fallen asleep.

Pam stared at him appalled. 'They wouldn't, would they?'

Alan grimaced as he shrugged on his Home Guard jacket. 'I wouldn't put it past them. And I suppose the council inspector could still turn us down.'

'Don't,' Pam shivered. 'We must look on the bright side. And we must do everything in our power to convince them we are the right people to have him.'

Later she was on the landing having just checked on George, when Bertie came in.

Bertie glanced at the door behind her. 'Is he here?'

Pam nodded stiffly. 'Yes, he's here.'

'Can I see him?'

She could hardly refuse. Silently she pushed the door open again and waved him in. 'For God's sake don't wake him,' she said.

Bertie would have to leave them, she thought, as she went back downstairs. Having a conscientious objector in the house might well prejudice the council's decision. She knew the Teacrosses didn't like it. She would make Alan talk to him. Tonight. As soon as he came in from Home Guard duty.

It was several minutes later that she realised she hadn't heard Bertie leave George's room. Quickly she ran back upstairs and tiptoed along the passage. The door was still open but there was no sound from inside.

Going in, to her astonishment she found Bertie standing a yard from the small bed with tears dripping unhindered down his face.

In horror she glanced at George, but he was sleeping peacefully, slewed across the bed, one small pyjamaed arm up on the pillow.

Pam took another step forward. 'Bertie?'

For a moment he didn't speak then he drew his arm across his eyes and sniffed back his tears. 'I know what you are thinking, Mrs Nelson,' he said in a low husky voice. 'I know you want me to go. But you needn't worry. I'm going.' He took a quick breath. 'I'm going to join up. I've decided.'

Pam couldn't believe her ears. She opened her mouth to speak, but nothing came out.

He squared his shoulders. 'I've been thinking about it ever since Sheila died. I still think fighting is wrong,' he said quickly. 'But I can see now that there's no choice. I thought we should negotiate like Russia negotiated. But since Hitler has invaded Russia there's no excuse any more. And I don't like people thinking I'm a coward.'

Pam felt oddly moved. She didn't quite follow his logic but there was no doubt the spirit of it was good. 'I'm very impressed,' she said at last. She saw his faint scepticism and touched his arm. 'I really am, Bertie. It's a brave decision. And your parents will be so proud of you.'

He looked shocked. 'Please don't tell my parents, Mrs Nelson. Not yet. Mr father will want me to join his old regiment and I don't want to. I don't want him interfering. Not after the way he's treated me. I want to do it my own way. As anonymously as possible.'

Katy stared at Mr Poole in horror. 'What do you mean a delay?'

It was already the end of July. Her mother was due back next week. And Katy wanted it to be all finished by then. She had hoped to be opening by the middle of August. She simply couldn't afford to keep paying rent on the building. It needed to start earning. And earning soon. What money she had was running out faster than she had anticipated. The redecoration was costing more than the brewery had agreed to pay. And there was so much equipment to buy. Glasses, ashtrays, tables, chairs, let alone all the bits and pieces she had needed to make the flat upstairs habitable again. Even with Aaref's help it was hard to find the things she wanted. Even basic things like linen and blankets. And scarcity made everything so expensive.

If it hadn't been for her friends and neighbours she knew she would have been doomed. But thanks to their generosity she was beginning to make progress. Pam Nelson had given her free run of her wardrobe. The Miss Taylors, had said she could have anything salvageable from their house. Mrs Frost wrote to say she had a piano in storage in Croydon which, if Katy could collect, she could borrow. Even the mysterious Mrs d'Arcy Billière had appeared one morning with four enormous red velvet curtains.

Gradually the pub cellar was becoming more and more like a junk shop and Katy was desperate to get it sorted out so she could clean up before the beer arrived.

She looked at Mr Poole now and frowned. 'How long a delay?'

Mr Poole shuffled his feet and avoided her eyes. 'A couple of weeks, I reckon.'

Katy's eyes narrowed. 'Tell me straight, Mr Poole. I don't want any more vague estimates. I'm about to hire staff and put in my drinks orders and I need to know. When will it be ready?'

Ken Poole took the pencil out from behind his ear and scratched his head with it. 'It's hard to say, Mrs Frazer,' he said nervously. 'You see, there's a problem getting the piping for the water pipes.' He saw Katy's expression and hurried on. 'They was all damaged in the explosion. We hadn't realised and now we've got to take up the floors again. And then there's the glass for the windows . . .'

'Mr Poole,' Katy said firmly. 'I don't want excuses, I want a date. I want a date we can all stick to. I shall be sending out invitations to the opening night and I don't want my customers having to clamber about over a building site to get a drink.' Forcing herself to meet his eyes she folded her arms across her chest and looked at him expectantly. The invitations had been Louise's idea. Better than advertising, they agreed. More personal. And it was something for people to put on their mantelpiece. Something to talk about. To get the word round.

Mr Poole certainly looked impressed. He sucked his yellow teeth and eyed her warily. 'OK.' he said, reluctantly, at last. 'I reckon we'll be through before the end of the month.'

Katy took a quick breath. 'In that case,' she said firmly, 'We'll open on the twenty-fifth of August.' Ignoring a sinking feeling in the pit of her stomach, she held out her hand with a smile. 'Shall we shake on it?'

Mr Poole shook his head sadly but took her hand. 'You're a hard woman, Mrs Frazer.'

Katy almost laughed. If only he knew. Inside she was shaking like a jelly. But she knew she had to act tough. It was her only chance. She couldn't afford to let them get the better of her.

It was Molly Coogan who had told her she was being too soft with the workmen. 'Take a leaf out of Sister Morris's book,' she had advised. 'Nobody gives her any nonsense.'

Katy had giggled. 'Nobody would dare.' But she knew Molly was right and she was determined to be stricter, not only with the workmen but also with her staff.

Which was another problem. As yet she had no staff. She reckoned she needed a full time barman, an evening helper and a twice-weekly pianist.

Several men on hearing that the pub was reopening had called to offer their services, but none of them had seemed quite right. Either they were over-confident or they were slimy. Mostly they had been condescending. One had even laughed openly at the idea of working for a woman. After her experiences with Barry Fish, she wanted men she could trust.

Ideally she wanted Aaref Hoch. But Aaref had refused. He would help in an emergency, he said, but he didn't want to be tied down.

So she asked Pete Carter one evening when she found him tinkering with the clock in the cellar.

'I know you're busy with Mr Poole during the day, but I thought you might like to earn a bit extra in the evenings.'

But Pete Carter, blushing to the roots of his hair, had refused too. 'I'd like to, Mrs Frazer, I really would,' he mumbled. 'But I'd never manage all them different drinks.'

'I'm sure you'd pick it up quite quickly,' Katy said hopefully. 'We'll have a list of all the prices.'

But he shook his head. 'That's the problem,' he said, twisting a small spanner through his fingers. 'You see, I'm not much of a one for arithmetic.' He flushed even darker and scuffed the floor. 'I never really got the hang of adding up.'

'Oh.' Mortified for embarrassing him, Katy desperately tried to think of something positive to say but before she could he had looked up at her eagerly. 'What about my brother Mick, Mrs Frazer? He's in need of a job. And he's all right with figures and that.'

'Mick?' Katy stared at him appalled. Mick Carter was a horror. A menace. A complete pain in the neck. He always had been. And yet he'd held down his job at the brewery until his father's misdemeanour had got him the sack. And he knew about beer. And he was young enough to do what he was told and strong enough to heave barrels about.

Suddenly it didn't seem such a bad idea.

But when she asked him the following day, Mick Carter seemed hesitant. 'What I really want is to join the merchant marine,' he admitted shyly. 'I've put in a form. But I don't reckon as they'll take me because I'm too young and I haven't got a reference.'

Katy frowned. 'Well,' she said bracingly, 'if you work for me for a few months you'll be a bit older and I'll give you a good reference and then you'll stand a better chance.'

Mick nodded thoughtfully. 'All right then,' he said with a sudden cheeky grin. 'I quite fancy lording it about behind the bar.' Then he looked away, shuffling his feet awkwardly. 'I'm a bit cack-handed though. You won't be cross if I break anything, will you?'

Katy bit back a smile. 'I'll be very cross,' she said severely. 'Anything you break will be docked from your pay.'

Mr Cox of Cox's Ironmongers reminded Joyce of the rogue hen. He had the same way of poking his head forward to look at you and the same beady eyes. Unfortunately where the rogue hen mistrusted men, Mr Cox appeared to have a similar mistrust of women. It hadn't been easy to persuade him to see them.

'I'm not used to doing business with ladies,' he said after Celia and Joyce had looked round the dark old-fashioned shop and pronounced it a perfect size and location for the café. There was even a small kitchen at the back.

Celia smiled. 'I'm not used to doing business at all,' she said. 'But I dare say we shall manage. How much rent would you want for the shop, Mr Cox?'

Mr Cox looked rather taken aback at such a direct approach. He pulled his head back sharply. 'Well, hmm, I'd really rather discuss those details with your husband, Mrs Rutherford.'

'My husband?' Celia looked astonished. 'But it's nothing to do with my husband . . . oh!' She stopped abruptly as Joyce trod heavily on her foot.

'Mr Rutherford is away at the moment,' Joyce said quickly. She lowered her eyes significantly. 'On government business.'

'Oh.' Mr Cox looked momentarily impressed then he frowned and poked his head forward, eyeing Mrs Rutherford beadily. 'But he does know about this, er . . . venture? I assume it has his full backing?'

There was a moment's hesitation and Joyce's heart sank. Then Celia pushed her handbag up her arm and nodded. 'Yes, of course,' she lied crisply. 'It has his full support.'

Joyce sighed in relief but Mr Cox still looked doubtful. 'Well, I'll have to think about it,' he said. 'The price and that.'

Celia looked disappointed, but Joyce quickly cut in again. 'Of course,' she said briskly. 'But you'd better let us know as soon as you can because we've got a couple of other places to look at and it would be a shame to miss the boat.'

Back on the street, Celia looked at Joyce in admiration. 'You're a wonder, Mrs Carter,' she said. 'So where are these other properties, that's what I'd like to know!'

Joyce chuckled. 'Stands to reason,' she said. 'You don't want to seem too keen. Else he'll put the price up. Anyway,' she added with a grin, 'You gave him a bit of whitewash too, over your husband and that.'

Celia made a guilty face. 'Thank goodness Greville is away.' She hesitated for a second and glanced at Joyce who was still smiling at the thought of Mr Cox's sudden anxiety when she'd invented the other properties. 'What about your husband, Mrs Carter? He's not going to like our little plan very much either, is he?'

Stanley. Joyce sobered abruptly. Stanley wasn't going to like it at all. Momentarily she relived the brutal punching he had given her after that hen incident the other day and a cold, steely resolve spread through her body. 'Don't worry about him,' she said grimly, and as she said it a shiver suddenly ran down her spine. 'I want this far too much to let Stanley get in the way.'

For the first two weeks of August the news was mainly of the German advance into Russia and the devastation left in the wake of the Russian retreat as everything of possible use to the German invaders was destroyed in accordance with Stalin's scorched-earth policy. Already Tallinn, the capital of Estonia, in the north had been gutted by fire and a similar fate was expected for Odessa in the south as the Germans pushed on towards the Black Sea.

Japan was flexing its muscles in the Far East. Fighting continued on the Egyptian borders and in the Mediterranean, repeated attacks on British shipping were causing problems both to military and civilian supplies. And night after night British planes bombed German cities.

Listening to the gloomy news, Katy wondered if she was stupid to be attempting to reopen the pub. In the likelihood of renewed bombing and an expected autumn invasion it did indeed seem crazy.

But it was too late now. The invitations had gone out. Suddenly Saturday, the twenty-fifth of August had taken on a new significance. The Miss Taylors were even coming up from Bristol for it, and Jen and Mrs Frost had managed to arrange a night off from a series of concerts in Winchester.

And then Bertie Rutherford announced his change of heart and offered to help Katy out in the evenings until his call-up papers came through.

Suddenly it was all looking more hopeful. She'd found workers she could trust, and her friends would be on hand to give moral support, and Louise had promised faithfully to bring some people from Gregg Bros. Katy's mother's physiotherapy was progressing well down in Surrey. And with the newly signed Atlantic Charter it looked as though it was only a matter of time before America came into the war.

The only person who wasn't pleased was Molly Coogan. 'Now you've got all your fancy friends coming you won't need me,' she said crossly one evening as she helped Katy measure Mrs d'Arcy Billière's red velvet curtains against the windows in the saloon bar. 'I might as well tell Sister Morris I'll work that weekend after all.'

Katy glared at her. 'Don't you dare,' she said, through a mouthful of pins. 'I need you more than anyone. I especially need you to keep an eye on my mother. I don't know how she's going to take it all. I get the impression she's still quite worried about it.' She grimaced slightly. 'She's not the only one.' Then she took the pins out of her mouth and smiled. 'Anyway, Aaref will be there. He's promised to help behind the bar if it's busy.'

Molly flushed. 'Yes, but so will beastly Louise be there,' she said gloomily. 'Which means he won't give ugly old me a second glance.'

'You're not ugly,' Katy said hotly. 'Anyway, looks aren't everything, everyone knows that. I'm living proof. If it was just down to looks, Ward would have married Louise.'

Molly shook her head. 'You're pretty,' she said. 'And you've got character. You've got drive and ambition and guts. You've got everything.'

'I haven't got Ward,' Katy said.

For a moment they looked at each other in silence, then as Molly flushed scarlet and started stammering out an apology, Katy made a rueful face. 'And I haven't got those other things either,' she said. She waved her hand round the half-finished room. 'All this organising business is an act. You know that. Underneath I'm the same pathetic creature that cried every time Sister Morris told me off.'

Molly shook her head. 'You're not,' she said. 'You're different. I don't know why but you are.'

Katy laughed. 'If I was that different I would have found a pianist by now. I spent a fortune getting Mrs Frost's piano shifted up from Croydon and now I've got no one to play it. Let alone to sing.'

Molly frowned. 'What about that Jen? Why don't you get her to sing?'

Katy shook her head. She remembered only too clearly the occasion once before when she had asked Jen to sing in the pub and Jen had refused point blank. 'Jen's a professional singer,' she said now. 'She doesn't sing in pubs. No,' she sighed and picked up the red material. 'I'll find someone.' She giggled suddenly as she began to climb the step ladder. 'After all there's always Mr Fish.'

'No!' Molly grabbed her skirt and pulled her back. 'You're not going up there. The last thing we need is for you to fall down and have a miscarriage.'

★　★　★

Louise was listening to *The Brains Trust* on the wireless in the drawing-room when she heard her mother call. She groaned. It was bound to be about blasted Bertie. Yesterday Bertie had come round and announced that he'd decided to join up. There'd been a bit of a scene. Celia had got all emotional and had wanted him to move back to Cedars House until he was called up and Bertie had said he'd stay where he was thank you very much. The Nelsons hadn't been ashamed to take him in and he didn't see why his parents should take any credit for his change of heart.

As her father was away anyway, Louise had thought the whole thing was a fuss about nothing, but her mother had been quite upset and kept asking her to go and talk to Bertie.

'Louise?' Her mother's voice broke into her thoughts again. 'Are you coming or not?'

'What is it?' Louise called back irritably. 'What do you want?'

'There's someone on the telephone for you,' Celia called back. 'A young man. I didn't quite catch the name. It's not a very good line. Mack somebody, I think. Or Jack perhaps. Do you want me to ask?'

For a second it didn't sink in. Then Louise was out of her chair running into the hall like a rabbit out of a snare. Snatching the receiver out of her mother's hand, she pressed it to her ear.

'Hello?'

'Louise? This is Jack Delmaine. I don't know if you remember me, we met a—'

'Yes,' Louise interrupted breathlessly, aware of her mother's startled expression. 'I remember. Lucinda's party.'

'I'm glad you remember,' he said and even over the crackling line she sensed a smile in his voice, and wished she hadn't sounded quite so eager. 'I've been held up here,' he went on, 'But I'll be back in London for a night at the end of next week and I've managed to get hold of a couple of tickets for that Noël Coward play, *Blithe Spirit*. It's had rather good notices. I wondered if you'd like to go with me.'

466

'I'd love to,' Louise almost shouted down the receiver. 'When is it? Which night?'

Even as she asked the question, she knew what the answer was going to be.

She was right.

'It's the Saturday,' he said. 'The twenty-fifth.'

Louise closed her eyes and lowered the phone.

She couldn't believe it. How could she be so unlucky? Opening her eyes again she stared miserably at the wall. She couldn't let Katy down.

Or could she?

She frowned. Katy would understand. Wouldn't she? There'd be other people there after all. Other friends.

Friends. Louise groaned inwardly.

She heard Jack Delmaine's voice coming through the receiver and put it back to her ear. 'Louise? Are you still there?' The sudden urgency in his voice sent a shiver of excitement curling round her stomach. 'This is a trunk call. I haven't got long.'

Louise swallowed hard. 'Jack, I . . .' She stopped and clenched her eyes for a moment as the conflicting emotions closed her throat. 'I . . . I can't make that night,' she said bravely. 'A friend of mine is opening a pub just down the road. I've promised to be there. I can't let her down.'

'A pub?' Jack Delmaine sounded astonished and Louise's heart twisted. She heard his exhaled breath. 'Oh well. Not to worry. Maybe another time.'

Louise felt awful. She didn't want another time. She wanted this time. Suddenly she hated Katy and her beastly pub. But before she could change her mind she heard the operator telling him his time was up.

'Louise, I've got to go,' he said. 'I'm sorry I won't see you, but I hope the er . . . pub opening goes well. Goodbye.'

Louise felt the tears in her eyes. It sounded so final. 'Why don't you come?' she shouted down the line. 'Give the theatre

467

tickets to someone else. Most people would kill for tickets to that show.'

She heard him laugh. 'I already killed someone to get them.' There was a second's pause then his distant voice. 'I'll see what I can do.' Then the line went dead.

Chapter Twenty-Six

In the end Mrs Parsons came home on the twenty-fourth of August, the day before the pub was due to open.

Katy went down to meet her at Clapham Junction. As they came back up the hill on the bus, Katy brought her up to date on the local news, how poor Pam and Alan Nelson were even now in court, hearing whether their application to adopt George Whitehead was approved, how Celia Rutherford and Joyce Carter were trying to get a premises for a café while Mr Rutherford's back was turned, and how in his absence Bertie Rutherford had decided to join up.

But her mother seemed more concerned by the state of the area than by the local gossip.

'It's all so dirty,' she said despondently as they walked along Lavender Road. 'And so grey. Goodness, you should have seen it down in Haslemere. Green as anything. You'd never have known there was a war on.'

Suddenly Katy was glad she had asked Mr Poole to finish painting the outside of the pub this morning, so the remaining scaffolding and ladders could be down for her mother's arrival. Even if the rest of Lavender Road was potholed with rubble filled craters and the houses shabby and boarded up, at least the Flag and Garter façade would shine out like a beacon of newness.

And shine it did. Stopping them in their tracks in amazement as the hot August sun almost blinded them as it reflected off the new paintwork. Even Katy was surprised. Then she realised what it was.

'The paint's still wet,' she said, laughing nervously. 'It'll be all right when it dries.' She stood back, admiring the effect. 'What do you think of the blue? It's the closest match to the old colour we could find.'

Her mother didn't answer and glancing round Katy saw her eyes were riveted to the new licence board over the door neatly inscribed with the words, 'Licensed proprietors: Mrs M. Parsons and Mrs K. Frazer.'

As the import of those few words sank in, for a second Katy's courage nearly failed her. What had she done? All the stifled fears of the last few weeks suddenly welled together in a choking stab of emotion. Was it going to work? Would they get enough customers? Would she be able to manage the accounts? The intricacies of the beer? Would they make any money or would the whole thing collapse, leaving them saddled for ever with debt?

Standing there looking at the building she had so painstakingly had rebuilt and redecorated, Katy wished she was a child again and could bury her face in her mother's shoulder, or better still run inside and hide in a cupboard until someone came to tell her that it was all over. She glanced hopefully at her mother, longing to abdicate all responsibility, or at least to share the burden, longing for the comfort of maternal reassurance.

But it didn't come. Her mother was suddenly white faced and trembling. And quickly, before her own nerve broke, Katy opened the door and ushered her inside.

Here again she was pleased to see that Mr Poole had followed her instructions. The paint-spattered dustsheets had been removed and the somewhat motley selection of tables and chairs had been neatly arranged around the fireplace.

Katy's eyes flicked quickly round the room, seeing it as though for the first time. It was the same wooden bar, not as smooth as it had been in her father's day, admittedly, but quite serviceable. She and Mick Carter had sandpapered and waxed it endlessly to cover the dents and blemishes from the blast and restore the shine.

Behind it the dresser was less recognisable. Too badly burnt in the flash fire caused by the spilt spirits to be left as bare wood, Katy had got Pete Carter to fix in some new shelves and then rub it down and paint it the same blue as the façade. It looked a bit empty now but once the bottles and tankards were on it, she thought it would look pretty good.

Next to the dresser was the gap where the grandfather clock would go if ever Pete managed to fix it. She glanced at her mother, remembering that was the spot her father had died, and quickly moved on to the saloon bar.

Mr Poole and one of his workmen were up on a trestle finishing off round the windows. Behind them the Miss Taylors' old armchairs, retrieved from the ruins of their house, made a cosy circle by the fire and on the counter Mrs d'Arcy Billière's cut-down red velvet curtains waited to be hung. Just inside the door two buckets of sand, a broom, a red fire bucket and a stirrup pump were lined up against the newly painted wall. Katy grimaced slightly as her mother's gaze stopped on them for a moment. Perhaps she should have kept them out of sight. But having gone to all this effort, she was damned if a stray German incendiary was going to spoil it again.

Climbing down off his ladder Mr Poole wiped his hand on his overalls, ready to shake hands.

As Katy introduced them, she waited for her mother to take control. To stake her claim on the business. To make her number with the workmen.

But she didn't, and suddenly Katy realised she wasn't going to. Her mother had never been strong, she remembered; it had always been her father who had made the decisions, her mother who had worried about them. Suddenly in a flash of understanding she realised why Sister Morris had sent her mother away – to give Katy a chance to take control.

Certainly after an initial hesitation, Mr Poole seemed to have no doubt about who was still in charge. 'We've only got the bits and pieces to finish off now,' he said deferentially to Katy. 'The light fittings and the curtain rails and that. But we'll see to those tomorrow.'

Tomorrow. Jerking herself out of her thoughts, Katy looked around. There were so many things still to be done before six thirty tomorrow night. The drink to unpack, the beer to prepare, the price list to work out, the glasses to wash and polish, the curtains to hang, the flowers to pick. Feeling her heart quail, she glanced bravely at her mother.

'You see,' she forced a bright confident smile on to her dry lips. 'We're nearly ready.'

'So,' Katy said as they went upstairs a minute later. 'What do you think?' To her dismay her mother's eyes filled with tears. 'Mummy, what's the matter? Don't cry. Don't you like it?'

'Of course I like it,' Mary Parsons sobbed. 'It's just like it was when Malcolm and I first moved in all those years ago. All clean and spick and span.' She wiped her eyes and dabbed her nose pitifully. 'But we can't run it, Katy. Not you and me. You don't know what it's like. It's a man's job.'

Katy sat on the chair opposite and leaned forward. 'Of course we can run it,' she said. 'We've got men to help us with the heavy jobs. Mick Carter and Bertie.'

Her mother looked at her strangely. 'You're so strong, Katy. You're stronger than me. It's funny. I never knew.'

Katy shook her head. 'I'm not strong. Not really.' She hesitated. 'It's just that we haven't much choice. We have to earn some money somehow. If it doesn't work we'll have to give up the lease at Christmas anyway.'

'You should have stayed with that nursing.'

Katy looked down at her hands. At the two rings on her third finger. She swallowed. She dearly wanted to tell her mother about the baby. Luckily the lump was still small enough to be concealed beneath her loose summer blouse. Sooner or later she would have to confess. But suddenly she knew that now wasn't the moment. Her mother was too anxious about the pub venture as it was. How on earth would she react if she thought that by Christmas they would be having to cope with a baby as well?

'We need somewhere to live,' Katy said. She stood up and took a steadying breath. 'And of course, it's still possible that Ward will come home.'

Her mother dabbed her eyes. 'But what if he doesn't? Who will look after us then?'

Katy looked down at her. 'We'll manage,' she said lightly. As she went into the kitchen to make the tea she put a hand on her stomach and added quietly to herself, 'We'll have to.'

Joyce was panting as she let herself into the house. It was a baking hot afternoon. And it had seemed a long pull up from the shops. If she hadn't had a letter from young Angie in Devon saying she was hoping to come up for a few days next week she wouldn't have bothered. Stanley and the boys could lump it as far as she was concerned, but if Angie was coming she'd have to try and give her some decent food. But it had been a job deciding what to get and the Friday afternoon queues had nearly finished her off.

She was looking forward to a nice cup of tea and a nice quiet read of the evening paper. Expecting the kitchen to be empty she was disconcerted to find Mick standing at the sink and even more disconcerted when she saw the dark red bruise around his eye.

'What happened to you?' she asked, putting her shopping basket on the table.

Mick flushed slightly. 'Tripped over a dustbin in the blackout last night.'

Joyce frowned. She'd used that excuse too often herself to be taken in by it. 'You want to watch out getting into brawls,' she said.

'Katy Parsons won't want you serving behind the bar with a black eye.'

Mick swung round angrily. 'I wasn't in a brawl,' he said. To her astonishment there were tears in his eyes. 'It wasn't my fault. Why do you always think the worst of me?'

Joyce looked at him in some surprise. She did always think the worst of him. Everyone did. It was true. It had become a kind of habit. She shrugged her shoulders. 'I don't know,' she said.

'Well, it's not fair,' Mick said. 'It's not my fault things go wrong. I know I've done things wrong in the past but I've been trying to be better. I've been trying to keep my nose clean. But it's not easy round here. I didn't want to lose my job. But nobody feels sorry for me, do they? Oh no, nobody cares about me.' He kicked the floor bitterly. 'I was doing all right at the brewery and all until Dad started there.'

He stopped for a second and then went on bitterly, 'I wish I'd shot Dad that time, not Lorenz. That Lorenz is all right. Better than Dad. Well, I'm going to show you all. I'm getting out of here as soon as I can. Before I get dragged down.'

Joyce stared at him. She had always thought Mick was so fond of his dad. Always trying to impress him. Suddenly she knew what had happened. Why he was so bitter. She looked at the bruise more carefully. 'It was your dad what hit you, wasn't it?'

Mick hesitated. 'You ought to know,' he muttered. Then as she flushed angrily he went on quickly, 'You don't have to get angry. I know how he treats you. It's not right. Mr Nelson doesn't hit Mrs Nelson around.'

Joyce gritted her teeth. 'Why did he hit you? What did you do to annoy him?'

'It's what I didn't do,' Mick said. He suddenly slumped down at the table and put his head in his hands. 'What I wouldn't do. I don't want to get dragged into it. I want to do something with my life I don't want to spend it in and out of jail.'

To her surprise Joyce felt a stab of respect for her errant son

Reaching for the kettle she filled it and lit the gas ring on the stove. Then she sat down opposite him. 'What did he want you to do?'

There was a long pause. Then Mick looked up bleakly. 'He wanted me to get a copy of the pub key for him.'

Joyce blinked. 'The pub?'

He nodded wearily. 'The Flag and Garter. They want to clean it out. It's that bugger Fish what used to be the pianist. He's been badmouthing Katy Frazer around the place. Says she did him down on money he was owed.' Mick's jaw clenched. 'Dad reckoned it would hurt Rutherford & Berry too, but I don't know. I reckon it would just hurt Katy. And it's not fair. She's a good sort.'

Joyce felt the rage mount in her like a red hot furnace. 'The bastard,' she whispered. 'The absolute bastard.'

Mick swallowed. 'When I said I wouldn't do it, Dad hit me.' He shivered suddenly and looked at Joyce with scared eyes. 'I don't know what to do, Mum.'

'Well, I know exactly what to do.' Joyce slammed her hands down on the table and stood up. 'I'm going to the police. God,' she could hardly speak for anger, 'to think what that Katy has gone through already.'

It was Mick's turn to look amazed. 'You wouldn't?'

Joyce reached grimly for her coat. 'I would.'

Mick stood up and grabbed her arm. 'Mum, you can't. You can't trust the police. He'd kill you if he found out.'

They both jumped as a knock came at the front door. Hurrying along the passage Joyce took receipt of a telegram. She looked at it blankly and then at Mick.

'It's for you.'

With trembling fingers Mick opened the flimsy envelope. Then he paled. Joyce saw the breath rise in him as he looked up, a mixture of excitement and fear shining in his eyes.

'It's the merchant marine. I'm to join a ship in Liverpool . . . tomorrow.'

Suddenly Joyce felt a stab of emotion. There were tears in her eyes.

For a moment they stared at each other then Mick cleared his throat. 'I'll see to the police,' he said, shakily. 'Tomorrow morning. Dad and Fish are pulling a job down St John's Road after the shops shut. I heard them talking about it. If the coppers time it right they'd catch them red-handed.' He looked at Joyce nervously. 'I'll be long gone by the time they find out.'

Pam and Alan sat on the hard bench with George between them and watched the judge ponderously rearranging the documents in front of him. The council report had been given. The Teacrosses' consent papers were in order. Now they just waited for his decision. They had been waiting months for this moment. Let alone all day.

Looking across George's head at Alan, Pam saw the tension in his jaw and felt her own stomach clench. Inadvertently she squeezed George's hand too tight and he made a slight squeak of protest.

At once the judge looked up, his expression stern. Meeting his steely eyes for a moment, Pam felt her heart contract. He's going to refuse, she thought. I know it. He's going to turn us down.

She was so convinced of it, that for a moment she couldn't make sense of what he was saying. It was only when Alan pulled her to her feet that she realised they had been asked to stand.

The judge's voice was unemotional. 'I am required to ensure that due consent has been given and that the adoption is in the best interest of the child.'

There was a long pause during which Pam found she was shivering convulsively and then he went on. 'I am satisfied that these tests have been met.'

He tapped his desk sharply. 'I hereby make an adoption order in respect of George Joseph Whitehead in favour of Mr and Mrs Alan Nelson of Lavender Road, Clapham.'

For a second Pam stood rigidly still and then she sank back into her seat and burst into tears. The next thing she knew George was clinging to her arm shouting that he didn't want to be sent away. 'I won't go,' he screamed. 'I want to stay with Auntie Pam.'

As the ushers came hurrying forward in shocked alarm, dimly she heard Alan trying to reassure George that it was all right. That they had won the case. That nobody could take him away now.

'Why is she crying, then?' George shouted, pummelling Pam's back. 'Why is she sad?'

Pam pulled him into her arms. 'I'm not sad,' she said. 'I'm crying because I'm happy.' She looked up and met Alan's gentle eyes. 'So happy.'

Katy stared at the barrel of draught on the counter and felt her knees shake. Picking up the mallet determinedly she told herself not to be so pathetic. It was only a matter of driving in the spike, turning it gently to let a bit of gas out then tightening it up to keep the beer nice and fresh until she put the tap in later. She'd seen her father do it often enough.

For a second she closed her eyes and leaned on the counter. If only Ward was here. He'd know how to do it. She felt a sob rise in her throat and tried to bite it back. She was tired. Tired and scared. It was all very well pretending to be confident and in control. But it was exhausting.

She had hardly slept a wink last night. The news that Mick was abandoning her for the merchant marine had been a body blow. Since she had reluctantly taken him on he had worked hard, willingly heaving furniture around, sorting out the deliveries, taking time to learn the prices. She knew she was going to miss his rough and ready good humour. And when she finally had slept, her usual dream of Ward's prostrate body being riddled with German bullets was interspersed with people banging their glasses on the bar shouting for service, and angry men complaining about the beer.

Earlier this morning in desperation she had accepted Bob Carter' offer of help.

'But I thought you had a bad back,' she said doubtfully, thinkin, of all the crates that still needed hauling up from the cellar.

He grinned. 'Not so bad I'd turn down a couple of quid,' he saic 'That's what Mick said you'd give me.'

Somewhat daunted Katy nodded. 'Well, yes, but it's hard work What with the barrels and that.'

Bob tapped his nose conspiratorially. 'Between you and m Katy, there's nothing wrong with my back. It's just that I've g this little chorus girl up in the West End and to be honest I'd rathe spend time with her than dodging bullets. Know what I mean?'

Katy did know and she didn't like the thought that she wa hiring a deserter. But beggars couldn't be choosers, she told herse sternly, as she sent him down to help Bertie in the cellar.

She had the same thought again half an hour later when a rathe seedy-looking fellow knocked furtively on the door and presente himself to her as a pianist and singer. Heart sinking, she showed hir to the piano and asked him to play a couple of numbers and althoug his tempo was somewhat awry, and his voice thin, he did appear t know one or two tunes.

'All right,' she said helplessly. At least it would be backgroun noise if nothing else. 'We'll see how it goes tonight. Will you mak sure you're here by six thirty?'

He stood up and smiled ingratiatingly. 'Wouldn't say no to a touc of money up front, love. Just to keep me going, like.'

Guessing that if she refused, she'd never see him again, Katy sighe and went to the till and took out half a crown. 'Mind you com though,' she said sternly as he pocketed the coin. 'Six thirty.'

Now as she leaned wearily on the counter, she suddenly kne he wouldn't come. Maybe nobody would come and she would b doomed.

She glanced at her watch. Her mother should be back from th shops soon, hopefully armed with the doilies and wood polish Kat had asked her to buy, and then she would be into another round of patient reassurance.

Earlier her mother had started worrying about the glasses. 'They're all different sizes. You can't serve drinks in all different sizes.'

Katy had gritted her teeth. 'They're the only ones we could find,' she said. 'Glasses aren't that easy to come by at the moment.'

Her mother had sniffed back a tear. 'Your father was always most particular about his glasses.'

Katy sighed. If only one of her friends was here to give her some moral support. But Molly was on duty until five, Louise didn't finish her shift until six and Jen hadn't arrived yet from the South Coast. The Miss Taylors were here, she had met them off the train earlier and taken them down to Cedars House where Mrs Rutherford had kindly offered to put them up. But she could hardly go and cry on their shoulders. They were worried to death about Ward as it was.

No, Katy lifted the mallet and the spike and squared her shoulders. She was on her own and she might as well get used to it.

'Bertie? Bob?' She shouted imperiously. 'Come up here a minute. I want to show you how to spike the draught.'

And then she lost Bertie. She couldn't believe it. They had just arranged the shorts and spirits on the dresser, fixed the new optics and stood back to admire the effect when Pam Nelson rushed in with little George at her heels brandishing a telegram for Bertie.

Katy knew instantly what it was going to be, and closed her eyes in despair.

'Oh, my God,' Bertie exclaimed, reading it in dawning horror, 'I've got to report to the Winchester depot at eight o'clock tomorrow morning.' He looked up incredulously. 'But tomorrow's a Sunday.'

'I don't think Sundays make much difference if you're at war,' Pam said dryly. 'Hitler certainly doesn't seem to notice them.'

'Mr Hitler is a horrid man,' George chipped in suddenly. 'He killed my mummy and my daddy. When I'm grown up I'm going to go and kill him. He lives in Germany.'

As Bertie and Bob grinned uneasily, Katy and Pam exchanged a glance. 'I hope we don't have to wait that long,' Pam murmured.

Bertie laughed nervously. 'Maybe I'll kill him,' he said. 'That would be a turn-up for the books, wouldn't it?' When nobody answered immediately, he flushed slightly. 'I suppose I ought to go and get myself sorted out, but . . .' He glanced hesitantly at the phalanx of glasses waiting to be washed and polished and then at Katy.

Katy braced herself. Thank goodness she still had Aaref in reserve. 'You go,' she said. 'There must be a million things for you to do. Come back later for a goodbye drink.'

Bertie nodded. He suddenly seemed rather pale as he tried to smile. 'Thanks,' he said picking up his jacket and slinging it over his shoulder. 'I will. In any case I'll need a drink by then.'

'Poor bloody blighter,' Bob muttered as he went out. 'Rather him than me.'

Pam touched Katy's arm. 'Is there anything I can do to help?'

Katy shook her head. 'It's all right. Miraculously, everything's pretty much ready. It's only really the glasses to do now and Mummy will be back in a minute. I'll set her to work on those. It'll give her something to do.' Mindful of her business, she glanced at Pam hopefully. 'You and Alan are coming back later too, aren't you?' She nodded across at George who was now perched happily on top of the pile of empty crates. 'After all, you've got something to celebrate now.'

Pam smiled. 'It's wonderful, isn't it? I still can't quite believe it.' She hesitated. 'We'd love to come, but we can't really bring George in, can we?'

'Why not?' Katy said. 'The more the merrier.' She grinned ruefully. 'At the rate I'm losing staff, I might be glad of him behind the bar.'

★　★　★

Joyce couldn't settle. She was like a cat on hot bricks. Since Mick had left this morning she'd had an ear on the front door. All afternoon she had been expecting a knock on the door, a policeman to be standing there, to tell her Stanley had been arrested, so when Stanley himself strolled in she nearly jumped out of her skin.

His eyes narrowed suspiciously as she stared at him in horror. 'What's the matter with you?'

'Nothing.' But she could feel the guilty flush staining her cheeks. She realised he was looking pleased with himself, that smug look he had, the secret smile and the glittering eyes that boded ill for later. Of all his looks she hated that one the most. I hate him, she thought. I really hate him.

He took a menacing step towards her. 'Then what are you looking at?'

She flinched back and hated herself for it. 'Nothing.'

He laughed sourly, pleased by her fear, and pushed open the sitting-room door. 'Then bring me a cup of tea, woman, and make it snappy.'

In the kitchen she found her hands were shaking. What had gone wrong? Where were the police? Mick's information must have been wrong. The wrong place. The wrong time. Or when it came to it, had Mick chickened out?

Bloody Mick. She was shaking so much she scattered the tea leaves over the table and had to spend a minute scraping them up.

As she poured in the boiling water she realised she didn't know what to do. Should she go to the police herself? Or was it too late? Or should she warn Katy? Or what?

She looked at the clock. Six o'clock. The poor child would be opening up soon. She couldn't worry her with it now. She was bound to be nervous enough as it was.

Joyce's own nerves were jangling as she carried the tea through to Stanley. If she stayed in the house a moment longer she would flip.

'I'm going over to the pub,' she said abruptly. 'See if I can give Katy Frazer a hand. She's opening in half an hour.'

Stanley barely looked up from the paper. 'I'll be over myself in a minute.' He smiled to himself. 'Don't want to miss opening night at the Flag. I reckon she should do quite a bit of business tonight.'

Chapter Twenty-Seven

Katy was frantic. It was twenty past six and her mother still hadn't come back from the shops. In the saloon bar Louise and Molly were arguing about the arrangement of the cushions. Mrs Frost was busy hemming up a curtain that had dropped. Jen had gone off to fetch the Miss Taylors. At the other end of the bar, Mrs Carter, looking drawn, was carefully stacking the last of the glasses.

Five minutes ago Aaref had arrived with a huge bunch of flowers. Immediately Katy had grabbed him. 'You're going to have to help after all. I've lost Bertie.' She thrust her carefully copied price list under his nose. 'Here. Can you try and learn these? There's no Irish whiskey, remember, nor much in the way of liqueurs. And only two dozen Guinness. But there's plenty of beer. Both draught and light. But mind you don't get too much head on it.'

Aaref looked bemused. 'Head? What is this?'

As Katy groaned, Bob leaned over the bar. 'Don't worry, Katy, love. I'll show him, I've got the hang of it now.'

Aware that in the process of getting the hang of it, Bob had poured and consumed several pints of beer himself, Katy nodded nervously and hoped that when the doors opened the rush of customers would prevent him from partaking of any more.

Already she could hear them queuing up outside.

Time was getting tight. The pianist predictably hadn't arrived. Calling to Molly to stop anyone coming in until six thirty, Katy thrust the flowers at Louise and was just about to run upstairs to change when a great shout came from the cellar.

Pete Carter had got the clock going.

'Quick!' Running back down the stairs, Katy called to Bob and Aaref. 'Can you help him bring it up?' It was her dearest wish to have her father's old clock ticking in the bar on opening night. It was like a symbol. Almost as though her father himself was present.

As she turned round, Molly grabbed her arm. 'Katy, there's two men at the door asking for Bob.'

Katy blinked. 'What sort of men?'

Molly grimaced. 'Soldiers.' She lowered her voice. 'I think they might be military police.'

'Oh no!' Katy stared around frantically. One glimpse of Bob heaving the heavy old clock up the cellar steps would be enough for the policemen to know he was a malingerer. And then she'd have lost yet another barman. Already she could hear the two boys groaning below as they took the clock's weight. 'Stop them,' she hissed at Molly. 'And tell Bob for goodness' sake to stay out of sight while I try and get rid of them.'

But getting rid of the military policemen was not all that easy. 'He's not here,' she said. 'I believe he's gone up to the West End tonight.'

The taller of the two sighed. 'Damn. We'll never find him up there.' They looked around hopefully. 'Just opening, are you?'

'Well, yes, but . . .' Katy stopped and stared at them aghast as she realised their intention.

They grinned. 'We'll stay for a couple of pints, then. If that's all right?'

Katy heard Molly's choked chuckle behind her. 'Of course,' she said helplessly. 'But I'm afraid you'll have to wait outside until half past six.'

The clock was blocking the cellar steps completely now. Aaref seemed to be trapped at the bottom. There was no sign of Bob Carter.

484

'He's scarpered out the back,' Molly said. 'I reckon that's the last we'll see of him tonight.'

Katy grabbed Pete's arm. 'Pete. You'll have to serve.'

Pete recoiled in horror. 'I can't, Mrs Frazer. Please. I told you, I can't add up.'

There were people outside. Katy could see them through the glass. She could hear them grumbling. It must be half past six. She looked around frantically. In a minute she was going to have to open the doors. Let them in. To a bar with no staff.

And then behind her the door opened and she heard her mother's voice. 'Katy? Look who I found.'

Swinging round she felt all the blood drain from her face. Standing there in the doorway, arm in arm with her mother, was Barry Fish.

Mary Parsons was smiling happily. 'Now we'll be all right. Barry will look after things for us.' She turned to her companion and looked up at him trustingly. 'Won't you?'

Barry Fish's ingratiating smile was hampered by his wary glance at Katy. 'With pleasure, Mary. With pleasure.'

Katy ran forward and stopped in front of them, barring their way. 'No,' she heard herself say. 'Mr Fish will *not* look after things for us, Mummy.'

Her mother looked shocked. 'But Katy, he knows all about it.'

'He knows far too much about it,' Katy said grimly. 'And he's not setting another foot in my pub.'

Behind her she sensed Pete Carter muscling forward. She was aware of a rustle of interest in the crowd on the pavement. She was aware she was making a fool of herself but she suddenly didn't care. It was her pub, her business, and she wasn't going to have beastly Barry Fish spoiling it for her.

'Come on now, Katy,' Barry Fish murmured. 'Be reasonable. Let bygones be bygones, eh?' He winked at her mother. 'Who's in charge here, anyway?'

Hearing footsteps behind her, Katy glanced round and found Molly and Louise shoulder to shoulder with Pete, their faces grim.

Behind them stood Mrs Frost and Joyce Carter, white faced and grimmer still.

Turning back to Mr Fish, Katy met his challenge head on. 'I am,' she said grittily.

And then before anyone could move, suddenly there was shouting in the street, a scuffle. Katy heard the word 'police'.

As the crowd parted nervously, in the middle of the road she saw Stanley Carter flailing and struggling as grim-faced policemen dragged his arms behind his back. 'Oi, what you doing?' he was shouting. 'I ain't done nothing.'

Another policeman was pointing at Barry Fish. 'That's him,' he shouted. 'That's the ringleader. Stop that man.'

Instantly Barry Fish broke and ran, barging through the crowd with Mary Parsons still attached to his arm. Frantically he tried to shake her off. 'Let me go, you stupid bitch,' he screamed at her as she clung on helplessly. But it was too late. Her leechlike grip had held him up and the two military police darted out of the crowd and were on to him, felling him to the ground almost before anyone knew what had happened.

If it hadn't been so awful it would have been funny. But even as the Clapham policemen snapped on the cuffs and led their victims away, Mary Parsons, alone and abandoned in the road, started to cry.

At once Katy left her position on the step. 'Mummy,' she said, running forward. 'It's all right. You weren't to know. But Barry Fish was a criminal. He'd stolen from Daddy.'

But her mother was inconsolable. 'I can't bear it,' she wailed, gripping Katy's arm with the same vicelike grip she had used on the pianist. 'I can't bear it.'

Helplessly, Katy glanced round. Now the fun was over, the crowd was getting restless again. They wanted to drink. But her mother seemed reluctant to go back to the pub.

'I can't, I can't,' she wailed. 'There's too many memories.'

Suddenly Katy found Jen and Molly Coogan at her side. 'Take her to Mrs Nelson,' Jen suggested. 'She'll look after her.'

'But what about the pub?' Katy said. 'Aaref's trapped in the cellar.'

'Goodness,' Molly giggled. 'You're out of date. One sniff of the police and Aaref was over that clock and out the back door.' She saw Katy's horrified expression and squared her shoulders. 'Don't worry. Us girls will manage for now.' She glanced grittily at Jen, her old rival. 'After all, what are friends for?'

Taking her mother to Pam Nelson was a good idea of Jen's. Not surprisingly, after years of dealing with poor Sheila Whitehead, Pam was good at coping with hysterics. She seemed to know exactly what to do. Nevertheless Katy had to wait until her mother was comfortably settled at Pam's kitchen table with a cup of tea before she felt she could make her escape.

'We'll bring her over with us in a little while,' Pam murmured as Katy edged towards the door. 'Once she's feeling more like it.'

Having been desperate to get away, once she was back in the street Katy found she had a strange reluctance to go back to the pub. As she looked down the road at its bright blue façade, the newly painted black and red sign, she could feel her heart thudding in her chest. What was going on in there? What was happening to her carefully prepared beer?

For a second she had a vision of thirsty men falling on her precious bottles in a gleeful free-for-all, and all her profits flying out of the window. Then, wiping her damp palms on her skirt, she began to run down the road.

As she approached, two men went in and as the doors swung she could hear the strains of music. Music and laughter and voices raised in song.

Closer again she could hear the clink of glasses, the murmur of conversation, the squeak of leather soles on lino.

At the door she took a long steadying breath, then she pushed it open and went in.

At once the noise hit her like a wall.

Startled she stopped and stared. She had never seen anything like it. The pub was in chaos, packed so full people could hardly move. For a second she nearly panicked, but then she realised it was orderly chaos. Everyone was smiling. Everyone seemed to have a drink. There was a queue at the bar but no unseemly grappling. There were just masses of people, a thump of music and over it all a blue haze of cigarette smoke.

Unseen, Katy stood on tiptoe to see where the music was coming from and the breath caught in her throat.

Over in the corner Mrs Frost was at the piano and beside her Jen, as though born to be a tap-room singer, was belting out the words to 'Roll out the Barrel'. As she swept her arm theatrically around the room, rousing her chorus of drinkers, she caught Katy's eye and raised her hand to her forehead in an ironic salute.

Suddenly Katy realised what was happening and she felt choked with emotion.

The girls were in control.

Standing on a box behind the bar, Molly Coogan was cheerfully pulling pints. Beside her Joyce Carter was calling out the prices.

Through the gap, in the saloon bar, Katy could see Louise carefully measuring out a dry Martini and the fat woman from Louise's factory was collecting up dirty glasses. In the corner, the Miss Taylors were comfortably installed in their own armchairs, Winston, the dachshund, looking rather astonished by their side.

Then even as the tears filled her eyes, Katy caught sight of the two military policemen helping Pete Carter manoeuvre the grandfather clock up the cellar steps.

At once Molly Coogan started shouting for people to make way. 'Come on, shift over, give the lads a chance.'

'Cor,' someone exclaimed good naturedly as the clock's case bumped past their legs. 'It's that bleedin' clock. Wondered what had happened to that. Wouldn't be the same pub without that clock.' He winked at Molly as the military policemen began to sweat. 'Must weigh a bit though, eh?'

'If you don't move sharpish, you'll soon be finding out how much it bloody weighs,' Molly retorted. Then she grinned at the policemen. 'Hurry up, boys, I want to have it up and going by the time the boss comes back.'

Looking around vaguely, wondering who she was referring to, Katy suddenly felt a bubble of excited pride. That's me, she thought. I'm the boss.

Half laughing half crying, deeply touched, she rubbed the tears away with the back of her hand and began to push her way forward to join her self-appointed staff.

Joyce was glad to be busy. Once the first rush of orders was over she'd rolled up her sleeves and begun washing the empties. It kept her mind off Stanley's expression as he was hauled away by the police. Even though she had wanted it to happen, it was still a shock. He'd gone. Stanley. Her husband. Bubbled by his own son.

Trying not to think about it, she found herself worrying instead about her lack of any means of support. Winter would be on them soon with all the extra expenses of heating and clothing that cold weather involved. It was all very well for Mrs Rutherford to keep going on about the café, she thought, as she rinsed the glasses and stood them upside down on the drainer, but there was no sign of it actually happening. That hen-faced Mr Cox, the ironmonger, still hadn't made up his mind and Mr Rutherford would be back next week, and unless they'd got the lease on his shop signed and sealed before that, Joyce reckoned they might as well forget it.

With a deep sigh she looked up for the next tray of dirties and was startled to find Mr Lorenz watching her from the other side of the bar.

Resting his hands on the counter he leaned forward slightly. 'I'm sorry about your husband,' he murmured.

Joyce stared at him. Nobody else had had the guts to mention it, although she had noticed quite a few people casting her curious glances, whispering about it behind their hands when they thought she wasn't looking. Funny that Lorenz of all people should be the one to sympathise.

'I'm not sorry,' she said. 'He was a vicious, thieving bastard and I'm glad to be shot of him.'

Lorenz looked somewhat taken aback by her bluntness. She saw the quick sweep of his long black lashes behind his spectacles, the slight colour tingeing his sallow cheeks and felt guilty for embarrassing him. She forgot sometimes that other people didn't always call a spade a spade.

Then he looked up again and she saw sympathy in his eyes and something else, a certain shy awkwardness that made her frown. 'I was wondering,' he said hesitantly, his voice so low among the general clamour in the bar that she had to strain to hear it, 'If you would do me the honour of having dinner with me one night?'

Dinner? Joyce could hardly believe her ears. With Lorenz? As his words sank in she almost burst out laughing. Then she saw the flicker of disappointment cross his face and quickly stopped herself. Why shouldn't she let Mr Lorenz take her out to dinner after all? It couldn't do any harm. Stanley would soon be safely behind bars. She could do what she damn well liked. Suddenly she felt a tingle of excitement. Nobody had ever taken her out to dinner before. Not to a proper restaurant. The best she'd ever got off Stanley was fish and chips.

She had a momentary vision of being shown to her seat by a white-coated waiter, spreading a napkin elegantly over her lap, then suddenly her face fell.

'I can't,' she said. 'I'd like to. I'd like to very much but . . . I haven't got anything to wear. Not to a smart place.' She stopped abruptly, surprised by the force of her disappointment.

But Lorenz was leaning over the counter eagerly. 'Oh don't worry about that, Mrs Carter,' he said quickly. 'I still have that outfit you had earlier in the year.' He saw her surprise and spread his hands. 'I didn't like the thought of anyone else wearing it, so I kept it out the back.' He hesitated for a second then went on cautiously, 'Oh, and a rather nice coat came in yesterday. Lamb's wool, very warm. I think it would suit you rather well for the winter.'

Joyce felt a strange feeling of warmth coursing through her blood. She smiled and saw the answering smile in his dark eyes.

'All right then,' she said. 'You're on.'

'Katy.' Molly was at her side. 'We're running low on draught. There's plenty more in the barrel, but we can't get it out.'

Following her back to the bar, Katy frowned. 'We need to tilt it. I remember now, Dad used to have a kind of wedge. You don't want to keep tipping it or it stirs up the sediment. Here, I'll hold it. See if you can find something suitable.'

As she grappled with the barrel Molly groped under the counter. 'Here, what about this?' She stopped and her eyes widened incredulously. 'It's a blasted Bible. What are you doing with a Bible under the counter?'

Katy felt herself colouring. 'It's the one Sister Morris gave me,' she said. 'She thought it might come in useful.'

Molly giggled. 'She was right,' she said. 'It's the perfect size.'

'Molly, you can't,' Katy was shocked.

'Why not?' Molly slid it under the barrel. 'Look, it's made to measure.'

'It is a neat fit, but . . .' Cautiously releasing the barrel, Katy looked round nervously. 'Do you think God will mind?'

'Mind?' Molly sniffed. 'He should be pleased to help out. Let's face it, he's done bugger all else for you. It's about time he gave you a helping hand.'

Joyce found she wanted to tell someone about Lorenz's invitation. And somewhat to her surprise the person she wanted to tell was Mrs Rutherford. But peering round the heaving bar she was disappointed to realise that Mrs Rutherford wasn't there.

The Miss Taylors were there, though, in the saloon bar, and drying her hands quickly on an already damp cloth, Joyce left her post and pushed her way over to them. The old ladies were looking a bit tired and sad, she thought, as she approached. Poor old things. They had been badly brought down by Ward Frazer's disappearance.

But when they caught sight of her their wrinkled old faces lit up at once. 'Mrs Carter, how lovely to see you. We so enjoyed having you to stay with us that time.'

Gratified, Joyce didn't know whether to mention Ward or not. Deciding not, she asked about Mrs Rutherford instead.

'You're staying with her, aren't you? I know pubs aren't really her thing but I thought she might be coming down as it's the opening night and that. Did she say anything when you left?'

'Charming woman,' Esme said. 'Very courteous. Infinitely preferable to that dreadful husband of hers.'

'She was going to come with us,' Thelma said. 'But then a man called and she stayed behind.'

'A man?' Joyce asked in alarm. 'What sort of man?' Surely the dopey old women hadn't left poor Mrs Rutherford alone with some strange man.'

'Rather an odd-looking man actually,' Esme said. 'Did you notice, Thelma? He had an awfully scrawny neck.'

Joyce grabbed her arm. 'Like a chicken?' she asked urgently. 'Did he look like a chicken?'

Somewhat taken aback, the two old ladies looked at each other nervously. 'Well, yes,' Thelma ventured cautiously. 'Now you come to mention it, he did look a bit like a chicken.'

'Oh my goodness!' Joyce exclaimed and was all set to run straight up to Cedars House when the pub door opened and Mrs Rutherford came rather hesitantly through the blackout curtain.

Peering at her anxiously, Joyce saw her recoiling at the force of the noise, saw her uneasy glance round the smoke-filled room and then their eyes met and suddenly her face was wreathed with smiles.

'Mrs Carter,' she hurried forward, bumping through the drinkers, 'you'll never guess!'

'I will,' Joyce said. 'We've got it, haven't we? Cox's place?'

'How did you know?' For a second Celia looked as though the wind had been taken out of her sails, but then she was clutching Joyce's hands. 'Oh Mrs Carter, I'm so excited. I made him sign everything up tonight. Just to be certain. And I've paid the deposit and everything. It's ours. Our café.'

Joyce stared at her. She didn't know what to say. She wanted to hug her. To kiss her. But thankfully she managed to restrain herself. This was Mrs Rutherford she was talking to after all. Her boss.

Our café. Our café. Joyce could hardly control her excitement. Glancing across to the bar she saw Lorenz's eyes on her.

'We've got it,' she yelled across to him. 'Cox's place.'

And then suddenly Lorenz was smiling too. A smile that she had never seen before, a smile that lit up his whole face and made his dark eyes sparkle. Quickly he stood up and came over. 'I'm so pleased for you,' he said gravely. 'Very pleased.' He spread his hands courteously. 'Perhaps you would allow me to buy you both a drink to celebrate.'

'Oh, Mr Lorenz,' Celia said. 'How very kind.'

I'm looking forward to that dinner, Joyce thought proudly. Quite a lot.

It was some time later when Jen drew Katy on one side. 'Are you all right?'

'I think so,' Katy said. 'But what about you?' Jen seemed to have sung solidly all evening. Popular song after song, she and Mrs Frost seemed to know them all and if they didn't they had a good stab at it.

'Oh, I'm fine,' Jen said. She grinned. 'I've got some news for you.'

Katy was intrigued. 'What?'

'I've been offered a job in London.'

'Oh Jen!' Katy stared at her in delight. 'That's wonderful. You're coming back? Here? To Lavender Road?'

Jen nodded. 'It's stupid really. This time last year all I wanted was to get away.' She shook her head. 'I thought I hated bloody Lavender Road, but all the time I've been away I've been miserable.' She made

493

a face. 'Pathetic, isn't it? Mind you,' she went on more soberly, 'It's been a right bugger of a year, hasn't it?' She hesitated and touched Katy's arm. 'Especially for you.'

Katy looked round the bar. Everyone was there now. Joyce Carter, Mr Lorenz, Mrs Rutherford, Louise, Bertie with little George Whitehead on his shoulders, Mrs Frost, the Miss Taylors. Even her mother was there, sitting uneasily with Pam and Alan Nelson in the saloon bar. They had all had their fair share of misery in one form or another. It hadn't been an easy year for any of them. But they had all survived, just as London itself had survived. Battered, but ready to fight again.

She turned back to Jen and shook her head. 'It's been bad for all of us,' she said, trying not to think of Ward, wondering just how fatally bad it had been for him.

Guessing her thoughts Jen made a sympathetic face. 'No news?'

'No,' Katy said flatly. 'Nothing.' Not about Ward at least. For a second she toyed with telling Jen about the baby but decided against it. There was plenty of time after all. And she had a nasty feeling that if she mentioned it just now she might cry.

Jen obviously thought she was going to anyway because she thrust her glass into Katy's hand. 'Here,' she said gruffly. 'Drink that. It'll get you through the rest of the evening.'

'Jen.' Katy caught her arm. She smiled awkwardly. 'Thanks for the singing and that. I'm really grateful. I promise I won't ask you again. I know it's not good for your voice.'

Jen laughed. 'You didn't ask me. It was that ghastly little nurse friend of yours that shamed me into it.' She shrugged. 'Anyway, oddly enough I've enjoyed it. Makes a change from horrible old factory canteens. I'm going to do 'Sergeant Sally' next.' She grinned. 'That'll get them going.'

Louise was surprised by how much she was enjoying herself. Considering the opportunity she had given up to be here, she was

494

having a remarkably good time. At first she had thought collecting up the empties was a menial task but at least it meant she could stop for a chat here and there with the Gregg Bros people Doris had brought with her, and everyone was in such high spirits. Several complete strangers had bought her drinks. She knew she was getting tiddly because when Doris told her that Ken was getting sacked for failing to meet his quota two weeks in a row she couldn't stop laughing. And she laughed even more when she discovered he was being replaced by a girl.

'Poor old Ratface,' she giggled. 'How frightfully infra dig.'

She was still smiling when out of the corner of her eye, she saw a new arrival grappling with the blackout curtain at the front door.

'Oh my God.' She swallowed her laughter in a gulp of horror and swung back to her colleague. 'Pinch me if I'm wrong, Doris, but has a tall sandy-haired man just come in?'

Doris squinted across the room. 'Yes. Rather a nice looker? Do you know him?'

Louise swallowed hard. 'Yes, yes I do.' She was about to turn round again when a thought occurred to her. Stopping in horror she glanced at Doris. 'Quick. Tell me. Honestly. How do I look?'

Doris's multiple chins wobbled in amusement. 'You look terrible.'

For a second Louise hoped she was joking, but a quick furtive glance in the mirror told her that Doris was speaking the truth. She was sweaty, her hair was plastered to her face and she was bright red. She was also clutching half a dozen empty beer glasses to her chest.

Frantically she looked for some means of temporary escape but it was too late. He had seen her in the mirror and was beginning to make his way over.

'Louise?' His cultured voice was as low and husky as she had remembered and it had exactly the same effect on her heartbeat. 'It's been quite a job finding you. This is the third pub I've tried.'

'Jack,' she muttered, nearly dropping the glasses as he leaned forward to kiss her damp cheek.

'Here, let me help you with those,' he said relieving her of two of the glasses. 'You look exhausted.'

'We're all exhausted,' Doris chipped in good naturedly. 'We've all been slogging our guts out. We had the police in earlier and all the bleedin' barmen scarpered.'

As Jack Delmaine's eyebrows rose in astonishment, Louise groaned inwardly. She should never have set foot in Gregg Bros, never allowed herself to be befriended by blasted Doris. Now, as both Jack and Doris were looking at her expectantly, there was no option but to introduce them.

'Pleased to meet you,' Doris said coyly as they shook hands. 'Louise has told me all about you. You're in the navy, ain't yer?' She giggled. 'Can't remember which one, though. Merchant or Royal?'

Jack Delmaine cleared his throat. 'Royal, actually,' he said.

Wishing the floor would open up and receive her, Louise saw his blue eyes slide incredulously around the noisy, smoky room and her heart sank even further. In the public bar Jen Carter was singing some raucous number that was making everyone laugh, George Whitehead was racing round trying to catch the Miss Taylors' smelly little dachshund and in the corner under the clock two military policemen were slumped apparently unconscious.

It could hardly be more different to the refined atmosphere of their previous encounter at Lucinda's private party at the Dorchester if it tried.

Oh God, she thought desperately, casting him an agonised glance, why on earth did I ever suggest he came? But then dimly she realised he was smiling at her. A warm, amused smile that curled slowly round her heart.

'I get the impression you're all several glasses ahead of me,' he said. 'I'd better get myself a pint and try to catch up.' Loosening his tie, he grinned at Doris. 'What's your tipple, Doris? What can I get you?'

Louise felt the relief coursing through her blood like the alcohol had done earlier. He's nice, she thought. He's a nice man. And he's given up precious theatre tickets to come and see me.

It seemed to Katy that as the beer went down the noise level rose. She never remembered it being so noisy in her father's day. It was partly Jen's fault of course, she had them all singing along to 'Run Rabbit Run' now, a great swell of noise as they reached for the high notes, a great cheer at the end and at once the stamping applause and the eager, shouted requests for the next number.

And then the rush for the bar. That was the best bit as far as Katy was concerned. Every time she looked in the till she felt a kick of excitement. There was so much money in there. Everyone seemed to be celebrating; Mrs Carter and Mrs Rutherford had got their café; Louise seemed to have got her man; Pam and Alan had got their child. In the tap room, Pete Carter and Mr Poole were well into their fifth pint in celebration of the restoration of Big Ben. Even Mr Lorenz, to everyone's amazement, seemed unusually free with his orders. And earlier when she had been putting up the blackout she had seen Aaref slip warily back into the bar, seen him return Molly's shy smile with one of his own, and wondered if in due course there might be something to celebrate there too.

After a couple of recuperative brandies, even her mother was looking more relaxed, and the unexpected arrival of Sister Morris hadn't dampened things down for too long. On the contrary, once Sister Morris had got over her indignation at having her bottom patted as she passed through the rowdy tap room and recovered from the shock of seeing her precious Bible propping up the draught, she had taken the sight of the two semi-conscious military policemen in her stride.

Settling her down with a small lemonade between her mother and the Miss Taylors in a comfortable armchair, Katy felt a stab of affection for her former mentor. Very much on her dignity in her desperately outdated tweed coat and skirt, she couldn't have looked more like a fish out of water in the noisy jovial atmosphere if she had tried, but she hadn't had to come. And having come, she hadn't had to stay.

But stay she did, sitting bolt upright in her chair with her hands folded in her lap, until the atmosphere got to her and even she began to unbend. Looking across at her now, Katy saw her exchange a nostalgic smile with the Miss Taylors as the three of them hummed along to one of Jen's more soulful songs and suddenly Katy felt some of the evening tension leave her shoulders.

Yes, she thought, leaning on the bar with a surge of relief, even though she had no staff for tomorrow, and at this rate probably no beer, at least tonight was going well. At least the new Flag and Garter had got off to a good start.

As Big Ben struck nine o'clock, she turned on the wireless for the news. That had been Aaref's idea. 'Get them used to hearing the news,' he had said, 'And they'll be in for it every evening.'

And tonight the news was better than usual. That morning British and Soviet troops had successfully invaded Iran, securing the precious oilfields and encountering only token opposition from the German troops stationed there. After what seemed like months of unmitigated bad news, even a small victory was something to celebrate, and once again there was a rush on the bar.

Katy had just turned off the wireless and was turning to help with the orders when Molly Coogan touched her arm.

'Katy,' she murmured. 'Have you seen who's just come in?'

Something in her voice caused a flicker of alarm to chill Katy's skin. Looking up slowly she felt the breath catch painfully in her throat.

By the door, dressed incongruously in a long elegant evening gown, a small mink stole round her shoulders, was Helen de Burrel.

As Katy moved numbly to the end of the bar, everything seemed to switch into slow motion. Although she was only on the other side of the room. Helen suddenly seemed a long way away.

Slowly Katy began to walk towards her, but it took a long time for her to realise that the whole room had fallen silent. That Jen had stopped in mid-note. That the loud frantic ticking she could hear was not Big Ben gone berserk, but her own pounding heart.

It took even longer for her to realise that Helen was smiling.

'Katy,' she said, reaching out her hand, her voice unusually breathless, unusually slurred with emotion. 'I've got news. We just heard from the Red Cross tonight. I had to come straight away. Ward is safe and well in a prisoner-of-war camp in Germany.'

Katy stared at her. She couldn't believe it. She felt tears welling in her eyes. She had been so certain he was dead. And now suddenly he was alive. Lovely, wonderful Ward. Her husband. Alive.

Her sudden choking unbelieving sob was drowned by a sudden burst of applause. Even those who didn't know why, joined in enthusiastically.

And when the clapping and stamping and cheering died away, Katy heard a strange knocking noise. For a dim moment she thought something had gone wrong with the beer pump, but then she realised to her astonishment it was Alan Nelson tapping on the counter. Shy, reticent Alan Nelson.

'Ladies and gentlemen,' he said. 'I would like to propose a toast. This last year has not been an easy one. But through it all a group of people have struggled with courage and fortitude. One person in particular has fought against the odds and it is due to her that we are here tonight. But it is to them all that I wish you to raise your glasses.' He raised his glass solemnly. 'To the ladies of Lavender Road. Let us hope that tonight marks the end of the old and the beginning of the new.'

As the scraping of chairs and the voices rose and fell and the sound of swallowing faded, Katy suddenly clutched her stomach.

At once Molly Coogan was at her side. 'Are you all right?'

Slowly Katy straightened up and turned to face her. 'It's the baby,' she said in wonder, a slow smile tugging at her mouth. 'I think it's kicking.'

Her baby. Ward's baby. Suddenly there were tears pouring down her face.

And then her mother was running forward, pushing through the startled drinkers. 'A baby? Oh Katy! Oh Katy!' Her whole face was lit with joy. 'You clever girl. How wonderful!'

Staring at her in astonishment, Katy started to laugh. The baby, she thought, as her mother threw her arms around her neck. I should have told her about the baby. It would have made all the difference.

As she looked over her mother's shoulder at the kindly, smiling faces of her customers, her friends, the Miss Taylors weeping openly in their relief about Ward, she suddenly heard the piano strike a sonorous chord. Looking up sharply as everyone turned round, she caught Jen's ironic smile across the room.

And only then did she recognise the tune. 'Land of Hope and Glory'.

Land of hope and glory, Mother of the free . . .

As Jen's beautiful, pure voice filled the still room, for the first time in months Katy felt her spirits lift. It's going to be all right, she thought. I really think it's going to be all right.

Author's Note

South London suffered very badly during the Blitz. There were three specific targets which the Luftwaffe were tasked with trying to destroy, Battersea Power Station, Clapham Junction railway interchange (one of the busiest in the UK); and the anti-aircraft guns on Clapham Common. And yet so many of the stories people told me spoke of extraordinary grit and resilience. I often wonder whether we would cope any where near as well if it happened again today.

As always I have made my historical detail as accurate as possible but, in the end, *Some Sunny Day* is a novel, the Lavender Road of the story is a figment of my imagination and the people who live in it are fictional.

Once again I would like to thank the huge number of people who have so generously given me details of their wartime experiences. Special thanks go to May Bridger, Alan and Wendy Simpkins, Billie Cullen, Jo Howe, Phyllys Stevens, Mary Ridgeon and Frank Putner. This book would have been impossible without them.

Helen Carey
www.helencareybooks.co.uk

If you'd like to read more about the women of Lavender Road during the Second World War, here's the prologue of Helen Carey's latest novel in the series . . .

London Calling

Prologue

12 December 1942

With considerable relief, Molly Coogan pulled her cloak round her, checked that her nurse's cap was pinned on securely, ran down the last few stairs and crossed the dimly lit lobby towards the heavily sandbagged doors.

Her hand was already on the handle when she heard someone speak behind her.

'I wouldn't go out there if I was you.'

The voice was portentous, almost gleeful in its gloomy menace, and Molly turned to see one of the hospital porters pinning a poster up on the wall next to the empty reception desk.

'That sounds ominous,' she said. 'Why not?'

It struck her suddenly that the whole lobby was unusually empty. Visiting hour was long past, but there were normally a few staff coming and going. She knew it wasn't an air raid. Even in the depths of the Wilhelmina septic wards she would have heard the sirens. She had heard them often enough. And the planes that followed.

Much of south London had been smashed to smithereens by Nazi bombs over the last couple of years. But the Wilhelmina Hospital had been built to withstand the Zeppelin raids of the Great War. It was proving equally effective against the Luftwaffe, despite its proximity

503

to tempting targets like the Clapham Junction rail interchange and the Battersea power station.

In her darker moments Molly sometimes wished that the Wilhelmina would suffer a direct hit and put everyone out of their misery. Throbbing and humming gently, insulated from the real world by its emergency generators, it was like some sinister old submarine. And she hated it. She hated the boarded windows, the hushed gloom, the ghastly competing scents of sepsis and iodine, the dogmatic senior nurses and the smug, complacent doctors. Most of all she hated the constant presence of death.

She didn't know how much more she could take. Even tonight . . . She stopped and shook her head.

'Why not?' she asked again. 'What's going on outside?'

'Fog,' the porter said.

He took a spare drawing pin out from between his teeth and stood back to admire his handiwork. Even in the muted light, Molly could see that it was a picture of Winston Churchill.

'Fog?' Molly repeated. 'I'm not scared of a bit of fog.'

But then she hesitated. It was an excuse not to go up to the Flag and Garter. A legitimate excuse. She could go back to the nurses' home instead, crawl into bed and block out the day, block out the thought of a young girl dying of septic infection only ten days after pricking her finger on a rose bush.

'That's easy to say, but it's a right old pea-souper tonight,' the porter said. 'Just like the old days.'

Molly felt torn. She was dog tired. But she had promised her friend Katy Frazer that she would help up at the pub.

'You can't see your hand in front of your face,' the porter added.

Wondering what other platitudes he would come out with, Molly took a step forward to read the slogan under Winston Churchill's face. *We will go forward together.*

That was all very well for him, Molly thought. Going forward for old Winnie probably meant being tucked up in front of a log fire somewhere nice and safe with a big fat cigar in his hand and a map of the world on his lap. But for her it meant struggling up to Lavender Road to spend the evening behind the bar in a noisy, smoky pub.

She nodded an unenthusiastic good night to the porter and pushed out through the heavy doors. She had to go. It was her last chance to give Katy a hand. She was back on nights again tomorrow, and by next weekend, fingers crossed, she would be at the maternity hospital in Croydon, starting midwifery training.

It wasn't much of a change. There'd still be scrubbing and cleaning and starchy old ward sisters to contend with. But at least she would be ushering life into the world rather than out of it. And if nothing else, it would get her away from the Wilhelmina, from London, from Lavender Road. And from Katy and her lovely Canadian husband Ward Frazer.

She would try to make a fresh start. It would be a wrench. A terrible wrench. But she knew it had to be done. For the sake of her sanity.

If you can't wait to find out what happens next in LONDON CALLING, you can order a copy now at www.headline.co.uk

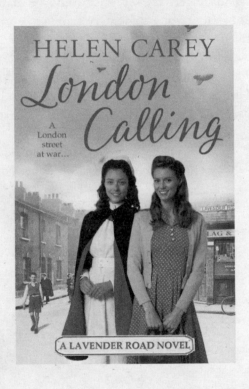

Helen Carey's earlier three novels in the Lavender Road series – LAVENDER ROAD, SOME SUNNY DAY and ON A WING AND A PRAYER – will all be available from Headline in 2016.